W9-AZV-178

WITHDRAWN

THE GEORGIA REGIONAL
LIBRARY FOR THE BLIND
AND PHYSICALLY
HANDICAPPED IS A FREE
SERVICE FOR INDIVIDUALS
UNABLE TO READ
STANDARD PRINT.

ASK AT OUR CIRCULATION
DESK HOW TO REGISTER
FOR THIS SERVICE, AS WELL
AS OTHER SERVICES
OFFERED BY THIS LIBRARY.

**Also available from
Linda Lael Miller
and HQN Books**

The McKettricks of Texas
McKettricks of Texas: Tate
McKettricks of Texas: Garrett
McKettricks of Texas: Austin
A Lawman's Christmas

The McKettricks series
McKettrick's Choice
McKettrick's Luck
McKettrick's Pride
McKettrick's Heart
A McKettrick Christmas

The Montana Creeds series
Montana Creeds: Logan
Montana Creeds: Dylan
Montana Creeds: Tyler
A Creed Country Christmas

The Mojo Sheepshanks series
Deadly Gamble
Deadly Deceptions

The Stone Creek series
The Man from Stone Creek
A Wanted Man
The Rustler
The Bridegroom

The Creed Cowboys
A Creed in Stone Creek
Creed's Honor
The Creed Legacy

Coming soon
Big Sky Mountain

LINDA LAEL MILLER

BIG SKY *Country*

COVINGTON BRANCH LIBRARY
NEWTON COUNTY LIBRARY SYSTEM
7116 FLOYD STREET
COVINGTON, GA 30014

DOUBLEDAY LARGE PRINT HOME LIBRARY EDITION

HQN™

This Large Print Edition, prepared especially for
Doubleday Large Print Home Library, contains
the complete, unabridged text of the original
Publisher's Edition.

ISBN 978-1-61793-995-2

BIG SKY COUNTRY

Copyright © 2012 by Linda Lael Miller

All rights reserved. Except for use in any review, the
reproduction or utilization of this work in whole or in
part in any form by any electronic, mechanical or
other means, now known or hereafter invented,
including xerography, photocopying and recording,
or in any information storage or retrieval system, is
forbidden without the written permission of the
publisher, Harlequin Enterprises Limited, 225
Duncan Mill Road, Don Mills, Ontario M3B 3K9,
Canada.

This is a work of fiction. Names, characters, places and incidents are either the product of the author's imagination or are used fictitiously, and any resemblance to actual persons, living or dead, business establishments, events or locales is entirely coincidental.

® and TM are trademarks of the publisher. Trademarks indicated with ® are registered in the United States Patent and Trademark Office, the Canadian Trade Marks Office and in other countries.

Printed in U.S.A.

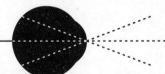

This Large Print Book carries the
Seal of Approval of N.A.V.H.

Dear Reader,

Welcome to a new community, Parable, Montana—a small town of the type I know and love so well. The people of Parable are good, decent, hardworking folks who pull together in times of trouble and never miss a chance to celebrate the good things in life.

In this first story, *Big Sky Country,* you'll meet Sheriff Slade Barlow, the dark-haired hunk who happens to be pretty disillusioned with love, and Joslyn Kirk, his equally love-skittish lady. Joslyn, after all, has returned to Parable only to right an old wrong, one she didn't actually commit, and she's planning to move on as soon as possible.

But here's the thing about small towns—and about love: there are threads that pull a person into the picture, whether they choose to be part of it or not. What are these threads? Friends, old and new, human and animal. Memories. The glorious process of making *new* memories. The laughter and the tears and, of course, there's always the biggest blessing of all: Love. In all its fascinating forms.

So welcome to Parable. You'll fit right in.

My very best,

Paula Jud Miller

In loving memory of my
beloved beagle, Sadie.
I'm grateful for every moment
of the eleven years we shared.

CHAPTER ONE

Parable, Montana

"You weren't at the funeral," Slade Barlow's half brother, Hutch Carmody, accused, the words rasping against the underside of a long, slow exhale.

Slade didn't look at Hutch, though he could still see him out of the corner of one eye. The both of them were sitting side by side in a pair of uncomfortable chairs, facing what seemed like an acre of desk. Maggie Landers, their father's lawyer, who had summoned them there, had yet to put in an appearance.

"I went to the graveside service," Slade replied evenly, and after a considerable length. It was the truth, though he'd stood at some distance from the crowd, not wanting to be numbered among the admitted mourners but unable to stay away entirely.

"Why bother at all?" Hutch challenged. "Unless you just wanted to make sure the old man was really in the box?"

Slade was not a quick-tempered man—by nature, he tended to think before he spoke and offer whatever response he might make with quiet deliberation, traits that had served him well over the several years since he'd been elected sheriff—but the edge in his half brother's tone brought heat surging up his neck to pound behind his ears.

"Maybe that was it," he drawled with quiet contempt as the office door whispered open behind them.

Hutch, who had just shoved back his chair as if to leap to his feet, ready to fight, thrust a hand hard through his shock of brownish-blond hair instead, probably to discharge that rush of adrenaline, and stayed put. He all but buzzed, like an electric fence line short-circuiting in a thunderstorm.

Slade, though still confounded by his own invitation to this particular shindig, took a certain grim satisfaction in Hutch's reaction. There was, as the old saying went, no love lost between the two of them.

"Good to see you haven't killed each other," Maggie observed brightly, rounding the shining expanse of the desk to take the leather chair behind it. Still gorgeous at fifty-plus, with short, expertly dyed brown hair and round green eyes, usually alight with mischievous intelligence, the lawyer turned slightly to boot up her computer.

"Not just yet, anyhow," Hutch replied finally.

Maggie's profile was all he could see of her, but Slade registered the slight smile that tilted up one corner of her mouth. Her fingers, perfectly manicured every Saturday morning at his mother's beauty shop for the last quarter of a century, flicked busily over the keyboard, and the monitor threw a wash of pale blue light onto her face and the lightweight jacket of her custom-made off-white pantsuit.

"How's your mother, Slade?" she asked mildly without glancing his way.

Maggie and his mom, Callie, were around the same age, and they'd been friends for as long as Slade could remember. Given that he'd run into Maggie at his mom's Curly-Burly Hair Salon just the day before, where she'd been having a trim and a touch-up, he figured the question was a rhetorical one, a sort of conversational filler.

"She's fine," Slade said. By then, he'd gotten over the urge to commit fratricide and gone back to mulling the thing that had been bothering him ever since the formidable Ms. Landers had called him at home that morning and asked him to stop by her office on his way to work.

The meeting had to be about the old man's last will and testament, though Maggie hadn't said so over the phone. All she'd been willing to give up was, "This won't take long, Slade, and believe me, it's in your best interests to be there."

Hutch's presence made sense, since he was the legitimate son, the golden boy, groomed since birth to become the master of all he surveyed even as, motherless from the age of twelve, he ran wild. Slade himself, on the other hand, was the outsider—born on the proverbial wrong side of the blanket.

John Carmody had never once acknowledged him, in all Slade's thirty-five years of life, and it wasn't likely that he'd had a deathbed change of heart and altered his will to include the product of his long-ago affair with Callie.

No, Slade thought, Carmody hadn't *had* a heart, not where he and his mother were concerned, anyway. He'd never so much as spoken to Slade in all those years; looked right through him, when they did come into contact, as if he was invisible. If that stiff-necked son of a bitch had instructed Maggie to make sure Slade was there for the reading of the will, it was probably so he'd know what he was missing out on, when all that land and money went to Hutch.

You can stick it all where the sun never shines, old man, Slade thought angrily.

He'd never expected—or wanted—to inherit a damn thing from John Carmody—bad enough that he'd gotten the bastard's looks, his dark hair, lean and muscular build, and blue eyes— and it galled him that Maggie, his mother's friend, would be a party to wasting his time like this.

Maggie clicked the mouse, and her printer began spewing sheets of paper as she turned to face Hutch and Slade head-on.

"I'll spare you all the legal jargon," she said, gathering the papers from the printer tray, separating them into two piles and shoving these across the top of her desk, one set for each of them. "All the facts are there—you can read the wills over at your leisure."

Slade barely glanced at the documents and made no move to pick them up.

"And what facts are those?" Hutch snapped, peevish.

Pecker-head, Slade thought.

Maggie interlaced her fingers and smiled benignly. It took more than a smart-ass cowboy to get under her hide. "The estate is to be divided equally between the two of you," she announced.

Stunned, Slade simply sat there, as breathless as if he'd just taken a sucker punch to the gut. A single thought hummed in his head, like a trapped moth trying to find a way out.

What the hell?

Hutch, no doubt just as shocked as Slade was, if not more so, leaned forward and growled, "*What* did you say?"

"You heard me the first time, Hutch," Maggie said, unruffled. She might have looked like a gracefully aging pixie, but she regularly chewed up the best prosecutors in the state and spit them out like husks of sunflower seeds.

Slade said nothing. He was still trying to process the news.

"Bullshit," Hutch muttered. "This is *bullshit.*"

Maggie sighed. "Nevertheless," she said, "it's what Mr. Carmody wanted. He was my client, and it's my job to see that his final wishes are honored to the letter. After all, Whisper Creek belonged to him, and he had every right to dispose of his estate however he saw fit."

Slade finally recovered enough equanimity to speak, though his voice came out sounding hoarse. "What if I told you I didn't want anything?" he demanded.

"If you told me that," Maggie responded smoothly, "I'd say you were out of your mind, Slade Barlow. We're talking about a great deal of money here, in addition to a very profitable ranching operation and all that goes with it, including buildings and livestock and mineral rights."

Another silence descended, short and dangerous, pulsing with heat.

Hutch was the one to break it. "When did Dad change his will?" he asked.

"He *didn't* change it," Maggie said without hesitation. "Mr. Carmody had the papers drawn up years ago, when my father and grandfather were still with the firm, and he personally reviewed them six months ago, after he got the diagnosis. *This is what he wanted,* Hutch."

Hutch snapped up his copy of the document and got to his feet. Slade rose, too, but he left the papers where they were. None of this seemed real to him—he was probably dreaming. Any moment now, he'd wake up in a cold sweat and a tangle of sheets, in his lonely, rumpled bed over at the duplex where he'd been living since he came back to Parable ten years ago, after college, a stint in the military and a brief marriage followed by a mostly amicable divorce.

"I'll be *damned*," Hutch muttered, his voice like sandpaper. He was dressed for ranch work, in old jeans, a blue cotton shirt and a pair of well-worn boots, which probably meant he'd had no more notice about this meeting than Slade had.

"Thanks, Maggie," Slade heard himself say as he turned to leave.

He wasn't grateful; he'd spoken out of habit.

She got up from her chair, rounded the desk and pursued him, forcing the printout of his father's will into his hands. "At least read it," she said. "I'll set up another meeting in a few days, when you've both had time to absorb every-thing."

Slade didn't answer, but he accepted the paperwork, felt it crumple in his grasp as his fingers tightened reflex-ively around it.

Moments later, as Slade opened the door of his truck, Hutch was beside him again.

"I'll buy your half of the ranch," he said, grinding out the offer. "I don't give a rat's ass about the money—I've got plenty of that anyway—but Whisper Creek has been in my family for almost a hundred years, and my great-great-grandfather built the original house and barn with his own hands. The place ought to belong to me outright."

The emphasis on the phrase *my fam-ily* was subtle, but it was an unmistak-able line in the sand.

Slade met his half brother's fierce gaze. Reached in to take his hat off the passenger seat where he'd left it earlier, resting on its crown, before heading into Maggie's office. "I'll need to give that some thought," he said.

With a visible effort, Hutch unclamped

the hinges of his jaws. "What's there to think about?" he asked, after another crackling pause. "I'll pay cash, Barlow. Name your price."

Name your price. Slade knew he ought to accept the deal, and just be glad John Carmody had seen fit to claim him, albeit posthumously. All he had to do was say yes, and he could buy that little spread he'd had his eye on for the past couple of years, pay cash for it, instead of depleting his savings for the down payment. But something prevented him from agreeing, something that ran deeper than his utter inability to act on impulse.

Indirectly, John Carmody had, at long last, acknowledged his existence. He needed to be with that knowledge for a while, work out what it meant, if anything.

"I'll get back to you," Slade finally reiterated, climbing up behind the wheel of his truck and putting on his hat. "In the meantime, I've got a county to look after."

With that, he shut the truck door.

Hutch thumped the metal hard with

the heel of one palm, then turned and stormed away, rounded the hood of the Whisper Creek pickup, yanked open the door and jumped into the driver's seat.

Slade watched as the other man ground the engine to life, shoved it into Reverse and threw some gravel in the process. He was all sound and fury, though. Half again too smart to actually break the speed limit with the sheriff looking on.

With a wry twist to his mouth, Slade waited a few moments, started his own rig and pulled onto the narrow side street. He was supposed to be in his office over at the courthouse, assigning his day shift deputies to patrol various parts of the county, but he headed for the highway instead. Five minutes later, he pulled up in front of his mother's place, an old trailer with rust-speckled aluminum skirting and a plywood addition that served as living quarters.

As a kid, Slade had been about half-ashamed of that jumble of metal and wood, jerry-rigged together the way it was, lacking only waist-high weeds, a few rattletrap cars up on blocks and household appliances on the porch to qualify as out-and-out redneck. Callie nagged him into power-washing the two-toned walls of the trailer—the part that housed the shop—at least twice a year, and he painted the rest of it regularly, too.

This week, all the words on the dusty reader-board at the edge of the gravel parking lot were even spelled correctly. *Acrylic nails, half price. Highlights/ perms, ten percent off.*

Slade smiled as he shut off the truck and got out.

The shop didn't open for business until ten o'clock, but Callie already had the lights on, and, most likely, the big coffeepot was chugging away, too. As Slade approached, the door opened, and Callie, broom in hand, beamed a greeting.

"Hey," she called.

"Hey," Slade replied gruffly.

Callie Barlow was a small woman, big-busted, with an abundance of auburn hair held to the top of her head by a plastic clasp roughly the size of the jaws-of-life, and she wore turquoise jeans, pink Western boots and a bright yellow T-shirt studded with little sparkly things.

"Well, this is a surprise," she said, setting aside the broom and dusting her hands together. Her expression was warm, as always, but her gray eyes showed puzzlement bordering on concern. She knew Slade took his job seriously, and it wasn't like him to drop in during working hours. "Is the county running itself these days?"

"My deputies are holding down the fort," Slade answered. "Is the coffee on?"

He knew it was; he could smell the rich aroma wafting through the open doorway, along with tinges of industrial-strength shampoo and a variety of mysterious hair-bending chemicals.

"Sure," Callie responded, stepping back so he could come inside the shop. "That's about the first thing I do every morning—plug in the coffeepot." The faintest ghost of a frown lingered in her eyes, and then her natural bluntness broke through. "What's wrong?" she asked.

Slade sighed, took off his hat and set it aside on the counter next to Callie's cash register. "I don't know if *wrong* is the word for it," he said. "I just came from Maggie Landers's office. It seems John Carmody remembered me in his will."

Callie's eyes widened at that, then narrowed in swift suspicion. "What?" she asked and had to clear her throat afterward.

He hooked his thumbs through the belt loops of his jeans and tilted his head to one side, watching her. If Callie had known about the bequest ahead of time, she was doing a damn good job of hiding the fact.

"Half," he said. "He left me half of everything he had."

Callie sank into one of the dryer chairs, nearly bumping her head on the plastic dome. She blinked a couple of times, and one of her false lashes popped loose at the outside corner of her eye. She pressed it back down with a fingertip.

"I don't believe it," she murmured.

Slade raised the dome above the chair next to his mother's and sat down beside her. Took her hand just long enough to give it a slight squeeze.

"Believe it," he said, not knowing where to go from there. He loved Callie and they were close, but she hadn't raised him to come running home to her with this or any other kind of news.

"What happens now?" she asked in a small voice. Her lower lip wobbled a little, and her eyes, usually bright and mischievous, looked dull, almost haunted.

"I have no idea," Slade answered quietly. "Not surprisingly, Hutch didn't take it real well. He's already offered to buy out my share of the ranch."

Callie closed her eyes for a moment, and when she opened them again, the shine was back. She was tough—she'd had to be, orphaned young and later giving birth to a child out of wedlock in a town where such things mattered, and mattered a lot—but her problems hadn't hardened her the way they would've some women. She'd taken things as they'd come, made the best of them and raised Slade to respect her—and himself. She was one of the most emotionally balanced people he'd ever known, but he wondered sometimes how much of that was an act.

"Once or twice, when you were growing up," she recalled now, her tone musing and a little distant, "John slipped me a few dollars for groceries or light bills or something you needed for school—things like that—but I never thought he'd do this. Not for one moment."

"He was full of surprises, I guess," Slade said with a touch of irony.

"He was full of *himself,*" Callie said. "He was so afraid I'd up and name you after him and make the scandal worse than it already was, but when I called you 'Slade,' he said I'd been watching too many TV Westerns. I never bothered to tell him that I got your name from a story I read in *Ranch Romances.*"

Slade smiled. She'd told him about the magazines she'd loved to lose herself in back in the day, and how she'd named him after one of her favorite heroes.

She hadn't gone to Carmody's funeral, hadn't even mentioned the man's name in recent memory, and only then did it occur to Slade that she might be grieving his loss just the same. She must have loved John Carmody once.

"You all right?" he asked.

She nodded. Swallowed. "Are you going to take Hutch up on his offer?" she finally inquired.

He sighed again. "Damned if I know," he said. "On the one hand, I could see myself accepting, buying that land I've had my eye on all this time—building a house and putting up a barn. But on the other . . . well, there's a part of me that wants to claim my birthright and have the whole world know it."

Callie patted his hand, rose from the dryer chair and crossed to the coffee-pot, a gleaming metal monstrosity that sounded like an old-fashioned steam boiler when it was plugged in.

"I guess that's understandable," she said, keeping her back to him as she filled a good-sized foam cup and popped a lid onto the top. "Wanting folks to know the truth, I mean."

Slade was on his feet, retrieving his hat from the counter, turning the brim slowly in his hands. "I don't reckon it will surprise anybody," he reminded her, recalling the gossip that had started so many schoolyard brawls while he was growing up.

Callie had been barely twenty years old when she'd taken up with Carmody; naive and alone in the world, and fresh out of some fly-by-night beauty school in Missoula with nothing but her license to cut hair, the old trailer she'd grown up in and the two hardscrabble acres sloping down to Buffalo Creek behind it. Her beloved "granddad" had been dead two years by then.

"I'm sorry, Slade," she said now. "For all you had to go through on my account, I mean. Practically everybody I knew said I ought to put you up for adoption, once I knew John had intended to marry someone else all along, but I just couldn't do it. I guess it was selfish of me, but you were *my* boy and I wanted to see you grow up."

"I know," Slade said, as he stooped to kiss her forehead. He'd heard all of it before, after all, and while he understood Callie's personal regrets, the fact of the matter was, he was glad she'd kept him. She'd sacrificed a lot, working long hours to build the business that had supported them both, though just barely sometimes, passing up more than one chance to get married, move away from Parable and finally enjoy a degree of respectability.

Instead, she'd stuck it out, right there in the old hometown, where she believed she had every right to be, as did her son, whether John Carmody, his high-society bride or the snootier locals had liked it or not.

Slade had tried to put it into words how grateful he was for the rock-solid courage she'd always shown, for the example she'd set by working hard, standing her ground and just plain showing up for life and doing what she could with what she had. Because of her, he'd grown up strong, sound-minded and at home in his body, with a quiet confidence in himself and in his own judgment that had never failed him, even during a tour of duty in Iraq and the rough patch when his marriage ended.

He paused in the doorway, hat in hand, looking back at her. "You can retire now," he said. "Maybe go on a trip or something."

Callie laughed, the sound almost musical. "That'll be the day, Slade Barlow," she replied. "If you think I'm going to accept a big check from you and spend the rest of my life eating bonbons and taking tours of other people's gardens, you'd better think again. Why, I wouldn't know what to do with myself if I didn't have this place—and what would all my clients do without me?"

Slade shook his head, a grin quirking up one corner of his mouth. "Just give it some thought," he said, full of a strange, sweet sadness. "There's a whole world beyond the borders of this town, Mom."

Callie waved a dismissive hand and reached for the broom again. "Maybe so," she said, "but I'm staying right here."

"You're stubborn as hell, you know that?"

"Where do you think *you* got it?" she countered.

Like his looks and the framework of his bones, he'd always figured most of his pigheadedness had come down from John Carmody, but now he recognized the quality as the downside of his mother's fierce persistence.

He waved once, crossed to his truck, got in and drove away.

He should have been at work half an hour ago.

By this time, he reckoned, all his deputies and Becky, the longtime receptionist, were probably fixing to send out a search party, complete with cadaver dogs and a plan drawn out on a grid.

The idea made him smile as he headed back toward the courthouse.

Joslyn Kirk overslept that morning, and when she opened her eyes, it took her a few seconds to recognize her surroundings and realize she was right back in the one place she'd sworn never to set foot in again—Parable, Montana.

Joslyn sat up in her sleeping bag— she'd arrived late the night before and hadn't bothered to put sheets on the antique brass bed—and looked around, taking in the cabbage-rose wallpaper, the worn planks in the floor and ornate woodwork, the heavy wardrobe that served as a closet.

She was in the guesthouse behind the mansion that had been her home for most of her childhood. Memories swamped her—on the other side of the broad green lawn, her mother would have been sitting on the screened-in sunporch on a bright morning like this one, sipping coffee and reading the newspaper. The housekeeper, Opal, would have been busy in the huge kitchen, preparing breakfast.

Now, her mom was in Santa Fe, living with husband number three, a successful artist. Husband number two, Elliott Rossiter, had died in prison of an embolism, and heaven only knew where Opal was by now. She and Joslyn had parted tearfully, with promises to stay in touch, but they'd lost each other's trails years ago.

Joslyn sighed, pushed back her long brown hair and wriggled out of the sleeping bag. There was no sense in moping about the past—she'd come back to Parable for a reason, and she needed to get on with the plan.

So she could leave again.

After a brief stop in the bathroom and a quick splash at the sink, she padded barefoot into the tiny kitchen and groped through various plastic shopping bags until she unearthed the cheap coffee-pot she'd purchased the day before, along with a few other essentials, at the big discount store out on the highway.

She fumbled with the pot, then the small can of ground coffee beans, then the old-fashioned water spigot.

A rap at the door interrupted the process, but only briefly. She'd be useless without coffee, and, besides, she knew who the visitor was.

"Come in!" she called.

There was a metallic jiggle at the front door, and a moment or two later, Kendra Shepherd, Joslyn's best friend since forever, stepped into the kitchen.

Blonde and elegant like a ballet dancer, Kendra looked ready to take on a new day in her crisp green suit and high heels. She ran Shepherd Real Estate, and she was clearly making a success of the enterprise.

"You really should lock the door at night," Kendra said, right off. "Parable has its share of petty crime, you know."

"As long as it's petty, why worry?" Joslyn said offhandedly with a little shrug, leaning to peer at the buttons on the coffeepot, looking for one labeled On. Finding it, she jabbed at it with the tip of one index finger. She straightened, smiled at her friend, feeling not the least bit self-conscious in her flannel pajama bottoms and oversize T-shirt.

"I'm serious," Kendra fretted. "Coming from Phoenix like you do, I'd think you would be more careful about your personal safety."

Joslyn plundered the shopping bags again, this time looking for cups and artificial sweetener. "Okay," she said, distracted by the desperate need for a caffeine fix. "Point taken. I'll lock every door and window from now on, and maybe adopt a rottweiler with overt killer instincts."

Kendra smiled and drew back a chair

at the compact kitchen table, which seated two. "Still a smart-ass after all these years," she remarked, sounding almost wistful.

"It's a coping mechanism," Joslyn said, only half kidding. She pushed her hair back again and regarded her friend with affection. "Thanks for doing this, Kendra—giving me a job and letting me rent the guesthouse, I mean."

Kendra straightened her elegant spine. She'd pinned her pale, silky hair up in a loose knot at her nape, and her simple jewelry—gold posts in her earlobes and one bangle bracelet gracing her right wrist—looked quietly classy. Her eyes were a pale, luminous green.

"I've missed you, Joss," Kendra said, as Joslyn pulled back the other chair and sank into it. "It's great to have you back in town . . ." She paused then, lowered her eyes.

"But?" Joslyn prompted gently.

"I can't quite figure out why you'd *want* to be here, after what happened." Color rose in Kendra's cheeks, but she met Joslyn's gaze again. "Not that any of it was your fault, of course, but—"

The coffeepot began to make sizzling noises, and a tantalizing aroma filled the air. "I have my reasons," Joslyn said. "I'm counting on you to trust me, Kendra—at least for the next few months. When I can explain, I will."

"People have been getting mysterious checks in the mail lately," Kendra said speculatively, "from some big law firm in Denver. And I know you sold your software company. . . ."

Joslyn bolted to her feet, hurried over to the square foot of counter space where the coffee machine stood, turned on the water in the sink and hurriedly rinsed the two plain mugs she'd purchased the day before. "I sold the company," she admitted, feeling a wrench of loss as she said the words, even though it had been a done deal for weeks now. "But I don't see what that has to do with people getting unexpected checks."

"The recipients of the checks have one thing in common," Kendra persisted. She hadn't gotten where she was by being slow on the uptake.

"They'd all invested in your stepfather's—business."

A knot clenched Joslyn's stomach and moved up her windpipe and into her throat. "Coincidence," she murmured, when she could manage to speak.

Her hands trembled a little as she pulled the carafe out from under the trickling stream of coffee and sloshed some into each of the mugs.

"If you say so," Kendra said mildly.

As Joslyn turned, a cup in each hand, Kendra pushed back her chair and stood. "I'd better run," she added. "I have a closing this morning, and then I'm showing a chicken farm for the seventeenth time to the same potential buyer." She looked down at her shoes. "Do you think I should wear boots instead of these heels?"

Joslyn was so relieved by the change of subject that she didn't protest. "Probably," she agreed, imagining Kendra high-heeling it around a chicken farm.

"Would you mind stopping by the office once or twice, just in case someone drops in wanting to look at a property? Slade Barlow has a habit of coming over to ask if the Kingman place has sold."

The name registered in an instant, like a sharp dart to the esophagus, and Joslyn had to swallow before she could nod. As kids, she and Slade had lived in different worlds, hers rich, his poor. Back then, she'd been his brother Hutch's girl, which hadn't helped, either. Although Slade had never actually come out and said as much—he'd barely spoken to her at all, in fact—she'd known what he thought of her: that she was spoiled, self-centered and shallow.

Worse, he'd been right.

When the financial roof had caved in and all those honest, hardworking people realized they'd been cheated out of their savings by the town's onetime favorite son—Joslyn's stepfather, Elliott— her charmed life was over. Once popular, Joslyn had found out who her real friends were, and fast. Only Kendra and Hutch had stuck by her. Soon after Rossiter's arrest, she and her mother had packed what they could into Opal's old station wagon and left town in the dark of night.

The recollection still shamed Joslyn. Running away went against everything she believed in.

"It wasn't your fault," Kendra reminded her. She'd always been perceptive—so perceptive, in fact, that sometimes she seemed to be a mind reader. Like now, for instance. "Nobody blames you for what happened, Joss."

That lump was back in her throat, aching and bitter, and it was another moment before she could say anything. Joslyn put the mugs down on the table, nearly spilling their contents, and forced herself to meet Kendra's eyes.

"But you still think I shouldn't have come here," she said, her voice small and uncommonly shaky.

Kendra reached out and touched Joslyn's arm. "Most folks around here understand that you didn't have anything to do with the scam," she said. "For pity's sake, you were just a kid. But some are still carrying a grudge. They might say things, *do* things—"

Joslyn closed her eyes tightly for a

moment, then resolutely opened them again. Nodded her understanding.

She was doing what she knew she had to do, even if she couldn't precisely explain the reasons, but one thing was definite: it wasn't going to be easy.

CHAPTER TWO

Once Kendra had gone, Joslyn showered, pulled on jeans and a short-sleeved cotton top, white with tiny green flowers, slid her feet into her favorite pair of sandals and got to work.

She unpacked the two large suitcases she'd brought from Phoenix and put away her limited clothing supply, then rolled up the sleeping bag and looked around for a place to store it. This was a challenge, since space was at a real premium in the guesthouse, but, with some effort, she managed to stuff the unwieldy bundle under the bathroom cabinet. Next, she helped herself to a set of time-softened sheets that still smelled faintly of fresh air and sunshine and hastily made up the bed.

Riding a swell of ambition, Joslyn set her high-powered laptop on the small desk in front of the living-room window, but she couldn't quite bring herself to fire it up and log on. She'd worked too many eighteen-hour days designing and redesigning software, marketing the innovative game she'd developed and patented and finally selling the whole enterprise to a multinational corporation for big bucks.

She'd been a very rich woman—for about five minutes. Now she had a secondhand car, enough money in the bank to cover a year's living expenses—if she was frugal—and, for the first time since she was seventeen, some peace of mind.

Arriving in Parable by night had been one thing, though, and venturing out in broad daylight, where she was bound to run into the locals, was another. Still, she needed groceries, since she'd only bought nonperishables the day before, and she *had* promised Kendra she'd stop by at the office and keep an eye out for drop-ins.

Plus, she reminded herself stalwartly, she hadn't come back to Parable to hide.

The reasons for her return were far from concrete, as many times as she'd rolled the whole situation through the cogs and gears of her brain. Obviously, she wanted to make things right with the people her stepfather had cheated. At the same time, she knew she wasn't responsible for another person's actions.

So why *had* she come back? Why had she sacrificed so much, giving up a good job, selling the company she'd built by working nights and weekends, forsaking her luxury condo and her dream car?

The only answer Joslyn could have given, at that moment or any other, was that something—her overdeveloped conscience?—had driven her back. The compulsion to return had been cosmic in scope, as impossible to ignore as a tsunami or an earthquake.

The mandate, it seemed to her, had arisen from some secret part of her soul, pushing her to take the next step and then the next, operating almost entirely on faith.

It was like walking a tightrope blindfolded. There was no turning back, and if she didn't keep moving, she was sure to lose her balance and fall.

Joslyn sighed and headed for the door, moving resolutely.

Visiting Kendra's office meant going inside the main house, of course—and she knew she'd be beset by all sorts of memories as soon as she set foot over the threshold—but there was something to be said for just getting things like this over with. Kendra lived on the second floor and ran her real-estate firm out of the huge living room, where, as of Monday morning, Joslyn would be working full-time.

Might as well bite the bullet and brave the first and inevitably emotional reentry while she had some privacy. After sucking in a deep breath and squaring her shoulders, Joslyn crossed the wide lawn where flowers of all sorts and shades and fragrances rioted all around her, climbed the wooden steps to the enclosed sunporch and reached for the handle of the screen door. Locked.

Joslyn sighed, recalling Kendra's remarks about Parable having its share of petty crime these days. Evidently, her friend practiced what she preached, but, since she hadn't offered a key, the front door was probably open.

Joslyn descended the steps and followed the familiar flagstone path around to the side of the house, running parallel to the glittering white driveway with its layers of limestone gravel.

The front yard, like the back, nearly overflowed with flowers, and Joslyn heard the somnambulant buzz of bees and the busy chirping of birds as she paused to look around. For a moment, she felt like Dorothy in the movie version of *The Wizard of Oz,* thrust with tornado force from a black-and-white world into a breathtakingly colorful one.

Except for a tasteful wooden sign suspended from a wrought-iron post by brass chain—Shepherd Real Estate,

Locally Owned—everything looked the same as it had when she lived there.

Four Georgian pillars supported an extension of the roof, and the windows, mullioned glass salvaged from some country house in England in the aftermath of World War II, shone in the sunlight like so many diamond-shaped mirrors. The front doors were mahogany, hand-carved with leaves and birds and unicorns and all manner of ornate curlicues. A heavy brass knocker in the shape of a lion's head added to the grandeur of it all.

After steeling herself for another emotional jolt, Joslyn tried the knob. It turned.

Joslyn pushed open the door and moved into the shadowy coolness of the massive foyer. Soaring two stories high, the entryway echoed with the ponderous ticking of the oversized grandfather clock dominating the inside wall.

Multicolored light spilled through stained-glass skylights, and two grand staircases stood on either side, sweeping upwards to the second floor. The one on the left opened on to the side of the house where her room—more of a suite, really—had been, along with spacious quarters for guests and a private sitting room with its own fireplace. The master suite, with its decadent bath, an honest-to-goodness ballroom, and a sizable library occupied the opposite side of the structure.

Joslyn took a step toward the stairs, like someone hypnotized, but stopped herself before she could go any farther.

This wasn't her home anymore. It was Kendra's, she reminded herself silently.

Yes, Kendra was her friend—probably her *best* friend—but that didn't mean Joslyn could go poking around in the old house, looking behind doors to see what had—and hadn't—changed in the years since her departure.

She peeked into the living room—Elliott had always referred to it as "the parlor"—and saw that Kendra had made good use of the space. There were two desks, both antiques, both equipped with computers and modern phones. The bookshelves on either side of the gray-white marble fireplace were stuffed with manuals but otherwise tidy.

The elegant round table in the center of it all sported a sparkling cut-glass bowl with an exquisite pink orchid floating inside.

Joslyn blinked, and, for the merest fraction of a second, the room was the way she remembered it—cheerfully cluttered, with the bookshelves spilling paperbacks and hardcovers and DVDs, and two huge sofas, upholstered in beige corduroy, flanking the hearth. The TV was blaring, newspapers and magazines littered the floor, and Spunky, the cocker spaniel, barked joyfully, as if to welcome her back after a long absence.

Another blink, and, of course, it was all gone.

They'd taken Spunky with them the night they fled, she and her mom and Opal, and he'd lived to a ripe old age.

Joslyn shook off the twinge of longing she felt and moved farther inside the room. A comfortable seating area filled one corner, but there were no customers waiting, so it was an all-clear. She'd done her duty as far as her friend was concerned, she decided, at least for the time being.

Turning on one heel, Joslyn practically ran out of that house, haunted, as it was, by the ghosts of her pampered youth, and zipped around back to the cottage to fetch her purse and car keys. She needed to cook—like reading, making her favorite dishes and trying new recipes were forms of personal therapy for her—and that meant a trip to the market.

The limestone gravel crunched under the wheels of her car as she drove onto Rodeo Road and turned right.

Parable, population 10,421 according to the sign at the outskirts of town, boasted at least two supermarkets and the discount store she'd visited the day before to buy necessities, but Joslyn liked Mulligan's Grocery, the mom-and-pop establishment across the street from the Curly-Burly Hair Salon, because the meat and produce were organic.

It had been a lot of years, though. Was Mulligan's even there anymore? Or had the small family business gone under, done in by competition from the bigger stores and the rocky economy?

Her heart lurched a little when she rounded the corner and saw cars in the store's grassy parking lot and an open sign in the front window. The soda machine, probably a valuable collector's item by now, still stood next to the screen-door entrance, along with an ice holder and rows of propane tanks for barbecuing.

Cheered, Joslyn parked her car, got out and headed for the door, looping her purse strap over one shoulder as she went.

The same sense of déjà vu she'd experienced in the living room of Kendra's house swept over her as she stepped inside.

She might as well have entered a time warp, things had changed so little. The bread and candy racks were right where she remembered them being, and the floors were still uneven planks, worn smooth by several generations of foot traffic and stained from a thousand spills. The brass cash register, another relic of days gone by, like the soda machine, occupied the same counter in the same part of the store. Only the people were different.

Mr. and Mrs. Mulligan, already old when she'd known them, were probably long dead. Joslyn didn't recognize the gangly man behind the counter or any of the other customers.

The tension that had drawn up her shoulders, without her really noticing, eased so suddenly that it left her a little dizzy. Her mind occupied with memories and ingredient lists, she'd forgotten to dread encountering one or more of her stepfather's numerous victims.

That was bound to happen, sooner rather than later, most likely, but for now, Joslyn dared to hope she'd wandered into a confrontation-free zone.

Please, God.

Except for a nod of greeting, the clerk at the counter didn't pay her any particular attention, and neither did the few shoppers gathering food from shelves and coolers.

Joslyn took a cart, one of the half dozen available—it had a rattle and one hinky wheel—and started down the first aisle. She hadn't bothered to make an actual list, since she needed practically everything.

She was standing in front of the spices, picking out the must-haves, like paprika and poultry seasoning, when she suddenly realized someone was watching her.

Joslyn looked up into a pair of eyes so blue that they might have trapped fragments of a sky darkening its way toward evening. Her heart fluttered up into the back of her throat and flailed there as she registered the man's identity.

Slade Barlow.

A badge glinted on his belt, reminding her that he was the sheriff of Parable County now, and he carried his hat in one hand and a bottle of water in the other.

Be out of town by sunset, Joslyn imagined him saying, in a slow, thoughtful drawl, befitting his jeans, Western shirt and polished boots.

"Hello," she said, sounding stupid in her own ears and feeling as stuck as a deer caught in the dazzle of oncoming headlights.

A slight frown creased Slade's tanned forehead. His hair was dark and short, though not *too* short, and those new-denim eyes were slightly narrowed.

"Joslyn?" he asked.

She bit her lower lip, nodded, wishing she'd worn a pair of shades and a baseball cap, so she could have pulled the brim down over her face.

Or, better yet, one of those dime-store disguises with the big plastic nose and mustache attached to a pair of horn-rimmed glasses.

Slade's white, even teeth flashed as he grinned. "Well, now," he said, still watching her.

Well, now? Just what did *that* mean?

Joslyn racked her brain, trying to recall if Sheriff Barlow had been caught up in Elliott's scam, but it didn't seem likely. He'd grown up in the trailer across the road from Mulligan's, the shy son of a single mom, holding down a paper route until junior high and washing cars and helping out with hay and wheat harvests after that. He'd driven an old car with rust spots on the chassis and the muffler duct-taped to the undercarriage.

A far cry from the flashy red car she'd been given the day she'd gotten her driver's license.

Nope, Slade wouldn't have had the means to sign up for pie-in-the-sky with Elliott Rossiter. Lucky him.

"I was sorry to hear about Elliott," he said.

Here it comes, Joslyn thought, inwardly bracing herself. "Sorry?" she echoed, stalling.

"That he died?" Slade prompted with just the hint of a grin dancing in his eyes and flirting with the corners of his mouth. For the most part, though, his expression was solemn. Thoughtful. Like she was the last person on earth he'd expected to run into in Parable, Montana, or anywhere else.

"Thanks for not adding 'in prison,'" Joslyn said, without intending to say any such thing.

"I reckon that part goes without saying," Slade replied easily. She knew he wanted to ask what she was doing back in Parable, and of course she couldn't have told him, even if she'd been inclined to do so, because she still didn't know herself. He nodded, started around her and her cart. "Anyhow, good to see you again," he said.

It was a lie, of course, though cordially told.

"Same here," Joslyn fibbed.

She'd have avoided Slade if she could have, but she had to admit, if only to herself, that Callie Barlow's baby boy had grown up to be one good-looking hunk of cowboy.

Once he'd rounded the display of boxed doughnuts at the end of the aisle, Joslyn tried to concentrate on spices again, but all she added to the seasonings already in her cart were salt and pepper.

The shopping cart wheel creaked and grabbed at the floor with every revolution as she pressed on toward the meat, fish and poultry, showcased in a refrigerated cooler, sure that everyone in the store must be staring at her by now, suddenly recalling her former association with Elliott Rossiter.

She selected a package of tilapia, an

organic game hen and some lean hamburger, trying to distract herself by ogling the prices—which were outrageous. She'd go broke if she did all her shopping at Mulligan's, that was for sure, nostalgia or no nostalgia.

But she didn't stay distracted for long.

Slade Barlow not only filled her thoughts, he seemed to *permeate* her body, too, as though there had been some quantum-level exchange of energy.

He was taller than she remembered, broader through the shoulders. It wasn't even noon, and he had a five o'clock shadow, and, furthermore, that quiet confidence of his both drew her and made her want to sprint in the opposite direction.

What was *that* about?

She heard him exchange pleasantries with the clerk as he paid for the water, heard the little bell over the front door chime as he went out.

She stood frozen in front of the meat counter, strangely shaken, half expecting the sky to cave in, shattering the not-so-sturdy roof of Mulligan's Grocery and landing all around her in big, blue chunks snagged with wispy strands of cloud.

"Aren't you Elliott's girl?" a quavery female voice asked.

Startled out of her daze, Joslyn turned and saw Daisy Mulligan herself standing at her side, shrunken and white-haired, with pink patches of scalp showing between her pin curls, but very much alive. Her blue eyes were watery behind the old-fashioned frames of her glasses.

Joslyn caught herself just before she would have blurted, "I thought you were dead," and rummaged up a warm smile, putting out her hand. "Joslyn Kirk," she said pleasantly. "Elliott was my stepfather."

Daisy nodded slowly, her rheumy gaze watchful, as she shook Joslyn's hand. "Nobody around here thought the Rossiter boy would grow up to be a crook," she remarked. "His father and grandfather were both doctors. Solid citizens. We should have known there was something wrong with Elliott when he didn't go to medical school."

Joslyn tried to read the old woman, but it was impossible. Either Mrs. Mulligan was about to shout down the ceiling, calling Joslyn the spawn of Satan and ordering her out of the store, or she was just making conversation.

There was no way to tell.

"And when he didn't marry a home-town girl," Daisy added ruefully, following up with a sigh. She looked fragile as a bird in her cardigan sweater and simple cotton dress, though she walked without a cane and her shoes weren't orthopedic.

Uh-oh, Joslyn thought.

"Not that your mama wasn't a nice-looking woman," Daisy allowed.

"Is," Joslyn corrected awkwardly. "My mother is still—around."

Daisy reached out and patted Joslyn's left hand, where it rested on the handle of the rickety shopping cart. "That's good to know, dear," she said. Behind the smudged lenses of her glasses, her eyes grew a size. "Some of us thought you'd come back and marry up with Hutch Carmody, since the two of you seemed so crazy about each other, but the majority expected you to steer clear of Parable for good."

Joslyn gripped the shopping cart handle with both hands now, her knuckles turning white. Daisy went on before she could think of anything to say.

"Fred's brother-in-law lost a bundle in that mess of Elliott's," the old woman reminisced. "Died before that outfit in Denver started sending out checks."

"Checks?" Joslyn managed, almost croaking the word.

"A settlement," Daisy Mulligan said. "That's what the letters from the lawyers said it was. Most everybody Elliott bamboozled got their money back, with interest, but it was too late for some."

Joslyn's throat tightened. She swallowed again. She'd known some of the people Elliott had fleeced were gone, known she'd have to face the living ones who remembered. But knowing hadn't prepared her for the actuality, and neither had all the sensible answers she'd rehearsed on the drive up from Phoenix.

Daisy didn't break her conversational stride. "Folks figure the tax people or the accountants or somebody must have tracked that money down to some foreign bank where Elliott stashed it before he went to jail, then gone in there and seized every nickel. It was like a miracle when those checks started showing up in people's mailboxes."

Joslyn nodded, and her smile felt plastered onto her face, about to crumble and fall away. "That must have been what happened," she said, though she knew full well that none of the stolen money had been recovered. Elliott had certainly squandered most of it, if not all.

Daisy smiled benignly. "I can't imagine what you're doing back here in Parable," she mused aloud, her tone sweetly confidential, as though she were sharing a secret. In the next instant, her wrinkled face brightened with speculation. "Unless you're going to marry Hutch Carmody after all," she said, almost breathless with excitement. "He could sure do with a wife. Might settle him down a little—he's got that wild streak in him, you know, like his old daddy had. And his mama's people, why, they might have acted fancy, but they made all their money bootlegging back in the 1920s. Before then, they were nothing but a bunch of hillbillies."

Joslyn felt like someone trying to board a moving freight train. "Umm— no," she finally said, stumbling lamely into an answer. "There isn't going to be a wedding. I mean, Hutch and I are friends, but there's nothing romantic going on between us."

Daisy's eyes twinkled. "Not so far, anyhow," she said.

With that, having said her piece, Mrs. Mulligan nodded once, turned and walked away.

Joslyn finished her shopping, paid up at the register and headed for her car, pushing that stupid cart through the gravel.

A dog, a thin, dirty yellow Lab with burrs in its coat, sat near the front bumper, like some disconsolate hitchhiker hoping to cadge a ride.

Joslyn hadn't had a pet since Spunky—she'd been too busy to give a dog or a cat the attention it would need—but she was a soft touch when it came to any animal, especially when it was so obviously down on its luck.

"Hey, buddy," she said, after putting her groceries in the backseat of the car and pushing the cart aside. She could see that the dog was wearing a collar, and there were tags dangling from it. She could also see his ribs. "Who do you belong to?"

He shivered visibly, but he didn't run away. Maybe he didn't have the strength, the poor thing. From the looks of him, he'd been on his own for a while.

The best thing to do, Joslyn instructed herself silently, was get into her car and drive off. Just go home, put away the groceries, check Kendra's office again and cook something. The dog had tags, after all. Someone would see that he found his way back to wherever he belonged.

Or not.

It was just as likely, she supposed, that he'd been dumped by some heartless jackass who hadn't bothered to take off the collar. Joslyn took a cautious step toward the creature, one hand extended so he could get her scent. He sniffed her fingers warily, shivered again, but remained where he was.

"You wouldn't bite me now, would you?" she prattled, moving closer, her hand still in front of the dog's muzzle. "Because I'm not going to hurt you, fella—I just want a look at those tags, that's all."

She crouched in front of him, looked into soulful brown eyes, full of baffled sorrow and the faint hope that some small kindness might befall him. Carefully, Joslyn lifted the first of two tags. The numbers on the pet license had been partially worn away, but the second tag was more informative. The dog's name was Jasper, and there was a local phone number.

Joslyn rummaged for her cell phone and dialed. One ring. Two. And then a recorded voice, deep and more formal than friendly, sounded in her ear. "This is John Carmody," the voice said. "I can't come to the phone right now. Leave your name and all that and I'll get back to you, if I think it's a good idea."

Despite the warmth of that June day,

a chill prickled down both Joslyn's arms, raising the fine hairs as it passed.

She'd been away from Parable for a long time, but she'd known about Hutch's dad's death. Kendra had emailed her the news, and she'd sent a condolence card immediately. Obviously, no one had gotten around to erasing Mr. Carmody's voice mail, with the peculiar result that, even though she knew better, Joslyn felt as if she'd just had a conversation with a dead man.

And here was that dead man's dog. Not seeing the point of leaving a message, she simply closed the phone and dropped it back into her purse.

"I'm so sorry, boy," she said, stroking the dog's head gently.

He shivered again.

She straightened, moved to open the back door of the car and began transferring her grocery bags to the trunk.

Jasper watched her the whole time, still hopeful.

"Come on," she said, when the back-seat was clear. "Let's get you home to Whisper Creek Ranch."

Jasper hesitated, as though debating

the matter, then limped obediently over
and jumped into the backseat, landing
with a little whimper.

Was the dog hurt? Should she take
him straight to the nearest veterinarian?
Her head was beginning to ache.

Joslyn slipped behind the wheel of
the car and glanced into the rearview
mirror. Jasper's big mug filled the glass.

"Everything's going to be all right,"
she promised him.

He sighed and settled in to wait for
further developments.

Joslyn got her cell phone out again.
She didn't have Hutch's number, but
Kendra was on speed dial.

Her voice mail came on, and Joslyn
figured her friend was either at the real-
estate closing she'd mentioned earlier
or busy showing somebody around the
chicken farm.

"Give me a ring, ASAP," she said. "I
need Hutch's number."

She hadn't even gotten out of the lot
before Kendra called her back.

"Why?" Kendra asked, not bothering
with a hello.

Joslyn stopped the car, making sure

she wasn't blocking incoming or outgoing traffic, and sighed. "Why, what?"

"Why do you need Hutch Carmody's
phone number?" Kendra was probably
trying to sound nonchalant, but it wasn't
working.

A slow smile spread across Joslyn's
mouth. Kendra Shepherd and Hutch
Carmody? They were polar opposites,
those two—she was prim and proper,
some would say a control freak, and
Hutch was a hell-raiser who liked to
take life as it came.

And those things were just the *beginning* of their differences.

Still, stranger things had happened,
especially in the realm of romance.

"I need the number," Joslyn replied
smoothly, "because I'm looking for a
night of wild, irresponsible sex, and I
figure Hutch will make as good a partner as anybody."

Kendra sucked in a breath—and then
laughed. "Well, if you're looking for 'irresponsible,'" she quipped, "Hutch is
definitely your man."

Zing, Joslyn thought, still smiling.

"Actually, I found his father's dog just

now, and the poor thing looks pretty bedraggled and very much in need of some tender loving care."

"Jasper?" Kendra asked. "You found Jasper?"

"Yes," Joslyn replied patiently. "That's what his name tag says. And when I called the number, I got John Carmody's voice mail."

"That must have been strange." There was a pause. "Hold on. I'm scrolling for Hutch's contact information."

"Holding," Joslyn confirmed, thrumming her fingers on the top of the steering wheel.

"555-6298," Kendra finally said.

Joslyn wrote the number in the dust on the dashboard of her car, using her fingertip for a pen. "Thanks," she said. "By the way, I checked the office before I left home. Nobody there."

"That figures," Kendra said, sounding tired all of a sudden.

Since Kendra was usually annoyingly optimistic, Joslyn picked up on the contrast right away, subtle though it was. "Are you okay?" she asked.

"My feet hurt," Kendra said, "and still no offer on the chicken farm."

Joslyn chuckled. "You didn't change out of those high heels?" she chided. "It's the law of cause and effect, my friend. And maybe the eighteenth showing will be the charm, and the next great chicken farmer will sign on the dotted line."

The smile was back in Kendra's voice. "Right," she said, with wistful good humor. "Do you happen to have any wine on hand?"

"I beg your pardon? I just moved in, Kendra. I barely have staples."

"Wine *is* a staple," Kendra retorted. "The last client dinner party wiped out what was left of my supply, so I'll stop for some later, on my way home. We can raise a glass to old times. Red or white?"

Jasper leaned over the back of Joslyn's seat and ran his tongue along the length of her right cheek. It was a companionable gesture.

She laughed, making a face. "Red, I guess, since it doesn't have to be chilled.

I'm about to cook up a storm, so plan on arriving hungry."

They set a time—six o'clock—said their goodbyes and hung up.

Joslyn immediately dialed the number etched into her dashboard dust.

Another recording. If the words hadn't been different, the effect would have been downright eerie.

Hutch sounded almost exactly like his father.

"Leave a message," he said tersely. "I might call you back and, then again, I might not. It all depends on what you want."

"I have your father's dog," Joslyn said after the beep and then realized the statement sounded like the preamble to a ransom demand. "I mean, it's Joslyn Kirk calling. You remember, from high school? I'm living in Kendra Shepherd's guesthouse now, and—well—I found Jasper and I'm sure you've been looking for him so—" She paused, blurted out her cell number and snapped the phone shut.

"What a charmer," she told Jasper wryly.

The lab gave a little whine of com-miseration.

"Guess you'll just have to come home with me for the time being," she told him with a surge of gladness that sur-prised her. If there was one thing she didn't need with her life in suspended animation, it was a dog.

Still, it wouldn't hurt to enjoy Jasper's company for a few hours. Would it?

After looking carefully in both direc-tions, Joslyn pulled out onto the high-way and pointed herself, Jasper and the groceries in the direction of Rodeo Road. It was time to push up her sleeves and get cooking.

The rest of that day was slow, which was good, Slade supposed, consider-ing the business he was in. He clocked out at five o'clock sharp, something he rarely did, and headed for home.

Letting himself into the one-bedroom duplex he'd rented after his marriage went to hell two weeks after he'd been elected sheriff, he looked around at the minimal furnishings, the bare walls and the scruffy carpet in a color his mother had dubbed "baby poop green."

The place had never been a home, just a place to wait out a transition—a campsite with walls and windows and a roof.

He hung up his hat, unhooked his badge from his belt and set it aside. He carried a service revolver, but that was locked up in a gun safe under the driver's seat of his truck.

From the front door, it was a straight shot to the open, one-counter kitchen, a hike of about a dozen feet, give or take.

Slade zeroed in on the refrigerator, which was the same uninspired color as the carpet, opened the door and assessed the contents. Two cans of beer, half a stick of butter and a shriveled slice of pizza from a couple of days back. He should have bought more than a bottle of water back there at Mulligan's Grocery, he reflected, taking a beer and shutting the fridge door on the dismal selection.

The truth was, he'd been too distracted to think straight ever since the meeting at Maggie Landers's office that morning, and running into Joslyn Kirk at the grocery store hadn't helped matters.

He popped the top on the beer, opened the sliding glass door next to the card table that served as a dining area and stepped out onto his miniscule brick patio. The grass needed mowing, and weeds were springing up everywhere.

On the other side of the low concrete-block wall loomed the old Rossiter mansion.

Slade sighed and sank into a beat-up lawn chair to sip his beer. A chuckle rumbled up into his throat as he sat there, watching the dandelions take over what passed for a lawn, and he shook his head.

Damned if he hadn't gone from solvent to out-and-out rich in the space of a single day. And then there was Joslyn.

A spoiled teenager with a bristly attitude when he'd last seen her, she'd rounded out into a warm-curved woman.

He'd barely squared that thought away in his mind when the familiar yellow dog sprang over the back wall and trotted right up to him.

CHAPTER THREE

Joslyn watched, taken aback, as Jasper, docile since she'd made his acquaintance at Mulligan's Grocery, suddenly transformed into a bionic robo-dog, streaking through the rose garden and the beds of nodding zinnias to take the rear wall in a single bound and launch himself into the neighboring yard like a missile.

Hutch, having just pulled up in an old pickup truck with mud drying on its sides, stepped down from behind the wheel, took off his hat, tossed it into the vehicle before shutting the door of the rig and grinned, resting his hands on lean hips.

"You reckon this means old Jasper isn't glad to see me?" he joked.

Joslyn smiled and started toward her old friend. "I don't know *what's* gotten into that dog," she said. "He's been on his best behavior since we met up in the parking lot—at first, I even thought he might be a little lame. So much for *that* theory."

She started off in pursuit of Jasper then, and Hutch fell into step beside her.

"It's good to see you again, old buddy," she told him.

"And you," Hutch responded gruffly.

Taking a sidelong glance at Hutch's ruggedly handsome face as they walked, Joslyn was surprised to see that he looked solemn. He was gazing in the direction Jasper had gone, and his mouth had hardened a little.

The grin was definitely a thing of the past.

He shoved a hand through his dish-water-blond hair and came back to himself, as if from some vast distance, just as they reached the gate between Kendra's property and the rental beyond.

Hutch opened the tall wooden gate with a jerk that made the partially rusted hinges squeal in protest and shouldered his way through.

Joslyn was right behind him. She felt responsible for Jasper—after all, he'd made his great escape on her watch.

Plus, she was curious.

In the old days, the gate had opened onto a vacant lot where she and the other kids in the neighborhood used to play softball. It hadn't occurred to her to wonder who lived there now that there was a house of sorts.

The sight of Slade Barlow standing on the little patio brought her up short.

So did the silent static immediately arcing between him and Hutch.

Jasper sat next to Slade, a little behind him, panting from the heat and recent exertion, calmly watchful.

"I thought this dog looked familiar," Slade said quietly, his arms folded as he regarded his father's son. Everyone knew that Slade and Hutch were half brothers, but it was a subject people whispered about—no one discussed it openly, as far as Joslyn knew.

"I'm here to take Jasper home," Hutch replied. Every muscle in his back and shoulders seemed tight, from Joslyn's perspective. He dropped his gaze to the dog, gave a low whistle. "Come on, fella." He beckoned. "Let's get going."

Jasper thumped his tail against the ground a couple of times, but he didn't move from Slade's side.

"I'm not sure he's ready to leave quite yet," Slade observed. His gaze moved to Joslyn, and he gave a slight nod to acknowledge her presence, his mouth quirking up ever so slightly at one corner, as though something about her amused him.

That got under her skin.

"He belonged to Hutch's father," she said helpfully, and immediately wished she'd kept her mouth shut. There was a lot going on here, and it wasn't entirely about the wall-leaping stray.

"I remember seeing him riding shotgun in Carmody's truck," Slade allowed.

Jasper still didn't move. Neither did Hutch.

Slade made a clicking sound and started in Hutch's direction, clearly hoping the dog would follow. Jasper stayed put.

Short of picking the animal up bodily and lugging him back through the gate to his pickup, Hutch seemed to be out of options.

"I'll be damned," he muttered.

Slade shrugged one powerful shoulder, and Joslyn found herself wondering, incomprehensibly, what he'd look like without a shirt.

To break the spell, she leaned down and patted her palms against her blue-jeaned thighs, summoning Jasper.

"Time to go home," she cajoled cheerfully.

Jasper merely gazed at her, switched his tail again, just once, and held his ground.

"Suppose I bring Jasper out to the ranch later on," Slade suggested easily. It was obvious that he was enjoying this little standoff, and that annoyed Joslyn—not that he would have cared whether she was annoyed or not. He was looking directly at Hutch, not at her; she might have been transparent. "I'd like to take a look around anyhow."

Beside Joslyn, Hutch stiffened slightly. "That figures," he said, and though he spoke mildly, the remark had a sharp point to it.

Slade didn't flinch. If anything, he seemed intrigued by the situation, charged though it was.

The scene reminded Joslyn of the famous gunfight at the OK Corral down in Tombstone. Except that nobody was armed.

Thank heaven.

"I'll bring the dog out to Whisper Creek in a little while," Slade reiterated.

Hutch didn't reply. He just nodded once, abruptly, and turned and headed toward the gate in the ugly wall. Maybe he hoped Jasper would follow, but that didn't happen.

Jasper had evidently made up his mind to stay.

Joslyn looked in Hutch's direction, then back at Slade.

Hutch might have gone, but the strange charge lingered in the air, a silent rumble like the prelude to a summer thunderstorm.

Slade lifted his eyes to the mansion behind Joslyn, and something flickered in their too-blue depths. "Are we neighbors?" he asked, his tone idle.

Joslyn felt her cheeks turn warm. "It would seem so," she said. "I'm renting Kendra's guesthouse."

"Ah," Slade said, as though her response explained a lot. Global warming, say, and strife in North Africa.

She didn't want to leave without the dog. It was the principle of the thing. So she tried one more time.

"Jasper?" she said, with just the faintest note of pleading in her voice.

Jasper cocked his head to one side, looking apologetic but remaining where he was. It was almost as though the dog had been searching high and low for none other than Slade Barlow and, now that he'd found him, it was trail's end.

He was home free.

Wondering why she felt so rattled— there was a thrumming inside her that was both unnerving and singularly

pleasant—Joslyn offered Slade a falter-
ing smile. "Well, I have company, so I
guess I'll go. . . ."

"See you," Slade said.

She turned and hurried through the
gate, leaving it open just in case Jasper
changed his mind.

Fat chance of *that* happening.

Doubling back through the flower-
beds and the rose garden, Joslyn saw
that Kendra was just pulling up in her
sporty blue convertible, a shiny BMW.
Hutch, probably exasperated over being rejected by his father's dog, especially in favor of Slade Barlow, stood
near his truck.

Kendra got out of the BMW, hauling
her gigantic purse with her.

Wine bottles clinked together inside.

"Hello, Hutch," she said, sounding
shy.

Hutch's tension eased visibly as he
looked at Kendra. "Hey," he said.

There it was again, Joslyn thought.
That weird zip in the air.

She felt superfluous standing there,
even intrusive.

"Hutch just stopped by to pick up

Jasper," she explained to Kendra, who hadn't asked. Hadn't even looked away from Hutch, as it happened.

"I thought dogs were supposed to be loyal," he said musingly with a little shake of his head. "I've been trying to track Jasper down ever since he ran off, the day Dad died."

Kendra was clearly puzzled, and a faint flush of apricot pulsed under her perfectly sculpted cheekbones. Her smile wobbled a little on her mouth and she cast a frantic say-something glance in Joslyn's direction.

"Why don't you join us for supper?" she asked Hutch.

Kendra's color deepened to pink.

Uh-oh, Joslyn thought. Wrong "something."

"Can't," Hutch said, almost too quickly. "I've got horses to feed."

Curiouser and curiouser, Joslyn reflected. "Another time, then," she said.

"Another time," Hutch agreed. Then, with a nod of farewell and one more glance toward the still-open gate leading to Slade's backyard, he sighed and got into his truck. He started the engine, rolled down his window and smiled at Joslyn, though his eyes were sad. "Thanks for looking after Jasper," he said.

"No problem," Joslyn answered.

With that, he was leaving, backing up, turning around, heading down the long, glistening driveway.

"What's going on between you two?" Joslyn immediately asked, turning to her friend.

Kendra's blush had subsided by then. She followed Hutch's rapidly disappearing truck with her eyes, looking every bit as sad as he had moments before.

"Nothing," she said unconvincingly.

"Let's open the wine," Joslyn said, resigned.

Kendra nodded, drummed up a smile, and the two of them walked toward the open front door of the guesthouse.

"If Hutch came by to pick up Jasper," Kendra ventured when they were inside and Joslyn was rummaging through a kitchen drawer for a corkscrew, "why did he leave without him?" She pulled two bottles of wine from her handbag and set them on the counter.

Joslyn found the corkscrew and broke into an Australian Shiraz. There weren't any wineglasses, but jelly jars would do. "It was the strangest thing," she answered, after a few moments of struggling with the cork. "Jasper and I were out in the yard—I figured the dog would be really glad to see a familiar face, after all he's probably been through—but all of a sudden, he just bolted for the back wall. Jasper, I mean, not Hutch."

Kendra smiled weakly at the clarification, accepted a jelly glass brimming with wine and waited for Joslyn to go on.

"You didn't tell me Slade Barlow lived next door," Joslyn said.

"You didn't ask," Kendra pointed out. "What happened next?"

"Jasper did some kind of instant-bonding thing with Slade. I called the dog. Hutch called the dog. And the crazy critter wouldn't move an inch. It was as if he'd belonged to Slade all along." She paused, frowned. "He's married, right?"

"Jasper?" Kendra said, with a sort of melancholy smile in her eyes.

Joslyn made a face at her.

"Oh," Kendra chimed, as though having some sort of revelation. "You meant *Slade*."

"Duh," Joslyn said, filling a jelly glass for herself.

"Divorced," Kendra said. "He was married to this gorgeous redhead with legs up to here and one of those smiles that knock men back on their heels. She was at his side while he campaigned for Sheriff, but once he got elected, she took the little girl and boogied for the big city and the bright lights."

Joslyn felt strangely diminished. She was moderately attractive, she knew, but no way did she qualify as "gorgeous," and she wasn't going to be knocking anybody back on their heels anytime soon.

Not that it mattered. Much.

"They had a child?" she asked, forgetting all about the toast she'd planned to make to her and Kendra's lasting friendship, and taking a big gulp of wine.

"*She* did. The smartest kid you've ever seen—Layne's a few years older than Slade, which might be one of the reasons things didn't work out." Kendra sniffed appreciatively. "What smells so good?"

"Supper," Joslyn said, immediately going on a hunt for pot holders. "And if I don't take it out of the oven, it's going to burn for sure."

Minutes later, Joslyn and Kendra were settled at the table, sharing a meal and talking about everything *but* Slade Barlow and Hutch Carmody.

Slade was about as still as the dog until several moments after Joslyn Kirk disappeared through the gate in the back wall; he had to fight down the damnedest urge to go after her.

And then what?

He sighed and looked down at the dog who looked back up at him, eyes luminous and full of peace.

Slade knew he resembled John Carmody—it was something he couldn't help—but surely this wasn't a case of mistaken identity. Dogs recognized their masters, no matter what.

"Want some water?" he asked the

animal, moving toward the sliding glass door leading in from the patio.

Jasper trotted after him, tags jingling merrily.

Slade got out the bowl he used for cereal, filled it from the faucet in the kitchen sink and set it down on the floor.

Jasper drank thirstily.

"You'll probably be happier out at Whisper Creek," Slade said, wondering if he'd been alone too long. After all, here he was, talking to a dog, which was the next worst thing to talking to *himself.*

"There's room to run out there," Slade went on. "A ranch is a good place for a dog." *Or for a man who'd rather be a rancher than a sheriff,* he thought.

Mercifully, the wall phone rang just then.

Slade grabbed for the receiver, which was mustard-yellow with a twisted chord.

"Slade Barlow," he said.

"Dad?"

Slade closed his eyes for a moment, glad his stepdaughter couldn't see him. The word *Dad* always lodged in the sorest part of his heart, sharp as a sliver. "Hello, Shea," he replied, his voice a little hoarse.

"She's driving me crazy!" Shea wailed. She believed in jumping right in.

Slade looked down at the dog, saw that he'd emptied the water bowl and was gazing up at him like Oliver Twist asking for more. "I guess by 'she,'" he replied, with a note of irony as he bent to pick up the bowl, "you mean your mother?"

"Whatever," Shea said. She'd been seven years old when Slade and Layne got married, and eleven when they divorced. Now she was sixteen with a driver's license, and the thought made the backs of his eyes sting. She was changing, moment by moment, and he wasn't there to see her grow up.

Or to protect her.

Slade didn't miss his ex-wife, and he was sure the feeling was mutual, but a day didn't go by that he didn't think of Shea and wish he and Layne had been able to hold the marriage together for the kid's sake, if not their own. Maybe even given her a sister or a brother, or both.

Slade refilled the water bowl and set it down for Jasper, who immediately started guzzling again. The Lab looked clean enough, but he was skinny as all get-out, and it was obvious that he was in the grip of a powerful thirst.

"I want to come and live with you," Shea said. Then, plaintively, "Please?"

"We've talked about this before," Slade answered, with an ease he didn't feel. If he'd been Shea's biological father, he'd have asked for joint custody, but he wasn't. Where she was concerned, he had no legal rights at all. "Remember?"

He could just see Shea rolling those wide lavender eyes of hers, dark bangs catching in her lashes. "You're not my real dad," Shea recited, singsong, because they had indeed had this discussion before—numerous times. "I *know* that. Mom's my mom and dear old Dad is some *sperm donor* who doesn't even care that I exist. So what does that make you? Huh? My stepdad—or just some guy who used to be married to my mother?"

Slade's heart cracked and quietly split right down the middle. In the few years they'd been a family, he'd come to love the girl as if she was his own. "I'll always be your stepdad," he said gently. Shea's father hadn't been a "sperm donor"—Layne had been married to the guy once upon a time—but there was no use in arguing the point. The kid wouldn't hear him.

Shea sniffled, and her voice got shaky. "She's impossible."

Slade smiled. Whatever their differences, hers and his, Layne was a good mother and an all-around responsible person. She'd set herself up in business in L.A., staging houses for real-estate firms, and made a success of it. "And you're a teenager."

"What's *that* supposed to mean?"

Slade ignored the question, since it had been rhetorical. "Shea," he said. "You and I both know your mom loves you. What's the real issue here?"

"She's sending me to boarding school next fall," Shea announced.

"What?" Slade thought for a moment that he hadn't heard correctly.

"Mom's in a relationship," Shea said, interspersing the words with a few more sniffles. "They're getting married."

"All right," Slade said, letting out his breath. *Boarding school? What the hell was Layne thinking?* "So what does your mom's relationship have to do with going away to school?"

Shea gave a long, dramatic sigh. "I might have been a little difficult lately," she confessed.

Slade leaned against the counter, pressing the receiver to his ear so hard that it started to hurt.

He eased up on the pressure, though his gut felt as tangled as the phone cord.

"This guy," he said, after clearing his throat. "Do you like him?"

"Bentley's all right," Shea admitted, albeit reluctantly.

Bentley? What kind of name was that?

"So—?"

"So maybe I acted out a little—and stirred up some trouble. Which is probably what made Mom decide that if she was going to have a shot at true love, she'd better get the kid out of the way for a while."

Slade moved to the fridge, opened the door, retrieved the arthritic slice of pizza and gave it to Jasper, who gobbled it up.

Had Joslyn given that critter water *or* food?

"Define 'acting out,'" Slade said, thinking he'd ask Shea to put Layne on the phone in a minute or two, so he could get some straight answers.

"I got a tattoo."

Slade swallowed a chuckle; he'd been expecting her to say she'd been doing drugs, or she was pregnant, or she'd been busted for shoplifting. The tattoo, while hardly good news, came as a relief.

"Doesn't that require a parent's permission?" he asked, watching Jasper lick his chops after scarfing up the pizza.

"There are ways around that whole permission thing," Shea said airily. "Anyway, Mom went ballistic when she found out. She and Bentley had a long talk and decided to incarcerate me for my last two years of high school."

Slade's mouth quirked up at the word *incarcerate*. "Is your mom around? I'd like a word with her."

"I'm not at home," Shea said.

"Tell me you didn't run away."

"Of course I didn't run away," Shea answered. "It's not like I don't know that's a bad idea, Dad. I'm at the mall, with a couple of my friends—I'm calling on my cell." She paused, drew in an audible breath and went on in a rush. "Can I come and live with you? Instead of going to boarding school, I mean?"

Loaded questions, both of them.

It might have been different if there were a woman in his life, a wife or even a steady girlfriend. But Slade was single, living in a one-bedroom dive of a place with an inadequate bathroom. His job was demanding and sometimes dangerous. Furthermore, he couldn't give Shea the kind of attention and guidance she needed—what did he know about teenagers, anyway? Especially those of the female persuasion?

Despite all those things, he wanted to say yes.

"Let's not get ahead of ourselves," he said finally, because he didn't want to cut the poor kid off at the pockets with an immediate "no." "I want to talk to your mother and hear her side of all this."

"She hates the tattoo. It's just a little, tiny bumblebee, on my right shoulder—it doesn't even show unless I'm wearing a tank top."

Slade smiled, picturing his ex-wife, a flawless auburn-haired beauty who wouldn't think of inking so much as a pore of her perfect skin. "You're sixteen," he reminded Shea. "That means your mom still makes the rules. I'll have a word with her and get back to you."

"She'll just convince you that she's right and I'm wrong and boarding school will be the best thing that ever happened to me," Shea argued.

"For now," Slade replied, gently but firmly, "this conversation is over. I'll call you back after I talk to your mother."

Shea huffed out another sigh. "Okay," she said, sounding as though she might start crying. He didn't think he could handle that.

"Shea?" Slade said.

"What?"

"I love you."

"Sure," Shea replied with mild skepticism, and they both hung up.

Slade kept a scrawled list of pertinent phone numbers taped to the inside of one of the cupboard doors; he pulled it open and scanned for Layne's information. Her office, home and cell were all listed, though most had been crossed out and replaced so many times that he had to squint to make out the most recent.

It occurred to him that everyone moved on with their lives—new homes, new numbers, new everything—except for him.

He was still stuck in the same dismal digs and the same job—one he'd wanted very much at the time he landed it. Over the past few years, though, he'd begun to get bored, yearned more and more for the life he *really* wanted to live: that of a rancher, with a wife and kids and a dog like Jasper.

Layne answered her cell phone on the second ring.

"Hello, there," she said sweetly with a warm smile in her voice. "Still breathtakingly handsome, I presume?"

References to his looks always embarrassed Slade a little, even from a woman he'd been married to; he regarded physical appearance as the least important aspect of a person. His marked him as John Carmody's son—the throwaway he hadn't bothered to acknowledge until after he was dead and gone.

"I'm fine," he said, watching as Jasper curled up in the middle of the floor and dropped into a deep snooze. "Listen, Layne, I just had a call from Shea and—"

"And she told you she's being banished to boarding school," Layne interrupted with a long-suffering sigh.

"Something like that," Slade said, turning one of the two folding chairs at his card table around and sitting astraddle of the seat. "What's going on, Layne?"

Again, Layne sighed. Slade pictured

her shaking back her mane of thick russet hair, which, the last time he'd seen her, had just brushed her shoulders. "She's—rebellious. I'm worried about her, Slade. Some of her friends have gotten themselves into real trouble."

"And in every case it started with a tattoo?" Slade teased, keeping his tone light, though he was concerned about Shea, too, of course.

"Bentley and I have tried everything," Layne said, quietly earnest and, unless Slade missed his guess, somewhat desperate, too. "Family counseling. Long heart-to-hearts at the kitchen table. Even a trip to Europe during her spring break. Shea closes herself off from me—I can't seem to get through to her."

"And you think boarding school is a solution?"

"I'm willing to try almost anything at this point," Layne admitted sadly. "Short of putting her up for adoption or just plain wringing her stubborn little neck."

"She wants to come here, to Parable."

"I'm not surprised," Layne answered.

"*You're* in Parable, after all. And I suspect that's the crux of the problem— right now, you're still her stepfather. She can pretend that you and I will reconcile at some point. Once Bentley and I get married . . ."

Slade closed his eyes for a moment. "Yeah," he said, when her words fell away. "I see what you mean. But don't you think sending her off to boarding school is a little drastic? Where is this place, anyway?"

"Havenwood is just south of Sacramento," Layne replied quietly. "It has a wonderful reputation for getting troubled kids back on track, and the level of education is unequalled."

"What makes you think Shea's going to cooperate, Layne?"

"I'm not sure she will," Layne said. "But I'm out of choices. I love my daughter, Slade, but I also love Bentley. I'm still relatively young and I want another shot at happiness. Is that wrong?"

"Of course it isn't wrong," Slade said.

"If you have a suggestion, cowboy," Layne told him, "I'd love to hear it."

That was when he said it, the thing

he hadn't planned to say. The impossible, crazy thing he had no right to say.

"You could send her here, to Parable, just for the summer."

There was a brief and, Slade thought, *hopeful* silence.

"You mean it?" Layne asked, very tentatively, after a few moments.

"Yes," Slade said, as surprised as anybody. "I mean it."

All the while, his brain was reeling. Where was he going to put a sixteen-year-old kid? And what if, like Layne, he simply couldn't get through to Shea? If she got into trouble, it would be his fault.

"Okay," Layne said. "Let's give this a try. If Shea calms down a little after a summer away from home, we can revisit the whole boarding school question in the fall."

"Okay," Slade echoed.

Layne laughed softly, but there was something broken in the sound. "I wish we could have made it," she said. "You and me."

"Me, too," Slade said. "But we didn't."

"No," Layne agreed. "You're probably

the only person on earth I'd trust with my daughter—you know that, don't you?"

"Yeah," he said, his voice gravelly. He was moved, because there was no doubt that Layne was telling the truth: she could count on him and she knew it. "I appreciate that, Layne. It means a lot."

There was a brief pause, brimming with all that might have been.

"I'll speak to Shea and get back to you so we can agree on the travel arrangements," Layne said at length. "And, Slade?"

He waited.

"Thanks," Layne finished.

They said their goodbyes, and Slade hung up.

"What the hell am I going to do now?" he asked Jasper, who had surfaced, yawning, from his nap just as Slade replaced the phone receiver in its cradle.

Jasper gazed quizzically up at him, probably wondering what kind of yahoo asked a dog a question right out loud and half expected to get an answer.

He shoved a hand through his hair,

heaved a sigh. Headed for the dinky bathroom, with its dinky shower stall and dinky tub. He started water running in the shower and fetched a change of clothes from the bureau in his bedroom.

Jasper stayed right on his heels the whole time, sat right there in the bathroom doorway while Slade stripped, climbed into the shower and scrubbed until he felt refreshed.

After that, he dried off with a ratty-looking towel—he'd need to get new towels before Shea arrived, for sure. Hell, he'd need a new *house.*

Fifteen minutes later, he and Jasper were in the truck and headed for Whisper Creek Ranch.

There was still a lot of daylight left, but the sky was turning a pinkish orange where it rimmed the distant mountains, soon to be followed by a lavender twilight and then moon-laced darkness.

If he wanted a good look at the ranch that was legally half his, he'd have to wait for tomorrow, but at least he could get Jasper back home, where he belonged.

The Carmody house was a long, rambling structure, two stories high. The lawn looked one hell of a lot better than Slade's own, and some kind of fluffy flower grew everywhere, in a profusion of pink and red, yellow and white.

He stopped his truck in front of the house, and before he shut off the engine, Hutch came out of the front door and stood on the broad porch, looking unfriendly.

Slade got out of the pickup. "I brought your dog back," he said.

CHAPTER FOUR

Jasper hunkered down in the passenger seat of Slade's truck, suddenly as unwieldy as a feed sack stuffed with scrap iron.

Hutch, an incongruous sight in that yard full of flowers, looked mildly amused as he came through the gate in the picket fence to watch the struggle.

"I'll tell you something about that dog," Hutch offered after a few beats. "He can be real cussed."

"Ya think?" Slade countered, exasperated. By now, Jasper wasn't just a dead weight; he'd turned slippery as a brook trout in the bargain. And he was still in the truck seat, where he clearly intended to remain.

Hutch laughed. Stood nearby with his arms folded and his head cocked to one side. He must have resembled his late mother, Lottie Hutcheson, Slade thought distractedly, because he didn't look a thing like the old man.

No, that was *his* cross to bear—never looking into a mirror without seeing a younger version of the man who had denied him since birth.

"You might just as well take him back home with you," Hutch continued, surprising Slade. "Jasper's like Dad was—once he's made up his mind about something, he's not likely to change it."

Slade slanted an appraising look at the man who was, biologically at least, blood kin. They were nothing alike, the two of them. Or were they? Down deep, at the DNA level, there had to be some similarities.

"Got any suggestions?" Slade finally asked.

Hutch considered the question at his leisure before offering an offhanded reply. "Like the ranch, I reckon old Jasper is half yours and half mine. Since he's taken a notion to be your dog from here on out, you might as well stop trying to wrestle him out of that truck and spare him the long walk back to town. You leave him here, he'll follow you home for sure."

Slade rubbed the back of his neck, pondering Hutch's words. He didn't need a mutt any more than he needed the responsibility of looking after a six-teen-year-old girl, but he figured Hutch was right. For whatever reason, Jasper had appointed himself sidekick. For the duration, evidently.

Slade knew he'd welcome the com-pany, though—he'd kept his life and his heart closed up tight since the divorce, doing his job, showing up, putting one foot in front of the other. Maybe it was time to open up a little, let somebody in.

Even if that somebody happened to have four feet and a tail.

It was a beginning, he supposed, though he wasn't sure of what.

"All right," he agreed slowly and shut the truck door with Jasper still inside.

"I'd swear that critter looks out-and-out relieved," Hutch said drily. "And in case you're wondering, I never mistreated him. Jasper was always a one-man dog, and Dad was that man. Now, I guess, the torch has been passed."

Slade studied his half brother for a long moment. Hutch's manner wasn't exactly cordial, but he wasn't waving a loaded shotgun and ordering him off the property, either. "Thanks," he said.

"You given any more thought to selling me your share of Whisper Creek?" Hutch asked after waiting a moment or two.

"I've given it plenty of thought," Slade answered, squinting a little against the last dazzling light of another summer day, "but I haven't come to any decision."

Hutch absorbed that response with a slight but oddly affable frown creasing the skin between his eyebrows. Then he gestured toward the house. "At the moment, the place is as much yours as it is mine," he said, and there was no reading either his tone or his expression. Carmody would be able to hold his own in a high-stakes poker game, that was for sure, Slade reflected—and he wouldn't need a hooded sweatshirt, a baseball cap or wraparound shades to manage it. "You might as well come inside and take a look around."

Slade looked past Hutch, taking in the rambling lines of that house. He'd never set foot in the place, and now fifty percent of it was legally his. It was a hard thing to take in.

"All right," he said after a long hesitation. He looked back at Jasper, who sat like a sentry in the truck seat, watching him through the partially rolled down window. The dog would be fine by himself, Slade decided, at least for a few minutes. He followed Hutch through that white picket gate, along the flagstone walk, up the porch steps.

He'd wondered about the inside of that house for as long as he could remember, though he'd never aspired to live there, or even step over the threshold. Now that he had a dog, and Shea was coming to spend what remained of the summer with him, however, he was a lot more interested in real estate.

Tomorrow was his day off—he'd check in with Kendra, maybe take another look at the Kingman spread. The house was nothing fancy, being nowhere near the size of this one, and it had sat empty for a long time. Still, with a little elbow grease and a lot of hot, soapy water, it would be livable.

They'd still be short one bathroom, though.

Inside Hutch's domain, Slade was immediately impressed with the high-beamed ceilings and the open floor plan. Despite all those flowers in the yard, the interior was singularly masculine, with sturdy leather furniture, plain, heavy tables and zero clutter. A few Navajo rugs and some high-quality Western art provided muted splotches of color here and there. The space had a quiet, meditative quality that surprised Slade a little, given Hutch's wild-man reputation.

What had he expected? Mirrors on the ceilings? A functioning saloon straight out of an old John Wayne movie or maybe a mechanical bull in the middle of the living room?

Slade indulged in a small, rueful grin, gone in an instant.

"Look around all you want," Hutch said, in the same casual tone as before. "I think you'll agree that as big as the place is, it won't accommodate both of us."

Slade grinned again, not about to let on that he felt a little sheepish all of a sudden, like he'd barged in or something. "You're right about that last part," he said. "And I've seen all I need to. It's getting late, and Jasper'll need some gear if he's going to move in with me."

Hutch assessed him in silence for a long moment, then said, "There's a bag of kibble in the pantry, and Jasper's got a bed and a couple of bowls and a few toys. You're welcome to the stuff if you want it."

"Sure," Slade said, mildly embarrassed. It only made sense to accept Jasper's belongings—the things would be familiar to the dog and therefore comforting, and besides, it would save a shopping trip to the big discount store out past the city limits. "Thanks," he said again.

"This way," Hutch said, turning.

Slade followed him through a set of swinging doors and into a big kitchen with dark-stained wooden floors, like those in the front part of the house, tall windows and a lot of gleaming steel appliances. The island in the center of the room was bigger than Slade's whole kitchen back at the duplex.

Hutch disappeared into what must have been the pantry and brought out a big sack of kibble, still three-quarters full. He set it down near one of the counters—there seemed to be miles of them, all smooth gray granite—and gathered up two ceramic dog dishes.

"Jasper's bed and the toys are in Dad's room," Hutch said. "I'll get them."

Slade nodded. "That'll be good," he replied, intending to lug the kibble and the bowls out to the truck while Hutch was fetching the other things.

Instead, though, he just stood there, after Hutch was gone, in that big kitchen.

He imagined his father reading the newspaper at the long table while he drank his morning coffee with Jasper at his feet.

Something about the image made Slade's throat tighten painfully.

He collected the dog food and the bowls—one of which had Jasper's name painted on it in jaunty letters shaped like bones—and got out of there, quick.

Jasper poked his muzzle out of the truck window and gave a little yelp of glad welcome when he saw Slade approaching.

Slade hoisted the bag of kibble into the back of the truck and placed the bowls at a careful distance from each other so they wouldn't bang around during the drive back to Parable.

Hutch reappeared, carrying the fanciest dog bed Slade had ever seen. It was a large canoe, made of brown fleece, and, like the bowl, it was marked with Jasper's name. There was a bright red leash, too, and a paper bag brimming with chew toys and other canine paraphernalia.

"Dad was downright foolish over that dog," Hutch explained, seeing the look on Slade's face and reading it accurately—as amused disbelief. He tossed the canoe-bed into the back of the truck, along with the other things, and dusted his hands together afterward, though not in a good-riddance sort of way. "The old man bought him Christmas presents and remembered his birthday, even."

That was more than Slade could have claimed. Still, he chuckled and gave his head a shake. "I'll give Jasper a good home," he said, because he knew that mattered to Hutch.

"If I didn't think that," Hutch countered matter-of-factly, "you wouldn't be taking him anywhere."

Slade nodded and rounded the truck. He'd been in more than one brawl with Hutch Carmody over the years, but he'd mostly been indifferent to the man. Or so he'd thought, until now. Given the exchange of the dog, Slade was seeing his father's son in a new light.

What kind of man *was* Hutch, anyway? The question would definitely require further consideration. Not that they'd ever be buddies, he and Hutch, let alone relate to each other the way real brothers would, especially if Slade decided to hold on to his share of Whisper Creek Ranch instead of selling out to Hutch—which was a distinct possibility.

It was clear, though, that there was more to this half brother of his than a hot temper, a penchant for partying and a reputation for leaving a trail of brokenhearted women behind wherever he went.

Hutch turned and went back inside the house as Slade shifted the truck into gear and headed for the main road that would take them back to Parable.

Jasper's lips were pulled back against his jawbones, as though he was smiling. He'd gotten his way, and now he seemed to be gloating a little.

"Don't go expecting presents at Christmas," Slade warned the dog, glad not to be returning to that crappy duplex alone, as he had so many other nights. "Or a cake on your birthday, either."

*   *   *

Although Joslyn wasn't supposed to start her job until the following Monday, she stopped in at Kendra's office bright and early Friday morning anyway, because she'd already done her yoga routine, spiffed up the guesthouse and scanned her email. Without Jasper around to fuss over, she was at loose ends.

Kendra was on the phone when she came in, looking cool and blonde and beautiful, as usual, in a crisp pair of linen slacks and a simple, airy white top. She smiled at Joslyn and held up an index finger to indicate that she'd be finished with the call in a moment.

"That's wonderful, Tara," Kendra said into the receiver, rolling her eyes comically at Joslyn. "You'll make a *wonderful* chicken farmer." A pause. "No, really," she insisted graciously. "How hard can it be? Yes. I'll bring the papers by this afternoon, and you can take the weekend to look them over." She nodded, "Yes," she repeated. "And Tara? It's short notice, I know, but I'd love to throw a barbecue in your honor tomorrow afternoon, here at my place. Can you make it?" Another pause, then a genuine smile. "Great! Two o'clock. No, you don't need to bring anything except yourself and any guests you'd like to include."

Joslyn, who couldn't help overhearing, concluded that, one, Kendra had finally sold the chicken farm she'd shown so many times, and, two, she, Joslyn, would be expected to show up at the barbecue. Along with half the town, most likely. In Parable, parties weren't generally private—they tended to be community events, because in some ways, the inhabitants were like one giant family.

She fought down a mild swell of panic. Her encounter with Daisy Mulligan the day before hadn't been bad, but who knew how the *next* person might respond? On the other hand, that person—and many others—had to be faced.

Kendra ended the call and stood up, smiling. "If you're here to start work," she teased, "you're a couple of days early."

Joslyn sighed, looked around. The

surroundings were certainly pleasant and less emotionally charged than the last time she was there. "I just stopped in to see if you needed help with anything," she said. She tilted her head to one side, smiled back at her friend. "Congratulations are in order, it would seem. You sold the chicken farm?"

"Finally," Kendra said with delighted emphasis. "No one can accuse Tara Kendall of making a snap decision. She's been looking at that place on and off for a couple of years."

"Is she from around here? The name doesn't sound familiar."

Kendra shook her head. "Tara's from New York," she replied. "She heads up the marketing department of a big cosmetic company, I think."

"It's quite a jump from a marketing job in the Big Apple to running a chicken ranch outside of Parable, Montana," Joslyn observed, already intrigued by this Tara person. At least, as an outsider, she wouldn't turn out to be one of Elliott's many victims.

"She's reinventing herself following a bad divorce, as I understand it," Kendra said, starting in the direction of the kitchen and leaving Joslyn with no real choice but to follow. "I sure hope there isn't a 'reality' series in the offing."

Joslyn laughed, though she felt a little nervous as she stepped into the room where Opal had presided for so many years. "*That* would be the biggest thing that's happened in this town since—"

Remembering what the last big thing in Parable was—Elliott Rossiter's investment scandal—Joslyn let the sentence go unfinished, and the laugh died, aching, in her throat.

Kendra looked back at her over one shoulder. Clearly, she knew what had brought Joslyn up short. "Let's have some coffee," she said kindly.

Joslyn looked around, relaxed a little as the instant shame over her stepfather's actions subsided. Kendra had made the kitchen her own, just as she'd done with the front room, where the office was now. There were no ghosts here.

"Does it bother you?" Kendra asked, approaching the coffeemaker—one of those flashy single-cup things—and pushed a couple of buttons. "Being in the house again after all this time, I mean?"

"I thought it would," Joslyn admitted. "And I guess it did at first, but I'm over that, it seems. After all, it's the people who live in a house, not the former occupants, who give it character—you're here now, and the place reflects you, as it should."

Kendra looked thoughtful, maybe even a bit sad, as she busied herself brewing coffee. "If you say so," she said in a musing tone.

Joslyn waited, standing behind one of the sleekly modern chairs at the sleekly modern kitchen table. In the old days, the furnishings and appliances had been antiques, right down to the wood-burning cookstove Opal had insisted on using to prepare family meals.

Kendra looked in Joslyn's direction and managed a feeble little smile. Gave a slight shrug of one shoulder. "Wasn't it John Lennon who said, 'Life is what happens when you're making other plans'?" She set a steaming mug of coffee on the table and indicated that Joslyn should sit down. Then she sighed and shook her head, as though to fling off some unwanted thought.

"What were your 'other plans,' Kendra?" Joslyn asked gently, pulling back one of the huge chrome-and-glass chairs and sinking into the seat.

"The usual," Kendra said, with an unconvincing attempt at sounding breezy and unconcerned. She prepared a cup of coffee for herself. "A husband. Babies. A great career." She paused. "I guess one out of three isn't bad."

Joslyn knew her friend had been married, very briefly, to a wealthy Englishman with a title, but that was the extent of the information Kendra had been willing to share. As close as they were, both of them had their secrets.

"You're young, Kendra," Joslyn pointed out, treading carefully. "You can still have the husband and/or the babies if you want. There are a lot of options these days."

Kendra brought her cup to the table and sat down opposite Joslyn. She looked down into her coffee, but made no move to drink it. "Call me old-fashioned," she said very softly, "but if I'm going to have children, I want to be married to their father. And I'd have to believe in love to get married."

"You don't believe in love?" Joslyn felt a pang of sorrow. Kendra had always been the romantic; even with her 4.0 grade average in high school, she'd been voted Most-Likely-to-Live-Happily-Ever-After by the rest of the senior class.

"Not anymore," Kendra said.

"Does this have something to do with Hutch Carmody?" Joslyn ventured, thinking of the odd charge in the air the day before, when Hutch stopped by to pick up Jasper.

Kendra's cheeks flamed. "No," she said very quickly and very firmly.

Joslyn winced slightly. "I'm sorry," she said. "I can't seem to open my mouth without putting my foot in it."

Kendra smiled, but her eyes remained sad. "I didn't mean to snap at you," she said. "But fair is fair, Joss. Why should I tell you my deepest secrets when it's so obvious that you're holding a lot of things back? We're supposed to be best friends, aren't we? And BFFs exchange confidences."

"You're right," Joslyn said. "What do you want to know?"

"Why you came back to Parable, for a start. I know that someway, somehow, you're behind all those big, fat checks that have been raining down on this town for the past couple of months, whether you'll admit it or not. What I don't get is why you're so secretive about it—or why you would do something like that in the first place. Like I said before, you're not responsible for what Elliott Rossiter did way back when."

"Okay," Joslyn replied, when the constriction in her throat loosened up enough to let a word pass. "Yes. I sold my software design company for megabucks, and I arranged for a law firm in Denver to track down everyone my stepfather stole from and see that they were repaid."

"Why did I have to drag that out of you?" Kendra asked mildly, raising both her perfect eyebrows in an expression of perplexed good will.

Joslyn took her time answering; some soul-searching was required to translate a lot of confused feelings into words. "I don't know," she said after a few long moments. "Not exactly, anyway. Parable was always . . . well, it was *home,* and it's been calling to me all this time to come back. I agree that what Elliott did wasn't my fault, but it shouldn't have happened—good people were all but ruined, after all—and since I had the means to make it right, I did."

"Why keep it a secret, though?"

"Because I want to be accepted in Parable on my own merit, not because I *bought* my way back into the town's good graces."

"You have a very expensive conscience," Kendra observed with a little smile that, though wobbly, was genuine enough. "But I do understand. And your secret is safe with me."

"Good," Joslyn said, relieved. "Now it's your turn. Why don't you believe in love anymore?"

Kendra's eyes filled with such pain

that Joslyn was immediately sorry for pressing the issue. Still, as Kendra herself had said, fair was fair.

"Because of Jeffrey," she said. "My ex-husband."

"What did he do?"

Kendra considered for a long time before replying, "He swept me off my feet, married me and promised me the moon. For a while, he even delivered. We traveled all over Europe after the wedding—it was a small, justice-of-the-peace ceremony—but oddly enough, we never got around to visiting his family in England. They didn't approve of me, as it turned out, but Jeffrey said I shouldn't let that bother me. Love conquers all, et cetera. We came back here, bought this house from the Rossiter estate and made plans to start a family of our own. He had plenty of money, and I was stupid enough to think I'd found someone to take care of me."

"And?" Joslyn prompted, when Kendra fell silent.

"And a week after we closed on this monstrosity of a house, his father fell ill and Jeffrey flew straight home to London. Next thing I knew, he was calling to say so sorry for any inconvenience, but he wanted a divorce. It had all been a colossal mistake, our getting together. Several million dollars suddenly appeared in my personal bank account, and his 'solicitors,' as he called them, sent me the deed to this house. That was it. The fairy tale was over."

"Ouch," Joslyn said, reaching across to give her friend's hand a light squeeze. "That's brutal. Did Jeffrey ever give you a reason?"

Kendra swallowed visibly and shook her head. "He didn't have to," she replied presently. "I don't know if his father was really sick, or it was just a ruse to get Jeffrey to come home, but once he got there, the home folks wasted no time convincing him that what we had together was just an unfortunate fling that must be curtailed at once, and damn the cost. Apparently, Jeffrey came around to their way of thinking. They raised the drawbridge and slammed the caste gate shut in my face and that was that."

"The bastard," Joslyn said with spirit.

"Amen," Kendra said.

Joslyn bit her lip, hesitant to speak but in the end unable to resist putting in her two cents' worth. "Still," she said, "to give up on love seems a little rash, doesn't it? I mean, how likely is it that *that* will happen again?"

"I loved him," Kendra said simply.

"Yes, but—"

"I'd better get back to work," Kendra interrupted. "I have to prepare the contracts for the chicken farm and get copies to both parties, and, of course, there's the barbecue to plan."

"Right," Joslyn said, standing up and carrying her cup and Kendra's to the sink.

"I could really use your help figuring out the food," Kendra said.

Inwardly, Joslyn sighed. There was no way out—Kendra had given her a job and a place to stay, and, besides, they were friends. She'd have to join in the festivities, like it or not.

And she was more than willing to help.

"How many people are you inviting?" she asked in cheerful resignation.

"You'd better figure on at least a hundred," Kendra said. "Probably more."

By then, heading for the inside door, she had her back to Joslyn and probably thought her friend hadn't seen her swipe at both cheeks with the heels of her palms as she dashed out of the kitchen.

Shopping was not Slade's favorite way to spend his time off.

He and his newest deputy, Jasper, were on their way home from the big discount store that morning, in Slade's pickup, when Layne called him on his cell phone.

"I think I'm insulted," Layne said without preamble, as usual. "Shea wants to leave for your place by yesterday, at the latest. She's all packed and every five minutes she wants to know if I've bought the tickets yet."

Slade chuckled, though he had a sinking feeling in the pit of his stomach, too. He loved Shea, no question about it, but he wasn't set up to give her a proper home, not yet, at least.

"You're putting her on a plane, then?"

"Yes," Layne replied. "If you're still up for this, that is. Believe me, Slade, if you want to back out, I'll understand."

"We'll make it work somehow," he said.

"If you don't mind, I'll come along with Shea. Just to help her settle in and everything."

Layne would probably take one look at his bachelor's quarters and hustle her daughter straight back to the airport in Missoula and onto the first outward-bound plane, no matter where it was headed.

"Okay," Slade said. He had to talk to Kendra, pronto, he decided. Even if he bought the Kingman place that day, which he didn't intend to do, the deal wouldn't close for at least a month. Maybe he could make arrangements to rent the house until he'd made up his mind about accepting Hutch's offer to buy out his share of Whisper Creek, though.

"Try to contain your enthusiasm," Layne teased. "I'll only be in Parable for a couple of days, and your virtue is safe, cowboy. I'm madly in love with another man."

Slade waited for the pang of regret Layne's statement should have caused him—he'd loved her, once—but it didn't come. He did wish he could have responded that he was "madly in love" with some hot woman, though.

One like Joslyn Kirk, say. He felt a stirring that did not bode well for getting out of the truck anytime soon, at least, not in the middle of town, where there were so many people around.

"I'll reserve you a room at the Best Western hotel," he said. "When are you planning on getting here?"

"Day after tomorrow?" Layne said, making it sound like a question.

Slade suppressed a sigh. "Shall I pick you up at the airport in Missoula?"

"Definitely not," Layne answered happily. "We'll rent a car."

"Fine," Slade replied. "I'll make the room reservation. Text me your ETA when you can."

"Will do," Layne said.

Slade was about to say goodbye and hang up when she murmured his name.

"Yeah?" he asked.

"Thanks," Layne answered. "I've been at my wits' end over Shea."

Slade wasn't a glib man. He was intelligent, and he was educated, but folks said he was as stingy with words as a miser was with money, and he couldn't refute that. "Everything will be all right," he said.

The call ended, and he headed for Kendra's place.

Once there, he parked alongside the mansion in the blindingly white driveway and spoke to Jasper.

"I won't be long," he said. "Mind your manners until I get back."

Jasper merely sighed.

Inside the big house, Slade found Kendra's office empty.

"Hello?" he called, just to be sure.

A woman's voice answered, from a distance, though it wasn't Kendra's.

"In the kitchen!" someone sang out.

Joslyn Kirk?

Oh, hell, Slade thought. It hadn't occurred to him that he might run into her, though he supposed it should have, since she lived on the property and she and Kendra were good friends. He cleared his throat, debating between sticking around and beating it.

Before he'd decided either way—he'd been leaning toward the first option because the second seemed pretty chickenshit—Joslyn appeared in the big arched doorway joining the office area to the formal dining room.

She had flour in her hair. Slade's heart did a weird little jig and then seized up briefly.

"Oh," Joslyn said, her eyes widening slightly and a blush climbing her cheeks. "It's you."

Slade gave a raspy chuckle. "It's me, all right," he agreed. "Is Kendra around?"

Joslyn shook her head, and her soft brown hair seemed to dance around her oval face. Her eyes were wide-set, her mouth full. . . .

Why was he thinking about her mouth?

"She finally sold the chicken farm," Joslyn said. "She's off delivering contracts." She hesitated, moistened her lips briefly before going on and thus ignited an achy flame in Slade. "Is there something I can help you with?"

Oh, yeah, Slade thought, grimly wry. *But it probably isn't the kind of help you have in mind.*

"I wanted to talk to her about the Kingman place—see if she'd get in touch with the owners and ask them about renting the house to me. I'll catch up with her later."

Joslyn swallowed, nodded. He wanted to touch his lips to the pulse leaping at the base of her throat.

Glad he'd brought his hat with him instead of leaving it in the truck, Slade held it in both hands at belt-buckle level. He hoped the move seemed casual.

"I'll tell her you stopped in," Joslyn said.

He took some consolation in the fairly obvious fact that he wasn't the only nervous person around.

"That would be great," he said. It was the perfect time to leave, but, probably for the same reason he was holding his hat in a strategic position, he didn't.

Joslyn dusted her hands together. "I don't know how to contact the owners," she said, "but if you want another look at the ranch house, I'm sure the lockbox keys are around here somewhere. I could get them and let you inside."

In the next moment, she looked confounded, as though she hadn't planned to say what she had.

Slade didn't need yet another tour of the ranch house—he'd been there with Kendra a dozen times. He knew every inch of the place, which floorboards creaked and the state of the plumbing. He knew just how each room would look, once he'd completed the necessary renovations, which he'd planned in detail.

"I'd like that," he said, careful not to let his gaze drift any lower than the base of her throat. He was already in over his head; no sense making things worse.

CHAPTER FIVE

Joslyn wasn't a licensed real-estate agent; she'd been hired, she reminded herself sternly, as a *receptionist*—a job she hadn't even started yet. For all that, here she was, having just tracked down the lockbox keys to a hook in Kendra's office-supply closet, heading out to show Slade Barlow through a house he'd already seen a dozen times, by his own admission.

She could have simply handed him the keys and sent him off to the King-man place on his own—he was, after all, the county sheriff and could certainly be trusted to enter an empty house unsupervised—but that didn't seem like the right thing to do, either. Every business had its protocols. There were ways to do things, steps that had to be taken, procedures to follow.

"No sense in taking two rigs," Slade said practically, opening the passenger-side door of his extended-cab truck and gently herding Jasper, who had been sitting in front, over the console and between the seats to the back. With a blush that might have arisen from self-consciousness, the cowboy-law-man brushed off the seat, raising a little red-gold cloud of dog hair in the process.

Amused—and strangely touched— Joslyn forgot her own concerns for the moment and indicated, with a gesture of one hand, that she was wearing old jeans and a T-shirt and therefore wasn't worried about getting a little messy.

Slade stepped back, still holding his hat in one hand, and waited for her to climb inside the truck.

Joslyn did so. Felt a blush of her own rise along her neck to the backs of her

ears as she made a major production
of fastening her seat belt.

Jasper, evidently glad to see her even
if he had forsaken her temporary care
to appoint himself Slade's dog, greeted
her by nuzzling her cheek once with his
cold, moist nose.

"Hello to you, too, you traitor," Joslyn
said fondly, smiling, while Slade rounded
the front of the truck and got in on the
driver's side.

Even being in the same room with
this man minutes before had all but
jolted Joslyn back on her heels, as if
she'd grabbed hold of a live wire or
poked a finger into a light socket. Being
in the same *truck,* sitting side by side,
ratcheted the sense-riot to a level of intensity that nearly took her breath away.

What *had* she been thinking to suggest this particular outing in the first
place, let alone agreeing to ride with
Slade instead of taking her own car?
The answer was all too obvious: she
liked the risky, even dangerous, feeling
of being so close to all that quietly un-
compromising masculinity. She was
electrified, her heart pounding, every

nerve in her body thrumming with all sorts of unwise instincts, each more primitive than the last.

Slade was as handsome in profile as he was head-on, and while she couldn't quite resist a glance in his direction, she made sure it was a short one and shifted her gaze to the windshield as soon she could tear it away.

Not usually a prattler, Joslyn prattled. "I'm afraid all I can really do is let you into the house, once we get out to the ranch," she said unnecessarily. The silence was simply too volatile to endure, for her at least, though it didn't seem to bother Slade at all. "I mean, I'm not a broker or an agent, so of course I couldn't make any binding agreements—"

A corner of Slade's mouth quirked. He was looking straight ahead, concentrating on his driving. Having a conversation with him would probably be like trying to herd cats into a culvert.

Having sex with him, on the other hand—

Well, never mind—better not to think about that. *At all.*

Except she couldn't seem to help it.
It was a thrilling prospect—one that
brought another hot blush surging into
her cheeks and made certain her insides felt as though they were melting.

Get a grip, she told herself silently.

"That's all right," Slade said, in that
slow, easy drawl of his. By then, Joslyn
had forgotten what they were talking
about, and he seemed to realize that,
because he added, "That you can't actually sell me the ranch, I mean."

Pause. Joslyn felt as though she'd
suddenly wandered onto a field of ice;
inwardly, she was flailing for balance.

"I understand you've looked at the
place before," she said presently, striv-
ing for a normal tone, and then wished
she hadn't spoken at all. He might think
she was implying that he was indeci-
sive, what people in the real-estate
business called a looky-loo.

Again, she caught herself. So what if
he did think that? Who really *cared* what
Slade Barlow thought, anyhow? *Besides you, you mean?* she asked herself.

Joslyn huffed out a sigh of pure frustration. She was, it seemed, carrying on two parallel conversations, one with Slade and one with herself.

This was unlike her. She was a self-possessed, independent woman. Why should this one man's opinion matter to her at all, let alone enough to rattle her so?

He chuckled—it was almost as though he'd guessed what was going on in her brain and body—and gave her another of those lethal blue-denim glances, the ones with all the impact of being sideswiped by a speeding car.

By then, they were on Main Street, nearly at the town limits. They passed Parable High School and the conveniently located hamburger franchise next door to it, and then they were in the country.

"I'd pretty much decided on buying the Kingman place," Slade told her, "but then—well—another opportunity came up, one that complicates things. I'm thinking of renting the house short-term, since my stepdaughter is coming to spend the summer with me and I basically don't have anywhere to put her."

Joslyn was still digesting what, for Slade anyway, amounted to a lengthy discourse as they cruised on by Mulligan's Grocery and the Curly-Burly Hair Salon on the opposite side of the highway. Both parking lots were semi-full.

Slade honked the horn once, probably saying "howdy" to his mom, Callie, who ran the salon, though he didn't look in that direction.

"I see," Joslyn said, though she *didn't* see. That strange, charged silence was really getting to her now. It was like dancing barefoot on a hot tin roof, this feeling. She should have stayed put in Kendra's kitchen, she decided peevishly, where she'd been whipping up a batch of her special garlic-rosemary focaccia bread to serve at Kendra's upcoming barbecue. At least there she'd only had to deal with memory-ghosts, not a long, lean, red-blooded cowboy putting out vibes that might make her clothes fall off if she wasn't darned careful.

Approaching a side road marked by a wooden For Sale sign and a rural mailbox that leaned distinctly to the right,

Slade geared down, signaled and turned. The truck bumped over a cattle guard.

"What brings you back here, Joslyn?" Slade asked, easily navigating the narrow, winding, rutted road leading uphill. "To Parable, I mean?"

There it was again, she thought. The question she wouldn't be able to avoid answering for much longer. It made her bristle slightly, that particular inquiry, even though it was perfectly reasonable. She supposed.

"I needed a change," she said.

"From what?" Slade wanted to know.

"My old life," she replied.

"Which was where?"

"Am I under investigation?" She was half-serious, though her tone was light.

Slade flashed her yet another devastating grin. "Nope," he said. "If you were, it would have been a matter of a few strokes on a computer keyboard to find out all I needed to know."

Joslyn sighed. It was true enough that her pertinent details were posted somewhere online, which gave rise to an interesting insight. Slade was curious about her past, that was obvious, and he could easily have run a search, but he was asking her face-to-face instead. What a concept.

Of course, he might *already* have run a background check on her and just wanted to see what she'd say.

Joslyn was still grappling with the possibilities when they crested one final hill, and the old house and barn sprang into view. Behind them, in the backseat, Jasper gave a happy little yip of anticipation. Clearly, the dog was already sold on the place, even if his master wasn't.

"I've been living in Phoenix since I finished college," Joslyn said quietly, because she knew there was no avoiding the topic of where she'd been all these years.

"And now you're back in Parable." Slade brought the truck to a halt between the two decrepit buildings that seemed to lean toward each other, as though silently sharing their secrets.

He didn't move to get out of the truck, and neither did Joslyn.

Jasper began to pace back and forth

across the backseat, his paws making an eager, scrabbling sound on the leather. He was anxious to explore the property on his own, evidently.

Joslyn still felt a little testy over Slade's remark.

And now you're back in Parable.

"Is there some law against my being here, Sheriff Barlow? A local ordinance, maybe? 'No one remotely associated with Elliott Rossiter shall set foot in our fair community from now until the end of time'?"

He arched one of those dark eyebrows, and his lips twitched almost imperceptibly.

What, Joslyn wanted to know, did he think was so darned funny?

The dog, meanwhile, was getting more restless with every passing moment, so Slade finally got out of the truck, opened the rear door and stepped aside so Jasper could leap nimbly to the ground. He watched as the animal ran wildly around the overgrown yard, barking exuberantly.

"Are you coming inside or waiting here?" Slade asked Joslyn, his tone as calm and easy as a creek flowing over time-polished stones. This after practically giving her the third degree about her return to Parable.

Pride-wise, remaining in the truck was out of the question—not that the idea didn't have a certain snit appeal—so Joslyn shoved open her door, grabbed her purse, and scrambled down out of the high seat. She marched around the front of the pickup, digging through the jumbled contents of her bag for the lockbox keys as she went.

She was so intent on the search— she'd often said her purse was like a portal to a parallel universe, and things disappeared into it, never to be seen again—that she arrived at her destination sooner than expected and nearly collided with Slade.

He laughed, low in his throat, and steadied her by taking a light hold on her shoulders. "Whoa," he said, blue devilment lighting up his eyes. "I was just trying to make conversation before. If you don't want to tell me what you're up to, you don't have to."

Again, Joslyn took umbrage. She had

Kendra's keys clenched in one hand by then, and she practically brass-knuckled Slade with them, shoving them at him the way she did.

"What I'm *'up to'?*" she demanded, careful to keep her voice down. "What the heck is *that* supposed to mean?" She sucked in an angry breath and exhaled a rush of words with it. "Maybe you think I came back to Parable to steal whatever money my stepfather may have missed? Is that it, Sheriff?"

Slade let his hands fall from her shoulders, and, to her eternal chagrin, she actually *missed* his touch. That annoying little quirk appeared at the corner of his mouth again, and his eyes twinkled. Maybe *she* was all shook up, but *he* was clearly enjoying the situation—a lot.

"No," he said matter-of-factly. He'd been holding his hat until that moment; now, he set it on the truck seat, crown side down, and shut the door. He rested his hands on his hips as he studied her, paying no heed to the wildly happy dog dashing hither and yon through the tall grass, chasing butterflies. "That's old news, what Elliott did."

"Then, what?" Joslyn pressed. "What could I possibly be 'up to'?"

Slade sighed again, ran a hand through his hat-rumpled hair. "I don't know," he replied quietly. Reasonably. "That's why I asked you."

The man was *maddening.*

Joslyn struggled to regain her composure. Finally, measuring her words out carefully, she said, "I grew up here, Slade—just like you did. Parable is home."

His jawline tightened, and his eyes darkened to a grayish shade of violet, reminding her of a once-clear sky roiling with sudden thunderclouds. "You couldn't wait to get out of here, if I remember correctly," he said.

Joslyn narrowed her eyes in consternation and tilted her head to one side as she studied him. So it was still there, that old boy-from-wrong-side-of-the-tracks hostility.

"Yes," she said crisply, squaring her shoulders. "Having all four major TV networks converge on a person's front lawn will do that." Her stepfather's very public fall from grace had been a feeding frenzy for the media; everyone wanted a comment from her, from her mother or even from poor Opal.

"You were making noises about getting out of Parable for good long before the authorities caught up with Rossiter," Slade said, unwilling, it appeared, to give an inch. The laid-back way he'd behaved before must have been an act. "I remember how you were back then, Joslyn. You made it pretty damn clear that you thought you were too good for a hick town in Montana and most of the people in it. So I can't help wondering—what's the big attraction now?"

The words struck Joslyn like a slap. She'd been a spoiled brat back in the day, and there was no getting around it. She'd had too much of everything—too much money, too much popularity, too many honors, like being prom and rodeo queen, class president and the captain of the varsity cheerleading squad. But all that had been *years* ago, and she'd grown up since then. She'd accomplished a lot of good things, become a genuinely nice person.

"People change," she pointed out snippily.

"Not in my experience, they don't," Slade immediately replied.

With that, he turned and headed for the lockbox beside the front door of that ramshackle ranch house, his strides long.

Joslyn watched, still smarting with indignation, as he stepped up onto the sagging wraparound porch, opened the lockbox and took out the actual keys to the house, stored there by Kendra.

He glanced in her direction once, then unlocked the front door, opened it and went inside. Jasper, butterflies forgotten, bounded after him, tail wagging.

"Jerk," Joslyn said under her breath.

And she wasn't referring to the dog.

In the next moment, a wasp buzzed her like a pesky little airplane, driving her along the weedy front walk toward the door.

Not that she needed an excuse to go inside the house and look around or anything like that. She was here on Kendra's behalf, albeit unofficially, and besides, if she stood out there in the yard, or waited in the truck, Slade would have won at whatever game he was playing.

Joslyn wasn't about to let him intimidate her.

So she marched right up the porch steps and on into the house.

She stopped just over the threshold, struck by a strange, sweet sensation of nostalgia; even though she'd never been there before, it was as though the house were welcoming her back from a long and difficult journey, almost *embracing* her.

It was at once pleasant and downright spooky.

She blinked a couple of times, listened to the sound of Jasper's toenails clicking on the hardwood floors in a nearby room, heard Slade speaking to him in low, affectionate words she couldn't quite make out.

Slowly, she shut the door behind her and looked around the shadowy interior of the medium-sized living room.

The place was surprisingly clean for an abandoned house—Kendra or the

owners must have hired a cleaning service to come in at regular intervals—
and it had a certain quiet charm, too.
The fireplace was formed of simple red
brick, with a wide wooden mantel above
it, and there were built-in bookcases on
one of the outside walls, framing a set
of bay windows with a bench seat un-
derneath. The floors were varnished
wooden planks, a soft butternut in color,
and instead of nails, they'd been secured with pegs.

It was easy to picture that room with
prints on the walls, comfortable furniture of the shabby-chic persuasion, colorful throw rugs scattered about, books
crowding the shelves, a fire snapping
on the hearth while fat flakes of snow
drifted past the windows. Even a glittering Christmas tree wasn't that big of a
stretch.

Joslyn reined in her imagination with
a sigh and a shake of her head. She'd
gotten carried away for a moment there,
but she was all right now. Really.

Except that something sweetly vis-
ceral flicked at her nerves just then, first
in her solar plexus and then all over her

body, and she turned to see Slade watching her from a nearby doorway, Jasper beside him.

For a few seconds, she and Slade simply looked at each other.

Then, in his forthright way, Slade said, "I'm sorry, Joslyn. About what I said outside, I mean."

She swallowed and tried to smile, but couldn't quite manage the feat. The truth was, he'd hurt her, this man whose opinion she did not want to value.

"All right," she said. Now *there* was a witty reply.

He crossed to where she stood, faced her.

She looked up at him. Breathed in the fresh-air scent of his clothes and skin. Let the heat of him warm her bones. If he were to kiss her right now, she thought dizzily, there wouldn't be a thing she could do about it.

Only he didn't. He simply watched her for a long moment, with a crooked little smile and a light in his eyes, and then he asked, "What do you think?"

What did she think? Of what? Being kissed? *Not* being kissed?

"Oh, you meant what do I think about the *house.*"

He grinned, amused all over again. "Yeah," he said. "About the house."

"It's—" Joslyn looked around, sighed softly. "It's lovely, what I've seen of it, anyway. Not at all what I would have expected, seeing it from the outside."

"Come on," he said, offering his hand. "I'll give you the tour."

He led her through the place, room by room. They checked out the large, old-fashioned kitchen, the single bathroom with its huge claw-foot tub, the downstairs bedroom with its glaring lack of closet space. There were three more bedrooms upstairs.

"I missed houses like this when I lived in Phoenix," Joslyn confided when she and Slade and the dog had gone full circle and returned to the living room.

Slade arched an eyebrow, asking "why" as effectively as if he'd spoken the word out loud.

"There are so many modern housing developments these days," she explained, feeling oddly self-conscious again. "All the houses seem to be built to the same general plan, of the same materials, and they look pretty much alike. Places like this, well, they're unique—they have character and personality."

"I agree," Slade said.

"You have a stepdaughter?" The question just popped right out of Joslyn's mouth, without her intending to ask it. It was weird the way her mind leapfrogged all over the place when she was with Slade.

She saw a gleam of pride in his eyes. "Yes. Her name is Shea and she's sixteen, going on forty-five."

"Kendra mentioned that you had a wife," Joslyn said. *Keep digging yourself in deeper and deeper,* advised the voice in her mind. *Why don't you just bump his hip with yours and ask him if he's looking for a good time?*

"Past tense—I *used* to be married. Layne and I have been divorced for a while now." Without touching her, he somehow managed to steer her toward the front door.

She missed the strength of his hand curved loosely around hers.

"Oh," Joslyn said, glad he couldn't see how happy she was to have his marital status clarified.

That didn't preclude a girlfriend, though.

"You?" he asked, as they stepped out onto the porch. He busied himself locking up again, while Jasper sniffed around in the grass.

"Single," Joslyn told him. "I've never had the time to fall in love."

He rested a hand lightly at the small of her back as they descended the rickety porch steps. "It takes time?" he teased. "I've always thought of it as something sudden, like getting struck by lightning."

She smiled at that, incredibly nervous though she was.

They reached the truck, and he opened her door for her, simultaneously whistling for the dog.

"Well, yes," Joslyn went on, as though there had been no gap in the conversation. "It takes time. You have to go out, circulate, meet new people, take chances. I was always too busy working."

Or too much of a coward to risk a broken heart.

Slade didn't move; he just stood there looking at her for a long moment, one hand on the door's edge, while Jasper trotted toward them, tongue lolling. She would have sworn the man was about to say something, but, in the end, he didn't.

Instead, he loaded the dog into the back, secured the door and came around to get behind the wheel again.

They were back on the main road and well on their way toward town when he finally spoke again. "What kind of work kept you too busy to fall in love?" he asked in a tone that might have been described as conversational—if anyone but Slade Barlow had been doing the talking.

The man did not engage in idle chit-chat. Joslyn had figured out that much. "I was a software designer," she said. "Computer games, that sort of thing."

He shifted the truck from second gear to third, and out of the corner of her eye, Joslyn saw the muscles bulge in his forearm. He'd rolled his sleeves up at some point.

"Impressive," he said without looking at her.

Joslyn swallowed. It was just too easy to make the jump from admiring his tanned, well-formed arms to imagining what it would be like to be *held* in them. And more.

"Not really," she answered, practically croaking out those two simple, innocuous words. "It's a matter of learning computer languages and practicing them until you're fluent."

He spared her a sidelong glance. "Is *that* all?" he said. He spoke lightly, but behind those blue eyes, Joslyn had no doubt, the wheels were turning and the gears were grinding. "Must be interesting work."

"It's demanding, too," Joslyn said with a nod of agreement. "There's a lot of pressure to come up with the next big, new thing, while the *last* big, new thing is still on the drawing-board. So I guess I'm a little burned out."

There, Sheriff Barlow. Chew on that for a while.

What he said in response surprised
her. "Me, too," he said, with a sigh. "I
loved being sheriff once upon a time,
but now I'd just as soon do something
else."

"Like what?" she asked, intrigued.
And very glad that they were talking
about his life now, instead of hers.

"Ranching," he replied. Why use ten
words when one would suffice?

"That's a tough business these days,"
Joslyn said. "Ranching, I mean."

As if she knew one darned thing
about the subject. She hadn't ridden a
horse in years, and, even when she had,
she'd been a terrified fraud.

"Every business is tough these days,"
Slade answered.

They were both quiet for a while as
they rolled on toward town.

Joslyn lapsed into a reflective mood,
thinking about the house they'd just left
and how different the inside was from
the outside, with its peeling paint and
sagging boards and the gap-toothed
state of the shingles on the roof.

For some reason, she thought of Kendra. On the exterior, her friend was a

beautiful, confident woman with a thriving business and an amazing house. On the interior, though, Kendra was as insecure as anybody else. She'd lost faith in the very thing that seemed to be most important to her: love.

Joslyn jumped back into the present moment, landing with all the gentle grace of a paratrooper wearing steel-toed boots. "You don't want to be sheriff anymore?" she asked.

Slade chuckled. "You don't do segues, do you?"

"No," Joslyn admitted. "Mostly not."

He slowed to the in-town speed limit as they passed the high school, shifting gears again. Flexing those muscles. "I haven't made a formal statement to the effect that I won't be running for reelection," he said mildly.

"But?"

"But," Slade conceded, with a smile, "I'm not wild about the man I believe will take my place if I leave."

He signaled a turn, and they were back on Rodeo Road.

"Who would take your place?" Joslyn asked.

Slade hesitated, bringing the truck to a stop in front of Kendra's palacelike home and place of business. His gaze was fixed on something beyond the windshield while he considered his answer—if indeed he planned on giving one.

"Never mind," he said, at last. "You don't know him."

"I might," Joslyn replied, peeved again.

"I've said all I plan to say on the subject," Slade informed her, pushing open his door.

She didn't wait for him to get around to her side but unbuckled her seat belt and got out of the truck on her own while he was still walking around it. "Then I guess you shouldn't have brought the matter up in the first place," she challenged as she worked the latch on Kendra's front gate.

"You're right," Slade said, standing on the sidewalk. "I shouldn't have."

She looked back at him, exasperated all over again, but determined to be polite, businesslike. Or at least *civil*.

"Shall I have Kendra call you?" Joslyn concluded that, since her friend's car wasn't in the driveway, she was probably still out.

Slade shook his head. "No need," he said. "I'll catch up with her before the end of the day." With that, he got back into his truck and drove away.

Joslyn hurried into the house and made a beeline for the kitchen. She washed her hands, pulled on the apron she'd been wearing before Slade interrupted her day and got back to work on her baking project for tomorrow's barbecue.

By the time Kendra got back an hour or so later, Joslyn was mostly over the encounter with Slade, and the kitchen smelled marvelously of fresh bread laced with herbs.

Kendra carried a grocery bag in each arm. Joslyn hurried over to relieve her of one of them, setting it on a nearby counter, and both women spent the next few minutes carrying in the rest of Kendra's purchases, jammed into every nook of her small car. When she threw a party, evidently, there were no-holds-barred.

She'd bought soda for the children, wine and beer for the adults, enough steak, hamburger and hot dogs to feed the cast and crew of a sword-and-sandal movie, plus condiments, paper napkins, plastic cups and cutlery.

"The rest is being delivered," she told Joslyn when they'd brought everything in.

"The *rest?*" Joslyn echoed with a small grin. "What else could you possibly need?"

"Potato salad, of course," Kendra said breezily. "They're making that up special at Mulligan's, along with a few desserts."

"Good heavens," Joslyn said, unpacking bags and stowing things in the refrigerator. Fortunately, the appliance was huge, and there was plenty of room inside, since Kendra seemed to live on yogurt and string cheese. "You must have invited half the county."

Kendra smiled and kicked off her high heels with a little wince of relief. "And they'll bring the other half," she said.

"I showed a property today," Joslyn admitted, still emptying bags.

Kendra padded over to a cupboard, took a tall glass down, got herself some ice and poured in a diet soda. "So I hear," she said, with just a hint of merriment in her voice. "I ran into Slade a little while ago at Mulligan's. He was buying canned dog food—turns out Jasper is something of a picky eater."

The mention of Slade's name gave Joslyn that now-familiar teetery feeling, so she got even busier putting away groceries. "Jasper," she said, "is a force of nature."

Kendra chuckled. "So is Slade," she replied. "Of course I invited him to the barbecue. Shea and her mom, too, if they get here on time."

Joslyn absorbed that. *Of course* Kendra had invited Slade. He was an old friend, a neighbor, a pillar of the community. If Joslyn herself was a little uncomfortable with the idea, well, that was *her* problem, wasn't it?

"Did he ask you about renting or leasing the ranch house he's been looking at?" she asked, hoping she sounded casual.

"It's a done deal," Kendra answered,

after taking a sip from her glass of soda. "I called the heirs—they're distant cousins of the original owners with no interest whatsoever in a run-down Montana ranch—and they're open to a six-month lease."

"That's good," Joslyn said.

"Stop fiddling with those bags," Kendra commanded good-naturedly, "and sit down for a minute. I need a break, and so, obviously, do you, my friend."

Joslyn took a seat at the fancy modern table, even though it was about the last thing she felt like doing at the moment.

Kendra eyed her speculatively.

"What?" Joslyn finally asked with a touch of impatience.

Kendra smiled. "I thought so," she said.

"*What?*" Joslyn repeated, wanting to make some excuse and bolt.

Kendra looked delighted. "You have a thing for Slade Barlow," she said.

CHAPTER SIX

"I do *not* have a 'thing' for Slade Barlow!" Joslyn replied too quickly.

"Says you," Kendra challenged, smiling. Idly, she rattled the ice cubes in her nearly empty glass of soda. "You blush every time you hear the man's name, and whenever the two of you happen to be in the same room together—"

The timer dinged on the super-stove, a six-burner monstrosity imported from England, and Joslyn was grateful for the excuse to jump up from her chair at the table and hurry over to take four fragrant loaves of bread out of the oven.

"Nonsense," she said, but she didn't sound very convincing, even to herself.

"He's available, you know," Kendra said coyly, pushing back her chair and standing. "Slade, I mean. And he's one of those rare men who actually *like* being married."

Joslyn shoved four *more* pans of bread dough into the oven to bake, set the timer and went back to unloading grocery bags. She didn't respond, but Kendra went right on talking just as if she had.

"Slade probably thinks you're still interested in Hutch Carmody," she said. "And, as you must remember, those two have issues with each other."

That statement stopped Joslyn with her hand still inside a bag full of hot dog and hamburger buns. She knew that Slade and Hutch were half brothers—everyone did—and she recalled the rows they'd gotten into as boys, but they were grown men now. Surely they were over all that now.

"Once and for all, Kendra," she said evenly. "I don't *care* what Slade Barlow thinks."

In a pig's eye, you don't, taunted that annoying voice in her head.

"I don't believe you," Kendra said, closing the refrigerator door and joining Joslyn at the long counter, still lined with bulging bags of supplies for tomorrow's barbecue.

"Besides," Joslyn said, with considerable bag-rattling, "Hutch and I went together in *high school,* a hundred years ago. I still consider him a friend, but whatever the attraction was when we were kids, it's gone."

Kendra tried to hide it, but she was clearly relieved. Maybe the whole point of the conversation, from her perspective, had been to find out if Joslyn still cared for Hutch in a romantic way.

The thought cheered her a little. Okay, so Kendra claimed she didn't believe in love anymore. But that, it seemed to Joslyn, was like not believing in gravity, or the phases of the moon. Some things simply *were,* whether a person believed in them or not.

"I know you're attracted to Hutch," she told Kendra gently. "You're both adults, presumably unattached, so why not go for it?"

Kendra bit her lower lip, looked away briefly. "We're too different, Hutch and I," she said.

Joslyn merely raised both eyebrows and waited.

Little red circles pulsed in Kendra's cheeks, like blooming flowers. "I'll admit there's a certain—well—*spark* between us."

"Think so?" Joslyn teased.

Kendra sighed. "We were discussing you and Slade," she pointed out, "until you cleverly turned things around."

"There is no Slade-and-me," Joslyn said. "Yes, he's hot. Yes, I've thought about what it would be like to go to bed with him. But, fortunately, I came to my senses. He's got a chip on his shoulder, Kendra—to him, I'm still the spoiled little rich girl speeding around town in a convertible and looking down her nose at everybody."

"He *said* that?" Kendra asked, after drawing in a breath. Evidently, she'd forgotten to breathe for a few moments there.

"In so many words, yes," Joslyn answered.

"Oh," Kendra said, sounding deflated.

Joslyn patted her friend's arm. "Let's get these groceries put away," she said.

They worked well together, their movements quick and efficient, and there was no more talk about Slade Barlow *or* Hutch Carmody.

"I appreciate your help, Joss," Kendra said when the last of the bread was cooling on the counter and all the bags had been emptied, folded and stuck into the recycle bin. "Stay for supper?"

Joslyn shook her head and smiled. "No, thanks," she said. "Maybe I'll have a bowl of cereal or a sandwich later, but right now, I'm on food overload. All I want at the moment is a bubble bath and a good book to read."

Kendra smiled back and nodded. "Sounds like an idea to me," she replied.

After a quiet "sleep well," Joslyn left by the back door, crossing the screened-in porch that had been her mother's sanctuary for so long. With a pang, she realized how much she missed her mom and how much she still missed Opal. And she had the strangest sense of having lived two distinctly separate lives, albeit as the same person—the young, self-absorbed Joslyn and the woman she was now.

It was late afternoon by then, and the flowers nodded in their beds as she passed, heading for the side door of the guesthouse.

She stopped a few feet short of it, surprised to see a hefty gray cat sitting on the welcome mat, grooming one forepaw. The creature wore its bushy tail jauntily, like a boa, and its eyes were an arresting shade of amber.

The animal eyed her calmly, as if to say, "*There* you are—it's about time you got back."

First Jasper and now this cat. What was she? Some kind of magnet for stray pets?

Unlike Jasper, the cat wasn't wearing a collar. It looked clean and well fed, though, and surely belonged to some-one.

"Meow," it said conversationally.

"Go home," Joslyn said, though not

unkindly. "Someone is probably looking for you."

The cat didn't move, except to perk up its ears and cock its head to one side.

"Well, alrighty, then," Joslyn said, resigned. "You might as well stick around until I can find out who you belong to. I don't happen to have any cat food on hand, but how do you feel about fat-free coffee creamer?"

She stepped past the cat, opened the door and entered her tiny kitchen.

The cat followed, its fluffy tail switching gracefully back and forth, like a question mark in motion.

As she'd told Kendra, Joslyn wasn't hungry, but she figured the cat might be, so she poured creamer into a saucer, tore a piece of bread into bite-sized morsels and set the works down on the floor.

The new arrival began to eat without hesitation.

Joslyn filled a cereal bowl with water and put that on the floor, too.

Then she headed for the bathroom,

filled the old-fashioned tub with semi-hot water and stripped off her clothes.

She was soaking, bubbles tickling her chin, when the cat strolled in, leaped nimbly onto the closed lid of the toilet seat and regarded her with an expression of benign expectation.

"I'm not going to get attached to you," Joslyn said. "Either your owners will show up, or you'll decide you'd rather hang out with Slade Barlow, like Jasper did."

"Reoww," said the cat.

"Furthermore," Joslyn went on, feeling only slightly silly for carrying on a conversation with a four-legged companion, "I can't keep calling you 'the cat,' so you'll need a name. A temporary one, of course."

The cat did the boa thing with its tail again, and from her present viewpoint, Joslyn could tell the animal was female. Judging by the size of its belly, it was probably pregnant, too.

That's just great, she thought ruefully.

"To me, you look like a Lucy-Maude," Joslyn said aloud. "I've always liked that name."

Lucy-Maude regarded her calmly, all elegance, striking a coquettish pose.

After her bath, Joslyn pulled a cotton caftan on over her head and proceeded barefoot into the living room, where she booted up her laptop.

Lucy-Maude came along, taking up a new post, this time on the arm of the big easy chair, with its somewhat tattered floral slipcover.

The laptop came alive, and Joslyn, suppressing a sigh, sat down in front of it and logged on. There were half a dozen emails from her mother.

Dana Kirk—she'd taken back Joslyn's father's name after the divorce from Elliott and never bothered to change it when she got married for the third time—usually practiced a healthy detachment from the more mundane details of her daughter's life. They talked on the phone once a month and emailed each other fairly often between calls, but neither of them needed constant reassurance of the other's affection.

Dana had been a loving, attentive mother while Joslyn was growing up and a rock during and after the Elliott debacle, and Joslyn had always known her mom was in her corner.

Feeling mildly guilty for not checking in sooner, Joslyn tapped into the first message. Then the second, then the third.

The first few were calm and chatty— **how was the trip? What's it like to be back in Parable after all this time? Say hello to Kendra for me; she was always such a nice girl.**

After that, though, the messages took on a note of steadily rising anxiety.

You're all right, aren't you?

Then, **Joslyn Lee, what's going on?**

And finally, **Damn it, Joslyn, answer your email!**

Joslyn smiled as she opened a new message window to respond. **Sorry if I worried you, Mom,** she wrote, trying to sound reassuringly perky. **I'm fine, just busy settling in and all that. So far, nobody has taken a potshot at me, but I'm sure word's all over town that Elliott Rossiter's stepdaughter is back.**

She went on to update Dana on Kendra, mentioned tomorrow's big barbecue and finished with an account of Lucy-Maude's arrival on her doorstep.

All that time, Joslyn was just as aware of what she was omitting from the missive as what she was including.

She didn't say that Kendra's disillusionment with love hurt her heart, for example, though it did. Kendra was a class act, and she'd be a wonderful wife and mother, just as she was a wonderful friend.

She didn't say that she had real misgivings about the reception she might get from some of the townspeople at her friend's barbecue the next day or that she'd have to steel herself to go.

And she sure as heck didn't mention the crazy way Slade Barlow made her feel—all achy and sweetly scared, and not at all like her usual, practical, computer-savvy left-brained self.

Dana believed in an easygoing, one-step-removed approach to parenthood, especially now that Joslyn was an adult, but that didn't mean she wouldn't fret.

The email was lengthy by the time Joslyn ended it with, **love you**, and hit Send.

Because she hadn't been online since she'd come back to Parable, Joslyn's mailbox was full to bursting.

She deleted the junk, sent short, chipper replies to various friends in Phoenix, assuring them all that she was "fine, just fine," and answered a few technical questions for the IT people at the corporation she'd sold her company to.

And then she logged off.

It was time for a bowl of cereal and a good book.

Slade called Layne that night, told her he'd leased a house in the country and said he and Shea could make a run to Missoula one day soon to pick out furniture.

Layne sounded distracted—unlike him, she had a life—and said she and Shea would arrive in Parable sometime on Sunday afternoon. She'd call as soon as they were settled at the Best Western hotel.

Slade asked to speak to Shea, and Layne said she was at the mall with her friends, buying jeans, boots and tank tops to bring to Parable.

The image made Slade smile. He said goodbye, hung up the receiver and turned to Jasper, who sat in the middle of the kitchen floor, waiting patiently for his kibble.

Slade fed the dog, opened a beer and stepped out onto that pathetic little patio of his. The house on the ranch needed some work, and he and Shea would both be sleeping on air mattresses and eating their meals at a card table for a while, but it would sure beat living here.

Jasper joined him outside, once he'd finished his supper, and sat next to Slade's lawn chair, a companionable, peaceful presence.

Slade ruffled the dog's ears gently and thought about the woman on the other side of that back wall, living in Kendra Shepherd's guesthouse.

Joslyn's not your type, cowboy, he told himself silently. *She's big-city sophisticated and you're mud-flap country. And she's back in Parable for a reason, whether she'll admit it or not, and when she's done whatever it is she*

*came here to do, she'll hit the road and
be gone for good.*

He thought back to the days and
nights after Layne had left, taking Shea
with her.

In his heart, he'd known he and Layne
weren't a good fit almost from the first,
but he'd mourned the dream of what
they could have had, could have *been,*
together, if things had worked out. He'd
grieved hard and deep for something
he'd never really had, a fantasy no more
real than heat mirages shimmering
above hot pavement.

Since then, he'd been careful not to
care too much about anyone or anything. He'd kept real busy, throwing himself into his work. Jasper had already
gotten past his defenses, though. And
now, like it or not, Joslyn Kirk had gotten under his skin, too.

He'd nearly kissed her that day, in the
dusty living room of that old ranch
house—stopped himself just in time.
Instinctively, he knew that once he'd
tasted Joslyn's lips, he'd be consumed
with the need to have more of her, and
then still more.

And then, when she went back to the bright lights, as she inevitably would, he'd be wide-open to a whole new round of sorrow. Strong as he was, he wasn't sure he could go through that again.

Which meant he'd better watch his step around the lovely Ms. Kirk. He'd just begun to resign himself to that decision when Jasper took a notion to shoot off toward the back wall, like he was riding a well-greased zip line, and soar right over the top. A canine Pegasus.

"The *hell*," Slade muttered, crunching his empty beer can in one hand and tossing it into the garbage bin behind the small attached garage he never used, because his truck didn't fit inside.

He opened the gate onto Kendra's lush backyard, which stood in stark contrast to his own crop of weeds and dandelions, and gave a long, low whistle to summon the dog.

"Jasper!" he called, exasperated.

No response.

Damn fool dog. Slade followed the stone path to the place where it widened, next to the guesthouse. The side door was open, and he could hear Joslyn laughing inside. The sound, soft and reminiscent of distant chimes, wrenched at his insides, the way hearing "Taps" playing on a bugle did.

"Jasper," he repeated, stopping on the doormat, raising one hand to knock at the framework.

Joslyn appeared, one hand looped through Jasper's collar, looking five kinds of good in a long, soft robe of some kind. The fabric was bold, with lots of gold and turquoise and what was probably called magenta, and it ignited sparks in her eyes. Her feet were bare and she was smiling—until she looked up and saw him standing there.

"I guess he wanted to meet Lucy-Maude," she said, letting go of Jasper's collar so she could stand up straight.

Before that, Slade had had a tantalizing view of the upper rounding of her breasts, and he wished she hadn't noticed him quite so quickly.

There was a painful grinding sensation low in his groin.

He wished he'd brought his hat along,

decided that was a stupid thought and dismissed it.

"I'm sorry if he bothered you," some stranger said, hijacking his voice.

A pretty flush glowed under Joslyn's cheekbones, and her eyes made him dizzy, in a psychedelic, Lucy-in-the-sky-with-diamonds kind of way. Slade, who'd never taken an illicit drug in his life, was suddenly high.

"Jasper's just sociable, that's all," she said with an odd little catch in her voice.

What *was* that thing she was wearing? It wasn't a nightgown, and it wasn't a bathrobe, either, since it didn't zip up the front or tie at the waist, like the ones his mother wore. And by rights it shouldn't have been so sexy, since it covered most of her up, but imagining what was beneath it jammed his normally prosaic imagination into overdrive, just the same.

"I guess it's all settled, and the owners have agreed to let you lease the ranch house," Joslyn said and then blushed again, and looked as though she wished she hadn't said anything beyond, "Here's your dog, so long, what's your hurry?"

Slade stood sideways, because that glimpse of her breasts had made him hard, and he sure as hell didn't want her to notice.

"Yep," he said. "It's a done deal."

"That's nice," she said, lingering on the threshold even though Jasper, by that time, had returned to Slade's side. "When will your daughter be here?"

"Sunday," Slade said. "Shea and her mother will be staying at the Best Western hotel for a few days."

Joslyn looked disappointed. "Shea won't be at the barbecue tomorrow, then?"

"Nope," Slade said. Damn, but he was getting suave in his old age.

She swallowed visibly. "Will you be there?"

"It's a workday for me," Slade told her, thinking about the near-kiss again and sorely tempted to follow through on it now. He wasn't a man to leave things unfinished once he'd started them. "But I'll probably stop in at some point."

"Kendra will be pleased if you do," Joslyn told him. Her tone was light, but there was some kind of quaver beneath it.

"Reason enough to show up," Slade said. "Kendra's a good friend."

"Yes," Joslyn agreed. "She certainly is."

A silence fell then, hanging between them like a wet blanket suspended from a drooping clothesline.

"See you tomorrow, then," Slade said.

She swallowed again and then nodded, and it finally came to Slade that Joslyn was as uncomfortable around him as he was around her.

"Come on, Jasper," he told the dog and started for home.

Jasper hesitated for a moment, then followed.

Slade passed through the gate, across his disgracefully neglected yard and into the duplex through the patio doors. He intended to take a cold shower, but, as luck would have it, his wall phone was ringing.

He snatched up the receiver, glad to have something to focus on besides the

strong possibility that Joslyn was naked under that robe-thingy she was
wearing.

"Hello, Slade," a female voice chimed.
"Maggie Landers here. I'm sorry to call
after hours like this, but the funds from
your father's estate have been transferred into a holding account, and I'll
need your signature before I can release them to you."

He wasn't my father, Slade wanted to
say, but it wasn't Maggie's fault that his
dad hadn't been willing to claim him
while he was still breathing. She was
just doing her job as John Carmody's
attorney.

"Monday ought to be soon enough,"
he said.

Maggie was in lawyer mode, and she
steamrolled right over his words as
though she hadn't heard him. "I was
thinking I could bring the papers with
me to Kendra's barbecue tomorrow afternoon, if you're planning to be there."

He felt an odd tightening sensation in
his chest. "What's the big hurry, Maggie?"

"There's a lot of money involved here,

Slade," Maggie reminded him. "Don't you even want to know how much you inherited, over and above your share of Whisper Creek Ranch?"

"It doesn't matter," he said.

"The hell it doesn't," Maggie shot back, sounding irritated. "Even after taxes, fees and the like, you'll be a multimillionaire."

That got through to him, with roughly the force of a sledgehammer blow to the solar plexus. He'd been expecting a few hundred thousand, maybe. Respectable money, but nothing like this.

"Holy crap," he said.

He heard the smile in Maggie's voice when she replied. "When the dust settles, you'll have around five million dollars to call your own. Just think what you'll be able to do for Callie with that kind of money."

Slade was dazed. He was still grappling with the idea that John Carmody had left him anything at all, let alone a fortune.

"Slade?" Maggie prompted, with kindly amusement. "Did you faint?"

"I'm here," Slade told her in a gravelly

voice. He shoved a hand through his hair. "Are you sure there isn't some kind of mistake—?"

Maggie actually laughed then. "No mistake," she said. "John Carmody was a lot richer than most people ever suspected."

Slade flashed back to his younger years, when his mom had had such a hell of a time just putting food on the table, let alone keeping a growing boy in jeans and shoes and paying for routine medical care and regular dental checkups. And he seethed.

He'd long since come to terms with the way he'd been raised—he'd been happy and well-adjusted, growing up, thanks to Callie—but she'd gone years without buying a new pair of shoes, and most of her clothes came from a thrift store. Where had all the old man's fancy money been then, when Callie so desperately needed help?

"I'll see you at the barbecue," Slade finally managed to say. "Around three o'clock, unless I'm too busy."

"Fine," Maggie said. "Three o'clock."

The call ended then, and Slade hung

up. He'd forgotten all about the cold shower.

He'd picked up a few groceries at Mulligan's that day—that was when he'd run into Kendra and she'd made a quick call on her cell phone to ask the King-man heirs about renting out the house for a few months—and he realized that the frog race going on in his stomach was at least partially due to hunger.

He nuked a box of something fro-zen—meat loaf, according to the la-bel—and offered to share it with Jas-per, who turned up his muzzle, sighed in apparent disgust and walked away.

When Kendra threw a party, Joslyn thought the next morning, perched on a stepladder and hanging colorful paper lanterns from the branches of the ma-ple trees surrounding the mansion's outdoor kitchen, she didn't fool around.

The coals were already lit in the belly of the huge stone grill, though it would be hours before the food would be served, and the night crew from the Butter Biscuit Café was present, setting up rented tables and folding chairs while Kendra supervised.

The woman had even hired a band, a disturbing indication, at least to Joslyn, that the celebration of the chicken farm sale would probably go on until all hours.

Although Joslyn enjoyed a party as much as the next person, she was dreading this one, and not just because she was sure to encounter some of the people her stepfather had cheated. She knew Slade would be there, and that was unsettling.

"They look great," Kendra said, stopping at the foot of the ladder as Joslyn climbed down, admiring the paper lanterns.

Joslyn smiled her thanks and stood in the grass, looking up at her own handiwork for a moment before catching her friend's gaze. "That must be one heck of a commission check," she observed. "Just how much did that chicken farm go for, anyway?"

Kendra chuckled. "A lot," she said. "It includes its own creek, a small lake and

some five hundred acres of land, remember."

"Do you throw a shindig like this every time you sell a property?"

Kendra, still smiling, shook her head.
"Only when the buyer is new in town.
It's a good way to say 'welcome' and
help them meet their future friends and
neighbors."

"No wonder you're so successful,"
Joslyn said. "You take going the second mile to a whole new level, kiddo."

A shadow seemed to cross Kendra's
face, but it was gone again so quickly
that Joslyn wasn't sure she'd seen it at
all.

"Since you're my landlady, I have a
question for you," Joslyn said as she
and Kendra folded the ladder. "Are pets
allowed?"

They were crossing the yard toward
a large storage shed, and two young
men from the Butter Biscuit crew rushed
over to relieve them of the ladder.

"Pets?" Kendra asked after a nod of
gratitude to the helpers.

"It seems I've acquired a temporary
cat," Joslyn said.

"What is it with you and lost animals?" Kendra teased, her eyes warm and full of light. Today, they were the clear green color of old-fashioned canning jars left to mellow through decades of changing seasons. "It's as if they gravitate to you."

"There have been *two,* Kendra," Joslyn pointed out reasonably. "Count 'em. One dog, one cat."

"The 'temporary' cat is welcome to stay," Kendra said.

"I'm sure it belongs to someone," Joslyn said. "Lucy-Maude is healthy and well fed—she's even clean. And—"

"And?" Kendra asked.

Here came the part that might be the deal breaker, but Joslyn's conscience wouldn't allow her to withhold the information. "She's expecting kittens. Probably soon."

"Yikes," Kendra said, but then her eyes brightened. "Maybe I'll keep one for myself. I love kittens."

They were standing apart from the preparatory hubbub now, in the shade of another of the venerable old maples. As a little girl, Joslyn had climbed every one of those trees, skinning her knees in the process, and once, when she was eight, taking a tumble and breaking her left arm.

She'd had to miss swimming camp that year, and she'd moped around for days—until Elliott had brought Spunky home, a squirming, awkward pup parted too soon from its mother and the rest of the litter.

Elliott, Joslyn reflected, hadn't been all bad. She even missed him sometimes, missed the funny, gentle, generous man he'd once been.

Kendra interrupted her reverie with a tilt of her head and an inquiring smile. "What?" she asked.

"Every once in a while," Joslyn confessed quietly, "I stumble into a memory and get stuck there for a few moments."

"Don't we all," Kendra said, with a soft sigh. Then she looked at her watch, a graceful timepiece with tiny diamonds floating under the crystal. Instead of jeans and a tank top, which Joslyn wore, Kendra sported trim linen slacks and a yellow off-the-shoulder blouse with ruffles. "Our work here is done, for now, anyway," she said. "And I'm due at the Curly-Burly in ten minutes. Come along?"

Joslyn shook her head and smiled. "No, thanks," she said. And then she gave her friend a brief once-over. "What services could you possibly need at Callie's shop?" she asked. "You're already perfect."

That made Kendra laugh again. "Highlights," she said, with a toss of her head that made her blond hair, loose for once, shimmer in the sunlight. "I get them once a month, and today's the day."

With that, Kendra walked away, got into her car, where she'd already stowed her purse, and started the engine.

A moment later, she was gone.

Joslyn went inside the guesthouse, collected her own purse and told Lucy-Maude, who was sunning herself on a wide windowsill in the living room, that she'd be back shortly.

She drove out of town to the big discount store, since some of the things she needed wouldn't be available at

Mulligan's and she was in the mood for one-stop shopping that day.

She still had to wash and blow-dry her hair and figure out what to wear to the barbecue later on—nothing too dressy, she had decided, but nothing too casual, either.

Something—moderate.

But what? She lived in jeans and sun-tops most of the time, and she'd do-nated much of her wardrobe to a char-ity before leaving Phoenix.

The parking lot at the discount store was practically full—people probably came from all over the county to shop there, and, of course, it was Saturday.

Resolving to make it quick, Joslyn locked up her car, hurried into the store and grabbed a cart.

She bought kibble for Lucy-Maude, along with kitty litter and a plastic box to put it in. She selected a few cat toys, too, and a small, soft pet bed uphol-stered in a pretty pink floral fabric.

Wheeling back toward the front of the store, she passed the women's clothing section and stopped when her gaze caught on a display of sundresses. They were sleeveless pull-ons, and she liked the black-and-white geometric print.

Taking a size medium from the rack, she held it up to her chest and looked down at it. She'd have to shave her legs and paint her toenails, she reflected, but the dress was attractive and reasonably priced.

"That will look great on you," a familiar voice commented.

She looked up to see Hutch Carmody standing in the aisle, grinning at her. He wasn't pushing a cart, but he was holding a hardcover book and a can of shaving cream. The man was drop-dead gorgeous, with his dark blond hair and blue eyes, but he didn't do a thing for her.

Not the way Slade did.

"Well, then," she said with a smile, "that settles it." She tossed the dress into her shopping cart. "See you at the barbecue this afternoon?"

"Wouldn't miss it," Hutch answered. "I hear there's a band."

Joslyn nodded with a chuckle, and rolled her eyes. "Kendra's going all out," she said.

Something flickered in his eyes, vanished again. "She tends to do that," he said moderately. "Any excuse for a party."

Joslyn was mildly jolted by that remark. Kendra obviously enjoyed entertaining guests, but she wasn't a party girl. Not the way Hutch seemed to be implying, anyway.

Before she could come up with a response, though, Hutch nodded in farewell and walked away. He'd only gone a few steps when he looked back at her over one shoulder and said, "Save me a dance, okay?"

CHAPTER SEVEN

By two o'clock that afternoon, Tara Kendall, the new owner of the five-hundred-acre chicken farm just south of Parable, had arrived and so had half the town, it seemed to Joslyn. Even if she'd wanted to, she thought wryly, she wouldn't have been able to escape. The driveway was jammed with vehicles of all makes and models, sizes and sorts, and her car was hemmed in.

She felt that way herself, standing there on the fringe of the celebration in her discount-store sundress and sandals.

Kendra spotted her and, being Kendra, headed straight over and looped her arm through Joslyn's.

"Come on, Cinderella," Kendra whispered cheerfully, looking typically elegant in her gauzy white top trimmed with exquisite lace and pants to match. Only Kendra, Joslyn thought, would dare to wear white at a barbecue. "Time to let these folks see what a class act you really are."

Joslyn didn't *feel* very classy, especially next to Kendra in that breathtaking outfit, but she rummaged up a brave smile anyway, because it was definitely show time.

A few people nodded in recognition and acknowledgment as she and Kendra waded into the group, stopping in the very center, where a slender, dark-haired woman with expressive amber-brown eyes stood chatting with several men, a glass of white wine in one hand.

"Tara Kendall," Kendra said, "meet my best friend, Joslyn Kirk."

Joslyn blinked. This was Tara? The future chicken farmer? She looked more like a fashion model or a famous actress in her pale blue summer dress and strappy high-heeled sandals. Her dark hair hung well past her shoulders, and when she smiled, her entire face lit up.

"Glad to meet you, Joslyn," Tara said, extending her free hand.

Joslyn took it and gave the long, elegant fingers a brief squeeze in greeting. "Welcome to Parable," she replied, smiling.

People were milling all around them by then. The three-man, one-woman country band was tuning up, and the workers from the Butter Biscuit Café bustled around, setting out dishes of food, buffet style. Smoky aromas rolled on the soft summer breeze, and hunger curled in the pit of Joslyn's stomach but was quickly dulled by nerves.

"Thanks," Tara responded warmly and with a twinkle of humor in her eyes. She obviously realized she didn't look anything like a chicken farmer—whatever a chicken farmer was *supposed* to look like—and enjoyed getting a reaction to the fact. "I'm happy to be here."

Joslyn, well aware that she'd been

noticed, couldn't have said the same. Stares burned into her from all directions, and a thrumming hush had fallen beneath the squeak of a fiddle and the twangs of guitar strings. If she could have clicked her heels together and vanished, she would have done it.

Kendra, still standing beside Joslyn, gave her a light jab with one elbow. "Head high," she counseled. "Shoulders back, chin *up*."

Tara looked puzzled by this exchange but offered no comment.

Joslyn, however, took Kendra's cue and stood up straight and proud.

Deftly, Kendra snatched two glasses off a tray that was being passed around and fairly shoved one into Joslyn's hand.

"Here's to coming home!" Kendra said, making sure her voice carried, raising her glass high.

Both Joslyn and Tara raised their glasses, too, and there was a cheery clink of crystal as the rims touched.

Joslyn was briefly reminded of the three-of-cups, a Tarot card showing a trio of women raising chalices high over their heads in the same sort of pose.

She was struck by the strange poignancy of the moment, the beginning of some new era—one of those times when people and situations just fit together like the pieces of a puzzle.

Kendra and Tara seemed to feel it, too, because their eyes widened, and then they smiled.

All three women sipped from their wineglasses.

"You'll be all right?" Kendra said, giving the question the tone and inflection of a statement. She was, after all, the hostess, and she needed to move among her guests and make sure everyone felt welcome.

"I'll be fine," Joslyn said.

And the three of them, Joslyn, Kendra and Tara, were swept apart then, on the varying currents of the gathering itself, and Joslyn suddenly found herself practically chest to chest with Slade Barlow.

He must have been on duty, since he'd clipped his badge onto his belt, but otherwise, he was dressed like most of the other men at the barbecue, in jeans and polished boots and a long-sleeved cotton shirt, crisply pressed.

Joslyn's heart lurched at the sight of him and the scent of him, and the hard heat of his proximity to her.

"Afternoon," he said, with the slightest grin and blue mayhem dancing in his eyes. "Nice party."

Joslyn was hardly aware of the party, nice or otherwise. The man made her breath jam up in her throat and then swell there.

Or was that her heart?

That was when she realized that she'd spilled some of her wine on his white shirt when they collided.

"I'm—"

He cut her off by resting a fingertip on her lips. "Don't say you're sorry," he said.

She blushed, even as fire raced through her system, glad that the wine was white, at least. It probably wouldn't stain his shirt.

Still, she dabbed at the mark ineffectually with the fingertips of her right hand, having shifted the glass to her left.

"Joslyn," Slade said, closing his hand around hers, stilling the motion of her fingers. *"No harm done."*

She blushed and would have jerked her hand back if he hadn't still been holding it. "I guess I am a little nervous," she confided. She knew people were looking at her, talking about her—she could feel the vibrations in every nerve.

"Why should you be nervous?" Slade asked.

Men, Joslyn thought.

"You *know* why," she said, flustered. Slade hadn't let go of her hand yet, and that was both a plus and a minus—a plus because she sensed all that quiet, masculine strength coursing into her, and a minus because . . . she sensed all that quiet, masculine strength coursing into her. "Because of Elliott and what he did."

Slade absorbed that, then visibly dismissed it from his mind. "I have to get back to work pretty soon," he said, releasing her hand at last. "How about running interference while I cut in at the front of the grub line?"

Joslyn smiled at that. Since the "grub

line" hadn't formed yet, there wouldn't be any need to cut in.

Glad to have something to do, she led the way over to the barbecue grill and the long tables packed with salads and fruit, mounds of her focaccia bread, condiments and soda and beer and wine chilling in big tubs of ice, picked up a plate and handed it to him.

"There you are, Sheriff," she said. "Dig in."

One of the food service workers manning the barbecue grill forked a medium-size steak onto Slade's plate, and the two men exchanged the brief, easy words of people who have known each other all their lives.

Both of them probably took it for granted, Joslyn thought, mildly peevish. Would *she* ever belong like that—not necessarily in Parable, but anywhere at all?

The possibility that she wouldn't made the backs of her eyes throb. Again, she wanted to retreat—hide out in the guesthouse with the doors locked and the curtains pulled, just her and

Lucy-Maude, until all the party guests went home.

But she didn't. *Wouldn't.* After all, pride was about all she had left. She'd shed everything else like an extra skin—her business, her job, her condo in Phoenix with all its carefully chosen furniture—all so she could repay someone else's debt. She'd bid her friends—okay, they were mostly acquaintances, not friends—a breezy adieu and driven to Parable in her secondhand car, having no idea of what to expect.

Slade, holding a plate mounded high with food, broke into her thoughts. "Aren't you going to eat?" he asked.

"Later," Joslyn said with a shake of her head.

His eyes moved over her hair, as warm as a caress, before locking with hers. "Keep me company, then?" he asked. He sounded solemn, but there was a twinkle in those too-blue depths. "Otherwise, people are bound to gang up on me, wanting to know if I plan to run for reelection later this year."

Joslyn remembered their discussion the day before and cast a furtive glance around her as Slade took a place at one of the as-yet empty picnic tables set up for the occasion.

"Is he here?" she whispered.

"Is *who* here?" Slade asked, waiting until she sat down across the table before taking a seat himself.

She realized she was still holding her wineglass and set it aside, promptly forgetting all about it again. "The man you don't want to be elected sheriff in your place," she whispered, irritated because she knew he was playing with her.

Slade looked around, shook his head once and stabbed a plastic fork into his potato salad. "Nope," he said after chewing and swallowing. His gaze drifted briefly over the bodice of her dress and her bare arms before returning to her face. "I don't see him."

Another man approached through the crowd just then. Unlike the sheriff, his boss, Deputy Boone Taylor, was in uniform. Dark-haired and dark-eyed, Boone had been a heartthrob back in high school, and he was still mighty easy on the eyeballs, in Joslyn's opinion.

"You're supposed to be off duty," Slade told him, slicing into the steak on his plastic plate.

"McQuillan called in sick," Boone answered, sparing a how-ya-been nod for Joslyn. "Asked me to fill in for him."

A muscle bunched in Slade's jaw and smoothed out again, as if by force of will. "McQuillan called you?" he asked in a tone that sounded idle and was anything but.

"Actually, he sent me a text," Boone said, his gaze catching on Tara, the guest of honor, now being herded toward the buffet table by half a dozen male admirers. "Is that the chicken rancher? In the blue dress?"

"Yes," Joslyn said helpfully. There was a different kind of tension in the air now, and even though she sensed it had nothing whatsoever to do with her, she still felt uncomfortable. "That's Tara Kendall. I could introduce you—"

But Boone shook his head, dragging his attention back to Slade and, peripherally, Joslyn.

"What's wrong with Deputy McQuillan *this* time?" Slade asked Boone. He'd set his knife and fork down now, and his fingers were curled back into his palms, though not exactly fisted. "And why didn't he contact *me* if he needed a day off?"

Boone sighed and hooked his thumbs in his service belt. Some men could carry off a uniform without looking like an overgrown Eagle Scout, and he was one of them. "I don't know, Sheriff," he said, narrowing his eyes a little as he looked straight into Slade's face. "I guess you'll have to ask him that."

The atmosphere between the two men almost crackled.

"Get something to eat if you're hungry," Slade told his deputy. It was a dismissal.

Without another word, Boone headed for the buffet table.

"It's Boone Taylor," Joslyn chided, when she and Slade were alone in the midst of the swirling crowd. "*He's* the one you don't want elected sheriff."

Slade gave her a wry look and stabbed at another piece of his steak. Before, he'd seemed hungry, but now, Joslyn could tell, he was just going through the motions of eating. "Nice guess, but you're way off," he replied. "It's *McQuillan* who'd probably go after the job."

Joslyn raised one eyebrow, frowning a little. "That name isn't familiar. Do I know him?"

"No," Slade said. "And if you have any sense, you'll keep it that way."

"Harsh," Joslyn said, intrigued. "If you don't like Deputy McQuillan, why did you hire him in the first place?"

He gave her another look, one that clearly said, "Keep your voice down."

As if anyone would have heard her over the lively tune the band was playing. The lead singer was Cookie Jean Crown—she'd starred in all the musicals back when they were all attending Parable High. Everybody had expected her to go on to fame and fortune, she was so talented, but here she was, older, like the rest of them, harder around the edges and considerably heavier.

"I *didn't* hire McQuillan," Slade said, his voice taut and low. "I *inherited* him from my predecessor."

"Oh," Joslyn said. It seemed a fortu-
itous moment to change the subject;
she could ask Kendra about the deputy
and the roots of Slade's evident antipa-
thy toward him, later on. "Cookie Jean's
still quite the singer," she remarked. She
waggled her fingers at the other woman,
now crooning "Georgia" to the band's
accompaniment, and Cookie Jean saw
the wave.

She didn't return it, though, and she
didn't smile.

In fact, she glared hard and then, still
singing, pointedly looked away.

Joslyn felt as though she'd been
slapped. "Ouch," she said, to no one in
particular.

This was it. The kind of response
she'd been dreading.

Mentally, she went over the long list,
compiled by her attorneys, of people
slated to receive compensation checks,
but Cookie Jean's name wasn't on it,
as far as she could recall.

When she turned around on the
bench of that picnic table, Slade was
looking at her. And there wasn't any
doubt at all that he'd not only seen the

exchange between her and her onetime classmate and friend, he knew what it meant.

Of course.

"Who was it?" Joslyn asked, bruised.

Slade didn't need clarification. "Her uncle, George Tulverson," he replied. "Took out a second mortgage on the dairy farm—it wasn't much of a place, but it was in the family for almost a hundred years—wanting to get in on Elliott's get-rich-quick scheme. George lost his shirt, like everybody else, and the farm went along with it."

Joslyn automatically put a hand to her mouth.

Hungry only a little while before, she felt now as though she might throw up.

"Folks can be pretty quick to judge," Slade said, pushing his plate away, his meal unfinished. "Especially when there's money involved. What some of them seem to forget is that while Elliott Rossiter certainly played a key role in the whole mess, nobody put a gun to their heads and forced them to invest. There were some who saw the scheme for what it was and stayed clear, even warned their friends to do the same thing."

Joslyn nodded, swallowed. She could feel other people watching her again now, their glances weighted. Maybe they'd been looking at her all the time, but she'd forgotten for a while because of Slade.

Now he was about to toss his plate into one of the strategically placed trash bins and go back to work.

"Joslyn?" he said, on his feet by then.

She looked up at him, unable to hide her misery, as much as she wanted to do just that.

"Don't run," Slade told her quietly. "You've got friends here, as well as a few enemies. Remember that."

She didn't want him to go, but she'd no more have said so than booked a seat on a flight to beautiful downtown Baghdad. "I'll be just fine," she said, jutting out her chin and hoping he hadn't seen the little shiver that went through her. "But thanks for your concern."

He grinned. "You're welcome," he said.

With that, he was gone, disposing of

his plate and seeking out Tara Kendall, who was with Kendra and some others at another table.

Out of the corner of her eye, Joslyn watched as Slade spoke to Tara and laughed at something Kendra said.

She felt excluded, on the outside looking in, although she knew that was silly.

The air was full of delicious aromas and happy noise, but Joslyn had neither an appetite nor an inclination to celebrate with the rest of the community.

Given her druthers, she would still have hidden out in the guesthouse until everyone was gone, but that hadn't been an option before Slade's quiet, "Don't run" and it wasn't an option afterward, either.

Slade departed, leaving a hole in the fabric of the afternoon.

The party wore on. The band took breaks, eating and drinking with everyone else, and then went back to making music. People came and people went.

Joslyn circulated, following her

mother's time-honored rule: if you're uncomfortable at a social gathering, forget about yourself and try to make *others* feel comfortable. Some of the guests were cordial, others were cool, and a few went out of their way to avoid speaking to her, which stung.

Hutch Carmody showed up just as some of the other men were unloading planks from a flatbed truck parked in the alley. He helped arrange the lumber into a makeshift dance floor in the middle of Kendra's backyard.

Cookie Jean and the band finished their gig and were replaced by two guys with fiddles.

Seeing her former classmate cutting around the side of the main house, Joslyn threw caution to the wind and hurried after her.

"Cookie Jean?" she called.

The other woman stopped, stiff-spined, but didn't turn around. "I don't have anything to say to you, Joslyn Kirk," she said.

Under other circumstances, the irony of that remark would have made Joslyn smile.

"Well, I have something to say to you," Joslyn insisted, going around Cookie Jean on the stone path and then pivoting to face her. "I'm sorry," she said, after gathering up courage from her dwindling supply. "About what Elliott did, I mean. It was terrible. But I had no part in it, and you know that. We used to be friends, Cookie Jean. Remember?"

Cookie Jean's trouble-hardened face paled a little. She'd sung away her lipstick and, because of the heat and the exertions of performing, the rest of her makeup was rubbing off, too. Her over-dyed blond hair hung limp from the pins that held it up in an out-of-date French twist at the back of her head.

"You mean," she said angrily, "that I was part of your adoring *entourage*. Do you think I didn't know, Joslyn, about all those slumber parties here—" She indicated the monstrously large house next to them with a motion of her head. "The ones only the popular girls got invited to?"

There was no denying there had been slumber parties at Joslyn's place, ones that hadn't included Cookie Jean and the other kids who rode the school bus in from the countryside surrounding Parable. What she couldn't bring herself to explain was that Elliott had limited those gatherings to six girls, including Joslyn herself, and he was the one who made out the guest list.

"It wasn't what you think," Joslyn said lamely.

"Wasn't it?" Cookie Jean snapped, shaking a finger under Joslyn's nose. She drew in a moist, shaky breath, and Joslyn realized the other woman was near tears. Well, fine—so was she. "Why did you come back here, anyway? You're not welcome in Parable, Joslyn. You're a reminder of bad times, that's all!"

Joslyn refrained from asking if Cookie Jean or someone in her family had received a large check in the mail recently. She couldn't buy back what Elliott had so callously thrown away, the trust and livelihoods of people who had considered him a friend, and she knew it only too well.

If she was going to leave Parable as

a whole person, able to move on with her life, she would have to ride out encounters like this one—and some that were even worse, probably. Joslyn knew she ought to shut up, just cut her losses and run, figuratively speaking, but she couldn't. *Someone* had to face up to the harm and loss her stepfather had caused, and since he was dead and her mother didn't feel the same drive to make things right, the task had fallen to her.

She was a modern-day Don Quixote, tilting at windmills.

"What about the *good* times, Cookie Jean?" she persisted. "Remember the parties at the lake? The bonfires after the big game, whether our team won or lost? The proms and the school carnival? You and I worked the ring-toss booth together, remember? And we had a lot of fun."

Cookie Jean's eyes glistened, but she quickly blinked away the shine. "Look, Joslyn," she said finally, sounding and looking bone weary now, "maybe other people in this town are willing to act like nothing happened and go on from there, but I'm not. Uncle George lost his *farm* because of your thieving stepfather— and all the fancy things he bought for you and your mother—and because my little brothers and I lived with him and Aunt Sarah, we lost the only home we ever knew. Six months after the bank auctioned off the farm, Uncle George had a heart attack and died, and Aunt Sarah moved to Boise to live with her sister. I tried to keep things together for my brothers by getting married right af- ter high school—to the wrong man. Toby, my younger brother, is in and out of trouble all the time, and Bill's gone into the service, where God knows what will happen to him. Do you know what his dream was, Joslyn? Bill wanted to help run the dairy farm, take over for Uncle George one day, when it got to be too much—"

She looked away, shook her head.

Joslyn stood, as Kendra had advised earlier, with her shoulders back and her head high, but inside, she felt fractured. For all her efforts to pay back what had been stolen all those years ago, in so

many cases, the damage was irrevers-
ible.

The Tulversons' dairy farm was gone.
Cookie Jean had paid a heavy price, as
had her brothers, Toby and Bill. The
check that had probably gone to their
aunt Sarah couldn't begin to compen-
sate for all she and the family had lost.

"Just leave me alone from now on, all
right?" Cookie Jean said in parting, and
then she stormed across the front yard
and out through the gate and Joslyn
saw her get into an old car and start
the engine with a hard, grinding sound.

Smoke belched out of the tailpipe as
she drove away.

"Did you save me that first dance,
like you promised?" asked a voice behind Joslyn, gently gruff.

She turned, and there was Hutch,
looking at her with a pride-saving lack
of pity and an understanding grin. Like
Kendra, he'd never blamed her for Elliott's actions, and she loved him for
that.

"Yes," Joslyn said. A runaway tear
got loose and trickled down her cheek.

Hutch stepped forward, wrapped an

arm around her and used one thumb to wipe away the tear. "I reckon Cookie Jean has a right to be bitter," he said, "but she's got no business treating you like that."

Joslyn pressed her lips together for a long moment. Being held by Hutch Carmody was like being held by the brother she'd never been blessed with, and it felt good. "Elliott's dead," she said miserably. "My mother isn't here. Who else is there to take the rap for what happened?"

"The people who suckered for the scam in the first place, maybe?" Hutch suggested. He released her, took her hand. "Elliott came to my dad with that scheme of his. Dad said it sounded like a crooked deal to him, and a fool's game in the bargain, and Elliott got mad and called him a few choice names. I thought they were going to get into it, right there in our yard, but Elliott finally got back in his car and left, and Dad never said another word about it."

Joslyn took that in, hearing the echo of Slade's voice in her head. *Nobody held a gun to their heads and forced them to invest.*

"I wish this damn party was over," she said.

Hutch chuckled. Pulled her back along the pathway leading to the smoky barbecue and the country music and the mixture of friendly and hostile people.

"Well," he said, "it *isn't* over. The dancing's about to start, and the best thing you could possibly do is have yourself a bang-up good time and make sure everybody knows it."

"You're a good friend, Hutch Carmody," Joslyn said with a little sniffle.

"I'm a pretty fair dancer, too," he replied with a twinkle.

Soon they were on the improvised dance floor, and the band was playing an old Johnny Cash ballad. Joslyn was beginning to think she might make it through the evening after all.

Slade's gaze went straight to Joslyn the minute he returned to the party, his shift over for the day. On his way over, he'd stopped by the Curly-Burly to pick up his mom, and she was dressed to celebrate in one of her fringed cowgirl outfits.

His jaw tightened as he followed Joslyn with his eyes; she was dancing with Hutch, and the two of them were laughing about something.

Callie gave Slade a subtle jab in the ribs with her ever-ready elbow. "Pull your eyeballs back into your head, cowboy," she whispered, in a teasing undertone. "They're just dancing, that's all."

Slade felt a rush of irritation. There were times, like now, for instance, when he sorely wished his mother couldn't read him as easily as one of her tattered romance magazines. "You seem to have mistaken me," he drawled, "for someone who gives a damn what Joslyn and Hutch do on the dance floor or anyplace else."

Callie chuckled at that. "You could cut in, you know," she said, and then she zipped off into the crowd to find Kendra and meet Tara Kendall, the woman she'd heard so much about, and left him standing there like a fool.

Slade wished he'd stayed home with Jasper instead of showering after work, putting on fresh clothes and heading back here.

If it wouldn't have meant leaving Callie stranded—not that she couldn't have gotten a ride home from a dozen different people—Slade would have turned on one heel and hightailed it out of there. The very cowardice of the thought made him determined to stay.

By the time he made his way through the throng, Callie had greeted her hostess, introduced herself to the most unlikely chicken farmer Slade had ever seen and scrambled up onto the bandstand with the fiddlers. In two shakes, she had a microphone in her hand, and the guests were cheering and shouting for a song.

Grinning, Callie launched into a Dolly Parton number, slow and sweet. She could sing them all—from Patsy to Reba to Faith and Carrie and Jewel. And she didn't have a shy bone in her body, obviously. Callie Barlow was one of the most self-possessed people he knew.

Slade shook his head in wry admiration, grinning to himself, and walked right up to Kendra.

"May I have this dance?" he asked with exaggerated formality.

She looked a little blurry around the edges, he noticed, but she brightened as she smiled up at him. "Like I'd ever say no to a handsome hunk of cowboy like you," she responded.

And they stepped onto the dance floor together.

In Slade's opinion, Kendra Shepherd was darned near the perfect woman, beautiful, smart, personable—and certainly sexy. But there was no spark between them—she would have agreed if he'd asked her—and they were destined to be friends but nothing more.

Looking down into Kendra's upturned face, he thought of her loser ex-husband and hoped the bastard would stay clear of Parable—and Kendra—for good. She'd been crushed by the breakup, though she'd made a brave effort not to let on, and Slade suspected the damage was long-term, if not permanent.

"You sure do know how to throw a party, ma'am," he drawled in an old-time movie-cowboy voice. She seemed to be sagging a little in his arms, and her gaze strayed once to Hutch and Joslyn, then snapped back to Slade's face.

"They look good together," she said. She sounded sad and a little embarrassed that she'd revealed so much.

"Hutch doesn't do a whole lot for me," Slade responded in order to lighten the mood, "but I can agree that Joslyn looks mighty fine."

Kendra managed a slight grin. "If you think Joslyn looks good," she teased quietly, tiredly, while Callie's voice soared above the song of the two fiddles, "why are you dancing with me?"

He chuckled, but there was a tightness in his throat all of the sudden. He cared about Kendra, wanted her to be happy. And, for all her success, she wasn't.

"I figured you were the most likely to

say yes," he responded a beat or two later.

Her smile broadened. "So," she said, "are you ever going to make up your mind about buying the Kingman place?"

He raised an eyebrow. "Talking business at a barbecue? Kendra, that just ain't country."

Kendra rolled her pale green, luminous eyes. "I'll talk business anywhere," she replied, "and you know it. Are you going to buy that ranch or not, Slade Barlow?"

He sighed. "I don't know," he admitted as the song came to an end and Callie climbed down from the bandstand amid loud applause and requests for another song. They stood in the middle of the dance floor, he and Kendra, looking very much like what they weren't: a couple in the process of falling in love with each other. "It's complicated, Kendra. And this isn't the time or the place to talk about it."

She nodded. The music started up again, and suddenly Hutch was beside them, looking as cocky and arrogant as ever, putting out a hand to Kendra in an unspoken request for a dance.

For all that cool Hutch was projecting, Slade noticed the slight twitch in his half brother's cheek, and, deep down where no one could see, he smiled to himself.

CHAPTER EIGHT

Joslyn watched, a glass of punch in one hand, as Kendra moved somewhat reluctantly into Hutch's arms, and they began to dance to a slow and dreamy tune, under the first stars of a summer evening and the colored light of the Chinese lanterns dangling from the branches of the maple trees. The effect was almost surreal—in a magical, romantic sort of way.

With a sigh, Joslyn set her glass aside—it was immediately whisked away by one of the waiters—and wondered if she could safely retreat to the guesthouse now. She'd put in an appearance at the party, smiled until her face hurt and initiated as many conversations as she could, meeting with both cautiously pleasant responses and outright rebuffs in about equal measure. She'd danced and eaten too much and had had too much wine, necessitating the switch to fruit punch an hour before. Her feet hurt, and she was tired, and her heart felt strangely heavy in her chest as she watched Hutch and Kendra moving slowly around the dance floor, looking so right in each other's arms.

"Looks like there's a lot going on in there," Slade said, appearing suddenly, touching Joslyn's right temple lightly with an index finger as he spoke.

She smiled, feeling skittish and, somehow, revived. "I was just thinking," she said with a nod toward the couple she'd been watching before, "how good Hutch and Kendra look together."

A smile crooked at one corner of Slade's mouth. What would it be like to be kissed by that sensual, well-shaped mouth? Joslyn hugged herself to repress a weird little shiver of anticipation.

"Kendra said the same thing about you and Hutch," Slade remarked. Without asking—without *needing* to ask—he took Joslyn into his arms, and they began to move to the soft, sweet music.

Things quickened inside Joslyn; that was what close proximity to Sheriff Slade Barlow seemed to do to her. She looked up into his face, mildly bewildered.

"We're just good friends, Hutch and I," she said, a mite too quickly for her own comfort.

A light sparked in Slade's eyes—or had she merely imagined that? "Well," he drawled, with the slightest of grins, "I guess *somebody* has to be Hutch's friend."

Joslyn had the oddest feeling that all the seams in her sundress had suddenly given way, that the garment might simply fall apart, dissolve around her. It was disconcerting to imagine herself standing there naked.

Aggravation swept through her, followed, strangely enough, by relief. "Hutch has plenty of friends," she said quite stiffly.

But they went on dancing.

"It was a joke," Slade replied with exaggerated patience and no little amusement, though there was something watchful about his expression, too. A sort of alertness that looked like concern but probably wasn't.

"You just don't happen to count yourself among those friends?" Joslyn asked, chagrined to realize that, with this man, she was more comfortable opposing than agreeing. Crazy as it was, she felt safer this way.

"No," Slade said, straightforward as always. "I can't say that I do."

"Why not?" Joslyn was compelled to challenge him.

"Because I think he's a jerk," Slade answered. "And I'd bet the ranch—if I had one—that his opinion of me is the same."

"Hutch is not a jerk," she said. Let him draw whatever conclusions he wished from her statement, which had pointedly not removed *him* from the jerk column.

Slade's eyes twinkled. Damn him, he was enjoying this. Again. He seemed to love throwing her off balance, tossing a wrench into the proverbial works. He was—he was *contrary,* that's what he was. Stubborn and pigheaded and maybe even smug.

Joslyn hated smugness.

"Whatever you say, ma'am," he gibed.

The song the fiddlers were playing— and therefore the dance, as well— seemed interminable to Joslyn just then. "Can we just be done with this conversation, please?" she whispered angrily.

"Sure we can," Slade agreed affably, just as the music stopped.

They stood still, just looking at each other, for a few seconds. Then Slade went one way, and Joslyn went the other.

She fled to the cool quiet of the guesthouse and locked the door behind her, as though pursued. As far as she was concerned, the evening was over.

Lucy-Maude greeted her with an affable "Meow." The cat sat primly in the middle of the kitchen floor, bathed in a shaft of multicolored party light, her furry tail fluffed out and her ears perked.

Joslyn bent and patted the animal's silky head. "Maybe it *was* a mistake, coming back to Parable," she confided softly, sadly. "No matter what I do, I'll still be Elliott Rossiter's spoiled step-daughter, at least to some people. What made me think I could ever fit in here, even for a few months?"

"Reow," Lucy-Maude replied sympa-thetically.

Joslyn went to the cupboard, took out a box containing a selection of herbal teas, chose ginger-mint and filled a cup with water. While the microwave whirred, heating up the concoction, she parted the curtains over the sink and looked out into Kendra's backyard.

The two-man band was packing up to leave, and guests were saying their farewells and heading out. The helpers from the Buttered Biscuit had begun the clearing-away process, and the Chi-nese lanterns were snuffed out, too.

She looked for Slade, against her bet-ter judgment, but he had disappeared, along with his singing mother. Hutch was nowhere in sight, either.

Cars and trucks started up in the driveway and out on the street.

"Well, *that's* finally over," she told the cat, just as the timer bell on the microwave dinged. Turning away from the window to take her cup of soothing tea from the microwave, Joslyn added, "And I'm glad, too."

It was *almost* true that she was glad. Almost, but not completely. She'd enjoyed the evening, felt pretty in her sundress, loved the music and the food and, in spite of a few snubs, chatting with other guests. She was pretty sure she'd made a new friend in Tara Kendall, too.

Most of all, though—and no one ever had to know this because it was nobody's business but her own—she had enjoyed being held in Slade Barlow's arms as they'd danced.

Maggie Landers drove up just as Slade was about to pull away from the curb, his mom ensconced in the passenger seat, tooting the horn on her expensive little blue roadster. It was a classic, that car, imported from England, and he would have recognized it anywhere.

With a sigh, Slade waited, rolling down the driver's-side window.

Maggie minced up alongside the vehicle, teetering atop her shoes and holding a sheaf of documents in one hand. "I got held up at the office and missed the whole barbecue," she said, quite unnecessarily, tossing a warm smile to his mother. "Hi, Callie."

"Hi," Callie answered back. She'd had a good time at the party, Callie had, and she was still glowing from all those compliments concerning her singing voice.

"More papers?" Slade asked, with a marked lack of enthusiasm. He was tired, and his head was full of Joslyn Kirk, and he just wanted to get to some quiet place so he could think. Mull things over till they made some kind of sense.

Maggie beamed up at him. She looked so fresh and perky in her expensive summer pantsuit that it might as well have been morning, instead of nearly eleven at night. "You know the ones," she replied. "How about signing them so I can cross another item off my to-do list?"

"Has anybody ever told you you're a workaholic?" Slade asked. These, he figured, were the documents that would transfer a shitload of John Carmody's money into his bank account. He should have felt like a lottery winner—but he didn't. Seemed more like getting a license to beg, to him. "Hell, Maggie, it's the weekend. The banks aren't even open."

"True," Maggie agreed blithely, standing her ground. "But getting your signature now will save one or both of us a trip on Monday." She paused, drew in a breath, hiked up her chin a notch. "Besides, this isn't just about the money Mr. Carmody left you. There's another document there, in case you haven't noticed. It's a formal offer from Hutch to buy out your share of Whisper Creek, and it's a whopper. Frankly, I advised him against paying so much, especially in this market, but he's determined to have that ranch all to himself, I guess."

Slade's jawline tightened, and, though Maggie might not have noticed, his

mom did. Callie laid a hand on his forearm, very briefly, the way she'd always
done when she reckoned he was about
to say something he might come to regret later.

"Got a pen?" he snapped, flipping on
the interior lights so he could see what
he was putting his John Hancock to.
He wasn't *about* to sign off on his half
of Whisper Creek until he'd done a lot
more thinking, considered his options
from every angle.

It was just the way he did things. The
kind of man he was.

Maggie handed him a fancy ballpoint
pen and the wad of papers. He scanned
them, signed in several places and
handed back the documents.

Maggie looked at them, then back up
at him. "What about Hutch's offer?
Aren't you even going to look at it?"

That particular packet of papers was
still in his hand. "I'll look at it, all right,"
Slade said tautly. *"Later."*

Maggie stepped right up onto the
running board and peered past Slade
to Callie. "Will you talk some sense into

this lunkhead?" she asked her old friend. "There's a lot at stake here."

"It's Slade's decision, Maggie," Callie replied easily. "And he's perfectly capable of making it on his own. In fact, I wouldn't have it any other way."

"But—"

Slade cleared his throat. The last of the other vehicles was pulling away, leaving the street quiet and dark. He could even hear the grasshoppers rubbing their hind legs together. "Do me a favor, Maggie," he said gruffly. "Will you, please?"

"Sure," Maggie said, getting down off the running board with considerable grace, for someone in the kind of shoes she generally wore. "What?"

"Tell Hutch to back off," Slade answered. He was direct but not rude, because he liked Maggie, knew she was just doing her job. "The more pressure he puts on me to sell out, the less likely I am to do it."

Maggie sighed. "Get back to me whenever you're ready," she said with a little nod of glum acquiescence.

With that, she walked away.

Slade watched in the side mirror until he saw that Maggie was safely back inside her car.

"You're pretty testy," Callie told him, "for somebody who's set for life, financially, at least."

Maggie zipped past, and then Slade pulled the truck away from the curb. He'd drop his mother off at her place and then get back to the duplex, where he'd left Jasper amid piles of boxes and other detritus of moving.

Tomorrow afternoon sometime, Shea would arrive. She'd be staying at the Best Western hotel with Layne for a few days—long enough, he hoped, for him to get the rented place ready to live in. He needed to buy some real furniture, and some groceries, and some decent towels, among other things.

"I have a lot on my mind," he said.

"Yes," Callie said. He'd told her, of course, about Shea's impending visit and that Layne would be coming with her, so he figured she was referring to that. She surprised him, though, as she so often did. "I saw you dancing with Joslyn Kirk."

He sighed and shoved a hand through his hair. Before getting into the truck, he'd tossed his hat into the backseat. He wasn't usually careless with his hat.

He felt hurried, prodded. And he hated that. "It was just that, Mom," he said. "A *dance*."

Mischief chimed in Callie's voice. "Did I say it was anything more?" she countered. Then, holding out a hand, "Let me have a look at those papers."

He handed them to her without looking away from the road.

The interior light had gone off by then, but there was still enough of a glow from the moon and the streetlamps to read by. She flipped a few pages, then let out a long, slow whistle of exclamation.

"Hutch *really* wants to own every square inch of Whisper Creek Ranch," she said.

"Ya think?" Slade asked. He wasn't proud of his tone of voice, but it was too late now. He'd already cut loose with it.

"Slade." That was all Callie said, just his name. But the word was rife with meaning. *You're not fooling me,* it said. *There's a lot more going on here than you're willing to admit to.*

He didn't offer a reply, and they traveled in silence all the way to the Curly-Burly. There, he got out of the truck, walked around to Callie's side and opened her door.

No matter how anxious he was to get out of there, he couldn't leave until he knew she was inside with the lights turned on and everything okay.

So Slade walked with his mom to the door of the add-on, waited while she unlocked it, juggling her purse from one arm to the other in the process. He reached in around her to flip the switch, and the lamps came on, glowing.

"Come in for a minute?" Callie said softly. She was obviously expecting a refusal.

"Sure," he said, suppressing another sigh. "I can't stay long, though. I have to get home and let Jasper out before he disgraces himself."

Callie smiled at that and Slade closed the door.

She tossed her purse onto the narrow table nearby and kicked off her party boots, leaving them as they landed, at odd angles to each other.

"How about some coffee?" she asked.

"Thanks," Slade replied, staying where he was, taking in that familiar homey room. The furniture was service-able, if a mite shabby, and he wondered if the carpet, threadbare but invariably clean, still felt soft under bare feet, the way it had when he was a boy. "But I'd like to get some sleep tonight, so I'll pass."

"Decaf, then?" she persisted. Callie Barlow hadn't gotten as far as she had by giving up easily.

"You have some," he said, following her into the kitchenette, which was only slightly larger than the one he had over at the duplex. "I'll sit with you for a few minutes."

Callie looked back at him over one shoulder of her fringed cowgirl shirt and smiled. "Good," she said. "I always get a little wistful after a night of kicking up my heels."

Again, she'd surprised him.

He took one of the chairs at the table, leaned against the red vinyl back and folded his arms while she puttered around getting out a cup, a spoon, a jar of decaf. "What makes you wistful?" he ventured.

"There's something about parties," Callie admitted. "They make me forget, for a while, that I'm going home alone."

Slade felt a pang at that, did his level best to hide it. Callie had her pride, after all, and if she thought he was feeling sorry for her, she'd be hurt. "You don't have to be alone," he pointed out quietly. "Even in this one-horse town, there are plenty of men who'd like to put a gold ring on your finger."

"Or through my nose," Callie responded archly. Then she giggled. "I could get married again." She paused thoughtfully. "If I wanted to settle."

"Did you love John Carmody?" Slade asked after they'd both been quiet for a few moments, given to their separate introspections. He hadn't planned to put that particular question to her, but there it was, hanging between them.

She paused in the act of setting her coffee cup in the microwave, looked back at him. "Of course I did," she finally answered in a smaller voice than usual. "I had his baby, didn't I?"

Slade squeezed his eyes shut for a moment. There was a peculiar burning sensation behind them. "Love and babies don't necessarily go together," he said hoarsely. "Not then and not now."

Callie came to sit across from him, forgetting all about her instant coffee in the microwave. "I loved John, all right," she said very quietly. "And I believe he loved me, too."

Slade gave a mirthless little snort, meant to pass as laughter. "He had a hell of a way of showing it," he scoffed, but gently, because Callie had been over enough rough roads in her life, and he didn't want to add to her sorrows.

A look of reminiscence settled in Callie's eyes, and she smiled softly, distantly. "You don't understand," she said. "And who can blame you?"

The bell on the microwave rang, and Callie was on her feet in an instant, back in the present and evidently desperate for decaf.

"I'm sorry," Slade said, and he meant it. "For bringing him up, I mean."

"You're thinking about your father," Callie said reasonably, as she returned to her chair with her coffee steaming between her hands, "because you've always believed he didn't care about you, and now, all of a sudden, he's left you a lot of money and half of Whisper Creek Ranch. It's natural to feel some confusion—and some other things, too."

She was getting at something, but he wasn't sure what.

So he waited, knowing she'd work her way around to the point in her own good time. He might as well just stay put until she did.

"Do you really want to work Whisper Creek Ranch," she began when she was ready, "or are you just making things tough for Hutch because he's the legitimate son, the one John favored?"

Slade unclamped his back molars and rotated his lower jaw a couple of times to loosen it up. "I don't know," he said, because it was his curse to be honest, even when it would have been easier—even better—to lie.

"Don't you think you'd better figure it out?" Callie prompted.

It reminded him of old times, the two of them sitting there at that table late at night, talking things through. Discussing everything from after-school jobs to girls. "Give me a little time, Mom," he said. "It's only been a few days since I found out the old man had a generous side."

Callie looked disappointed. "It's wrong to hate your father, Slade," she said.

Slade leaned forward slightly in his chair and narrowed his eyes. "I *don't* hate John Carmody," he replied. "I'd have to care about him to do that."

"After all this time, you're still bitter," Callie replied, and moisture gleamed in her eyes.

"Yep," he agreed. "You could say that."

"I tried so hard to be both mother and father to you," Callie told him, blinking back the tears. "But I should have known—no matter how much I loved you, you still needed a dad."

He reached across the table, took her hand briefly and gave it a light squeeze. "Plenty of people grow up without one parent or the other," he said. "I turned out fine, and as a mom, you went above and beyond the call of duty. Anyhow, it's no use wishing things had been different."

"Suppose we change the subject?" Callie suggested, with weary brightness. "Are you excited about Shea coming to spend the summer?"

"I'm happy about it," Slade said, grateful to his mom for turning the conversation in another direction. "But I'll admit, I'm a little worried, too. What do I know about teenagers? Especially the female kind?"

Callie smiled. "You know plenty about teenagers," she said. "Just last month, you talked three of them down off the water tower before they could fall and break their fool necks."

"It's a rite of passage, climbing the water tower," he said. "I did it, and so did almost everybody I grew up with."

"What did you say to them, Slade?" Callie pressed, though she already knew. The incident had been a big deal at the time; half the town had gathered, holding their collective breath, to watch the drama unfold.

Drama was fairly rare in Parable, thank God, so when the opportunity arose, people got right on it.

"I said they wouldn't be in any trouble if they came down the ladder, slow and careful, but if I had to climb up there and get them, one by one, there would be hell to pay when I got them back to my office."

"See? You knew just how to handle them."

"My heart was in my throat the whole time," Slade admitted. "I might have looked and sounded calm, but I was scared as hell. Fifty feet is a long way to fall."

"Sure you were scared," Callie affirmed. "We all were—especially their parents. The important thing is, you didn't let it show. You gave those kids an out, a choice, and they took it. That was smart, Slade." She paused, swallowed, and her eyes widened a little. "You really climbed that water tower when you were young? Even after I told you not to at least a thousand times?"

Slade grinned. "I had to," he said. "Hutch Carmody dared me."

Callie threw out her hands in mock disgust. *"Well,* then," she said, *"of course* you had to do it!"

"I dared him back," Slade recalled. "And the damnedest thing happened when we got up there."

"What?" Callie asked after a moment.

"I never knew Hutch to be afraid of anything, but it turns out that he doesn't like heights. He froze up there—it was just the two of us—and I had to call him a two-bit, yellow-bellied coward to get him to come down."

Callie's eyes went even wider still. "And he never forgave you for calling him a two-bit, yellow-bellied coward?"

"He never forgave me for knowing he was scared," Slade clarified. "It was bad enough that he froze. To have me be the one to be there and see it was adding insult to injury. Once we got to the ground, we had a hell of a fight."

"Why did he go up there in the first place if he was afraid?" Callie asked.

She was looking for logic in a situation that had been awash in teenage testosterone, not reason.

"Because I dared him," Slade said simply.

"Slade Barlow," Callie scolded with a wave of one hand. "You could have gotten *both* of you killed."

"Didn't happen," Slade pointed out. He straightened. "Now, is this conversation over yet? Because if it is, I'd like to go home and let my dog out for a few minutes, take a shower and fall face-first into bed."

Callie smiled. "Bring Shea by to see me?" she asked. Slade was on his feet by then, so she stood up, too. "After Layne leaves, I mean?"

Slade pretended to be shocked, even horrified. "You don't want to see Layne?"

"Hell, no," Callie said, punching him lightly in the chest.

He laughed and kissed her forehead. "Good night, cowgirl," he said.

She smiled up at him. "Get out of here," she replied. "It's late and I'm tired of looking at you."

Slade laughed again and took his leave.

When he got home, Jasper was waiting eagerly beside the sliding doors, with his muzzle pressed into the crack.

Slade opened the way, and the dog shot out into the yard.

"Don't go over the wall," Slade warned him. He didn't want to deal with Joslyn Kirk—unless you counted sleeping with her.

He'd like to do that, all right.

Jasper behaved himself, though. Did his business and trotted back into the kitchen, tags jingling.

Slade refilled the dog's water bowl and gave him a little extra kibble, just for the heck of it.

"We're getting company tomorrow," Slade said, looking around at the boxes that contained all his worldly goods.

Except, of course, for the millions that would be transferred into his bank account Monday morning, and half of one of the finest ranches in the state of Montana.

He shook his head. *Unreal,* he thought. *I'm just the sheriff of a pissant county, and I don't have a clue how to run a place like Whisper Creek.*

"But half of that ranch is mine," he said, right out loud.

And that was as good as having half a father. How pitiful was that?

He locked up, checked his landline voice mail for messages—there weren't any—and meandered into his bedroom.

He tried to picture Joslyn in that room, in her sandals and her sundress and her damnable attitude. But he couldn't. Any way he looked at it, she wasn't the air-mattress type. If—*when,* for he knew it was certain to happen, for good or ill—he made love to Joslyn Kirk, it would be on clean, scented sheets, in a room with real furniture and a breeze blowing in through an open window. There might even be flowers around. Maybe some candlelight and soft music.

Hell, a man could *dream,* couldn't he?

Joslyn slept in late on Sunday morning; awakened to the sound of church bells pealing all over town and the weight of a cat standing on her chest.

"Meow," Lucy-Maude said, and her meaning was clear. *It's about* time *you woke up, you lazy human. I'm starving here.*

Joslyn laughed and stroked the cat's fuzzy head. The bells kept ringing, the separate sounds tumbling over each other in chaotic jubilation. The digital clock on her bedside table clicked over to eleven.

Lucy-Maude leaped off her chest and onto the floor, tail switching impatiently from side to side. A vivid image of a dish filled with kitty kibble sprang full-blown into Joslyn's mind, and she laughed again.

"Message received," she told the critter. "But could you give me a second? I'm still half-asleep."

A few minutes later, they convened in the kitchen, woman and cat, and Joslyn dished up the kibble before she even started the coffee brewing.

While Lucy-Maude was busy forestalling the threat of famine, Joslyn opened the back door, breathing in the fresh morning air. The sun was shining, the sky was blue, and the flowers were a feast to her soul. She took a while to absorb all that brilliant color, the blues and reds, yellows and golds, pinks and purples.

Except for the Chinese lanterns hanging dark and damp from the branches of the maple trees and a flat place in the grass where the dance floor had been, all evidence of the barbecue and subsequent festivities had vanished.

Lucy-Maude finished the kibble, moved to the threshold and began grooming herself in the warmth of the morning sunlight.

Some moments, Joslyn thought, were just plain perfect.

When the coffee was ready, she poured a cup and walked out into the backyard in her cotton pajama bottoms and long T-shirt, taking a seat in a nearby lawn chair. Lucy-Maude approached and wound herself around Joslyn's ankles a few times, then rolled in the grass, as happy as a kitten.

The screen door on Kendra's sunporch creaked open, and Kendra came through it, wearing cutoff jeans and a tank top but no shoes. Her hair was pulled back in a ponytail that made her look about fourteen years old.

"Is there any more of that coffee?" she called.

"Help yourself," Joslyn responded, smiling.

Kendra passed her, looking wan, entered Joslyn's kitchen and came out with a cup of steaming coffee in her hand. Joslyn had brought over a second lawn chair during the interim, and Kendra sagged into it. Her toenails were painted a bright shade of coral. "I drank too much wine last night," she confessed.

Joslyn grinned. "Is that why you danced with Hutch Carmody?" she asked lightly.

"Probably," Kendra replied, her tone rueful, though a smile twitched at the corners of her mouth. "What's *your* excuse?"

"For dancing with Hutch?"

"For dancing with *Slade*," Kendra said.

"I'm a sucker for punishment," Joslyn answered cheerfully. "There's something about him—"

"Raw sexual magnetism, maybe?" Kendra prompted, beginning to perk up as the caffeine hit her bloodstream.

"You noticed," Joslyn joked.

"It's hard not to," Kendra replied. "I think God was showing off a little when He decided to throw Slade Barlow together."

"Amen," agreed Joslyn.

Kendra chuckled. "And then there's Hutch."

Joslyn waited.

Kendra stared off into a distance that wasn't visible to Joslyn. "We dated for a while," she said, very quietly. "Hutch and I, that is."

"You didn't tell me that," Joslyn said almost accusingly. She'd known, of course, that Kendra was holding things back, just as she was. "What happened?"

"I met my husband," Kendra replied, after a long time. "Jeffrey."

"Oh," Joslyn said. "Love at first sight?"

"Hardly," Kendra said, avoiding Joslyn's gaze. "Hutch and I had had a fight—it was over something stupid, I can't even remember what—and we broke up. Even then, I thought it was temporary, but I hadn't counted on Hutch Carmody's thick skull or his pride. Things got out of control, fast, and the next thing I knew, I was getting married—hoping right up until the 'I do's' that Hutch would storm in and stop the wedding." She paused, let out a shaky breath. "He didn't, obviously."

"But the other day, you said—"

"That I blamed my husband for destroying my faith in love," Kendra interrupted quietly. "That's what I wanted you to believe—wanted *myself* to believe, but the truth is, Jeffrey didn't break my heart—*I* did. With some help from Hutch."

Joslyn took that in, sighed and finally nodded. People did crazy things when they were in love.

CHAPTER NINE

Sunday was a workday for Slade, and he was in his office bright and early, dismissing the night deputy and brewing himself a pot of strong coffee. Things were quiet, the jail cells empty except for the local derelict, Lyle Hoskins, who'd needed a place to sleep the night before and was now snoring away with all the delicacy of a dull buzz saw. When Lyle woke up, Slade would tell him to make use of the prisoners' shower and give him a county voucher for breakfast over at the Butter Biscuit Café. In the meantime, Slade accepted with resignation, he'd just have to put up with the racket.

He'd been checking APBs on his computer for the last little while, but now he looked down at Jasper, who was resting on the floor at his feet, brown eyes rolled up toward him. The effect was one of comical curiosity.

"You sound almost that bad when you're really zonked out," he told the dog companionably, referring to Lyle's resonant snoring.

Jasper whimpered slightly, but didn't raise his muzzle from his outstretched forelegs. He was just getting comfortable, according to his body language, and if Slade would just shut up and let him get some shut-eye, all would be right in his little dog world.

Slade looked around when the office door swung open and Deputy Treat Mc-Quillan swaggered in, wearing a fresh uniform and a grudging expression.

Slade wasn't surprised to see Mc-Quillan, since he'd summoned the man by radio soon after arriving at work half an hour before, but the deputy's attitude took him somewhat aback. Treat

McQuillan lacked for a lot of things, but brass wasn't one of them.

"You wanted to see me, Sheriff?" McQuillan asked, almost snarling the question. He was short, his body lean and lanky, and he had a beaked nose and bright, birdlike eyes that seemed lidless, since he so rarely blinked. Always on the lookout for a slight, that was McQuillan.

Why anybody, including a loving mother, would dub the guy "Treat," even as a baby, was a mystery to Slade. He must have looked like a California condor right from the first.

Maybe it was a family name. Or maybe it came out of a magazine, like "Slade," he thought, with a brief touch of amusement.

"I'm glad you could make it in," Slade responded, his tone deliberately mild. McQuillan got under his hide just by breathing, and that wasn't right. Where was all that self-control people credited him with? "Since you seem to have a challenge turning up for your regular shifts on time and all."

McQuillan glared at him. The nephew

of the late, great Wilkes McQuillan, who'd served as the sheriff of Parable County for over thirty years and been a very popular man throughout his tenure, Treat had expected to take over the job when his uncle died suddenly of a heart attack and left the office up for grabs. Treat had made no secret of the fact that he felt out-and-out *entitled* to the badge and everything that came with it, as if there was some kind of divine-right-of-kings thing going.

Treat had barely made it onto the ballot, though, and Slade's landslide victory still stuck in his craw, even after five-plus years. That much was obvious.

"Boone's been complaining about me again, hasn't he?" Treat demanded. His two front teeth overlapped slightly, and his eyes were set too close together, giving him a mean look that, unfortunately, tallied with his behavior.

Slade leaned back in his desk chair and reached down to scratch Jasper's ear when the dog somewhat belatedly got to all four feet and growled.

"We're not talking about Boone,"

Slade pointed out. "We're talking about you."

In a perfect world, McQuillan wouldn't stand a chance of getting elected sheriff if Slade stepped down—everybody knew he was a petty hothead with too many imaginary scores to settle—but it *wasn't* a perfect world now, was it? The plain truth was, nobody else wanted the job, with its long hours, famously low pay and almost constant tedium, so McQuillan would probably run unopposed.

And he'd make one lousy sheriff.

"You'd like to get rid of me, wouldn't you?" McQuillan challenged, clenching his fists at his sides. His size didn't do a hell of a lot for his self-esteem, Slade supposed. Treat was what Callie called a "banty rooster," always strutting around, hoping to run into trouble and willing to create some if he didn't. Yes, sir, Treat's whole life, it seemed to Slade, was about proving things.

Must have been exhausting.

Treat seemed to get angrier when Slade didn't respond to the accusation. "I'll *tell* you what your problem is, Barlow. I remind you too much of my uncle—the best sheriff this county ever had."

Slade sighed and left off scratching Jasper's ear to cup both hands behind his head, lean back in his chair and regard his deputy long and hard before he spoke again. "Don't flatter yourself, McQuillan," he said flatly. "Yes, Wilkes was a first-class sheriff and a good man. But all you have in common with him is your last name."

McQuillan reddened at that, tightened his fists so the knuckles showed white.

Bring it, Slade thought silently. *Come right over this desk and go for my throat, because that would give me the dual pleasures of firing your worthless ass and kicking it for good measure.*

Treat didn't bite, but he was still seething. "You've lost your edge, *Sheriff,*" he taunted. "Everybody knows you hate this job, that you'd rather dig post holes and drive cattle like some throwback to the Old West, so why don't you just resign and be done with it?"

"You're on thin ice here, Treat," Slade said without raising his voice.

Treat braced his hands on the edge of Slade's desk and leaned in. "You've even got money," he ranted, his ears going a dull red and sort of glowing, as if they were lit up from the inside, "now that old John Carmody took pity on you and left you what should have gone to Hutch. You know why John did that, Slade?"

Slade rose slowly to his full height. He was letting McQuillan get to him again, and he knew it, but knowing didn't make it better.

Treat McQuillan backed off a step or two, but he wasn't through running his mouth. "It wasn't because the old man finally decided to claim you, after all those years," he continued. "It was because he and Hutch never got along. Not from day one. Carmody wanted to get under Hutch's hide, pay him back for all the grief he caused, that's all, and what better way to do it than to practically disown him and make damn sure the whole county knew the story?"

Slade could feel a vein pulsing under

his right temple, and he saw red at the periphery of his vision.

His voice came out gravel-rough. "Get out," he said. "And don't come back until I put your name on the duty roster."

Jasper must have been as fed up with McQuillan as Slade was, because he growled in earnest now and made a move to round the desk.

Swiftly, Slade bent to grab hold of the dog's collar and restrain him.

"That dog makes a move on me," Treat sputtered, already heading for the door, "and I'll shoot him."

"Don't even think about doing that," Slade said. All his life, he could have said what he'd do in any given situation. He was all about self-control, balance, calm consideration of every angle. But here, in McQuillan, was the exception.

Under certain circumstances, Slade knew, he could hurt this guy.

Maybe McQuillan saw that disturbing truth rise in Slade's eyes, or maybe he just sensed it. In any case, he finally figured out that he ought to leave and stalked out of the office, slamming the door so hard behind him that the glass panel bearing Slade's name and title rattled in its frame.

Now that there was no immediate threat of mayhem, Slade let go of Jasper's collar and sank back into his chair, closing his eyes. He felt sick to his stomach, and that twitch in his temple was a hammering beat now, pounding a headache into the side of his brain.

He took slow, deep breaths.

His stepdaughter was on her way to Parable, he reminded himself. And she needed a father—not a maniac.

Lyle, no doubt awakened by the confrontation just past, rattled the bars of the holding cell just then and called out in a charitable tone, "You can let me out now, Sheriff. Once I grab a shower, I'll be good to go."

Slade smiled at the crazy normality of the moment and pushed back his chair, stood up and took the cell keys from a drawer in his desk.

Lyle was all gray bristle, from his almost nonexistent buzz cut to his beard. He was probably in his sixties, though it was hard to tell, since Slade couldn't recall him ever looking any other way than he did right now, and he seemed to consider being Parable's most eccentric citizen as his moral duty. Lyle didn't drink, but sometimes he didn't take his medications, either, and when that happened, all bets were off.

He might take a notion to strip off all his clothes and walk the white line on the highway like a tightrope, for example. Or decide to live in the town park, like a homeless person.

Once, when he'd been missing for several days, a thing that often happened with Lyle, Slade and Boone Taylor had searched for him, from one end of the county to the other, and finally found him hiding out in a culvert just outside of town. He'd been absolutely certain that civil war had broken out between Montana and Idaho, and the bombs were about to start falling at any moment.

"Spud missiles," Boone had cracked at the time. "The worst kind."

They'd taken Lyle to a mental hospital in Great Falls that day, in the backseat of Slade's truck. Soon as his medications had had time to build up in his system, Lyle had been released, and he'd caught the first bus back home.

"You hungry?" Slade asked, opening the cell door. The shower set aside for the use of inmates was down the hall-way—it wasn't as if this was maximum security or anything.

Lyle scurried past him and picked up the paper bag he usually had with him when he visited the county jail. From experience, Slade knew it contained fresh clothes, a bath towel from home, toothpaste and a brush. "Only if you're going to give me one of them meal tick-ets you always seem to have handy," he replied. "I spent the last of my allow-ance on an LED-powered hair-growing helmet I saw on TV, and they cut off my credit over at the Butter Biscuit months ago. Why, Essie won't even trust me for a slice of pie!"

Slade quelled a grin. "Of course you'll get your voucher," he said. "Go take your shower and I'll have it made out by the time you get back."

Clutching his paper bag, Lyle went off to do as he'd been told.

When he returned, ten minutes later, he glowed pink from a thorough scrubbing, and he had his eye peeled for the promised voucher.

To Lyle, a free meal was serious business—since his wealthy sister controlled the purse strings—and so, for some inexplicable reason, was growing a head of hair.

Lyle rubbed his stubby little hands together, probably anticipating his usual order of bacon, eggs and biscuits. He wore overalls, an old pair of high-tops with the laces broken off and a flannel shirt that wasn't fit for the average rag bag. "Hand over the coupon, Sheriff," he said. "I'm so starved, my stomach thinks my throat's been cut."

Slade studied Lyle's grizzled pate, frowning a little, as he held out the voucher.

"Did it work?" he asked finally.

"Did what work?" Lyle countered, snatching the slip of paper from Slade's hand.

"The hair-growing gizmo you mentioned," Slade said, careful to keep a straight face.

Lyle looked self-conscious for a moment and ran a hand over his nearly
bald head. "It hasn't got here yet," he
explained, aggrieved. "Delivery takes
four to six weeks, unless you pay extra
for the special shipping and handling."

Lyle enjoyed watching infomercials
on TV, between shopping channel mar-
athons, much to his long-suffering sister Myra's consternation. Myra had
never married and, in her opinion, the
responsibility for that, at least partially,
lay at her brother's door, him being cra-
zier than a bedbug and all. Fortunately,
she and Lyle had inherited a big brick
house and a sizable sum of money after both their parents had died of old
age, because neither one of them could
have earned a living, even when they
were young.

"Well," Slade drawled, "when it gets
here, let me know how it works."

Lyle, already on his way out, spared
him an exasperated glance. "Why?" he
asked. "You thinkin' of ordering one for
yourself? Don't know why you'd do that,
Sheriff—you already got plenty of hair."

Slade bit the inside of his lower lip so

he wouldn't grin. "Just curious, that's all," he said easily.

That pleased Lyle. He nodded, clutching his paper bag, which now contained the clothes he'd had on since the day before, if not longer, and headed out to have breakfast as a guest of Parable County.

Once Kendra had finished her coffee and gone, Joslyn went inside the guesthouse, took a quick shower and dressed in black shorts and a yellow sun top. She wound her damp hair up into a knot on top of her head, fixed it there with a plastic squeeze clip and fired up her computer.

As soon as she'd logged on, she ran a search for local lost-pet notices on the animal shelter's site, just in case someone was looking for Lucy-Maude.

The grainy photos of half a dozen found cats were posted there, along with several dogs and a couple of ferrets, all awaiting their owners at Parable's own Paws for Reflection.

Joslyn's eyes burned slightly as she studied the images. She wanted to bring them *all* home, cats, dogs *and* ferrets, but obviously that wasn't possible.

She glanced down at plump Lucy-Maude, sitting imperiously in the center of a hooked rug Opal had made years ago when she'd been on a crafting kick, and wondered where the animal belonged and if anyone missed her.

With a sigh, Joslyn reached for her purse, rummaged for her smartphone and snapped a picture of Lucy-Maude. Then, still impressed by the wonders of technology even after all her experience with it, she zapped the photo from her phone to her computer. Adding it to the other Paws posts took two seconds.

"Found," she wrote. "Healthy gray cat, age unknown, female, with amber eyes. Expecting babies, soon."

If Lucy-Maude's owners happened to see her picture on the site, they could contact the people at the shelter, who would in turn get in touch with Joslyn. She drew a deep breath, entered her phone numbers in the proper boxes, and then let out a very deep sigh as she clicked on the confirmation button. A part of her hoped that no one would claim Lucy-Maude, because then she could keep her.

Right, taunted her practical side. *Kittens and all.*

She imagined a litter of mewing gray fluff balls frolicking all over the guesthouse and smiled a bit sadly. *Instant Crazy Cat Lady,* she thought, considering the scene. *Just add me.*

Then she got up, crossed to Lucy-Maude and lifted her gently into her arms, nuzzling her silken ruff. "Don't you worry," she promised the purring feline. "I'll find your people—and homes for all your babies, too. Good ones."

"Meow," observed Lucy-Maude, brushing Joslyn's cheek with her cold little nose and tickly whiskers.

A knock at the open door off the kitchen, clearly visible from the living room because the whole place was space-challenged, made Joslyn straighten her spine and set the cat down carefully.

Hutch was standing in the opening, leaning indolently against the door frame, his fine mouth crooked up in a grin. "Hi," he said. "I just stopped by to see if you were up for some lunch over at the Butter Biscuit and maybe a horse-back ride afterward."

Recalling what Kendra had told her that morning, Joslyn hesitated. Then she told herself to stop being silly—Hutch was her friend, and there was no disloyalty in accepting at least *part* of his invitation.

"Yes to lunch, no to the horseback ride," she said, glad to see Hutch and, at the same time, grappling with the odd and totally unreasonable wish that the suggestion had come from Slade instead. "You know I'm hopeless with horses, my bogus stint as the Parable County Rodeo Queen notwithstanding."

Hutch laughed and stepped into the kitchen, looking loose-hinged and at ease inside his skin. "Don't you think it's time you made an honest woman of yourself, then?" he challenged. "Come on, Joss. Don't be chicken. It's a nice day and I've got just the horse for you—a little mare named Sandy. She's no more dangerous than a rocking chair."

The rest of Sunday stretched before Joslyn, long and lonely. Kendra had other plans—a shopping junket to Missoula that hadn't appealed to Joslyn, though Kendra had asked her to go along—which meant she might not see another human being before tomorrow morning. She was due to start working at the real-estate office then, and she was looking forward to having a job again.

She wasn't cut out for a life of leisure.

"I'm not chicken," she said in belated protest. "I happen to consider myself a very brave person."

"I'd say that's right on the money," Hutch agreed, looking more serious now, though Joslyn knew the twinkle in his eyes, having gone, would return momentarily. "It took guts to spend all that time right out in the open at Kendra's barbecue, fixed in everybody's crosshairs."

Joslyn sighed, found her sandals and slipped them onto her feet. "There were moments," she admitted as Lucy-Maude, taking no interest in visiting cowboys, jumped up into the seat of the overstuffed armchair and curled up for a nap.

"You'll want to switch out those shorts—good as you look in them—for a pair of jeans," Hutch said. Sure enough, the twinkle had already returned. "It would be a shame to scratch up a fine set of legs like yours cutting through the brush on a horse."

"Flatterer," Joslyn said with a grin, heading for her tiny bedroom.

"I call 'em as I see 'em," Hutch called after her.

She returned a couple of minutes later in well-worn jeans, sneakers and with a long-sleeved cotton shirt over her sun top. Looking down at her shoes, she said, "These are the best I can do, since I don't own any boots."

"Another thing that ought to be rectified," Hutch teased. He'd moved to the armchair, where he sat perched on one wide arm, stroking Lucy-Maude's sleek back. "You do realize that this critter has something in the oven? Six or eight somethings, probably?"

Joslyn, oddly touched by the sight of a rough-and-tumble cowboy like Hutch petting a cat, sighed. "Yep," she said. "I picked up on that."

Hutch ran his eyes over her once with platonic appreciation and cocked another grin. "Maybe we can rustle you up a pair of boots when we get to my place," he said. "Dad kept some of my mom's things when she died, and she did a lot of riding before she got sick."

Joslyn's throat tightened, just briefly. She remembered Lottie Hutcheson Carmody's long illness and subsequent death; her mother and Elliott had gone to the funeral, leaving her at home with Opal, much to her secret—and guilty—relief.

She and Hutch had both been twelve at the time and already good friends, in the gibe-and-shove way of prepubescent kids. More than once, Joslyn had wished she'd insisted on attending Lottie's services, if only so Hutch would have seen her there and known she was sorry he'd lost his mother.

Losing her own was unimaginable, then as now.

Hutch laid a hand to the small of Joslyn's back and lightly steered her toward the door. Slipping her purse strap over one shoulder, she went along.

The Butter Biscuit Café was doing a brisk business, as it always did on Sundays. People came for breakfast before or after church, then for a late lunch or an early supper.

Essie Spotts, the middle-aged and inherently good-natured owner of the place, somehow conjured up a table right away. Essie's hair was dyed Elvis-black, and she wore it pinned up in a loose bun on top of her head, shot through with pencils of varying lengths. She hadn't been at the barbecue the day before, but she'd provided much of the food and the waitstaff.

If she'd lost any money in Elliott's investment scheme, she didn't appear to blame Joslyn for it, unlike a number of other, less charitable souls around town.

"Now, then," she said cheerfully, plucking one of the pencils from her hair and pulling a small order pad from her apron pocket. "Blueberry brunch balls are the special, since we're serving breakfast all day. Comes with scrambled eggs and either bacon or sausage on the side. Toast is extra, since you've got your carbohydrates in the brunch balls."

A benign smirk curved Hutch's mouth as he sat down across the table from Joslyn and intertwined his fingers, in no apparent hurry to consult a menu. "What the heck," he began, "is a blueberry brunch ball?"

Essie, who happened to have a hefty vinyl menu tucked under one pudgy elbow, bopped Hutch lightly on the head with it. "It's a mess of *blueberries,* you dumb cowboy, mixed with pancake dough and deep-fried."

Hutch laughed. "It's all right, Essie," he teased. "You not wanting the word to get out that you're crazy in love with me, I mean. I understand completely."

Essie, who had to be past fifty, blushed behind the powdery circles of rouge on her cheeks. "You stop that nonsense right now, Hutch Carmody," she scolded, clearly delighted, "and tell me what you want to eat. In case you haven't noticed, the place is full to the rafters, and I don't have all day to stand around here yammerin' with the likes of you."

"I'll have the special," Joslyn interjected politely. "Please."

Hutch was still grinning. "And I'll take a cheeseburger, fries and a double chocolate shake, just like I always do."

Essie clucked her tongue, shook her head, spiky with pencils, and turned to hurry off and put in the order.

"Blueberry brunch balls?" Hutch asked, looking at Joslyn.

"Oh, stop it," Joslyn said. "You just like *saying* that."

"You've got to admit," Hutch replied, "it's alliterative."

"'Alliterative'?" Joslyn smiled. "I don't think I've ever heard you use that word."

"I'm not really a dumb cowboy," he confided mischievously in a whisper, "whatever Essie says to the contrary. I've even read a book or two in my time—in fact, I'm seriously considering getting myself one of those electronic readers and downloading a whole mess of Shakespeare."

Joslyn chuckled, and Essie returned with Hutch's milk shake and the orange juice and coffee expertly balanced on a small, round tray. She served the drinks and trotted off toward the door to greet another batch of customers and say goodbye to some on their way out.

"You and Shakespeare," Joslyn said with a mock frown. "Not a combination I would have come up with in a million years."

"Forsooth," Hutch said.

"That's all the Shakespeare you know?"

Hutch laughed again. "Pretty much," he admitted.

The food arrived and in the next instant, his grin faded, and the laughter drained from his eyes.

Joslyn turned to look back over her shoulder to see what—or who—had been able to effect such a lightning-fast change of mood.

Slade Barlow had just come in. He saw the two of them right away, nodded cordially enough, took off his hat and spoke quietly to Essie, who was, once again, all smiles and blushes.

Hutch slid back his chair. Stood. "I'll

be right back," he said to Joslyn without looking at her.

She didn't like the glint in Hutch's eyes. "Wait—" she said.

But he was already walking toward Slade.

It seemed that the whole place went silent just then. Nobody spoke or even clinked a fork against a plate or a cup against a saucer. No pans rattled in the kitchen.

Because there was no other sound, Slade's words, though spoken in a low rumble, were clearly audible.

"Hello, Hutch," he said.

"You take a look at my offer yet?" Hutch countered without returning the greeting first. His back, turned to Joslyn now, was rigid, and she could tell that his arms were folded. "To buy your share of Whisper Creek, I mean?"

Slade took in their surroundings with an eloquent—and irritated—glance. He was a private man, Joslyn knew, one who didn't run from public confrontations but didn't much enjoy them, either.

"Maggie gave me the papers last

night," he said evenly. "I haven't had time to give the matter a whole hell of a lot of thought, as it happens."

Hutch seethed at that. "All the better to jack me around, right?"

"Now, Hutch," Essie said, handing Slade the take-out cup of coffee he must have ordered when he came in, "don't you go starting anything. I mean it."

Slade set the coffee casually aside on the register counter, along with his hat. "Yeah," he echoed. "Don't start anything, because you might have your hands full finishing it."

Hutch wanted to hit Slade; Joslyn and everyone else in the Butter Biscuit knew that. "All I want is an answer," he growled, and it was obvious from his stance that he was still looking directly at his half brother.

"All right," Slade said, measuring out his words. "In that case, I guess it has to be no." There was a long, dangerous pause before Slade went on, "I've been thinking of getting myself a couple of horses. Which half of the barn at Whisper Creek is mine?"

Essie squeezed between the two men and put a manicured hand on each of their chests, fingers splayed.

"Hutch," she said, "you go and sit down with your lady, *right now.* And, Slade, you take your coffee—it's on the house this time—and go about your business."

Joslyn felt something akin to amazement as, however reluctantly, both men obeyed Essie's motherly command.

Slade picked up his cup of coffee and walked out the door.

Hutch returned to the table where he'd been sitting with Joslyn and pushed away what remained of his cheeseburger.

"*Damn* it," he said after a charged moment.

Joslyn considered reaching out to him, maybe patting his hand, but that seemed almost—well—patronizing under the circumstances, so she held back, staring down at the blueberry brunch balls on her plate, her appetite completely gone.

"Let's go for that ride," Hutch said after a few very long moments.

Joslyn nodded, and Hutch settled up the bill, and they left.

Talk closed behind them like briefly parted waters as they went through the door of the Butter Biscuit Café.

Essie's words rang in Slade's mind as he climbed into his truck, parked in the gravel lot beside the café, balancing his coffee in one hand and juggling his hat with the other. *You go and sit down with your lady,* she'd told Hutch moments before.

Since when was Joslyn Hutch's "lady"?

Some of Slade's coffee squeezed past the lid and spilled as he jammed it into the cup holder, burning the web of skin between his thumb and forefinger.

Slade swore. Jasper, riding shotgun, looked at him with concern.

"Get a grip," Slade said, talking to himself now and right out loud, too. Not, as he figured it, a good sign. "Hutch and Joslyn were having a meal together, not rolling around naked in high grass."

Jasper's expression went from concern to pity. He gave a low, throaty whine.

"It's all right, boy," Slade told the dog. "I'm only about half as crazy as I sound, and you're in no danger."

He took a couple of deep breaths, then started the truck, shifted it into Reverse, and backed up. He'd stick with the original plan, he decided—take a spin by the Best Western hotel at the edge of town to see if Shea and Layne had arrived yet.

That would get his mind off Joslyn and Hutch. He hoped.

They were just getting out of a white rental car in front of the Best Western hotel when Slade pulled in with Jasper. Layne, coolly elegant in a red-and-white polka-dot dress and big sunglasses, waved and smiled. She was gorgeous, his ex-wife, but she didn't make his breath catch or his heart rate speed up.

Shea, standing by the passenger door in jean shorts and a short pink T-shirt that left part of her midriff showing, jumped up and down as she recognized him—he guessed that, without her friends there to see, she didn't have to put on that disdainful front so common to teenage girls.

"Hey," he said, getting out of the truck, leaving his hat and his dog behind.

Shea, small with a head of dark hair and huge violet eyes, squealed with delight and flung both arms around him, pressing her forehead hard into his breastbone. "Hey," she said, choking a little on the word.

Above Shea's head, Slade's and Layne's gazes met as she took off her sunglasses. Layne nodded cordially, and Slade nodded back and hugged Shea just a little more tightly than before.

Living with a teenager *and* a new dog was going to liven up his summer, all right, even before adding Joslyn Kirk to the mix.

CHAPTER TEN

After the confrontation with Slade, back at the Butter Biscuit, Joslyn could see that Hutch was even more set on the horseback ride than before.

Settled in the passenger seat of the beat-up old ranch truck he drove over the bumpy roads leading to Whisper Creek Ranch, she bit her lower lip.

"Do you want to talk?" she asked.

Hutch scowled, though he kept his eyes on the dusty swath of oil-stained gravel and dirt in front of them. "About what?" he snapped.

Joslyn simply looked at him.

To his credit, Hutch immediately threw her an apologetic glance. "Sorry," he said.

"What's going on between you and Slade?" Joslyn persisted. She'd gleaned a lot from things that were said earlier at the café, but she wanted to hear Hutch's take on the situation, so she pretended to know nothing.

He was looking straight ahead again, and his jaw tightened until the bone bulged. "Same old, same old," he said presently, trying for a light tone and failing big-time. "Cain and Abel, that's us."

"I think it's more," Joslyn ventured. She'd always known that the two men were half brothers, one legitimate and the other not, just as everyone else who'd ever spent more than a day in Parable did. It was old news, which indicated that some new dynamic must have entered the equation.

Hutch glanced her way and signaled a turn onto a familiar side road, next to a sturdy mailbox with the name "Carmody" stenciled on the side. Drove too fast over the ruts and bumps. "A few days ago," he said, without looking in her direction, "Maggie Landers called Slade and me into her office for the reading of my dad's will. Half of everything the old man owned goes to Slade."

Joslyn absorbed that without comment. Splayed her fingers on her blue-jeaned thighs and made a concentrated effort not to bite her tongue as they bounced along that pot-holed driveway.

She'd been under the impression that John Carmody had never been willing to admit Slade was his flesh-and-blood, born of a long-ago affair with Callie. It was one of those secrets that wasn't much of a secret.

"Half of everything," Hutch reiterated grimly, bringing the truck to a jerky stop, at last, between the two-story colonial house and the long, low-slung barn, with its weathered red paint and white shutters at the windows. "Including this ranch."

"Oh," Joslyn said lamely.

"Yeah," Hutch bit out, *"oh."*

She summoned up a wavery smile. "So this means you're going to wind up in the poorhouse?" she teased, her tone tentative.

Still lame, she decided.

Hutch made no move to get out of the truck. He shut off the engine, though, and gazed off toward some horizon she couldn't quite see. "Money's not the problem," he said, after a long, uncomfortable silence. "There's plenty of that to go around. It's the land. It's been in the family for more than a century, Joslyn. There are Carmodys *buried* here. It's wrong to break this ranch into pieces."

"Does it have to be that way?" Joslyn asked, very quietly. "Couldn't you and Slade work something out?"

"I offered him more money than he's ever seen for his share of Whisper Creek," Hutch said miserably. "He doesn't want the place—never showed any interest in staking any kind of claim before. And he could have done that, if he'd taken a notion to. Hired a lawyer, gotten a DNA test done, whatever." He paused, sucked in a breath, squared his shoulders. He still wasn't looking at Joslyn. "No, Slade's just jerking me around, that's all. Because he can, probably. Besides, this is his chance to get back at me for having what he never got, and he means to make the most of it."

Joslyn wanted to choose her words carefully, so she took her time putting them together in her head. While she hadn't known Slade any better when they were younger than she did now at this moment, he'd never struck her as the envious type. Slade had been quiet and kept mostly to himself and a small circle of friends, and he'd never had nice cars or expensive clothes, as she and Hutch had, but it was also true that he'd never shown any signs of wanting those things. Even as a youth, he'd been squarely centered in his own identity, it seemed to her, and comfortable there.

"I know you want things settled," she said, "but it hasn't been that long since your dad died, and now you've got the inheritance thing to deal with. Maybe if you just, well, *breathe,* and let the dust settle for a while, Slade will stop dig-ging in his heels and reconsider your offer."

Slade loved the Kingman place; she'd seen that when the two of them had gone out there together. Although he'd been slow to make up his mind about buying it, she figured he'd wind up living there when all was said and done.

Hutch sighed, shoved a hand through his hair. "In other words, I should back off a little? Is that what you're saying?"

She smiled. "That's what I'm saying," she confirmed. "Slade's stubborn. *You're* stubborn. What we have here is a good old-fashioned standoff, and turning it into a pissing match isn't going to solve anything."

At last, Hutch turned to look at her directly and gave her a sheepish grin. "Maybe I've been pushing Slade a little too hard," he admitted.

"Maybe," Joslyn chimed, singsong. "Now, let's have a look at that rocking-chair horse you told me about before I lose my courage completely and hike back to town."

Hutch chuckled, shoved open the truck door. "Come on," he said. "You're going to like Sandy. I promise."

"Liking something and wanting to take it for a ride are two very different things," Joslyn said, climbing out of the truck to stand on the ground.

Hutch's eyes sparkled as he came around to face her. "I'm not touching that one with a ten-foot pole," he told her.

She laughed, but her cheeks felt warm, too.

He led the way into the barn, which was lined with stalls on both sides, many of them containing horses, but just as many standing unused.

I've been thinking about getting my- self a couple of horses, Slade had said, back at Essie's diner. *Which half of the barn at Whisper Creek is mine?*

The mare, Sandy, was a tiny buck- skin, barely larger than a pony. She looked harmless enough to Joslyn, standing there in her stall, munching placidly on grass-hay as she whiled away a summer afternoon.

"See?" Hutch said, standing beside Joslyn and leaning on Sandy's stall door. "Perfectly safe."

Joslyn sighed. "Which horse are you going to ride?" she asked. Partly, she was trying to buy time, and she knew Hutch sensed that. Was amused.

Hutch pointed to a nearby stall. The gelding inside was big, a black-and-white paint with the long legs and stately head of a Thoroughbred. "I ride most all of these cayuses at one time or another, but Remington, here, is my favorite."

"Even Sandy?" Joslyn teased, smiling at the image of Hutch, the one-time rodeo champ and seasoned rancher, riding a near-pony.

"I used to ride her," he said, grinning. "When I was this high." He held up a hand to elbow height. "She's not much of a challenge now."

"Good," Joslyn said. "Because a *challenge* is not what I'm looking for here."

Hutch smiled at that, then went about saddling Sandy. When he'd finished, he led the mare out of the stall and handed the reins to Joslyn.

"Go ahead and lead her out into the sunshine," he said. "I'll get Remington rigged up and be right behind you."

Joslyn took Sandy's reins with some

trepidation and led the animal out of the barn. Since she and Sandy were practically at eye level with each other, she felt silly for being nervous.

Silly and oddly *happy,* too.

It had been a long time since she'd ridden a horse, and she hadn't been good at it even back then. Parable being a Western kind of town, where lots of people rode regularly, both Elliott and her mom had tried to josh her out of her fear, promising her riding lessons and eventually a horse of her own if she'd just give it a try.

It had been Elliott who had wanted her to compete in the rodeo queen pageant, though, and Joslyn had given just enough ground on the equestrian question to participate in that contest. She'd been amazed when she won, and the victory had quickly soured when she'd caught the tattered edges of the rumors that the whole thing had been fixed.

Elliott, she strongly suspected, had *bought* the title for her.

She'd been vaguely ashamed of the "win" ever since.

Only a couple of minutes had passed

when Hutch came out of the barn, leading Remington, who looked more like a spotted Clydesdale to Joslyn than a regular saddle horse with some racers in his background.

Joslyn's heart began to pound. Sure, Sandy was a plodder, and her back wasn't very far from the ground, but Remington looked ready to gobble up ground with those long, powerful legs of his. His deep chest, probably containing a ticker the size of a riding lawn mower, heaved with anticipation.

Suppose she and Hutch got out there on the range or on some hard country road, and Remington decided to break into a run? Even a tame horse like Sandy would probably feel obliged to keep up.

"I don't know," Joslyn murmured dubiously, looking from one horse to the other.

But Hutch wasn't going to let her back out now. "Dare ya," he taunted, grinning.

"You and your dares," Joslyn blustered, remembering how Hutch had gotten her to climb the water tower in town once, when they were in high school, while calling encouragement from the ground. And that was just one of several such occasions.

"Look," Hutch said, leaning in a little as though to impart some well-guarded secret, "I promise I won't let anything happen to you."

"What if Remington runs?"

"I won't *let* him run, Joss."

"How do I know you can stop him? He's bigger than you are."

"Trust me," Hutch said with a patient grin. "Remington's well trained. He won't run unless I give him his head, and I don't plan on doing that. At least not while you're riding alongside me."

"Okay," Joslyn huffed out. "Well, then." With that, she turned, grasped Sandy's saddle horn, which wasn't that much of a reach, stuck one foot into the stirrup, and hauled herself up onto the mare's back.

Sandy's haunches quivered, and her tail twitched back and forth.

"She's not fixing to buck or break into a dead run," Hutch assured Joslyn, accurately reading the expression of abject terror on her face. "She's just swat-ting away flies."

Sandy *didn't* run, as it turned out, and neither did Remington.

Hutch took it real slow, reining Rem-ington toward the grassy pasture, which probably went on for miles, and Sandy followed sedately, a half length behind.

After clutching the saddle horn until her palms were sweaty, Joslyn finally managed to relax a little, enjoying the slow, predictable pace.

She and Hutch rode as far as the creek that gave the ranch its name—it took twenty minutes to cover the rela-tively short distance—and stopped there to let the horses drink. The water sparkled in the sun, pristinely clear.

"Doing fine?" Hutch asked.

"Doing fine," Joslyn confirmed. She was still jittery, but she felt empowered, too. She could get to like riding, she thought.

Someday.

"You didn't even need boots," Hutch observed drily on the return trip. Poor Remington was fidgety, like a race car gunning its engine with the emergency brakes on.

"I might get a pair," Joslyn said, her confidence buoyed by the afternoon's mild accomplishment. Surely, if she could face a town full of people her stepfather had ripped off, she could learn to ride for real. In rural Montana, it was practically a required skill.

"Good." Hutch grinned.

They went back to the barn, but he left Remington outside at the hitching rail, while he and Joslyn put Sandy away in her cozy stall.

The mare seemed relieved to see the end of dude duty and get back to her feeder and her supply of drinking water.

Hutch put up the saddle, blanket and bridle, then he and Joslyn headed outside again.

He gestured toward Remington. "That animal is never going to forgive me if I don't let him get some exercise. Do you mind?"

Joslyn smiled and shook her head. "Go for it," she said.

With that, Hutch untied the gelding and mounted up. Rode through the open gateway into the green, wind-rippled pasture. The big Montana sky arched over them like a blue bowl.

Joslyn climbed onto a fence rail and settled in to watch.

Hutch gave a sudden whoop of pure joy, and then he and Remington were off, a blended streak of man and horse, moving so fast and with so much grace that they almost looked ready to break free of gravity and fly.

Within a minute, they were around a bend and out of sight, and it seemed to Joslyn, sitting there with one hand shielding her eyes from the sun, that they were gone a long time. She was just beginning to fret a little when they reappeared, Remington moving at a trot, Hutch's pale caramel hair gleaming in the light. She could see his grin from a long way off, and a bittersweet feeling stirred in her heart.

As much as she liked Hutch, she knew he wasn't for her, and she wasn't for him.

What a pity. They would have made one heck of a pair.

* * *

Shea was busy exploring the house and grounds out on the rented ranch, with Jasper practically in lockstep, and Layne and Slade stood between their separate vehicles, awkwardly cordial.

At sixteen, Shea was headed into her junior year of high school, come fall, but she was still Slade's little girl, as far as he was concerned.

Layne smiled, watching her daughter poke around the outside of that tumbledown old ruin of a barn. "Strange, isn't it?" she mused aloud. "How Shea looks more like you than me, with that dark hair of hers?"

He felt a pang, as he always did, no matter how subtle the reminder, because Shea wasn't his biological child. He'd have given anything for that.

He nodded once, cleared his throat. "Layne, about the house—the way it looks, I mean—"

Layne was a generous soul, and she smiled. "We have a few days," she said. "Shea and I will help you set up housekeeping before I go back to L.A." She looked around. "Anyway, it's not so bad."

Slade shifted his weight from one leg to the other and sighed quietly as he watched Shea out of the corner of one eye. She seemed fascinated with that old barn; the trouble being that it might collapse at any time. One good gust of wind and the whole thing would be nothing more than a big pile of kindling.

He bit back the words he wanted to call out to Shea.

Be careful.

Teenagers tended to be rebellious, Shea more than most. He meant to keep her safe, but he didn't want to start off on the wrong foot by being too protective, either.

"How've you been, Slade?" Layne asked, breaking into his thoughts and bringing his gaze straight back to her face. Had he been mistaken, or had he caught a note of worried solicitude in her voice? "Since the divorce, I mean?"

His throat constricted. In the early days—and nights—following the split with Layne, he'd been pretty much a train wreck, though he'd managed to hide it from everybody but Callie. He'd consumed more beer than he ought to, in the beginning, at least, and sat in the dark listening to a ten-CD collection of bluesy jazz, over and over again, for weeks.

Even then, though, while he was figuratively a round-the-clock guest at the Heartbreak Hotel, he'd known the divorce was best for everybody concerned—Shea included. At least, in the long run.

"It's nothing I'd ever want to go through again," he said, in all honesty, "but I'm all right."

Shea came toward them through the tall grass, her smile luminous. Jasper, keeping up, stared at her in frank adoration.

"Can we get a horse, Dad?" Shea asked. Her pale purple eyes shone at the prospect. "I'd feed it and water it and everything."

To Slade, Shea seemed, in that brief moment, so much younger than sixteen. But she *was* verging on womanhood, this girl born of his heart if not his body.

"That barn isn't safe for field mice, let alone horses," Slade responded, but the fact was, he'd already decided that he and Shea would attend the livestock auction outside of Missoula the following weekend. He'd see what was on offer and make a decision then, but in the interim he wasn't making any promises.

"We could buy some lumber and some nails and make that barn good as new," Shea enthused, spreading her hands. She had one of those wash-off henna tattoos on her right forearm. At least, Slade *hoped* it was the wash-off kind.

Layne rolled her eyes at Shea's suggestion, but her expression was full of quiet love as she looked at the girl and shook her head. "Miss Fix-it," she said. "I can't even get you to change a light-bulb at home. Now you're ready to rebuild a barn?"

"Anything for a horse," Shea said, leaning down to pat Jasper's head. "Not that you're not awesome, boy, because you so totally are."

Slade grinned. Here was the thing he'd always known about Shea, even during the troubled times, the thing that made him sure she'd turn out all right. She had a tender soul.

He said, his voice a bit thick, "Let's go back to Callie's place. She's expecting us for supper."

"Whoop-de-do," Layne said, under her breath. A rueful little smile played on her lips, and she lowered her sunglasses from the top of her head to cover her eyes.

"Mom," Shea protested, as though horrified.

Now for the drama, Slade thought. It was odd, the things a man missed about being married and having a daughter.

Slade put one arm around Shea and gave her a brief squeeze to distract her. "It's all good, shortstop," he told the girl. "It's just supper. And if hostilities escalate, you and I can sneak off to McDonald's."

Layne gave him a look of mock desperation. "Oh, great. And leave me alone with a woman who thinks I keep a gang of flying monkeys in my attic."

Slade laughed. "Mom doesn't think you have flying monkeys," he teased.

"Though she may be surprised to find out that a house hasn't fallen on you."

"Hugely funny," Layne said as Shea opened the back door of Slade's truck so Jasper could jump in, shut it after him and climbed into the passenger seat.

"I'm riding with Dad," she called brightly, and somewhat after the fact.

"You'll be all right," Slade told his ex-wife, his mouth twitching at the corners. "As long as you don't let Mom talk you into a permanent or a dye job and—oh, yeah—you might want to let me taste your food before you eat it."

Layne looked at him in humorous misery. "Will you *stop* it, Slade? I've been traveling with a teenager all day and I'm jumpy enough already, thank you."

"Okay," Slade said, "I'll stop. You and Mom may not be each other's greatest fans, Layne, but she's wild to see Shea again, and she'll behave."

Layne sighed, gave a waggle-fingered little wave and got into her rental car.

By the time they reached the Curly-Burly, their two vehicles raising separate trails of dust on the unpaved roads, Callie had closed the shop for the day, put on a pink cotton T-shirt dress and jeweled sandals—sedate attire, for her—and even tied a ruffly apron around her waist.

Slade didn't recall seeing the apron before.

Now that Slade was grown up and gone from home, Callie generally lived on deli salads and things she could heat up in the microwave.

All of a sudden, it seemed, Callie was Martha Stewart, gone country.

She ran right out into the parking lot, smiled politely at Layne and threw both arms around Shea as soon as the girl got out of Slade's truck.

"Look how grown up you are!" Callie chimed, her eyes glistening with tears.

Shea hugged Callie back, laughing.

Slade hoisted Jasper down from the backseat, and the dog rushed over to join in the reunion, tail wagging.

"Come in, come in, all of you," Callie sniffled, beaming, one arm still around Shea. She looked down at Jasper. "Even you," she added. "Whoever you are."

"That's Jasper," Shea told her step-grandmother. "We were just out at Dad's new place, and he said maybe we could fix up the barn and get some horses—"

"Whoa," Slade interrupted affably. "That's not what I said."

Layne gave him an I-told-you-so kind of look, though he couldn't remember what it was she'd told him.

Something, probably. She'd always said that was one of their problems, that he didn't listen to her half the time.

They all trooped into the add-on beside the trailer that housed the Curly-Burly, Jasper included.

It was hot inside, even with several fans going, because Callie had been cooking. Hence the retro apron, no doubt.

Layne perched on the far end of the couch and fanned herself with a copy of *TV Guide* magazine. Callie was one of the last holdouts—she didn't own a DVR or a computer and therefore didn't depend on the internet for the latest entertainment info, like a lot of people did.

Jasper was happily underfoot, and Shea prattled about the flight from L.A., and the drive from the airport to Parable, and the friends she'd left behind for the summer.

"You'll make some new ones right here," Callie said with absolute certainty. "A lot of kids hang out at the park, since there's a pool."

Shea didn't seem overly interested in making the acquaintance of the local teenagers just then. "Can I check my email?" she wanted to know. She looked questioningly around the tidy room. "Where's your desktop, Grands?"

Callie smiled at the old nickname, probably relishing the sound of it. With Shea living so far away, she hadn't seen her since the divorce, and Slade realized, with a wallop, how difficult that separation had been for his mom.

"No computer," she said. "I like to do most things the old-fashioned way."

Layne, unobserved by her daughter and former mother-in-law, made a face at Slade.

He laughed. "Your email will keep for an hour or two," he told Shea.

The kid was already on to something new. "Is that lasagna?" she asked as

Callie grabbed a pair of pot holders and hoisted a casserole dish out of the oven, plunking it down on the counter.

"Sure is," Callie said, pleased.

"That's my favorite!" Shea responded.

"I remember," Callie answered. Her gaze found Layne's, caught for a moment, and veered away again, pronto.

Inwardly, Slade sighed.

Callie had never liked Layne.

Layne had never liked Callie.

But both of them adored Shea, which was most likely the only reason they hadn't already gotten into it over something. While Slade and Layne were married, the two women had observed a bristly détente, with occasional bursts of gunfire.

So far, though, Slade thought, so good.

After Hutch brought Joslyn back to the guesthouse from the ranch, kissed her on the forehead and left, she fed Lucy-Maude, refilled the cat's water dish and took a long, cool shower to wash away the sweat and dust.

Later, when her thighs began to ache

from the brief ride on Sandy, she took two aspirin, made herself a single serving of Chinese noodles in the microwave, ate and went through her dwindling stack of reading material.

Zip. She was one chapter from the end of the paperback biography waiting on her bedside table, and then she'd be fresh out. Since she hadn't gotten around to applying for a card at the Parable Public Library—there wasn't a bookstore in town as far as she knew—and she was too tired and sore to drive to Mulligan's or the discount store to see what they had to offer, this was a problem.

She peered out the front window, saw that Kendra's car was in the driveway covered in dust, with the top up. There might have been a light on in the mansion's kitchen, but she couldn't be sure, since the sun was still shining.

She paced for a few moments—realized that even that hurt—and stopped, reaching for her cell phone and tapping in Kendra's number.

Her friend sounded weary, but there

was something else huddled in her rather cool "hello," too.

"How was your shopping trip?" Joslyn asked.

"How was your horseback ride?" Kendra immediately retorted. Then she sighed and said, "I'm sorry, Joss. I shouldn't have snapped at you like that."

Joslyn, no longer used to the way news traveled in small towns, still felt stung, even after her friend's hasty apology. "No," she said moderately. "You shouldn't have."

"Don't be mad," Kendra said.

"I'm not," Joslyn told her truthfully. "A little confused, maybe. But mad? No."

Silence.

"Kendra?" Joslyn prompted after a few moments.

Kendra made a little choking sound, and Joslyn wondered if she was crying. "I'm sorry," Kendra repeated.

"We can talk about it another time," Joslyn said gently. "It's no big deal. I'll let you go so you can get back to whatever you were doing when I called."

"You must have called for some reason," Kendra sniffled, recovering a little.

"I was hoping to borrow a book," Joslyn said, wishing she'd never picked up the phone in the first place. Then, quietly, she added, "Not a boyfriend."

"Hutch isn't my boyfriend," Kendra assured her. "I don't know why I bit your head off like that, Joss—I guess I'm just tired, after the party and everything, and now I have PMS and—well—none of that excuses what I did, does it?"

"It's *okay,* Kendra," Joslyn said. "I'll see you in the morning. Nine o'clock sharp."

"Wait," Kendra almost pleaded. "Don't hang up. I have this great memoir that I just finished reading. It's about a woman who joined the Peace Corps back in the late sixties—I could bring it over. . . ."

Joslyn hesitated. "Fine," she said, at some length. "I'll be waiting."

She awoke slowly the next morning, after spending half the night reading the book Kendra had loaned her, and when she remembered that today was the day she was to start her new job, Joslyn gasped and bounded out of bed.

Lucy-Maude, curled up near her feet,

gave a disgruntled and drawn out "Meooooow" in protest.

Joslyn staggered into the bathroom, turned on the shower and stripped to the skin to stand under the spray, letting the water sluice away the last clinging remnants of an uneasy sleep.

Determined not to be late on her first day at Shepherd Real Estate, she hurried to finish, dried off, brushed her teeth and dressed quickly in black pants and a pale blue shell top. Since she didn't wear much makeup—just tinted moisturizer, a little mascara and a swipe of lip gloss—that task was soon finished, too.

Her hair was frizzy from the shower, though, and she wanted to look professional when she got to the office but not priggish. Therefore, instead of winding her long brown hair into an all-business bun, she quickly braided it into a single plait, then turned her head from side to side, assessing the look.

Just then, Lucy-Maude announced from the bathroom doorway that it was time she had her breakfast.

Joslyn prepared a cup of instant coffee—since she'd be across the lawn at Kendra's office for most of the day, it didn't make sense to brew an entire pot—and fed Lucy-Maude her morning ration of kibble, keeping one eye on the clock the whole while.

She sipped her coffee and thought about the night before when Kendra had practically insisted on bringing over the book. Joslyn had expected her friend to ask about the horseback ride with Hutch, but they'd both danced around the subject. Which might have been for the best.

Joslyn had wanted to explain that she and Hutch were truly just friends, but it seemed so pat, that phrase. "Just friends." People said it all the time, but what did it really mean?

After a quick scan of her personal email and the Paws for Reflection site, where there was still no indication that anyone was missing a cat fitting Lucy-Maude's description, Joslyn said good-bye to her feline roommate and set out for the mansion.

She went around the house to the

front entrance, found the door unlocked and let herself in.

"Kendra?" she called, moving toward the office.

Her friend sat at her desk, her eyes red-rimmed and puffy.

Alarmed, Joslyn immediately dumped her purse onto the desk that would be hers and crossed to Kendra, resting a hand on the other woman's slightly tremulous shoulder. "What is it?" she asked.

"There's— I've had news—" Kendra stumbled to reply. She didn't rise from her chair, didn't seem capable of it. "About Jeffrey."

"Your ex-husband?" Joslyn asked after swallowing. "Did something happen to him, Kendra?"

Slowly, Kendra nodded. "He's—very ill. Some kind of cancer. They don't expect him to live, and—and he's been asking for me. . . ."

Most of the starch drained from Joslyn's knees. She went to her desk chair, rolled it over beside Kendra's and sank into it. "He's in England?" she asked, very softly.

Kendra nodded. "His mother called me," she said numbly, staring into space. "Personally. You have no idea what it must have cost her to do that—and I'm not talking about the bill."

Joslyn bit her lip, recalling what Kendra had said about the breakup of her marriage to Jeffrey. His family had evidently despised Kendra from the beginning, done everything they could to undermine the relationship. "What are you going to do?"

Kendra's eyes filled with tears. "I have to go to him," she said. "It isn't a question of love, but Jeffrey was my husband—"

Joslyn took her friend's hand and squeezed. "Then go," she replied, very quietly. "Of course I can't list or sell properties without a real-estate license, but I'll cover for you in every way I can."

"Thank you," Kendra said. "I'm not sure how long I'll be away, but I'll check in whenever possible."

Joslyn didn't reply to that. She gave her friend a hug, and then she helped her pack and book a flight to London.

"One more thing," Kendra told her, as

she was getting into the car an hour later to drive to the airport in Missoula. "I hate to leave the house empty while I'm away. Would you mind moving in, just until I get back?"

CHAPTER ELEVEN

Things were relatively quiet around Shepherd Real Estate for the rest of the morning, and by the time Joslyn's lunch hour rolled around, she had already explained to several callers that Kendra had been called away on personal business and wasn't sure when she'd be back in Parable. She'd assured each one politely, evading all attempts to extract the exact *reason* for the sudden disappearance, that Kendra remained in contact with her office and any messages would be passed on.

Not particularly hungry, Joslyn was

already looking forward to going back to work after the break. She'd missed having a job, she realized, missed the routine of keeping regular hours and, especially, the challenge of learning new things.

Heaven knew, she had plenty to learn about running a real-estate firm.

Lucy-Maude was waiting patiently when she entered the guest cottage through the kitchen door after crossing the lawn from the main house.

"Guess what?" Joslyn told the cat, washing her hands at the sink in anticipation of whipping up a sandwich for lunch, unappealing as food sounded at the moment. Skipping meals tended to play havoc with her blood sugar levels, and then she got edgy and had a hard time concentrating. "We're moving."

Like lunch, the idea of spending even a short time back in the mansion did nothing for Joslyn, but she could understand why Kendra wanted the place to be occupied during her absence. So many things could go wrong when a house stood empty—burst pipes, electrical fires and numerous other disasters that had to be dealt with quickly. And naturally, vandalism and burglaries were less likely to occur if someone was around.

Still, for Joslyn, the place was her emotional Ground Zero; it was there that all their lives—her mother's, Elliott's, her own and even Opal's—had imploded. From that centerpoint, the calamity had spread, scorched-earth fashion, throughout the community of Parable and far into the surrounding area.

There had been so much sound and fury, not to mention years of fallout, that the aftershocks still rocked Joslyn—and certainly Elliott's surviving victims—on the deepest level.

Troubled, Joslyn refilled Lucy-Maude's kibble bowl, then made herself a turkey-bologna and lettuce sandwich on white bread, but two bites were all she could force down, despite her best intentions. Her throat squeezed shut and refused to let any more food pass, and her stomach threatened to rebel.

Once again, she asked herself what she hoped to accomplish by returning to Parable, anyway. Financial remuneration for Elliott's theft had already been made, wherever possible—what else could she do?

Besides lusting after a certain cowboy-sheriff who probably equated her with those dim-witted heiresses who were always turning up on tabloid TV. Best not to think about Slade Barlow and how he'd almost kissed her in the living room of that charming old ranch house he was renting, and how much she wished he had . . .

Whoa, she thought, with a guilty grimace, *rein it in, girl.*

Bottom line? She was stuck here, at least until Kendra got back from the U.K., and who knew how long that would take? In the meantime, there was a business to run, a promise to be kept.

"What do I know about real estate, anyway?" she asked Lucy-Maude, who was having no trouble at all gulping down the extra ration of kibble. "Nothing, that's what." Joslyn flung out both hands for emphasis. "Zip. Zilch. Nada."

Lucy-Maude paused to give her an I-get-the-picture-so-chill-out kind of look, then went back to kibble crunching.

"I am spending *way* too much time alone," Joslyn fretted, tossing the remains of her sandwich and then rinsing the plate and the butter knife at the sink before placing them carefully in the drain board. They looked lonely there, with only that morning's coffee cup for company—*and the dish ran away with the spoon.* "If you'll pardon the expression, because technically, with you around, I'm *not* completely alone, but, well, you *are* a cat."

Lucy-Maude gave her a look of tolerant affection and continued to dine.

Joslyn, over her rant, spent the next twenty minutes gathering necessities—toothpaste, toothbrush, pajamas, the memoir she'd borrowed from Kendra, et cetera—and stuffed them all into her suitcase for ease of transport. Then she collected Lucy-Maude's kitty paraphernalia—her blanket bed, litter box and litter, and the bag of kibble—and set everything in the middle of the cottage's living-room floor.

There was a preponderance of *stuff*

to be moved, Lucy-Maude's and her own, it seemed to Joslyn. She'd been traveling light ever since leaving Phoenix, and now she was accumulating things again.

Not good.

If there was one lesson she'd learned since selling her company, her condo and her car, it was how little a person truly needed.

On her first trek across the lawn to the mansion, she lugged her laptop and the suitcase, entering through the screen door of the sunporch, since she'd remembered to unlock it earlier in anticipation of the move.

Rather than in her old room or one of the mansion's several guest suites, Joslyn decided to take up residence in Opal's quarters, next to the huge kitchen. It was a way, at least figuratively, of keeping one foot outside the big house, in the hope that she wouldn't get sucked into some emotional vortex and then thrown back into white-water memories of a time she mostly wanted to forget.

To think she'd missed this great, hulking house and the life she'd lived within its walls. Now, it seemed almost oppressive.

Opal's former space was nearly as large as the cottage out back, with a private bath—was it even possible to buy sinks and toilets and bathtubs in that strange shade of pink anymore?—and a sitting room, even a little stovetop and a miniature refrigerator. Here, Kendra hadn't changed out the furniture—the inexpensive but serviceable couch, armchair, coffee table, floor lamps and TV set Opal had used were still there.

It was a poignantly spooky moment for Joslyn, standing there looking around at the familiar apartment—it almost felt as though the beloved housekeeper had just stepped out to run some routine errand in her old station wagon or take something out of the oven or the clothes dryer.

The backs of Joslyn's eyes scalded for a moment as she wondered, yet again, where Opal was now—if she was well and happy, if she was even still alive. Maybe later, when the workday was over, she'd go online, try to find her old friend.

And what would she say if she *did* locate Opal? "Remember me? Joslyn? I'm back at the Rossiter mansion—God knows why, really—some kind of self-punishment, I guess—and all that made me think about you"?

Hardly. Besides, Opal would be considerably older now; even if she hadn't passed away, she might well be infirm, closeted away in a nursing home somewhere. Better to leave the poor woman alone, Joslyn reasoned.

But still she *wondered,* because she'd loved Opal dearly.

Since there was more to be done in the apartment, Joslyn shook off the ache of nostalgia and began putting things away in the bedroom closet, the bureau drawers, the medicine cabinet.

When she'd finished with all that, she transported Lucy-Maude's things to the new quarters and, finally, Lucy-Maude herself, yowling indignantly inside a cardboard box with the flaps folded to secure the top and prevent escape, and turned the disgruntled cat loose in the small area they would be sharing until Kendra returned.

Stealthily, Lucy-Maude explored the space, checking out the small bedroom, the retro bathroom and the mysterious realm behind the couch.

Joslyn decided she'd go back for the few food items she'd left behind in the guesthouse later. She'd used up her lunch hour, and it was time to get back to work. Not that there was much to do.

Resigned, she washed her hands again, left Lucy-Maude to her explorations and made her way through the kitchen and the formal dining room to the former parlor, from whence Kendra ran her agency.

A sturdy gray-haired woman clad in capri pants, a plaid sleeveless shirt and a pair of oft-washed sneakers stood in the arched doorway, startling Joslyn a little, since she hadn't heard her come in. The visitor's eyes were tranquil, the color of clear creek water, and her skin, though wrinkled, glowed with good health and an amiable temperament.

Like so many people in Parable, this

woman looked vaguely familiar to Joslyn, but she couldn't quite place her.

"I'm Martie Wren," the caller announced, putting out a work-roughed hand in greeting.

Joslyn stepped forward, smiling, to shake Martie's hand. "Joslyn Kirk," she said. "If you're looking for Kendra, I'm afraid she's out of the office for the next few days—"

Weeks? Months?

"I was looking for you, actually," Martie broke in cheerfully. "I run the animal shelter, Paws for Reflection. I'm here about the cat you found—you posted a notice on our website?"

A tiny trapdoor opened in the pit of Joslyn's stomach—she was already attached to Lucy-Maude and wasn't ready to give her up, even though restoring her to her owners was the right thing to do—but she managed a smile. "Come in," she said. "Sit down."

"Can't stay long," Martie said directly. "The critters keep us hopping over at Paws, if you'll excuse the pun, and there's a lot to get done before I can do any significant sitting down."

Joslyn kept smiling, though the near certainty that Martie had come to take Lucy-Maude back to her rightful owners made her heart feel bruised. "I understand," she said quietly.

Martie assessed her astutely. "Seems like you might be a little taken with this particular animal," she observed.

"A little," Joslyn admitted. *That* was the understatement of the day. "But I imagine someone's looking for her. She doesn't strike me as neglected." *Pregnant, but not neglected.*

"I'd like a look at her in person, so to speak," Martie said with a twinkle. "I know you put a picture of her up on the site, but there are a lot of gray cats out there. If she's the one I think she is, she's been looked after right along. But that isn't the same as having a real home and being loved, now is it?"

Having a real home and being loved. What a concept.

"This way," Joslyn said, mulling over Martie's words as she led the way back through the dining room and kitchen to the staff quarters.

Lucy-Maude had installed her royal

self in the seat of the armchair, and she stretched luxuriously when Joslyn and Martie entered the sitting room, as regal as Cleopatra reclining on her barge.

"Yep," Martie said, advancing on the cat in a slow and nonthreatening way and putting out a hand for Lucy-Maude to sniff. "This is Carlotta, all right."

"Carlotta?" Joslyn echoed, knowing she must sound foolish. It wasn't as if Lucy-Maude had been born with the name she'd given her, after all. So why was it such a jolt to hear the cat called something else?

Martie nodded. "Carlotta's sort of a community cat, I guess you'd say. Belongs to just about everybody. We've been trying to catch her to have her spayed and see to her shots, but she's an elusive little dickens. She makes the rounds for meals and a safe place to sleep, if the weather turns bad or the coyotes are on the prowl."

Joslyn had forgotten the lonely and chilling screamlike wail of the coyotes who turned up in Parable now and then, usually in the dark. A shiver went through her, just to think of poor Lucy-Maude out there all alone, practically defense-less, taking her chances with hungry scavengers.

"How long has she been with you?" Martie went on, when Joslyn didn't say anything.

"A few days," Joslyn answered.

A broad smile broke across Martie's plain, likable face. "I've never known Carlotta to stay put longer than a day or so, and even then, she's elusive. Seems to me that she might have cho-sen to be your cat, exclusively, from here on out."

Joslyn felt a curious tangle of emo-tions in that moment. There was hesi-tancy—her plans for the future were hardly concrete. But there was also re-lief, because no heartbroken pet owner was out there, searching frantically for his or her lost cat.

Joslyn swallowed, scrambled for a response. "But I probably won't be stay-ing in Parable too much longer," she said awkwardly. "I wasn't really plan-ning on adopting a pet, and I'm pretty sure she's expecting—"

Martie's smile faded. "Oh, my," she

said, leaning to probe Lucy-Maude's belly with gentle fingertips and then nodding. "Sure enough, she's pregnant."

"And, like I said, I wasn't planning to adopt—"

Martie smiled when Joslyn's words fell away. "We'll worry about the kittens when the time comes," she said. "As for your being ready to adopt, well, in some cases it works the other way around, and the *pet* does the choosing." She paused, drew a beleaguered breath and let it out again. "I can take Carlotta to the shelter with me if that's what you want. As always, though, we've already got a pretty big backlog of pets in need of homes."

Joslyn flinched inwardly at the image of Carlotta/Lucy-Maude behind the door of a cage, however humane the surroundings, not to mention all the *other* cats and dogs and birds in shelters everywhere, waiting.

And waiting.

"I'll keep her, then," she said, and a sense of sad exultation swept through her. "Somehow, we'll make it work, Lucy-Maude and I, come what may."

Martie gave Joslyn an approving pat on the shoulder and smiled again. "That's the spirit," she said. Then, cagily, she added, "Feel free to stop by Paws anytime you want."

Effervescent on the inside, Joslyn gave a choked little laugh and barely kept herself from rolling her eyes. "Sure," she said. "And come home with a few more cats? Maybe a dog and a couple of rabbits for good measure?"

Martie laughed, too. "Can't blame me for trying," she said. Then her expression changed, and she looked around at Opal's little space. "It's odd to be back in this house," she added. "Never thought it would happen."

Joslyn had been about to promise to take Lucy-Maude in for shots and a veterinary exam immediately, but Martie's remark stopped the words in her throat. "You knew Opal?" she asked raggedly, after a moment or two of recovery.

Martie nodded. "We're good friends," she replied.

Joslyn caught her breath. "Then you're in contact with Opal?"

"Oh, sure," Martie said. "She's been living in Great Falls for years with her sister-in-law. Got married once, Opal did, but the fellow didn't live long."

Joslyn's heartbeat sped up a little. She opened her mouth, closed it again, unable to speak.

That cagey look was back in Martie's eyes, but this time, it wasn't as friendly as before, and recognition gradually dawned right along with it. "You said your name when I came in, but I didn't register it," she murmured. "You're Elliott Rossiter's stepdaughter. I thought I'd seen you somewhere before."

Joslyn swallowed hard. Short of apologizing for who she was, which she didn't intend to do, she didn't know what to say.

In an instant, though, Martie's face changed again, and she was once more the friendly, take-charge person who ran the Paws for Reflection animal shelter. She rested a hand on Joslyn's shoulder, lightly and briefly, and her smile conveyed both sadness and warmth.

"I heard you were back in Parable, but I guess it slipped my mind," the older woman said. "I'm just so darned busy all the time."

Joslyn had to ask the question, though she dreaded the answer. "Did Elliott— did he cheat you, too?"

Martie gave a grim little nod of confirmation. "We turned over our life savings to that rascal, Charlie and me," she replied. "Charlie was my husband at the time. We'd known the Rossiter family forever, Charlie and I, and we never dreamed Elliott wasn't on the up-and-up. His people were fine, upright folks. Just the same, we lost practically every nickel we had."

"I'm so sorry," Joslyn croaked.

"Don't be," Martie replied stalwartly. "It wasn't your fault, it was mine and Charlie's and Elliott's. Anyhow, I got a whopper of a check in the mail a few weeks back—even after splitting it with Charlie—we're divorced now—it's a pile. Without it, I'd have had to close the shelter by now, most likely, and that would have broken my heart for sure."

A pause. "Seems like everything worked out for the best, in the end."

Joslyn wondered if she'd ever hear all the stories—each of Elliott's victims had one, of course—even if she stayed in Parable for the rest of her life.

Not that she had any intention of doing that—she just hadn't figured out an alternative yet.

"Some good comes out of just about everything, I guess," Martie said. With that, she shook Joslyn's hand again and turned to leave the office.

"I'll take Lucy-Maude in for a checkup as soon as possible," Joslyn called after her.

"You do that," Martie replied kindly.

And then she was gone.

Joslyn went to her desk, logged on to Kendra's computer using the password her friend had given her before she left, and did her best to respond to the various nonpersonal emails that had been collecting in the virtual mailbox. Fortunately, there weren't many of those, but finding the answers took a while because Kendra hadn't had time to show Joslyn the ropes.

By midafternoon, she was all over the internet, looking for real-estate classes. Clearly, if she was going to get anything done around here, she needed a license.

She found an online course, vetted it with the state of Montana to make sure the school was legit and signed up.

The first files arrived minutes later via email, and she printed them out to study later after closing time.

Kendra called at a little after four; she had a two-hour layover in New York, and then she'd be on her way to London. She sounded numb, as though she were reading a prepared speech.

Joslyn ached for her friend. Wished she—or someone—were making the trip with Kendra, lending moral support. "I'll be here," she said. "If you need to talk, call me—and don't worry about what time it is."

Kendra gave a small, broken-sounding sigh. "Okay," she said in the same wooden tone, "thanks."

"Kendra—" Joslyn began, about to suggest that making this trip might not be such a good idea after all and maybe she should just turn right around and come back home, but there was a click on the other end and the connection was broken.

Slowly, Joslyn hung up the receiver and sat perfectly still for a few long moments, worrying about Kendra. After that, she rooted through the bookshelves for procedure manuals and did her best to familiarize herself with the inner workings of Shepherd Real Estate.

There was a lot to take in. Fortunately, she was a quick learner, and always had been.

At five-fifteen, she locked the front entrance, turned out the lamps and made her way through the kitchen to the little apartment that had once been Opal's.

Lucy-Maude greeted her with a purr that sounded like a lawn mower starting up and weaved her silken body between Joslyn's ankles.

With a chuckle—and being careful not to trip over the cat's continuous figure eights around her feet—Joslyn opened up a cupboard, found the familiar mishmash of dishes Opal had collected over the years, and helped herself to a bowl with a chip on the rim.

She filled it with a mixture of canned cat food and dry kibble, and set it down next to the water dish she'd put out earlier.

Lucy-Maude, tail twitching, ate ravenously. The animal was eating for two, after all—or six or eight.

Joslyn sighed. "You might as well know that it's a ninety-nine percent certainty that we'll be moving on one of these days," she told the cat, who ignored her and continued to eat. "Parable is a nice enough place, if you really belong, but my guess is we're just passing through, so don't get too comfortable here."

Naturally, Lucy-Maude didn't answer. She didn't even look up from her food.

When her cell phone jangled in the depths of her purse, Joslyn was glad of the distraction, because the thought of leaving town for good left her feeling strangely bereft.

"Hello?" she said without looking at the caller ID panel first.

"Is that my Jossie girl?" Opal asked, big-voiced and hearty, the way she'd always been.

Tears of joy filled Joslyn's eyes in the space of an instant. "Opal?" she cried.

"Who else?" Opal retorted good-naturedly.

Joslyn found her way to the easy chair and sank into it, the phone pressed hard against her ear. "Oh, Opal," she said, as Lucy-Maude finished her supper and began an elaborate grooming ritual. "I can't believe it's you."

"Believe it," Opal said, sounding gruff now. "My friend Martie called a little while ago, said my name came up in conversation, and from your reaction, she got the idea you might want to talk with me. I called the office right away, but nobody answered, so I tried this number and here we are, yammering away, just like old times."

A single tear trickled down Joslyn's right cheek, and she didn't bother to wipe it away. "How are you, Opal?" she asked, almost whispering the question.

"I'm just fine," Opal replied, with her usual staunch conviction. "Moving a little slower, maybe, and with a few more aches and pains than before, but for the most part, I'm as sturdy as a plow horse." She paused, chuckled warmly. "Probably weigh about the same as one, too."

Joslyn smiled. "That's good," she said.

"It's good that I weigh as much as a plow horse?" Opal joked.

Joslyn laughed, but it came out sounding like a cross between a gulp and a sob. "That you're fine," she clarified.

"How about you?" Opal wanted to know. "You doing all right, sweetheart?"

"I'm getting by," Joslyn said, because she'd never been able to lie to Opal, except by omission. And even that didn't always work, because Opal was perceptive to an almost preternatural degree.

"Getting by," Opal repeated, clearly disappointed. "I'm not sure I like the sound of that, girl. You married yet? Got any little ones?"

Joslyn shook her head before re-membering that Opal couldn't see the gesture. "No," she said. "I haven't really had time for that."

"Well, you'd better *make* time, then, hadn't you? You're not getting any younger, you know."

Joslyn laughed again, but this time, it was genuine. It was a release, like a good sneeze. "Fine," she agreed cheer-fully. "I'll go out and hog-tie a husband as soon as we hang up. Get pregnant on the honeymoon."

Opal laughed, too. Was there just a trace of tears in the sound?

"What the Sam Hill are you doing back in Parable?" the older woman asked without further ado.

So much for chitchat.

Joslyn fidgeted. The question had been inevitable, of course. "I'm trying to set some things right, I guess."

"What sort of things?" Opal asked warily.

Joslyn hesitated long enough to draw in a deep, steadying breath and thrust it out again in the form of a ragged sigh. "You know," she said finally. "Elliott did so much damage here, Opal. He hurt so many people—"

"And how is that *your* responsibility?" Opal retorted crisply, but with the old, stalwart caring she'd always shown Joslyn and her mother.

"It's not," Joslyn replied, sadly defensive. "But *someone* needs to make amends, don't they? If they can, that is?"

"Well," Opal said, after a few moments of silent rumination, her tone softer now, "in my opinion, you're way off base, but it's a gift from God Himself to hear your voice again, just the same." A pause. "How's your mama doing these days?"

Joslyn told Opal about Dana's new life in Santa Fe with her artist husband, Brian.

"That's mighty good to know," Opal replied, sounding gratified when Joslyn had finished. "I always liked Dana. Thought she was half again too good for Elliott Rossiter, though she sure enough seemed to love the man."

"She did," Joslyn affirmed, thick-throated again as she remembered the happy times before Elliott's greed took over.

Given that Opal had been working for the Rossiter family long before Joslyn and her mother came on the scene, it was significant that she still regarded Dana so highly. After all, there *were* people, like Cookie Jean Crown, who thought Elliott stole to keep his wife and stepdaughter living the good life. He'd outfitted Dana in designer clothes and taken her on expensive vacations all over the world, often by chartered jet, and Joslyn had lacked for nothing, either as a little girl or as a teenager. So maybe there was some truth to the idea.

"I've got half a mind to come and see you," Opal announced. "You happen to have a place to put me?"

Again, Joslyn laughed. Again, her eyes stung. "Are you serious, Opal? A visit from you would mean the world to me right now."

"'Course I'm serious," Opal said decisively. "You think I'm talking to hear my head rattle? Why, I can hop a bus with no trouble at all. I'll just throw a few things in that old suitcase of mine, buy me a ticket, and be on my way." She sounded just like her normal take-charge self. "Does the bus still stop at the service station right there on Main Street, just across from the Butter Biscuit Café?"

"Probably," Joslyn answered, thinking fast. Opal could stay in the guesthouse, since it wasn't occupied at the moment. "Wherever it stops, I'll be there to pick you up. Just let me know when you'll be arriving."

"I'll get right back to you," Opal said.

Twenty minutes later, she did just that.

It turned out that the bus still came through Parable every afternoon at three-forty-five sharp, and if there were passengers to let off or take on, it made a half-hour stop at the gas station so travelers could stretch their legs or grab a bite to eat over at the Butter Biscuit.

Opal promised to be onboard tomorrow's bus.

As soon as they'd hung up for a second time, Joslyn speed-dialed her mother's number in Santa Fe and spilled the news of Opal's impending arrival like an armload of Mexican jumping beans.

Dana was as delighted as Joslyn had been.

"That's wonderful, sweetheart," she said with a throaty laugh. "And may I say, it's good to hear you sounding, well, *happy*."

Joslyn blinked. Didn't she *usually* sound happy? Okay, sure, the last few years had been challenging; she'd worked too hard and gotten too lonely, but she hadn't been *un*happy, had she?

She decided to let the remark pass. "Why don't you join us, Opal and me?" she asked. "Here in Parable, I mean?"

Dana sighed. "Oh, honey, I'd love to see you *and* Opal, but Brian has a big gallery showing coming up in just two weeks, in Chicago, and we're both in an absolute frenzy, trying to get everything crated and ready for shipment—"

Joslyn closed her eyes for a moment, opened them again. "Oh," she said, unable to hide her disappointment.

There was a brief, injured silence on the other end of the line. "You think the show is just an excuse—that I'm afraid to come back to Parable, after all that happened, don't you?" Dana asked gently and without rancor.

"Of course not, Mom," Joslyn answered just as gently. "I know you're not a liar."

Dana let out a long breath. "We can't afford for Brian to miss this show," she went on. "He has a handful of dedicated collectors in Chicago, and with the economy the way it is, and art being regarded as a luxury . . ."

"I understand, Mom," Joslyn said. And she did. In boom times, Brian could hardly keep up with his commissions—portraits and landscapes were the meat-and-potatoes, colorful abstracts the gravy. These days, that gravy was probably pretty thin.

Dana's voice brightened. "I'll come for a visit *after* Brian's show," she said. "Tell Opal I've missed her, and I'll be in touch very soon to plan some kind of get-together for all three of us."

"Sure," Joslyn replied.

They chatted a little while longer, and said their goodbyes.

Within half an hour, Joslyn's stomach was grumbling, reminding her that she'd skipped lunch. She didn't feel right about raiding Kendra's freezer and pantry, even though she knew her friend wouldn't mind in the least, and the few things she'd left in the guesthouse refrigerator held no attraction whatsoever.

She didn't feel like cooking anyway.

On impulse, Joslyn decided to make a quick run to the Butter Biscuit Café, where she'd eaten with Hutch the day before, and order takeout. She was in the mood for comfort food—something Opal might have made, like fried chicken and mashed potatoes and gravy.

Yikes. Just the thought of all those fat grams made her clothes feel tighter. Still, when was the last time she'd indulged herself this way? Over the past few years, she'd done nothing but work and worry. And her doctor in Phoenix *had* advised her to put on ten pounds, hadn't he? She figured this one meal would be good for five.

"I'll be right back," she promised Lucy-Maude after filling the cat's bowl with kibble and refreshing the contents of her water dish at the apartment sink.

Five minutes later, Joslyn pulled into the parking lot beside the Butter Biscuit Café. The station where Opal's bus would stop was directly across the street, dusty and in need of a paint job.

Joslyn smiled, imagining the reunion and, at the same time, making a to-do list in her head: change the sheets in the guesthouse bedroom, clean the bathroom, give the place a good dusting and vacuuming, pick a bouquet of flowers from Kendra's gardens to provide a bright splash of welcome.

The Butter Biscuit was bustling with customers, and all the tables were full. Excited, dizzy with plans, Joslyn didn't immediately register the identity of the tall man standing next to the cash register, flanked by a model-beautiful woman with an amazing head of auburn hair and a very pretty young girl.

Slade Barlow gave Joslyn one of those slight, tilted grins that made her nerves jump to attention and then drawled a quiet hello.

Joslyn felt jarred—running into Slade

was something a person needed to *prepare* for—but she managed a smile and said hello back.

He introduced her to his ex-wife, Layne, and his stepdaughter, Shea.

Layne eyed her thoughtfully, though not rudely, and smiled to herself.

Shea, the teenager, was the outgoing type. "We're here for the meat loaf special," she said. "Dad says it's worth waiting for." Her eyes were pale violet in color and they shone with vivacity. "Maybe you'd like to sit with us?"

"I was planning on takeout," Joslyn said lamely. "Lots to do at home."

A wry twinkle flashed in Slade's blue eyes. "Next time, then," he said.

Joslyn helped herself to a menu and studied it as though it were the Rosetta Stone. "Sure," she agreed distractedly. "Next time."

CHAPTER TWELVE

Even after she fled the restaurant with a couple of foam food containers in hand, Joslyn Kirk's image stuck in the back of Slade's mind as surely as if it had been tattooed there, in full color and three-plus dimensions.

He could still smell the flowery scent of her hair.

Essie, having apparently forgiven him for his part in the near set-to with Hutch the day before right there in her place of business, smiled and sent two waitresses scurrying to clear and wipe down the first table that opened up, and he and Layne and Shea were seated promptly. They'd invited Callie to come along, but she'd politely begged off, since it was her week to host the game of ladies-only poker.

"With Mom," he'd told a visibly relieved Layne, "nothing comes before five-card stud."

"You haven't heard a word we've said over the last twenty minutes," Layne remarked now without challenge, when Shea excused herself from the meat loaf special to take a call on her fancy smartphone and thereby left the two of them alone at their table.

As sheriff, Slade had been known to work twenty hours at a stretch when circumstances warranted, but he figured grid searches and long, boring stakeouts had nothing on shopping with two women all day.

He'd have sworn they'd hit every store in Great Falls since morning, he and Layne and Shea, picking out furniture, electronics, towels and sheets, pots and pans—everything a person needed to outfit a house, according to them. Essie's meat loaf special was about the only thing he could think of that would have gotten him to leave the ranch house and lucky Jasper, whom he'd left snoozing in that fancy dog bed with his name stitched on to it.

"You always said that was our main problem," Slade remarked, knowing his response was a mite late, but too tired to care. "That I didn't listen to you, I mean."

"You didn't," Layne insisted, smiling. "I used to test you, just to prove the theory. I'd say things like, 'There are three pink elephants stomping down the flower beds in the backyard,' and you'd reply—distractedly, of course— that that was 'fine. Just fine.'"

Slade took a sip of his coffee and gave an idle grin. "So it was a set-up all along," he teased.

A brief silence descended then, the kind that settles between two friends with nothing to prove to each other.

"That woman we met while we were waiting for a table," Layne said, after scanning the surrounding area to make sure Shea was out of earshot and none of the other diners were bending an ear in their direction, "'Joslyn,' you said her name was?"

As if she'd forgotten. Layne had been chomping at the bit to ask about Joslyn ever since they'd run into her up front.

Slade set down his cup. "Yes," he said moderately. "Joslyn."

"You like her," Layne said.

Slade shifted in his chair. "Sure I like her," he answered. "We grew up together—sort of."

Even "sort of" is a stretch, cowboy, he chided himself, inside his weary brain, *and you know it. Joslyn was silk and diamonds, and you were leather and burlap.*

"No," Layne said, eyes twinkling, "I meant, you *like* her. The attraction was only slightly less noticeable than a billboard with moving parts and flashing lights—and I'd say from the way she turned pink and dived into that menu like it contained next week's winning lottery numbers, it's mutual."

Slade was vaguely uncomfortable with the turn the conversation had taken. He wished Shea would finish her call— she was still over there by the silent jukebox, chattering away, her expression animated—and come back to the table, but of course she didn't. That would have made things way too easy for him. He pretended an interest in what was left of his meat loaf.

Layne chuckled. "So are you going to *do anything* about this, Slade? Or do you plan to stand around being the strong, silent type until Joslyn gives up on you and finds herself another guy?"

"Why the sudden interest in my love life?" Slade snapped, careful to keep his voice down. Parable being a small town, there would be enough gossip about Layne's visit; no need to give folks anything extra to chew on.

"I want you to be happy," Layne said, pretending to be hurt. "What's wrong with that?"

"Did it ever occur to you that being single and being happy might not be mutually exclusive?" Slade countered. "And what makes you think I'm *not* happy?"

Layne sighed. "That apartment you've been living in, for starters. I know your tastes run more toward beer than champagne, but that place is *depressing.* A blow-up *bed,* for pity's sake? Sheets covering the windows, instead of drapes? And that *carpet*—I'm pretty sure that color is banned in California."

"This isn't California," Slade pointed out peevishly. "And would you mind keeping it down to a dull roar?"

Layne merely sighed and shook her head, regarding him with what looked like tender amusement. "Some men are meant to be married," she said, with quiet certainty. "They're born to be heads of households, pillars of the community, guardians of all that's right and good. They make ideal husbands and fathers. And you're one of those men, Slade."

Slade cleared his throat. "That's an interesting observation, coming from you," he said. There was no need to come right out and say that the divorce had been her idea, not his. He'd have stuck it out, come hell or high water, if only for Shea's sake.

Which wasn't necessarily a good thing, he realized now.

There were times when it was better to cut your losses and run.

"Ouch," Layne responded, making a face.

Slade didn't say anything. He'd not only depleted his quota of words for the day, he was well into tomorrow's.

"You married me because you wanted to be Shea's father," Layne continued presently, unruffled, "not because you wanted to be my husband."

Since there was some truth in that statement, Slade didn't refute it. He'd thought he loved Layne when they got together, but it had been Shea he'd been smitten with, Shea and the idea of being somebody's dad.

It was relatively uncomplicated.

That couldn't have been said, however, about what he'd felt for Layne. He supposed that had been more about hormones, and the person he'd wanted her to be.

The simple fact was, he liked Layne the way he liked Kendra and Boone Taylor and Maggie Landers, among others. As a friend.

"This Bentley yahoo," he said, after

casting another glance in Shea's direction. She was still talking on the cell, and the way she sparkled all over, he'd have bet there was a boy on the other end of that conversation. "He's all right?"

"He's wonderful," Layne answered, and a dreamy look shimmered in her eyes, only to be replaced by a mischievous twinkle. "Plus, he *listens* to me," she added.

Slade frowned and inclined his head toward Shea once again. "Does she always spend this much time on the phone?"

Layne grinned. "Separation anxiety," she said. "She's missing her friends back in L.A., that's all. It'll pass."

"I hope so," Slade replied. "It isn't natural for a kid to go around with a hunk of plastic glued to their ear."

"These days, it is," Layne answered lightly, pushing her plate away, folding her arms and resting them on the tabletop. "Shea's on her best behavior right now because she wants to impress you and she's angling for a horse, but just you wait, *Dad.* Under that sunny exterior lurks a bona fide, card-carrying

teenager. You've got your work cut out
for you, at least for the rest of the summer."

Shea ended the call, at long last, and
started toward them.

Slade smiled at the child he would always think of as his daughter, no matter
what kind of shenanigans she might
pull.

"A horse," he said, musing aloud,
"might be just what she needs right
now."

Back home in the maid's quarters off
Kendra's kitchen, Joslyn set her take-
out meal on the tiny table and nodded
an acknowledgment to Lucy-Maude's
meow.

"I was all set to pig out," she told the
cat ruefully. "And *then* I ran into Slade
Barlow, his ex-wife and his stepdaughter. I'm telling you, that woman—his
ex—looks like a *movie star,* or even
some kind of goddess."

Boldly, Lucy-Maude leaped up onto
the table and sniffed at the boxes containing the fried chicken dinner—complete with mashed potatoes and gravy

and green beans boiled up country style, with onions and bacon—Joslyn had picked up at the Butter Biscuit Café just minutes before.

With a gentle motion of one hand, she shooed the cat off the table.

"Frankly," she went on, "I've mostly lost my appetite." She began to pace, arms folded. "No man in his right mind would divorce that woman," she prattled on, needing to vent, since she might just burst if she didn't, "which means *she* must have kicked *him* to the curb, *which means* there's probably something wrong with him—"

Lucy-Maude gave her a look that seemed almost pitying and bounded gracefully up onto the back of the armchair. "Reow," she said.

"You're totally right, of course," Joslyn admitted. "I'm jumping to conclusions here." A tight-lipped pause. "I'm also *talking* to a cat. *Again.* Lucy-Maude, I have *got* to get a life."

"Reow," Lucy-Maude repeated and began to groom one delicate forepaw.

Suddenly, Joslyn had to laugh—at herself, at her situation, at the world in general. "Any suggestions?" she asked the cat. "On where I might pick up a life, I mean?"

As far as Lucy-Maude was concerned, it appeared, she was on her own.

So Joslyn wiped down the table, washed her hands at the sink and took a plate from the cupboard, flatware from a drawer. Then she sat herself down and resolutely ate her supper. Some of it, anyway.

After stowing the leftovers in the miniscule fridge, she washed the plate and the silverware she'd used, rinsed them and left them to dry in the drain board. Next, she spent two full hours going through the already clean guest cottage like a human whirlwind, scrubbing everything, whether it needed it or not, so the place would be shipshape for Opal. After that, she read over the printout of the first lesson in her online real-estate course, doing plenty of highlighting, following up with a long, luxurious bubble bath. Then she finally crawled into bed, taking several minutes to get settled. When she finally came to rest on her side, Lucy-Maude curled up behind her knees, purring contentedly.

Sleeping, even when she was exhausted, was usually a challenge for Joslyn, but that night was the exception. She dropped into the innermost depths of her mind like a sinking stone and didn't surface again until morning.

Face full of sunlight, she sat bolt upright as all the puzzle pieces of consciousness settled back into their proper places, and a surge of joy rushed through her.

Today was the day.

Opal would arrive in Parable for a visit—*Opal,* the cherished friend and second mother she'd missed so much and feared she might never see again.

They'd chatter like magpies, she thought happily, catching each other up on everything that had happened since they'd parted ways, and, for a few days at least, she, Joslyn, would have someone to talk to besides her cat.

It was a thrilling prospect.

She dressed quickly, donning the black-and-white sundress she'd bought to wear to Kendra's barbecue, fed Lucy-

Maude her breakfast and headed for the office to unlock the front door and boot up her computer.

She'd just finished making an appointment for Lucy-Maude at the veterinary clinic when the desk phone rang.

"Shepherd Real Estate," she answered sunnily. "May I help you?"

"Probably not," Kendra replied, with a tired smile in her voice. "But you've got the makings of a first-class receptionist, overqualified though you are."

Joslyn spoke carefully. "How was your flight?"

"Long," Kendra said. "I checked into my hotel and slept for a few hours, but I'm still pretty jet-lagged. Jeffrey's brother Dennis is on his way over right now—he's going to drive me to the hospital for a visit—"

"Oh, Kendra," Joslyn whispered.

"This is hard," Kendra confided. "On the one hand, I know I have to see Jeffrey and hear what he has to say, or I'll always wonder and wish I'd done things differently. On the other, I want to run as far and as fast as I can."

"I know the feeling," Joslyn agreed

gently. Returning to Parable was like that for her, and so, in a way, was the crazy mixed-up way Slade Barlow seemed to affect her. She was at once drawn to him and terrified of all he might cause her to feel, not just physically, but emotionally, too. "Just take it one step at a time, Kendra, and be kind to yourself along the way, okay?"

"Okay," Kendra said, with another sigh. After a few moments, she added, "Tell me something wonderful, Joss. I could really stand to hear some good news."

"Opal is coming for a visit," Joslyn replied immediately, brightening. "Can you believe it? After all this time, we're finally reconnecting." She paused. "I invited her to stay in the guest cottage, since I'm sleeping in the main house while you're away. That's all right with you, isn't it?"

"Of course it is," Kendra responded with more spirit than before. "Opal was always so kind to me—remember how she used to give us cookies and milk after school, and tell us all those long,

involved stories about when she was a
little girl in Arkansas?"

"I remember," Joslyn said softly. Back
then, Opal, quick to recognize that Kendra was a little-girl-lost in so many ways,
had taken the child under her wing,
loved and protected her as fiercely as
she had Joslyn. "I think she's only planning to be here for a couple of days."

"You tell Opal she can stay as long
as she wants," Kendra said.

"I'll do that," Joslyn answered.

They discussed the few telephone
and email messages that had come in
since they last spoke, Joslyn mentioned
that she'd begun studying for the real-
estate license exam, a plan Kendra
readily approved and encouraged her
to pursue during working hours, when
there was time, and then they rang off.

Joslyn had a hollow feeling in the
center of her chest as she let Kendra
go, wishing she could have done something, said something—anything to
make things easier for her friend.

The morning raced by, and, on her
lunch hour, Joslyn ventured out to raid
Kendra's gardens. She gathered a bou-

quet of brightly colored zinnias, day lil-
ies and roses, arranging the flowers in
a pretty glass vase she found in the
pantry of the main house, and set the
works on the bedside table out in the
cottage.

She was standing back to admire the
display when she heard the sound of
an engine and big tires grinding their
way through the white gravel in the
driveway.

She went outside and found Hutch
there, just getting out of his truck. His
expression had all the cozy warmth of
an impending tornado.

"Is it true that Kendra took off for England?" he demanded, bypassing
"hello" completely and shoving a hand
through his already rumpled hair as he
approached Joslyn.

Joslyn folded her arms and dug in
her heels just a little. "Yes," she said.
"Although I wouldn't exactly say she
'took off.' You made it sound like Kendra did something wrong by going, and
she didn't."

Hutch thrust out a sigh. "Talk around
town is, she's gone back to her ex-hus-

band," he said, looking so miserable in that moment that Joslyn immediately softened toward him.

Joslyn bit her lip, wondering how much she should say. Kendra's reasons for making the trip to Britain were private ones, but Hutch looked as though he'd been sucker punched.

He was even a little pale under that riding-the-range tan of his. And he was her friend, too.

"It's not a reconciliation," she said, very quietly. "Jeffrey's seriously ill, Hutch. Dying, from the sound of things."

Hutch's face changed, tightening a little, then relaxed as if by force of will. He muttered an exclamation, and his shoulders sagged slightly.

Joslyn reached out, touched his upper arm. She wanted to comfort him, but she'd probably already said more than she should have, so she held her tongue.

"What if she doesn't come back?" The question came from somewhere so deep inside Hutch that it sounded raw when he voiced it.

And Joslyn saw immediately that he'd

have taken the words back if he could have. Which was probably why she went ahead and pretended he hadn't said them in the first place.

Having nothing more to say, evidently, Hutch turned and started back toward the still-open door of his truck, climbed in and started the rig up again with a roar.

He raised a hand in brief farewell, and then he drove away.

Joslyn stood there in the driveway for a few moments, biting her lower lip and pondering Hutch's words as the dust slowly settled behind his truck.

It was obvious that he still cared for Kendra, though he'd probably never admit as much, as proud and stubborn as he was. And Kendra, who so obviously carried a torch for him, wasn't likely to fess up, either.

What a waste, Joslyn thought, as she returned to the main house. There was just no figuring some people out.

The irony of that reflection would only occur to her later—much later.

* * *

At three forty-five that afternoon, the bus pulled in, diesel fumes huffing from its exhaust pipe, directly in front of the filling station on Main Street.

Joslyn waited in the shade near the front door, beaming in anticipation.

Three passengers got off the bus, two young girls and an elderly man, followed by the driver, before Opal finally stepped down, tall and gray and with her big patent leather purse pressed hard against her side. She wore wire-rimmed glasses and a "church-going" hat with a wisp of a veil, and her shoes were freshly polished. Her crisp cotton dress, a bright floral concoction of magenta and orange and turquoise, didn't have a wrinkle in it, even though she'd traveled for some distance.

Joslyn hesitated, then hurried over to Opal, and the two of them hugged and cried and laughed, all at the same time.

The bus driver got impatient, waiting for Opal to point out which of the bags jammed into the undercarriage of the dusty-sided coach was hers, and she said, in her kindly authoritative way,

"Oh, just hold your horses for a minute, young fella."

The "young fella" was probably pushing fifty, but he looked as chagrined as a schoolboy as he stood there, sweltering in his too-tight uniform.

"Look at you," Opal said, holding her at arm's length, her strong hands gripping Joslyn's shoulders as she gave her a grandmotherly once-over. "You're too thin. You need some of my good cooking, that's what you need."

Joslyn laughed again and swiped at her right cheek with the back of one hand. "It's so good to see you, Opal."

Opal took pity on the bus driver then and told him the brown suitcase in the front, wedged in there between the two duct-taped coolers, was hers.

He unloaded it for her, and Joslyn took it from there, lugging the bag over to her car, raising the trunk lid with a press of one of the buttons on her key fob and hoisting the baggage inside.

Opal glanced around her. "This town doesn't look any different than it did when we lit out of here, you and your mama and me," she observed drily. "It's still forty miles up the back end of no-where." Her brown gaze swung straight to Joslyn's face then and connected. "You mind telling me what the heck you think you're doing, coming back here?"

"Later," Joslyn promised. "Let's get you settled first."

"Not much settling to do," Opal allowed, as she opened the front passenger-side door to get into Joslyn's car. "I only brought a few things from home, since I'm not planning to impose on you for more than a couple of days."

"You can stay as long as you like," Joslyn said. "Kendra asked me to let you know that."

"Where's she?" Opal asked, looking around again. "Busy working?"

Joslyn, seated behind the wheel, key in hand, drank in the sight of her old friend for a long moment. "Kendra's in England at the moment," she said.

"England?" Opal echoed, sternly baffled. Joslyn might as well have said Kendra had stepped into a parallel universe, from the woman's expression. "What's she doing way over there?"

"Long story," Joslyn replied. "It'll take

hours to tell you everything." She smiled, started the engine. "Let's go home."

Once the furniture had been delivered to the ranch house and the place was beginning to look like flesh-and-blood people lived there instead of just ghosts, Layne announced that she'd be heading back to L.A. the following day. She missed Bentley, and she didn't want to be away from her home-staging business for too long.

Slade noticed that his ex-wife was watching Shea closely as she spoke, there in the box-cluttered kitchen, probably trying to gauge the girl's reaction to being left behind.

Shea, her dark hair clipped in a wad on the top of her head and fanning out from there like a rooster's tail, grinned at her mother. She was wearing jeans and a pink tank top, and there was a smudge of dust on her right cheek— she'd been busy.

"Is this the part where I throw myself on the floor, wrap both arms around your ankles and beg you not to go,

Mommy dearest?" she asked Layne pertly.

Slade, just home from work, smiled into the cup of coffee Shea had handed him the moment he'd come through the back door. Her welcome had only been slightly less enthusiastic than Jasper's.

"Smart aleck," Layne said good-naturedly, putting her hands on her hips. Like Shea, she was dressed for housework—not her favorite enterprise, if Slade recalled correctly.

Shea laughed and slipped a daughterly arm around Slade's waist, resting her head against his shoulder for a moment. "Dad will take good care of me," she said. "Won't you, Dad?"

She looked up into his face when she asked that question, and Slade felt something scrape at the back of his heart.

"Bet on it," he said, somewhat gruffly. Then he straightened. "Which is not to say there aren't going to be any rules, because there are."

Shea frowned, wrinkling her turned-up nose, narrowing her eyes a little.

"Rules?" she countered. "What kind of rules?"

"The usual," Slade said, after exchanging glances with Layne.

Layne smiled, amused. Maybe even a little smug.

"Such as?" Shea persisted, still studying his face. Her arm had dropped to her side, though, and she'd put a step or two between them.

"No climbing the water tower in town," Slade began, setting his coffee aside to count on his fingers. "No friends over when I'm not around. No spending texting, watching TV or surfing the Net."

Shea frowned. "I wasn't planning on climbing the water tower," she said. "It's not as if I'm stupid or anything."

Layne folded her arms and watched the exchange, her expression still merry.

Slade noticed his stepdaughter hadn't commented on the remaining rules. "There's more," he said. "You have to clean up after yourself—no leaving the bathroom looking like a cyclone just hit it—and if you want to keep using that cell phone of yours, you'll need a job to pay for the service."

Shea blinked. "Where am I supposed to get a *job?*" she asked.

"Mom's always looking for somebody to sweep out the shop and book appointments," he said. "You might start by asking her."

Shea stared at him. "You mean, like sweeping up people's *hair* and stuff?"

"That's the general idea," Slade said.

"Mom just gives me an allowance," Shea replied.

Slade glanced at Layne, smiled. "For doing what?"

Shea looked honestly confused. "F being her kid," she murmured.

"Nice work if you can get it," Slade told the girl.

"I think I'd like to get back to our hotel room and start packing for the trip," Layne interjected cheerfully, twinkling at Slade. "Shall I drop Shea off at your office on my way to the airport?"

Slade looked to Shea for an answer instead of giving one himself.

The chances seemed pretty good that Shea would change her mind about staying in Parable, now that she knew she wasn't going to be able to do anything she pleased.

But the kid flashed the kind of smile that probably set the young bucks of her acquaintance back on their heels.

"I could just stay here, with Dad and Jasper," she said. "My room is almost ready, after all. Soon as those new sheets come out of the dryer, I can make up my bed."

"Best you spend one more night with your mother," Slade said after clearing his throat. Oddly, his eyes smarted a little, and he reached for his coffee again, needing to be busy with something. "Since you won't see her again for a while."

Shea sighed.

Layne gave Slade a grateful look.

And that was that.

Shea left with Layne in the rental car.

Slade finished his coffee, set the cup in the sink and looked around at the jumble of new stuff—dishes, a toaster oven, an electric mixer, for Pete's sake— that still needed to be put away.

Then he looked down at Jasper, who

was wagging his tail in happy anticipation of whatever development might come next.

Slade laughed and bent to rumple the dog's ears. "Come on," he said. "Let's go outside and take in some of those wide-open spaces Montana is so famous for."

Jasper took to the idea right off.

They wound up down by the creek, watching the water rush by, bending its way around rocks, sunlight dancing on its surface.

The moment was close to perfect—until Hutch Carmody ruined it by driving up in the rattle-trap old truck of his. With his money, Slade thought, you'd think the man would drive a decent rig.

Slade set his jaw. "Now what?" he muttered to Jasper.

Hutch parked the truck and came down the bank toward Slade and the dog.

Jasper wagged a greeting and allowed Hutch to scratch him behind the ears.

"What do you want?" Slade asked, not being one for small talk.

Hutch laughed, but the raspy sound wasn't reflected in his eyes. "Now that just ain't neighborly," he replied, laying on the hick vernacular.

"We aren't neighbors," Slade pointed out.

"We aren't a lot of things," Hutch answered brusquely. He made a point of taking in the creek, the expanse of good grazing land fringed at the horizon by tall pine and fir trees. "Nice place," he added.

"It'll do for the time being," Slade said. He knew why his half brother was there—to take another stab at talking him into selling his share of the Whisper Creek spread. What he *didn't* know was why the idea of letting go of a place he'd never wanted in the first place got under his hide the way it did.

Hutch was offering a price that was more than fair, after all, and Slade could understand why the man wanted to own that land outright instead of sharing it with a brother he'd have preferred to ignore.

Now, Hutch sighed and watched the

creek flow for a few moments, as though he found some fascination in it. And maybe he did.

It was a beautiful thing to see, that ribbon of moving light.

"I've got a proposition for you, Slade," he finally said, his gaze direct now.

"What kind of proposition?" Slade asked. In spite of himself, he was intrigued. "If it's more money, you can forget it. I've got all I'd need for ten lifetimes, let alone the one I've got."

Hutch smiled, but again there was no friendliness in him anywhere. Just a quiet persistence that matched Slade's own.

"I'm talking about a horse race," he said.

Slade was surprised, though he did his best not to show it. "I don't own a horse," he said and then felt foolish for stating the obvious.

"You might want to acquire one, then," Hutch replied easily. "The sooner the better."

"What the hell are you getting at, Carmody?"

Hutch bent down, picked up a stick and tossed it for Jasper, who dashed after it, joy on four legs.

"Like I said," answered John Carmody's legitimate son and heir, "I'm proposing a horse race. If you win, I'll move out of the main ranch house at Whisper Creek—build a place of my own or bring in a trailer or something—and you can live there instead. We'd share the responsibility for the operation fifty-fifty. If *I* win, which I admit is a sight more likely in my opinion, you accept the offer I made you and the spread is all mine."

Slade narrowed his eyes. Hutch had practically been born on a horse, but Slade could ride, all right. "When would this race take place?" he asked.

Hutch shrugged one shoulder, grinned and bent to take the stick Jasper had brought back to him and, much to the dog's delight, give it another throw. "I figure you need a while to practice, if this is going to be fair," he said affably, though there was an edge to his tone, and the light in his eyes was cold as January creek water. "So I think we ought to wait till Labor Day weekend.

We'll figure out the details in the meantime."

Slade unclamped his back molars.
Hutch made it sound as if he was some
kind of greenhorn, playing at being a
cowboy. The fact was, though, that
Slade had won his share of rodeo events
over the years. He'd ridden bad bron-
cos and even badder bulls, and he'd
been pretty fair at roping, too. He'd just
never felt he could justify the expense
of keeping a horse.

He looked Hutch straight in the eye.
Waited a beat before speaking.

"Little brother," he said, "you're on."

CHAPTER THIRTEEN

"Truth is," Opal said forthrightly, as she and Joslyn sat drinking tea at the big table in Kendra's kitchen, "I miss working for a living, like I always did. Willie left me well fixed, but don't you know, girl, I'm too *young* to be retired, and there are days when that sister-in-law of mine drives me right straight up the wall."

Joslyn smiled. She still couldn't get over it—Opal was back. Sitting right across from her in the very room where they'd had so many other conversations over the years, some of them profound, most of them reassuringly ordinary.

They'd been bringing each other up to date for some forty-five minutes, and Opal had already related that she'd been briefly married to a fellow she met at church and widowed only a year later. Her Willie, having enjoyed a long career as the manager of an auto parts store, had been a saver, and he'd made sure that both his wife and his sister were provided for when he passed away.

"I've missed you," Joslyn said.

Opal reached out to pat Joslyn's hand. Lucy-Maude regarded them both from a third chair at the table, looking as though she expected a cup of tea for herself.

"A day hasn't gone by when I didn't think about you and your mama," Opal replied. "I read about Elliott in the newspaper, how he died in jail and all, and I thought that was mighty sad, him ending up that way, especially when he came from such good people. Far as I could tell, there wasn't any kind of funeral or memorial service to go to, but I sure wondered how you and Dana were holding up. I'm no good with a computer—I don't see any point in learning how to work one of those things at this stage of the game—but I should have guessed you'd be in touch with Kendra."

Joslyn lowered her eyes. *She* knew all about computers, but she hadn't searched for Opal. Maybe she'd been afraid of what she'd find—and maybe she'd been too ashamed. Even though neither she nor her mother could be blamed for Elliott's criminal actions, she didn't feel entirely guiltless in the matter, either.

She'd certainly enjoyed all the perks of being a rich man's stepdaughter— living in a mansion, wearing the latest styles, driving a nice car as a teenager, one many hardworking adults wouldn't have been able to afford.

Though she'd never know for sure, her stepfather might have done what he did, at least partially, so he could go on indulging her every whim. Elliott had liked to show off his beautiful wife and his stepdaughter, and that took money.

Opal seemed to be reading her mind.

"It's right now that matters, honey," she said gently. "I reckon we both could have tried harder, but we had some healing up to do. Besides, it's not what happened yesterday, or ten years ago, or what happens tomorrow that matters. All we've got, any of us, is *now*."

Joslyn nodded, swallowed. Looking back over her life, it seemed to her that she'd always acted as though she had forever to do the things she really wanted to do—get married, have children, make new friends instead of being such a loner, perhaps even build a business she could keep instead of selling.

Slade Barlow came to mind then—he was never far away—and the mere thought of him made her blush.

"What are you doing back here?" Opal asked after refilling both their cups from the china teapot in the center of the table.

Joslyn chuckled, surprised that it had taken Opal this long to get back around to the subject, but at the same time, the threat of tears stung her eyes. "I've been wrestling with that question myself," she admitted. "I had the means to make some reparation for what Elliott did, so that was part of it. But now, well—" She paused to bite her lower lip before going on. "Now I'm beginning to wonder if it isn't because the words *home* and *Parable* have always been interchangeable for me."

Opal took that in, nodding. "Now we're getting somewhere," she said presently. "Guess I could say the same thing about this little town, that it feels like home, I mean. Great Falls is a real nice place to live, but Parable will always be the place where my life really began." She took a sip of tea, silent for a long moment as she relished it. Opal had always loved her tea—said it ran in her veins in place of blood. "Oh, I was born and raised in Arkansas, it's true," she went on finally, "but when I answered a newspaper ad and came out here to work for old Mrs. Rossiter—Elliott's grandmother, God rest her sweet soul—as a kind of lady's companion, I fit in right away." She smiled, remembering. "Back then, I was the only black person in Parable—maybe in the whole county. Folks were curious about me,

no doubt about it, but they were generally kind, and I don't mind admitting, I
enjoyed the attention."

"But you never married—until Willie, I
mean."

Opal shook her head. "Never met a
man I wanted to share close quarters
with before Willie." She smiled wistfully.
"I was his princess bride, he always
said. Good as that marriage was, it was
still an adjustment for both of us—he'd
been a widower for twenty years, and I
was a spinster, mighty set in my ways,
but it worked for us. We *made* it work."
Another pause came then, during which
she studied Joslyn thoughtfully before
asking, "What about you? How does it
happen that a pretty woman like you is
still single?"

"I guess I haven't met my Willie yet,"
she replied. "Are you hungry, Opal?"

Opal shook her head. "I packed a
lunch this morning before our neighbor
drove me to the bus station, ate it on
the ride over here. I mostly just have
toast and fruit in the mornings, and then
I eat a pretty good-sized midday meal.
That's enough food for me." Again, she

assessed Joslyn. "I'd like to fatten *you* up a little, though."

"Please don't try," Joslyn said, only half kidding. "You know I can't resist your cooking—especially the baked goods. Anyway, you're not here to cook. You're a guest, Opal."

"Be that as it may," Opal maintained staunchly, "there aren't many things I enjoy more than fixing up a good meal for somebody I care for."

Opal's words touched Joslyn—and a love of cooking was something they had in common.

Opal had taught her the basics years before, and she'd taken it from there, watching TV chefs, poring over cookbooks and experimenting on her own. She'd eaten well all along but not, evidently, enough to suit either her doctor back in Phoenix or Opal.

"That's the fun part," she agreed. "Preparing food and then sharing it with another person."

Opal nodded, started to speak, and then yawned instead. After that, she blinked her eyes a couple of times, behind the shining lenses of her snazzy modern glasses, smiled and said, "Got up pretty early this morning. I didn't want to miss that bus."

Joslyn smiled. It wasn't yet five o'clock in the afternoon, but Opal *did* look worn-out. "If you're sure you don't want any supper first, I'll walk you out to the guesthouse and you can settle in for the night."

Opal laughed throatily. "I'm sure," she said, her dark eyes twinkling. "Trust me, if I'm hungry, I eat." A breath, a shake of the head. "The *guesthouse,* is it? My goodness. Only time I ever set foot in that place before was to get it ready for company. Now, I *am* the company."

"Absolutely," Joslyn said, hugging Opal again once they'd both stood up. "Nothing but the best for you, my friend."

"Silly girl," Opal retorted, but she looked and sounded pleased.

"I'll get your suitcase," Joslyn told her, heading for her car, parked at the top of the long driveway, to retrieve Opal's bag from the trunk.

Opal followed, her polished shoes, now scuffed, crunching in the white gravel.

Once she and Joslyn were inside the cottage, Joslyn led the way into the bedroom and set the suitcase on the bench at the foot of the brass bed.

Opal admired the multicolored bouquet in the vase on the nightstand. "Flowers," she said. "You thought of everything."

"There are plenty of clean towels," Joslyn said, eager to make her friend comfortable, "and the coffeemaker is set to start brewing promptly at 7:00 a.m."

For as long as she'd known Opal, the woman had unfailingly arisen from her bed at that exact hour, sick or well, rested or tired. She'd always said it was because her body clock was tuned to seven, and her eyes flew wide-open at that time, on the dot.

"Good," Opal said quietly. "Believe I'll have a nice bath and maybe read in bed for a while. Helps me get to sleep."

"If there's anything you need—" Joslyn began. It would be hours before she herself was ready to turn in for the night, of course, but she could always tackle another lesson from her real-estate course.

"I'll be just fine," Opal told her firmly. "You go on back to the big house and look after that cat and whatever else you've got to attend to, and don't worry about me."

Joslyn nodded, hesitated another moment, then said good-night, hugged Opal once more and left the cottage for the main house.

That afternoon, it seemed bigger and emptier than ever before, and she was glad of Lucy-Maude's appointment at the veterinary clinic. The veterinarian, Dr. Ryan, ran a busy practice with several partners, and once a week, they kept the place open late.

Inside Kendra's house, Joslyn rounded up a disgruntled Lucy-Maude, tucked her back into the cardboard box she'd used to bring her in from the cottage and headed for her car.

"It's a little late for birth control," she told the angry cat, who was clawing and yowling inside the box, even though Joslyn had cushioned the bottom with a blanket and made sure there were plenty of air holes. "But you need your shots and a checkup."

Once again, she thought wryly, she was talking to a cat. As long as the cat didn't answer, she figured, she was all right.

Slade was never sure what made him do it, but the next morning, after Layne had driven off for the airport in her rental car and Shea was visibly bored hanging around his office while he took care of paperwork, he made up his mind that he had to see Joslyn.

Just like that.

As soon as he'd taken Shea over to the Curly-Burly to hit Callie up for a job, he and Jasper headed straight for Kendra's place before he could lose his resolve.

It was eight-thirty when he knocked on the door of the guesthouse, but it wasn't Joslyn who opened up.

It was Opal, the Rossiter family's longtime housekeeper and cook.

"Slade Barlow," the older woman cried, delighted. "Darned if you aren't even handsomer as a man than you were as a boy. How's that fine mother of yours?"

Slade, taken aback, grinned with pleasure. "Opal?"

She laughed. "Yep," she said. "It's really me. But I reckon I'm not who you were looking for."

Slade cleared his throat, remembered to take off his hat. "Is Joslyn around?" he asked. He couldn't believe he was doing this—he wasn't impulsive in the least, never did much of anything without thinking it through from just about every angle first.

Now, here he was, calling on a woman he barely knew at practically the crack of dawn, without the faintest idea what he'd say when he came face-to-face with her.

"She's staying in the big house while Kendra's away," Opal answered, looking at him closely enough to make him feel mildly uncomfortable, so that he shifted his weight from one foot to the other. "I figure I'm entitled to be blunt sometimes, now that I'm an old woman," she continued, after taking in the badge affixed to his belt. "Is this visit official, Sheriff, or is it social?"

Slade cleared his throat. Didn't it just beat all that, when he'd finally gone against everything in his nature and acted on what amounted to a whim, he'd wound up knocking on the wrong door?

"Neither one," he said awkwardly. "I just wanted to see her, that's all."

Don't ask why.

Opal smiled broadly. "Good," she said, looking as though she thought this unexpected call meant a whole lot more than it actually did. "That's good."

"Maybe I'll stop by later," he said, glad to see Opal again but anxious to be gone.

"You turned coward since I saw you last?" Opal asked, jutting out her chin a little ways. "Never thought I'd see the day Callie Barlow's boy was scared of anything."

He felt his neck heat up, knew it had turned red. This was a challenge he couldn't turn away from, and Opal damned well knew it.

"You think Joslyn's awake yet?" he asked.

"'Course she's awake," Opal retorted immediately. "She's got to open up Kendra's office by 9:00 a.m."

"Where's Kendra?" Slade asked, stalling to give himself time to consider his options, such as they were. Passing his hat from his right hand to his left and back again.

"I guess if Miss Kendra wanted you to know that," Opal replied, smiling, "she'd have made sure to tell you before she left."

Slade sighed. Smiled. "Fair enough," he answered. "You staying around Parable, Opal, or just visiting?"

Opal folded her arms, still grinning, letting him know without saying as much that she was reading him like the proverbial book. "I might stay on, if I can find myself a job," she said. "You know anybody looking for a mighty good cook and housekeeper, Slade?"

He thought about his cluttered ranch house and Shea, who'd have to be alone at least some of the time while he was working, and how he couldn't cook a lick. It wouldn't be healthy for his daughter *or* for him to take every meal at the Butter Biscuit Café or live on stuff he'd nuked in the microwave.

"Me," he said. Impulsive act number two, and the day had hardly begun.

Opal's eyes widened. "Are you serious?"

"Yes, ma'am," he said, with a smile. "I sure am."

Now, it was Opal who was rattled, instead of him. "I'd be expensive," she warned. "And I don't drive at night."

"No problem," Slade agreed happily. "I came into some money lately, and you wouldn't have to drive at all if you didn't want to. Shea—that's my daughter—has her license now. I'll have to see her in action for a while before I let her get behind the wheel, but if you were with her, I'd feel a lot better about it."

Opal's mouth fell open, closed again.

"I'd need to meet this young woman and get a look at the house I'd be responsible for keeping up," she said, just as the back door of the mansion's sunporch creaked open behind them, across the green, flower-dappled expanse of the yard.

Slade glanced back over one shoulder, saw Joslyn standing on the steps. She was barefoot and wearing the oversized T-shirt she'd probably slept in.

Heat pounded through him as he turned his full attention to Opal again. "I understand," he said. He took one of his cards from his shirt pocket, handed it over. "Give me a call when you decide."

Opal took the card, nodded.

Slade offered a gruff goodbye and turned to approach the back step of the main house where Joslyn was still standing.

It was that or run the other way.

Joslyn's chestnut-brown hair spilled around her shoulders in wild, spiraling curls. "Is anything wrong?" she asked.

It gave Slade a pang that she'd think that, especially right off. He supposed it was natural, though, since, as sheriff, he was often the bearer of bad news.

"Nothing's wrong," he said, coming to a stop in the grass, maybe a dozen yards from where she stood, with his imagination running wild behind what he hoped was a bland expression.

If he could have, he thought, dazed by the realization—if things were different between them, that is—he'd have closed the space between himself and Joslyn in a few strides. He'd have lifted her right off those naked feet of hers, kissed her hard and carried her to the nearest bed before either one of them came up for a single breath of air.

Joslyn tilted her head to one side, her arms folded self-consciously across her breasts, braless and shapely under that T-shirt she wore. "Why are you here, then?"

Again, his courage wavered.

He could have said he'd come to ask why Kendra had left town without a word to anybody.

He could have said there'd been a burglary in the area and he wanted to make sure Joslyn was locking her doors at night.

Neither of those things were true, though, and it was Slade's curse that he couldn't bring himself to lie, even when that would have been the best thing for everybody concerned.

He didn't have an answer at the ready, but one jumped right out of his mouth just the same, as fully formed as if he'd given it some thought. "There's a live-stock auction coming up this Saturday, just outside of Missoula, and I was thinking you might want to come along with Shea and me."

She sort of slumped against one of the two pillars that supported the porch roof. "A livestock auction?" she re-peated, looking completely baffled.

"I'm in the market for a horse or two," he said. His old practicality was coming back; he wished he'd never gotten the harebrained idea of asking Joslyn out, because it was a sure road to nowhere, as little as they had in common.

Failing that, he wished he'd suggested something a little more datelike than a livestock auction. Dinner and a movie, maybe. Even stopping by Sully's Tavern to dance to the jukebox and have a beer or two.

But asking her to stand next to a high fence in the roiling dust and the hot sun, watching as horses and cattle were sold off to the highest bidder?

Smooth, he thought, hoping Hutch would never catch wind of this. It was just the ammunition his half brother would love to get hold of.

"I don't know a whole lot about horses," Joslyn told him. She was still keeping her arms across her chest, and he was glad, because if he'd caught a glimpse of nipples pressing against the thin fabric of that T-shirt thing, he'd probably lose his mind.

"You were rodeo queen," he reminded her and immediately felt even stupider than before. She'd ridden a beautiful, coal-black mare around the arena at the Parable County Rodeo that year, her tailor-made Western getup and pink hat glistening with rhinestones, waving and smiling at the crowd.

"My dad borrowed the horse from a friend of his," she answered. "I was scared out of my mind the entire time."

Slade laughed. "You sure had everybody fooled," he said. "Looked like you knew what you were doing, anyhow."

She smiled. "That was the idea," she admitted.

There *had* been rumors back then, that Elliott Rossiter had bought the title of Parable County Rodeo Queen for his stepdaughter.

"Will your ex-wife be coming along, too?" she asked. "To this auction, I mean?"

Slade was caught off guard for a moment, but then he realized what the question meant, however casually it had been voiced. Joslyn was as nervous as he was.

"Layne?" he said, as though he had so many ex-wives that he'd needed to weed through them before he got to the one she was asking about. "No, she's gone home to L.A. to get ready for her wedding. It'll just be Shea and me and—hopefully—you."

"I've never been to a livestock auction," Joslyn said. There was a slight sparkle in her eyes, it seemed to Slade. "Maybe it would be fun."

Slade didn't know what to say to that. Livestock auctions were a lot of things—

noisy, crowded and more, but he wouldn't have described them as "fun."

Especially for a woman like Joslyn Kirk.

"Unless Opal is still here on Saturday, in which case I won't want to leave her," Joslyn said with a nod in the direction of the guesthouse, "count me in."

Slade didn't mention that he'd just offered Opal a job and was hoping the woman would stay on in Parable for good. For one thing, nothing had been decided yet—Opal might take one look at that rented ranch house of his and take to her heels.

"Good," he said.

"How's Jasper doing?" Joslyn asked, just when he would have said goodbye and walked away.

It was only then that Slade remembered he'd left the dog in his truck. It was cool out, since the day was young, and one of the windows was rolled partway down, so Jasper had plenty of air, but still. "He's all right," he answered. "Waiting for me in the rig."

Joslyn nodded, smiled. "He's a good dog."

"He sure is," Slade had to agree.

"See you Saturday," she said. "Un-less—"

"I know," he said. "Unless Opal is still in town. If she is, maybe she'd like to go along." Where the hell was he going with this? Damned if he knew.

He put on his hat, tugged at the brim. And he left, heading for the truck with long strides, avoiding the strong temp-tation to look back.

Opal joined Joslyn, who had gotten dressed by then, in the mansion's big kitchen and immediately began rum-maging through the refrigerator for the makings of breakfast.

"He turned out just fine, that Barlow boy," Opal observed. She found eggs and milk there and bread on the coun-tertop, since Joslyn had stopped off at Mulligan's Market on the way home from the veterinarian's office the night before.

Joslyn blushed. "Yes," she said. She'd agreed to go to a livestock auction with Slade and his stepdaughter on Satur-day morning. It couldn't be called a date, she supposed, but against her better judgment, she was looking forward to the occasion. The pull of the man was downright magnetic, but she'd be all right, she was certain. After all, what could happen at a horse sale?

"He ask you out?" Opal inquired, taking a copper skillet down from the hanging arrangement of pots and kettles above the center island. She knew her way around that kitchen, obviously, even though it no longer belonged to the Rossiters.

"Sort of," Joslyn said, after biting her lip.

"Sort of?" Opal repeated.

"He and his stepdaughter, Shea, are going to an auction Saturday, in Missoula. He invited me to come along."

Opal rolled her eyes. "Men," she said. "They don't have the first clue about flowers and moonlight."

"I won't go if you're going to be here, though," Joslyn hastened to add, letting Opal's observation pass without comment. "You and I still have plenty of catching up to do."

"If I'm still in Parable then," Opal said,

setting the skillet on one of the gas burners and turning up the flame beneath it. "I'll spend some time with Martie over at that animal shelter she runs."

Hope swelled in Joslyn's heart. She'd thought Opal meant to stay no longer than a few days, and Saturday was a way off. "Good," she said. "You're not in any hurry to leave."

Opal busied herself whipping up a batch of scrambled eggs and some toast. "You sit yourself down while I get your breakfast," she ordered. "And don't give me an argument about it, either, young lady, because I've missed tending to you."

Joslyn, at a loss for an answer, sank into a chair at the big table.

Opal chatted as she cooked. "I've already been offered a job, too," she went on. "How do you like that?"

"A job?" Joslyn managed. "How—? Who—?"

"Sheriff Slade Barlow, that's who," Opal answered, almost jubilantly. "Who else have I seen since I got here, besides you?"

"Slade offered you a job?" Joslyn asked, more than surprised.

"Yes, ma'am," Opal said.

"As what?"

Opal laughed. "Well, it wasn't a deputy's position," she teased. "As a cook and a housekeeper, silly."

"Oh," Joslyn said, not sure how she felt about this development. Of course she wanted Opal to stay on in Parable for as long as possible, but if she was keeping house for Slade Barlow, she, Joslyn, would run into him all the time.

Sure, she'd agreed to go to the livestock auction with him—what could happen there, especially with his teenage daughter along, too? But Opal was practically family, and Joslyn wanted to spend time with her.

If Opal worked for Slade, though . . .

"You'd be living at his place?" Joslyn asked, thinking of the charming, if rundown ranch house he'd just moved into.

"Probably," Opal replied. She brought the plate of scrambled eggs and toast to the table and set it down in front of Joslyn. "Eat," she commanded.

Joslyn obediently picked up her fork.

Beneath the table, a recently fed Lucy-Maude twined her sleek body around Joslyn's ankles. Joslyn had evidently been forgiven for last night's indignities—shots, a blood test, a thorough veterinary examination. It was official: there would be kittens, and sooner, rather than later.

Opal, meanwhile, went back to the counter to toast some bread for herself. "I told him I'd need to meet that stepdaughter of his and get a look at the house I'd be looking after," she went on, "but this has all the earmarks of an answered prayer, as far as I'm concerned. Like I told you, I miss working."

Opal's scrambled eggs were, as always, delicious. Joslyn ate hungrily.

"Are you sure you're up to it?" she asked between bites.

Opal brought her toast to the table on a small plate, fetched a banana from the bunch resting in the fruit bowl and sat down across from Joslyn. She didn't answer, just looked amused and puzzled, both at once.

"I mean, it's a big house, and nobody's lived in it for a while, so it needs work and—" Joslyn caught herself. What was she *doing,* making a case *against* the very thing she wanted so much—for Opal to stay in Parable? She swallowed hard. "And what about your sister-in-law? Wouldn't she be all alone if you left?"

Opal frowned, putting down her first slice of toast. "My sister-in-law," she said, "is as sick of me as I am of her. Besides, she's got a million friends."

Joslyn had a mouthful of scrambled eggs by then, so she didn't answer.

"Don't you want me to take this job?" Opal asked very quietly.

"Of course I do," Joslyn replied, as soon as she could speak. "It's just—well—you'd be working awfully hard, it seems to me."

Opal grinned. "And you think that might kill me off?"

Joslyn shook her head. "No, I just—"

Opal reached across the table, took her hand and squeezed it. "Work doesn't kill half as many people as retirement does, to my way of thinking," she declared. "Fact is, I've seen it do more than one person in before their time."

She paused, took another bite of toast, chewed and swallowed. "Anyhow," she went on, when she was ready, "I think Slade mainly wants somebody to look after that girl of his while he's working. You ever met her?"

Joslyn nodded. "Once," she said, remembering the encounter at the Butter Biscuit Café. "Her name is Shea, and she seemed nice enough."

Opal produced a business card from the pocket of her fresh cotton dress—this one was blue with little white flowers on it—and set it on the table for Joslyn to see.

"Fine, then," she said. "I'll give Slade a call in a little while. When you get off work this afternoon, you can drive me there to meet the child and eyeball that house."

And that was the end of it. Opal had spoken.

CHAPTER FOURTEEN

Slade was up on the ranch house roof when Opal and Joslyn drove up just before six that evening. He worked shirtless, rimmed in the last dazzle of sunlight, with his worn-out jeans riding low on his lean hips.

Joslyn's palms turned sweaty the instant she spotted him, and she tightened her fingers around the steering wheel of her car. Her heart pounded with a longing—even a need—she didn't dare recognize, let alone give a name to.

Opal, buckled in on the passenger

side, chuckled. "Now, *that*," she observed, ducking her head slightly to get a better look at Slade through the windshield, "is a man."

Amen, Joslyn thought. But what she *said* was, "You'd think he'd bother to wear a shirt when he's expecting company."

Her tone was downright grumpy.

Joslyn's remark made Opal grin broadly as she unhooked her seat belt and pushed open the car door to get out.

By then, Slade was climbing down the ladder leaning against the house, and Shea and Jasper spilled out of the back door just as he set his booted feet on the ground.

With a grin, he retrieved a navy blue T-shirt from the sawhorse he must have draped it over before the climb, tugged it on over his head. The hard muscles of his abdomen rippled as he completed the process.

Jasper trotted circles around Joslyn, barking excitedly.

Shea, clad in jeans and a loose pink

T-shirt, laughed and ordered kindly, "Jasper, *chill.*"

Joslyn wrenched her eyes away from Slade's midsection, but not quite quickly enough. The spark in his eyes, bluer than his shirt, said he'd caught her staring.

She blushed as a melting sensation warmed between her hip bones, but she managed a smile as Opal stepped forward in her colorful dress and a pair of crepe-soled shoes, holding out a hand to the teenager.

"I'm Opal," she said. "You must be Shea."

Shea nodded, clearly pleased, and shook hands with Opal. "Nice to meet you, Mrs.—?"

"Just Opal," Opal replied. "Unless, of course, you want me to call you Miss Barlow?"

Shea's glance at Slade was brief, but Joslyn noticed the fleeting expression of sadness in the girl's pale violet eyes. "My last name might have been 'Barlow,' if Dad had ever gotten around to adopting me while he and Mom were still married. It's Tarrington, by default."

Slade's mouth quirked at that statement, but he didn't comment.

"But I'd like you to call me 'Shea,'" the teenager finished, smiling at Opal.

"Then we're agreed," Opal answered, with gentle humor. Joslyn knew that, behind those dark, wise eyes, Opal's sharp brain was sifting and sorting through all the nuances of the dynamics between Shea and Slade. "You call me Opal, and I'll call you Shea."

Shea nodded. "Come inside and see the house," she said, including Joslyn in the invitation by catching her gaze and holding it for a moment.

Joslyn found herself liking the girl even more than she had on their first meeting. Sure, Shea was probably on her best behavior, but Joslyn sensed her good heart, her intelligence and her love for her stepfather, the man she called "Dad."

Shea and Opal led the way, with Jasper behind them and Joslyn and Slade bringing up the rear.

His hand rested lightly on the small of Joslyn's back with a sort of easy solicitude that made her feel safe even as her senses rioted behind what she hoped was a cool exterior.

"Don't mind the mess," Shea sang cheerfully as they entered the kitchen. It looked cleaner than it had on Joslyn's first visit but much more cluttered, with boxes and various grocery items stacked everywhere.

"Never met the mess I couldn't clean up," Opal said, looking around.

It was easy enough to picture the woman presiding over this kitchen and the rest of the house, too. She'd have every inch of the place in spit-shined order before the end of the first week, if she accepted Slade's job offer.

"Wait till you see the rest of it before you say that," Shea teased, her tone sunny, musical, as she and Opal and the dog continued the tour.

Slade and Joslyn wound up standing in the kitchen, just the two of them. Alone.

Joslyn backed up and found herself pressing against the edge of one of the counters.

Slade stood practically toe-to-toe with her; she was aware of his hardness

and his heat, his strength and his scent,
in every cell of her body, every nook
and crevice in her mind and her soul. A
primitive yearning thrummed through
her, a reverberation like the striking of a
bass chord.

Never in this lifetime or, she suspected, any other, had she wanted a
man the way she wanted Slade Barlow.

"Sooner or later," he drawled, the
sound of his voice coming to her as if
through a pounding void, his mouth still
quirked at one side but his eyes quizzi-
cal and wary, "we're going to have to
do something about this."

"About—what?" Joslyn practically
choked. She was terrified, but at the
same time she knew for certain that if
he started to move away, she would
bunch both fists in the fabric of his sexy
T-shirt and try to keep him right where
he was.

His chuckle was a rasp, and there
was a touch of irony in his tone when
he replied, "About *this.*"

And then he kissed her.

Tentatively at first, then with a com-
manding hunger that made her breath

catch and her knees go weak. His hands, first resting on the sides of her face, calloused and warm, moved to her waist, as if he'd sensed she needed help to stand.

Still, the kiss went on. Their tongues touched, sparred. Slade's erection, pressed against her, felt fiery and demanding and huge. She wanted him inside her.

Overhead, Joslyn heard Opal and Shea's footsteps on the second floor, the tone of their chatter, the rhythmic click of Jasper's nails against the wooden planks.

Joslyn's arms slipped around Slade's neck, and he raised his mouth from hers just long enough to allow them each a breath and then kissed her again, even more deeply this time.

He drew back just as they heard Jasper start down the stairway that led from the kitchen to the upper hallway.

Slade was breathing hard, and Joslyn felt dazed, downright drunk. And more in need of this man's intimate attentions than ever.

"Now what?" she whispered, as Jasper appeared in the kitchen, with Opal and Shea following close behind him.

Slade grinned, though he looked almost as rattled as Joslyn felt. "I have a few suggestions," he told her, and his gaze lingered on her breasts for just a moment, clearly enjoying the sight of her nipples trying to press through the fabric of her top and the bra beneath it.

There was, of course, no time to ask what those suggestions might be, because Opal and Shea were back in the kitchen.

Slade had moved to stand behind a chair, and though his stance was casual, Joslyn knew what he was hiding. She could still feel the weight of it against her upper abdomen and her stomach.

Flushed, she scurried to the sink, turned on the faucet and began splashing her face with cold water. It was that or let Opal and the girl see everything— *everything*—in her burning cheeks and hot eyes.

"Are you feeling all right, Jossie?" Opal asked, managing to sound concerned and amused, both at once.

Joslyn remained with her back to the room, her face dripping cold well water, and turned off the faucet. "No," she said, though it wasn't an entirely truthful answer, because, overheated as she was, there was also a strange and very powerful sense of jubilant anticipation building inside her. "I think I might be coming down with something."

She forced herself to turn around, swabbing at her face with a wad of paper towels plucked from the roll on the counter, just in time to lock gazes with Slade.

Still standing behind the kitchen chair over by the table, he looked back at her over one broad shoulder, his eyes twinkling. "Maybe you ought to go right to bed," he said easily.

If Joslyn had been closer, and if she'd been inclined toward physical violence, which she wasn't, thank you very much, she'd have slapped Sheriff Slade Barlow across the face. Hard.

"Well," Opal said, mercifully ebullient, "I like what I see. Shea's a fine girl, and this house needs me. If that job offer is still open, I accept."

Slade turned back to face Opal. "When can you start?" he asked.

Shea gave a squeal of delight, and Jasper added a happy yelp.

"Tomorrow," Opal replied, looking around again, taking in the boxes and the groceries and all the rest. "And that's none too soon, from the looks of this place."

Slade laughed. "Fine," he said, while Joslyn remained behind him, leaning against the counter, trying to recover her composure.

"Tomorrow?" she finally managed. "Opal, you just got to Parable—"

"And I'll *be* here, which means you and I will have plenty of chances to get together," Opal reasoned kindly. With that, she turned to Slade. "I'll need a car of some kind," she added. She'd never been shy. "A station wagon or a van will do. It doesn't have to be new, but I can't drive anything but an automatic."

"Done," Slade said.

"Now," Opal continued, rubbing her hands together, "where will I sleep?"

Shea and Slade conferred at that

point, agreeing that the big bedroom down the hall from the kitchen would probably be best for Opal.

"But there's only one bathroom in this whole place," Shea contributed, looking worried, in case that turned out to be a deal breaker.

"I reckon we'll manage," Opal replied gently.

Looking at Opal and Shea, the way they interacted even though they'd just met, gave Joslyn a sweet pang in the innermost regions of her heart. She saw her own younger self in the girl, a stepdaughter as she herself had been, never completely sure where she fit into the structure of the family, very much in need of the older woman's strong, steady affection and quiet attentiveness.

"Can I drive the station wagon, too?" Shea wanted to know. "I have my license, you know."

"If you're with Opal or me," Slade told the child. "Like I said before, I want to see what kind of driver you are before I turn you loose on Parable County."

Shea waved her stepfather's words

off with a dismissive motion of one hand, but her eyes told a different story. She adored the man.

"I suppose you're going to be just as stubborn about the horse," Shea challenged next, setting her hands on her hips.

"Maybe even more so," Slade said.

Shea gave a put-upon sigh, but the light in her eyes shone as brightly as ever. "I'm getting a horse," she told Opal and Joslyn excitedly. "Of my *own.* Dad's buying one for himself, too. We have to keep them at Whisper Creek, though, because our barn is unsafe."

By then, Joslyn was ready to flee. She was flushed and achy and anxious, and it surely showed on the outside.

Anyway, Slade was using up all the air in the room, leaving her breathless. Joslyn heard his voice in her head. *I have a few suggestions.* A hot shiver went through her. "We'd better be getting back to town," she said.

"I made up a batch of my special spaghetti and meatball casserole this afternoon," Opal announced to all and sundry. "Slade, why don't you and Shea come, too, and sit down to supper with us. It'll give you a chance to sample my cooking."

Joslyn fastened her gaze to the floor. Slade *I-have-a-few-suggestions* Barlow, in close proximity? Probably for several hours? Yikes!

"Yes!" Shea chimed in.

"Thanks, Opal," Slade said thoughtfully. Joslyn knew he was looking at her—she could feel it—but for the life of her she couldn't raise her eyes to meet his. "If you're sure it wouldn't be any trouble—"

"No trouble," Opal said, beaming.

Give me strength, Joslyn thought. Then she made herself smile in a way that took in both Slade and Shea, and she nodded, said stupidly, "Good—that will be—nice."

"Okay," Slade said, more breathing the word than speaking it. "Give us half an hour to get cleaned up, and we'll be on our way."

"We'll eat at Kendra's," Opal specified, as Shea hurried off, Jasper clattering after her, probably so she could stake first claim on the bathroom.

"We'll be there," Slade confirmed.

Joslyn scurried for the back door and practically ran to the car.

"Girl," Opal demanded, when she caught up and settled herself into the passenger seat. "What's gotten into you? You ran out of that kitchen like it was on fire."

It was, Joslyn thought. *We're talking flash point here.*

"You're imagining things," she replied, without so much as a glance in Opal's direction.

Opal gave a low chortle. "Oh, no, I'm not," she said.

All the way back to town, Joslyn racked her brain.

What was she going to *wear?*

The bathroom was still steamy from Shea's recent shower when Slade's turn came. He stood in front of the sink, wiped a circle in the glass door of the medicine cabinet and looked into his own face, five o'clock shadow and all.

"Who are you?" he asked, his tone gruff. "And what have you done with Slade Barlow?"

Damned if he hadn't practically *tack-led* Joslyn out there in the kitchen earlier, kissing her the way he had. *Twice.*

Not only that, but he'd talked some trash, too. All but told Joslyn straight out that he meant to bed her at the first viable opportunity. That much was true, but still. He could have been subtler about it.

He turned away from his scowling image, shoving a hand through his gritty, sweat-dampened hair, and leaned into the shower stall to turn the faucets on, full blast. Stripped while he waited for the spray to go from freezing cold to lukewarm—Shea had already emptied the hot water tank, apparently.

The pipes rattled behind the wall, reminding him that this was an old house, and there were thousands of things that could go wrong with it.

Grimly, Slade stepped under the showerhead, reached for a bar of soap and lathered himself from head to foot. Stood still as the chilly water sluiced over him, rinsing away the suds.

He supposed a semi-cold shower was just what he needed—and deserved. He'd been so hard it hurt while he was kissing Joslyn and for a while afterward, too.

And now he'd agreed to go to supper at her place. He was a sucker for punishment, it seemed.

Out of the shower, he dried off quickly, shaved and put on the fresh clothes he'd gathered and then stacked on the lid of the toilet a few minutes earlier—jeans, a blue cotton shirt, boots.

When he reached the kitchen, Shea was there, pouring Jasper's supper into a bowl and setting it down on the floor. She was wearing an actual skirt, a short, ruffled thing, white with black polka dots, and a black top.

"There's no bed in Opal's room, you know," Shea said. "We're going to have to shop again, unless you expect her to sleep on the floor."

Slade groaned at the prospect of another mall crawl, but he was grinning the whole time. He was foolishly happy, despite the jittery sensation in the pit of his stomach. "Hook up that fancy new computer we bought and order something online," he said. "Get the sheets and any other rigging you need while you're at it."

Shea looked at him curiously and with a degree of suspicion. "You're awfully free with your money for somebody who refuses to pay my cell phone bill," she told him. "What's the deal here?"

He laughed. "I'm not broke, Shea. Just careful."

"Did you win the lottery or something?" Shea pressed. Like her mother, she never let a subject drop until she was through beating it to death.

Slade found his keys, jingled them to indicate that it was time to leave. "It's the magic of compound interest," he teased. Since his inheritance still didn't seem real to him, he was hesitant to talk about it. "The habit is out of fashion these days, but they call it *saving.*"

Shea rolled her eyes, but a smile lurked at the corners of her mouth. "Don't moralize," she said. "And *anyway,* Mom and I are on the family plan, for the cell phones, I mean. She automatically pays for my service right along with hers."

"Then you can reimburse her," Slade

said, enjoying the exchange. He said goodbye to Jasper, who barely looked up from his kibble, and then he and Shea headed for the truck. "Speaking of that, how did things go at the Curly-Burly?"

Shea had gone to his mother's hair salon to apply for work, but they had yet to discuss the outcome.

"I'm hired, as if you didn't already know," Shea replied breezily. In the middle of the yard, she made a dive for Slade's keys. He held them out of her reach. "Why can't I drive?" his stepdaughter fussed. "I take Mom's car all over Los Angeles and I've never even had a warning, let alone a speeding ticket or an accident. And, besides, this is *Parable*. What can possibly happen?"

"You'd be surprised," Slade said, getting behind the wheel. Parable was a peaceful community—there were only three traffic lights in the whole county—but bad things happened everywhere.

Shea flounced up into the passenger seat, pouting a little. "I don't think a cow crossing the road would surprise me, Dad," she said with such studied disdain that he laughed again. "Especially when it probably only happens every third blue moon."

"Tell me about the job," Slade said, starting the truck and steering it down the long, rutted driveway toward the main road.

"I'll be sweeping up *hair,*" Shea said, with another roll of her eyes. "What's to tell?"

"There must be more to it than that," Slade persisted. He figured it was important to talk with kids, however mundane the subject matter, and Layne's accusation that he hadn't listened to her during their marriage was on his mind, too. He didn't want to make the same mistake with Shea, especially when they had such a short time together.

"I'll be washing out sinks, too," Shea replied. "And setting up appointments. And if I can drag Grands into the twenty-first century—in other words, if she'll spring for a computer—I can streamline the whole operation for her. Build her a website and everything."

"You can do that? Build a website?"

Slade was impressed. He used computers at work, of course, but the new desktop he and Shea and Layne had picked up on the big shopping expedition was only the second one he'd ever owned personally. The first was a dinosaur that took forever to boot up.

"Yes," Shea said. "I'm not stupid, you know."

That seemed to be a theme with her. "Nobody said you were," Slade answered. "I probably couldn't build a website if my life depended on it, and I'm not stupid, either."

"There are all kinds of templates and stuff," Shea said, but she looked guardedly eager now. "I could show you."

Templates?

"Okay," Slade answered. "I'd like that."

"You mean it? Or are you just humoring me?"

"Why would I want to humor you?"

"I don't know," Shea responded. "But I've never known you to talk this much, and that makes me think you're up to something."

Slade didn't comment. He just grinned.

Shea continued to speculate. "And then there's the money thing, and the way you and Joslyn looked all startled and messed up and stuff, when Opal and I came downstairs after I showed her around the house. You know what I think? I *think* the two of you were kissing."

The kid had gotten under his skin, no doubt about it, and he hoped she didn't notice that his ears were hot or the way his fingers tightened on the wheel.

"It's a free country," he managed after a beat or two. "Think what you like."

Shea laughed. "Don't look so shocked, Dad," she said. "The cat's already out of the bag. Right after we got back to the Best Western hotel, that night when we ran into Joslyn at the Butter Biscuit, Mom told me she thought you had a thing for her."

Slade said nothing. Didn't so much as glance away from the white line running down the middle of the county highway.

"Have you asked Joslyn out yet, Dad?"

Slade cleared his throat. He had to

say something if he wanted to keep the lines of communication open between himself and Shea, and he wanted that very much. He just wished they could change the subject, that was all. "She's going to the auction with us on Saturday morning," he said.

"You told me that already," Shea said patiently. "Dad? Hello? That isn't a *date.*"

Slade swore under his breath. "Maybe it's the best I could do on short notice," he answered.

"Now that's just pitiful," Shea decreed. "If the two of you went to dinner and a movie, or out dancing, *that* would be a date. Even if you took a horseback ride together, and maybe picnicked someplace where there was a view. But a *horse sale?* Dad, that is definitely *not* romantic."

"Does it have to be?" Slade asked, slowing for the outskirts of town. Off to his right, he spotted Lyle striding down the sidewalk, wearing his hair-growing helmet. The lights flashed in cheerful sequence, like on a Christmas tree.

Lyle smiled and waved as they passed.

Slade tooted the horn in response.

Happily, Shea was distracted from her lecture about what does and does not constitute a date. Her mouth fell open, and she watched Lyle, with his head full of LED lights twinkling away, until he disappeared into the blind spot. Then she spun around on her seat to confront Slade.

"Dad," she said. "We just saw a guy with blue lights on his head. And you just *drive on by?* What kind of sheriff are you?"

Slade smiled. "Far as I know, eccentricity isn't illegal in this state. I wouldn't have thought you'd be all that surprised by a man in a light-up helmet, given where you live."

"We have our share of grandmothers with battery-powered sweatshirts," Shea explained solemnly, "especially around Christmas. But *this* guy—"

"His name is Lyle," Slade said easily. "And he's harmless."

"He's weird."

"As I said, that's not a crime."

She favored him with one of her dazzling smiles. "Not here in Mayberry, anyway?" she joked.

"Not here in Mayberry," Slade confirmed with a grin, downshifting to make the turn onto Rodeo Road.

When they pulled into Kendra's driveway beside her imposing house, Shea sucked in an audible breath. "Holy sh—crap," she blurted, taking in the sights.

"Nice save," Slade said, stopping the truck, shutting off the engine.

Opal immediately appeared in the doorway of the screened sunporch, beaming as though they'd just come home from some war unscathed, and she'd been waiting to welcome them for the duration.

Slade wondered where Joslyn was—if she'd thought of some excuse to skip supper, annoyed because he'd put the moves on her back there in the ranch house kitchen—but Shea leaped out of the truck and hurried along the walk toward Opal.

"We're here!" she announced, quite unnecessarily.

Slade smiled to himself. For all that she was sixteen and growing up in a pretty sophisticated environment in L.A., there was still a lot of the child in Shea. He hoped that would never change.

"Come on in," Opal called, beckoning with one hand. She wore a ruffled apron over her dress and sported an oven mitt on one hand. "Supper's just about ready."

Slade's stomach rumbled slightly. Although he'd never sampled Opal's fare, having been the kid who mowed the lawn and weeded the flower beds when she worked for the Rossiters, he'd heard plenty about it over the years.

Back then, when the weather was hot, she'd always brought him out a pitcher full of her tangy lemonade, though, the sides slippery with condensation and the ice making a festive sound as she walked across the grass. He'd thanked her quietly, waited until she'd gone back inside the big house, and foresworn the glass, drinking thirstily straight from the spout of the pitcher.

The recollection made him chuckle.

Shea slipped past Opal and went on

into the house, but Opal lingered on the step, watching Slade approach.

"Joslyn's out in the guest cottage," Opal said with a gesture in that direction. The older woman was doing her level best to look and sound stern, but her gentle eyes sparked with mischief and amusement. "Lord knows what she's doing, since the place was already scrubbed to a high shine when I got here and I haven't had time to dirty it up none. Would you mind telling Joslyn that supper is about to go on the table and we'd appreciate the honor of her company?"

The sensation that swelled in Slade's middle wasn't hunger, not this time. It was pure nerves with a generous helping of anticipation. "Sure," he said, turning to head toward the cottage.

The cottage's side door stood open, and he rapped lightly at the door frame, much as he had the last time, when he'd followed Jasper over from next door.

"Come in," Joslyn called from somewhere inside.

He stepped over the threshold, waited

for his eyes to adjust from the bright sunlight outside to the cool shadows of the interior. "Joslyn?"

"Here," she said.

He followed the sound of her voice into the tiny living room and was mildly surprised to find Joslyn standing at the top of a shaky foot ladder, replacing a lightbulb in the old-fashioned fixture hanging from the ceiling. Instinctively, he went over and steadied the ladder.

She was wearing a pale pink sundress, and her legs were bare to the knees, smooth and smelling faintly of lotion.

He didn't dare let his gaze travel any farther than the hem of that dress. *Woman,* he thought, averting his eyes and gripping the ladder as if he expected a high wind at any moment, *are you* trying *to drive me crazy?*

"Got it," she said happily, starting down the ladder.

The mingled scents of soap and shower water and that lotion dazed him a little, and she brushed against him as she stepped to the floor.

"Opal said to tell you supper's on,"

he said and then felt three kinds of stupid. First he'd invited the woman to a livestock auction as if it was some kind of black-tie affair, and then he'd all but groped her in his kitchen—

And now this.

At this rate, she'd write him off as a hick at any moment, if she hadn't already done so.

Joslyn's smile made something flutter in his chest, and she stepped back, spreading her hands a little. "How do you like my dress?" she asked, her tone shy and a little reckless, both at once. "I borrowed it from Kendra's closet."

Slade opened his mouth, closed it again.

"I like it fine," he said finally, tongue-tied fool that he was. What had happened to that *other,* bolder Slade?

"Of course I'll have to be careful not to get any of Opal's spaghetti sauce on it," Joslyn fretted, patches of pink blooming on her cheekbones as she looked down at the soft confection of a dress. "It's probably expensive, knowing Kendra. Maybe I should change into something of my own?"

Slade imagined that cotton-candy garment being pulled off over her head. What a revelation that would be.

"Uh, I think it's all right—" he stumbled. *Oh, it's better than "all right."* "I mean, you look nice and everything."

"Good," she said and started toward the doorway, dusting her hands together. She stopped next to the switch and flipped the light on and off a couple of times, evidently admiring her handiwork. "There," she added. "That's better."

Slade automatically retrieved the stepladder, folding it and then leaving it against the wall because he didn't know where it went, and he felt foolish enough already, all things considered.

"Let's go," she said. "Opal is a terror if the food gets cold."

Slade followed her out of the cottage and into the yard where the first long shadows of twilight were just beginning to spill across the ground.

A strange, sweet pain gripped him somewhere deep inside and held on. "Joslyn?" he said.

A few feet ahead of him, she stopped,

turned her head to look back at him over one perfect, almost bare shoulder. "Yes?"

He'd been on the verge of apologizing for what had happened earlier out at his place, but seeing her standing there with the light shimmering through the borrowed dress and playing in the rich brown silk of her hair, he knew he couldn't say he was sorry, because that would be a lie.

He was sorry they weren't spending the evening alone.

He was sorry he didn't have his half brother's legendary way with women.

But he was *not* sorry for stating his intention to seduce her, because that hadn't changed.

"You look beautiful," he said instead.

CHAPTER FIFTEEN

For Joslyn, the meal in Kendra's enormous kitchen passed in a haze. She barely tasted Opal's famous spaghetti and meatball casserole—always one of her favorites—and she caught only a word or two of the conversation here and there.

Her mind, her body and all her senses were focused on the man seated next to her at the table—Opal's doing, of course—and if she hadn't known it earlier when he kissed her, she knew for sure now.

Slade Barlow was absolutely, definitely, inevitably going to make love to her.

And she was not only going to let him, she was going to respond with everything she had.

There was a strange, jangly kind of peace in this dazed clarity, along with a helpless sensation that frightened her a little. Joslyn felt like an asteroid straying too close to a massive black hole— once she was into this, whatever it was, she might never find her way back out again.

No matter what came afterward—in her mind, she capitalized *Afterward*— whether she moved away from Parable or got married to somebody else and had ten children or joined a convent, a part of her would always belong to the current sheriff of Parable County.

Lust, that's all it was, she insisted to herself. Just lust, not love. It *couldn't* be love. Not that she was an expert on the subject or anything.

Still, seeing Slade's dark hair damp from the shower and catching the clean scent of his skin and his clothes, she was ravenous, but not for food. This was a whole new kind of hunger, one she'd never experienced before.

And, she rationalized to herself, she was a mature woman, with healthy emotional and physical needs, and the birth control device she'd had implanted a year before, when she'd been briefly involved with a man she met at work, was still standing guard at the entrance to her womb.

Furthermore, she'd been alone, and lonely, for far too long, working ridiculous hours and living for one objective: to repay the people her stepfather had cheated so she could get past the whole thing, put it behind her once and for all and move on.

But move on to where? To do what, exactly? She hadn't thought that far ahead, not in any depth at least. Nor had she counted on Slade complicating her life.

She bit her lower lip and tried hard to tune in as Shea and Opal chatted about ordinary things, movies they'd both seen or wanted to see, a shared and generally secret penchant for bowling, and what to name the new horse. Slade,

Joslyn noticed, wasn't any more talk-
ative than she was, but that was normal
for him, wasn't it?

Eventually, the meal ended.

Opal reciprocated for Shea's tour of
the ranch house by offering one of the
mansion, a proposal Shea eagerly accepted.

Which left Slade and Joslyn alone together. Again.

Slade cleared his throat, as if he
meant to say something, but then he
looked away, stood up and started
clearing the table.

Joslyn posted herself at the sink, rinsing plates and silverware and glasses
before putting them into the dishwasher.

Given that the mansion was probably
five times the size of the rented ranch
house and taking Opal's fondness for
matchmaking into account, Joslyn reasoned, they'd be alone for a while.

Silently, when the kitchen was tidy
again, Slade took Joslyn's hand and led
her outside, into the cool fragrance of
the yard.

It still wasn't dark, but the moon was
out, full and fat and silvery, and the sky

was speckled with stars. They sat side by side on the steps of the sunporch, and Joslyn drew in the smells of freshly cut grass and the wide variety of flowers gracing Kendra's garden.

Slade was still holding her hand, their fingers interlocked.

"Do you ever miss this house—living here, I mean?" he asked.

Joslyn hadn't expected that question—didn't know *what* she'd expected.

She shook her head. "Not really," she replied presently, not looking at him, because she knew he might see too much in her eyes if she did. "We were happy enough here as a family, at least until—well, until everything came out, but the place never really belonged to me in any real way. It was my stepfather's home—looking back, it seems to me that Mom and I were sort of *temporary,* like pampered guests at some high-end spa."

His mouth crooked up at one corner, and she wanted to touch his hair, trace the strong line of his jaw and find the slight cleft in his chin with her fingertip. But she was content, for now, to hold his hand—the connection was charged, but it also seemed perfectly natural.

"If it were any of my business," Slade said quietly, rubbing a calloused thumb lightly over her knuckles, blissfully unaware, no doubt, that he was awakening senses in her that went far beyond the original five, "I'd ask Kendra straight out what she wants with this big place. She probably rattles around in it like a buckshot pellet in the bottom of a pail."

Joslyn smiled at the quaintness of the comparison and recalled the general outlines of Kendra's childhood, joined, as it had been, to her own. Kendra had grown up in her grandmother's cluttered double-wide, just barely on the right side of the railroad tracks, constantly reminded that she was underfoot, in the way, an unavoidable liability. She hadn't been physically abused, as far as Joslyn knew, but she'd certainly been neglected, tolerated at best. Not loved.

Any affection Kendra had received came from kindly teachers and from Opal, Joslyn's mother, Dana, and from

Joslyn herself. She'd had few friends, except for them.

Even as a little girl, Kendra had been ethereally beautiful, somehow wistful, like a lost fairy princess trying to find her way home to some faraway, enchanted land. Kendra had wanted to own this grand house, Joslyn guessed, because she'd been loved there, wanted and welcome.

"I think Kendra planned on filling the place with children," Joslyn heard herself explaining. "And living happily ever after with Jeffrey."

An instant after she'd spoken, Joslyn regretted blurting out something her friend would surely consider personal and private.

"Except the marriage didn't work out," Slade said, still caressing Joslyn's knuckles. "That's a problem I can relate to."

Joslyn felt a quickening inside. "Was it hard?" she asked. "Getting divorced, I mean?" Talk about your dumb question, she chided herself silently. When had getting a divorce ever been easy?

Slade glanced briefly back over one

shoulder, as if he expected Shea to be standing somewhere nearby, listening in. Then he sighed. "It was hard," he confirmed.

"What happened?" Joslyn couldn't resist asking, her voice soft.

He sighed, looking out at the gathering twilight, the garden and the lawn and the guesthouse. And still holding her hand.

"Nothing drastic," he answered after Joslyn had had a few moments to wish, yet again, that she'd kept her mouth shut.

Slade sighed, turned his head, looked down into her eyes. "Divorce is a strange thing," he replied quietly. "In my case, at least, it wasn't so much being apart from Layne that made it tough, but losing Shea, and never knowing the other kids Layne and I *would* have had if we'd stayed together."

It seemed only right to rest her head against the side of his upper arm. A perfect fit. "Life never seems to turn out the way we planned, does it?" she asked, thinking of all the things she'd put off so she could throw herself into the all-consuming task of making up for someone else's mistake.

The sudden awareness that she'd stepped out of her own life to make those amends, that she'd essentially abandoned herself, left her stricken and a little sick at heart.

All the time, she'd believed she was doing the right thing—she *still* believed the bilked investors had deserved to get their money back—but what had she sacrificed in the meantime? What had she missed out on?

"What was *your* plan, Joslyn?" Slade asked, and even though it was an uncomfortable question, it broke the spell of confused remorse that had gripped her moments before.

She sighed. "I didn't have one for a long time," she replied, lifting her head, sitting up straight, tugging the hem of Kendra's dress down over her knees. "It was all about coping, getting by. Surviving, I guess."

"Sounds grim."

"It wasn't so bad," Joslyn said. "Just not fulfilling."

Just empty. Just lonely. Just march-

ing in place while who knew how many chances to be happy went by.

"Define *fulfilling,*" Slade urged, with a spark of humor catching like starlight in his eyes.

"A career to be proud of—a home and a family—" Joslyn blushed, afraid she'd said too much. It certainly wouldn't have been the first time, after all. "What about you? What fulfills you, Slade?"

He thought for a long time. "I used to think I wanted to be sheriff until I reached retirement age," he finally said. "Now, I'm not so sure. It's going to sound crazy, but I'd like to work up an honest sweat every day, driving cattle, digging post holes, stringing wire, pounding nails. I guess I'm a throwback to the Old West, just like one of my deputies said."

"You want to be a rancher," Joslyn observed rhetorically, absorbing the knowledge.

"That's pretty much the size of it, yeah."

She smiled. "But you still can't make up your mind whether or not to buy the place where you're living now," she said.

Something changed in his face, hardened along the lines of his jaw. For a moment, Joslyn thought he was going to stand up and walk away, leaving her sitting there by herself, but, once again, he surprised her.

"As you probably know, John Carmody was my biological father. Turns out he left me half of Whisper Creek Ranch and a considerable sum of money when he died. I don't care about the money—I still haven't decided against giving it back or passing it on to some charity—but that ranch? It's symbolic, I guess, of everything I never had."

Joslyn simply watched and waited, amazed that he'd share something this intimate with her. He probably didn't know Hutch had already sketched in the outlines of the situation for her.

"Hutch has been trying to buy me out since the will was read," Slade went on. "We finally agreed to decide the matter with a horse race. He wins, I sell him my share and walk away and Whisper Creek is all his."

"And if you win?"

"I get the main house, he lives elsewhere on the ranch, and we run the outfit together, Hutch and I," he replied.

"Which is why you're going to that livestock auction on Saturday," Joslyn ventured, uneasy. What if Slade—or Hutch—got hurt or even killed in this horse race?

"Partly," Slade answered. "I doubt if there'll be any Thoroughbreds on offer, but you never know. Mostly, I'm going because I promised Shea a horse. The responsibility will be good for her."

She remembered something Shea had said earlier—that she and her dad would have to keep their horses at Whisper Creek because they couldn't use their own rickety barn.

Which would mean Hutch and Slade would be running into each other constantly, even before the stupid race took place. Given their volatile history, those repeated encounters might be more dangerous than the race itself.

She pulled her hand away. "That's crazy," she said.

Slade arched one eyebrow. "Buying Shea a horse?"

"No," Joslyn said tautly, stiffening her

spine and raising her chin. "I'm talking about the horse race. It's an insane idea, Slade."

"Tell that to Hutch," Slade said, letting go of her hand. "He's the one who came up with it."

Joslyn bristled. "I would have expected you to have more common sense than Hutch," she told him.

"Thanks," Slade said. "I guess."

"I mean, of the two of you, you've always been the practical one—"

"Maybe that's the problem," Slade mused aloud, getting to his feet. Reaching down to help her to hers. "Maybe I've been *too* practical."

In the next moment, he shocked her again—by pulling her close and kissing her, gently at first, then hard and deep.

As frustrated as she was, she melted against him, incapable of pulling away. It galled Joslyn to know that if he'd swept her up in his arms, carried her across the yard to the guest cottage and had his way with her, she wouldn't have offered a word of protest.

Even more galling was the fact that *he* was the one in control here.

Presently, he let her go, moved past her and crossed the darkened sunporch to step into the kitchen.

"Shea!" he called. "It's time to head for home."

Joslyn remained where she was, listening as Shea issued a good-natured protest, and Opal accepted Slade's polite thanks for the meal she'd prepared. And then she dashed for the guest cottage, to avoid saying good-night to their guests.

She waited in the dark cottage until she heard Slade's truck start up, drive away, tires crunching on the gravel.

When Joslyn returned to the main house, Opal was sitting at the table, sipping a cup of raspberry tea. Lucy-Maude was curled up in her lap, and Opal stroked the cat with her free hand, making her purr.

"Where did you run off to?" Opal asked, peering fretfully at Joslyn. "You didn't even say goodbye to our company."

Since Joslyn didn't have an excuse for disappearing, she didn't offer one.

Instead, she shook her head, sighed

and made herself a cup of raspberry tea, joining Opal at the table.

Opal, thank heaven, did not continue the lecture.

Slade was up long after Shea had disappeared into her room with her cell phone. He tore down the bed he'd just bought, maneuvered all the parts, including the mattress and box spring, down the stairs and into the room that would be Opal's.

There, he put it back together.

That job done, he dug out the air mattress he'd slept on at the duplex, carried it up to his room and plugged it in to power the pump.

There was a whooshing sound as the mattress inflated, and Jasper, seated in the doorway, looked wary of the whole process.

Once the too-familiar mattress was full, Slade threw on a couple of sheets and tossed his pillows in that direction also.

Then he shoved a hand through his hair and sighed, looking at Jasper again. He needed more to do if he was going to keep thoughts of Joslyn at bay, but short of adding on a room or building a barn, he was out of options. Immediate ones, at least.

"One more trip to the yard," he told his dog, "and we'll turn in."

Jasper seemed to understand; he trotted happily down the back stairway and across the kitchen to the door. There, he waited with his muzzle pressed to the crack while Slade caught up to him.

While Jasper explored the grass, Slade stood with his head tilted back, taking in the moon and stars. They'd seemed a little brighter and a lot closer to earth before, he thought, when he and Joslyn were looking up at them together.

The night was quiet, except for crickets chirping and the faint murmur of the creek down over the hill. In the distance, the lights of Boone Taylor's place gleamed, and beyond them, just the merest twinkle of a glow came from Tara's chicken farm.

Idly, Slade wondered how Boone was getting along with his new neighbor. A loner by nature, Boone had considered buying the chicken farm himself, just so nobody could move in next door.

Now, obviously, it was too late for that.

The thought made Slade smile, albeit a little sadly. It would be a good thing if Boone took a shine to Tara—he'd done nothing but work since his wife died a couple of years ago—it was time old Boone did some socializing.

Like you've got any room to talk, Slade reminded himself. From the day his divorce from Layne was final up to now, he hadn't done much "socializing" either. He'd picked up a few women, always in other towns, even other counties, but that had been more about sex than anything else—he couldn't recall even one of their names.

And now there was Joslyn. He'd never wanted any other woman the way he wanted her—not even Layne.

It scared him a little, the intensity of it, and while he wasn't the timid sort, he *was* a bit gun-shy. Joslyn, unlike everybody since Layne, was someone he could care about. She was smart—the

workings of her mind intrigued him almost as much as the lushness of her
body—and when she smiled at him, it
was like being knighted by the beautiful
queen of some finer, gentler realm.

But it wasn't love. He'd have known if
it was.

That decided, he whistled for Jasper,
and the dog came back to him, tongue
lolling. They went inside, but Slade still
wasn't ready to sleep.

So he took the new computer out of
its box and set it up on the kitchen table, for want of a better place. He
opened another box to find the router
and still another that contained the
printer. The instructions might have
been written by a dyslexic Martian, but
after several cups of strong coffee and
a lot of swearing under his breath, Slade
managed to get the contraption up and
running.

It was after midnight when Shea padded downstairs in her nightgown, patting back a yawn with one hand, to join
him in the kitchen.

"Dad? Do you realize it's the middle
of the night?" she asked, bending to

pat Jasper, who got to his feet and went to greet her. "What are you *doing?*"

"What does it look like I'm doing?" Slade countered reasonably, amused by the parental tone she'd taken.

"Don't you have to work tomorrow?"

Slade grinned, scraped back his chair, stood and carried his cup to the sink. "Yes," he answered, "I do. But I got to wondering if I could put this computer together and get it online, a backwoods rube like me, and then I had to find out, one way or the other."

Shea stood a few feet away, her arms folded. "Why don't you just admit it?" she countered. "You can't stop thinking about Joslyn Kirk. That's the *real* reason you aren't asleep."

He sighed. "Go back to bed, Shea. You'll need your strength, putting in a full day at the Curly-Burly tomorrow."

She made a rueful face, though her eyes, as usual, were smiling. "How much strength does it take to sweep up hair?" she retorted.

"Plenty," Slade said. "My mother believes in hard work—her own, and yours."

"I was thinking of taking the day off, actually," Shea announced, in a tone that said she was testing the waters. "You know, so I could stay here and help Opal get settled, put her things away and everything—"

Slade halted his stepdaughter's speech with a raised index finger. "One second," he interrupted. "You only *started* work this morning. Now, you want to take tomorrow off?"

"Special circumstances," Shea pointed out. "*You'll* be patrolling the county all day, ignoring people with electric helmets on their heads and whatever else you do. Who's going to make Opal feel welcome?"

"Opal," Slade said, in wry truth, "can take care of herself. I told her I'd leave the door unlocked in the morning, and it's pretty obvious what needs to be done around here." He spread his arms, indicating the clutter surrounding them both.

It was weird how he'd gotten by with so little stuff living at the duplex, and now, all of a sudden, he was surrounded by *things.*

"She doesn't even have a car," Shea persisted. Slade saw law school in her future; she was born to argue any case, no matter how flimsy. "How is she supposed to get out here in the first place?"

"Opal told me at supper that her friend Martie will drive her out," Slade answered with exaggerated patience. "And I've already got a line on a good used car for her to use in the future—Boone offered to sell me his late wife's compact. Now will you go back to bed?"

Shea hauled back a chair at the table and plunked herself down on the seat. "Sure, Dad," she said. "When you turn in, I'll do the same." A pause. "Did you say 'late,' just now? You're buying Opal a dead person's car?"

"As far as I know," Slade said, "it isn't haunted." Sadness touched the center of his heart, though, remembering Boone's pretty bride, Corrine. They'd been high school sweethearts, Boone and Corrine, "joined at the hip," as Callie liked to say, apart only when Boone served his hitch in the Marines.

Corrine had died a couple of years ago of breast cancer—at the age of thirty-two. Boone hadn't been the same since, and who could blame him?

"Stubborn," Slade said, shaking his head, bringing his attention back to his stepdaughter. "You're *stubborn.*"

"Believe it," Shea responded. "You'd almost think I was a Barlow."

Slade sighed again. Thrust a hand through his hair—again.

So that was it. There was still some breath and a heartbeat in the subject of the adoption that never happened, so she wanted to kick it around a little longer.

"Shea," he said, his voice quiet, "I can't change the past. I can't go back in time and adopt you, as much as I wish that were possible."

She was quiet for a long time. Then she asked, very softly, "What about now? Why couldn't you adopt me *now?*"

"Shea, that probably isn't even possible now that your mom and I are divorced. The legal complications boggle the mind—and besides, I don't think your mom would agree to that anyway."

"How do you know if you don't ask her?"

"Sweetheart, your real dad isn't going to win any prizes for parenthood, but he's out there somewhere. And even if your mom wanted to let me adopt you, this guy has rights where you're concerned."

"What rights? He was a sperm donor."

"Your mother was *married* to him, Shea."

"No, she wasn't."

"Of course she was."

Shea shook her head, and the expression in her eyes was obstinate. "I saw some paperwork—something to do with security clearance, so Mom can travel with Bentley sometimes after they're married—and it said Mom had had one husband. Count 'em. *One.* And that husband was you, Dad."

Slade frowned. Soon after he and Layne had met, she'd told him about Shea's natural father—said she'd known the guy in college, that they'd eloped, realized they'd made a mistake and parted ways, all within a few months. He'd known Layne was pregnant, this yahoo, and said he wasn't ready to take on the responsibility of a family.

At the time, Slade hadn't cared about his wife's past—only the present they shared and their future together. Responsibility? Bring it on.

Except there hadn't *been* a future together.

"It was a short marriage, Shea," he finally answered. "Maybe, in your mother's mind, it didn't count as the real thing."

"Oh, great. So that means *I* don't count? *I'm* not 'the real thing,' either?"

"I didn't say that," Slade said. Obviously, this wasn't going to be a short conversation—or an easy one. He took a chair at the table, reached out to take Shea's hand, give her fingers a brief squeeze. "Of course you count."

"Then adopt me."

"Shea—"

"At least *ask* Mom about it, Dad."

Slade took a moment to collect his thoughts. "Why is this so important to you, Shea? You're not a little girl anymore—in a couple of years, you'll be in college."

"It's important," Shea said, her eyes

filling with tears, "because once Mom and Bentley are married, with you mostly out of the picture, I'll be *his* stepdaughter. And he's a big advocate of me going to boarding school in the fall."

The truth hurts, Slade reflected glumly. He'd seen little of Shea since the divorce, mostly because of the distance between Montana and Southern California, and he wished he'd made more of an effort.

"An adoption is pretty much out of the question," he said. "But, tell you what, I'll ask your mother if you can stay here in Parable for the coming school year. How would that be?"

Shea sighed heavily. "Better than nothing, I guess," she conceded. Then she perked up again as another idea struck her. "What if you and Mom got back together? You could adopt me then, couldn't you?"

"That isn't going to happen, Shea," Slade said gently, wondering how long the kid had been hoping he and Layne would reconcile. From the beginning, probably. "The deal is, if your mother agrees, you can go to school here next year instead of that other place. Take it or leave it."

Shea considered the offer. "You think she'd say yes—let me stay with you, I mean?"

"She's letting you spend the summer."

Shea's face brightened. "Better than nothing," she decided aloud.

"Gee, thanks," Slade gestured.

"You'll ask Mom?"

"I'll ask her. Tomorrow."

Shea bounded out of her chair, threw her arms around his neck and hugged him. Then she stood back. "You won't regret this, Dad."

Slade laughed, but the sound was throaty, more like a cough. "Go to bed," he told her.

She kissed the top of his head. "Thanks, Dad," she told him.

And that was the whole conversation.

Without further argument, Shea went back upstairs to her room.

Jasper followed, stopping at the base of the steps to look questioningly back at Slade.

"Go ahead," Slade told the dog.

Jasper clattered up the stairs behind Shea.

And Slade sat alone in the kitchen for a while after they'd gone, thinking things through.

When, after almost an hour, he hadn't come to any new conclusions, he got up, locked the back door, shut off the lights and climbed the stairs where the air mattress waited.

After brushing his teeth and trading his clothes for a pair of sweatpants, comfortably worn, he stretched out on the inflatable bed, stared up at the dark ceiling and cupped his hands behind his head.

Morning would be a long time coming.

When Joslyn wandered out of the maid's quarters the next morning in search of coffee, she found Opal already in the kitchen, fully dressed, coiffed and busy at the stove.

"French toast," Opal announced, with a nod toward the pan she'd been standing over, spatula at the ready.

The aroma was a delicious swirl in

the air—Opal's French toast was special, more like a fried sandwich, always with some tasty filling in the center, like cream cheese and blueberries.

Suddenly hungry, Joslyn padded over to the counter, helped herself to a mug from the hooks Kendra had artfully arranged near the coffeemaker, and poured herself an eye-opener. "You're not supposed to be cooking," she grumbled, well aware that Opal would be taking off for Slade's place that very day and leaving her and Lucy-Maude alone in that big house. Glad as she was that her friend had decided to stay on in Parable, she also felt a little cheated at having their reunion cut short. "You're a guest, remember?"

"Drink that coffee," Opal commanded cheerfully. "Maybe a jolt of caffeine will improve your personality."

Joslyn laughed. "Sorry," she said. "I guess I *am* a little cranky."

"A little?" Opal teased.

Joslyn sat down at the table, the scene of last night's electrified supper with Slade Barlow seated practically at her elbow. Some of the buzz lingered, a silent zip that made her nerves leap under her skin.

"You just got here," she pointed out while Opal continued to supervise the French toast. "And now you're leaving again."

"It's not like I'm going to the ends of the earth, girl," Opal responded, plopping the food onto a plate and bringing it to Joslyn along with a knife, fork and spoon. The syrup had already been set out, though she probably wouldn't mess with perfection by adding any to her French toast. "I'll be just outside of town, and we can see each other whenever we want."

Joslyn took a few more sips from her coffee mug as Lucy-Maude meandered in, tail high and twitching lazily back and forth. She leaned down to stroke the cat once as she passed close to her ankles.

"I know," she said. "It's just—"

Opal refilled her own coffee cup and joined Joslyn at the table. "Just that it's Slade Barlow I'll be keeping house for, and seeing me will mean seeing *him,* too? Is that what you're trying to say?"

Joslyn set her mug down, picked up her fork, regarded her breakfast and laid the utensil back on the table. "I'm glad you're staying in Parable, Opal," she said carefully. "That's what matters. As for Slade, well, it's not like I'm avoiding him or anything. We *are* going to a horse auction together on Saturday."

Opal chuckled, shook her head. She looked younger than she had when she got off the bus in front of the service station, her eyes bright with purpose and mischief and that razor-sharp intuition Joslyn had forgotten the woman possessed. "Last night at supper," she said, "you looked like you were about to jump right out of yourself. So did Slade, though he managed to hide it a little better."

Joslyn sighed. "He makes me nervous," she admitted.

Opal reached over, picked up Joslyn's fork, and placed it in her hand. "Eat," she said. "And between bites, tell me what it is about that man that scares you so much."

One taste of the French toast led to another. It was scrumptious, of course.

And there didn't seem to be any point in trying to steer the conversation away from Slade, since Opal would only steer it right back.

Just the same, the truth—that she wanted him—was just too raw to tell, even to Opal. So she hedged a little.

"He's divorced, and he has a stepdaughter. The situation is complicated."

Opal sighed. "Lots of folks get things wrong the first time out, marriage-wise, and do better when they try again," she said. "Shea lives with her mother most of the year, from what she told me last night, while I was showing her through this big old house, and besides, I don't think she's the kind to cause trouble. As for complications—well, wake up and smell the bacon, girl—*life* is complicated."

Joslyn remembered being part of a stepfamily, how she'd felt different, somehow set apart, from the kids living under the same roof as both their natural parents. She'd been fond of Elliott, thought of him as her dad, but she'd also resented him for taking up so much of her mother's time and attention. Elliott and Dana had traveled a lot when they were married, and even when they'd both been at home, they'd tended to get lost in each other.

They'd tried to have more children, Joslyn knew, and when Dana hadn't conceived, their disappointment had been palpable.

In her little-girl mind, Joslyn reflected, she'd come to the conclusion that she wasn't enough for them. To be completely happy, her mother and stepfather had needed other daughters or sons.

If it hadn't been for Opal, Joslyn thought, still surprised at the insights that had just surfaced in her mind, seemingly out of nowhere, she might have felt as bereft as a child as Kendra had.

"Shea needs Slade's full attention right now," Joslyn observed in belated response to Opal's statement about life being complicated. "They've been apart, and now they're together, and they have to work out how that's going to be. I'd just be another problem to sort out."

Opal's eyes widened, then narrowed.

"A 'problem'? That's all you think you've got to offer that man *or* his daughter?"

"I don't have a place in the equation, Opal," Joslyn answered, believing it with her whole heart. She'd always been the extra puzzle piece, the one that didn't fit with the rest of the picture. "One plus one does not come out to three, no matter how you juggle the numbers."

Opal just stared at her for a long time, shaking her head. "I don't understand you," she said finally. "Jossie-girl, I don't understand you one little bit. Not right now, anyway."

Joslyn had no answer for that. She didn't understand, either.

CHAPTER SIXTEEN

There was a brief flurry of activity when Opal moved to Slade's ranch, driven there, with her one suitcase, by her friend Martie Wren, but then, for Joslyn, it was business as usual.

She worked hard at keeping busy over the next few days, managing Kendra's office as best she could, given her limited knowledge of real estate, responding to emails and answering the telephone, printing out lessons for her online course and gobbling them up practically whole. She'd almost forgotten her innate passion for learning, for experimentation, for discovery.

She'd been ready for hours that Saturday morning, the day of the livestock auction, when she finally heard Slade's truck tires rolling over the snow-white gravel of the driveway, but she took her time answering the brisk knock at the sunporch door.

No need to seem too eager.

And besides, Slade was taking her to a horse sale, not the Cattleman's Ball.

Deciding what to wear had been a no-brainer—jeans, sneakers, a long-sleeved green T-shirt that would protect her arms from sunburn—swipes of lip gloss and mascara for makeup. She'd done her hair up in a ponytail, so it was less likely to stick to her neck if she got sweaty, and borrowed a baseball cap from Kendra's closet so her nose wouldn't peel. The ponytail fit nicely through the hole at the back of the cap.

Dressed this way, Joslyn thought, as she crossed the sunporch to lift the hook on the screen door, nobody would think she was out to vamp Slade Barlow.

But there he was. Tall, dark and definitely handsome, standing on the back steps with his hat in his hand and his head tilted to one side, he was definitely ripe for vamping. He wore a light blue Western-cut shirt, open at the throat, jeans that rested easy on his lower body and polished boots.

His dangerously blue eyes took her in with a sweep of quiet appreciation. "Ready?" he asked. His voice was husky.

Joslyn, not trusting her own, merely nodded that she was.

Shea, meanwhile, waved from the truck. She was in the backseat with Jasper, and the girl's smile was dazzling, even from that distance. In fact, Jasper seemed to be grinning from ear to ear, too.

"I'm staying in Parable for a whole year!" Shea crowed excitedly, when Slade opened the passenger door for Joslyn and she climbed up into the seat. "Dad called Mom this morning and asked her if I could go to school in Parable, and she said yes!"

Shea's delight, like her smile, was effervescent and therefore contagious. Joslyn turned and smiled back at the teenager as she buckled herself into the seat belt.

"That's great," she said, confused.

But was it, really?

Once he'd walked around the truck and gotten behind the wheel, Slade smiled and shook his head. "We'll see if you're still this excited after school actually starts and you realize this definitely isn't L.A."

"Are you trying to get me to change my mind about staying?" Shea demanded, sounding a little hurt.

Slade chuckled, the sound almost hoarse. It relaxed Joslyn a little, realizing he was wound up as tightly as she was, though she couldn't be sure it was for the same reasons. "No," he said. "I'm glad about it."

As Slade backed the truck down the driveway and eased out onto the street, Shea chattered on, this time addressing Joslyn. "I asked Opal to come with us, but she's baking pies all day, and then she and Martie Wren are going to a bingo game over at the Legion Hall.

Opal sent to Great Falls for all her stuff, and it's arriving next week in a moving van, and—"

"Shea," Slade interrupted affably.

"What?"

"Come up for air," he replied with a short laugh. "Take a breath."

Shea pretended to get huffy, sitting back hard in the seat and folding her arms. "You don't have to *act* like a dad all the time," she pointed out, "just because you're in charge of me for a year."

Slade gave Joslyn a look, his eyes twinkling.

Meanwhile, Joslyn considered the ramifications of Shea's big news. It wasn't as if she and Slade were in a *relationship,* after all—but even if they had been, none of what was going on was her business in any way, shape or form. She had no right to object, and no real reason, and yet—

"I sure hope I find the perfect horse," Shea piped up, somewhat fretfully, when they were out of town and on the highway to Missoula. The drive would take about an hour, Joslyn knew, and

they'd pass through some breathtakingly beautiful territory along the way.

"Something tells me you're not going
to be all that hard to please," Slade remarked. "Not when it comes to horses,
anyhow."

At that moment, Shea's cell phone
played an ear-jarring guitar riff, and she
answered with an excited, "Tiffany? Hi!
Sure, I can talk now—"

Slade sighed. He'd rolled up his shirt-
sleeves before starting up the rig, and
the muscles in his forearm flexed powerfully as he worked the gearshift. His
fingers were long and deft. . . .

Great, Joslyn thought, bringing herself up short. She'd been in the man's
truck for all of ten minutes, and she was
already cataloging his body parts.

"So if Opal's baking pies and going
to bingo," she said, because the silence
between her and Slade was too awkward, "she must be feeling right at home
at your place."

Slade slanted a glance in her direction, and she thought she saw a flicker
of concern in his eyes. "It all happened
pretty fast," he said. "Opal moving in

with us, I mean. You'd just found her, as I understand it, and now she's gone again."

Slade's remark touched Joslyn's heart in an unexpected way, made her throat tighten up. She'd been on her own for a long time, and she valued her independence—would defend it fiercely if any kind of threat arose—but she *had* narrowed her life to the point where she practically had to live it sideways to squeak through. Now, suddenly, that nose-to-the-grindstone existence she'd created for herself was expanding, erupting, breaking open.

She was terrified.

Still, it was comforting to know her feelings concerning Opal's abrupt departure for his ranch house mattered to Slade, even just a little.

"Opal wasn't happy being retired," she said after swallowing. "She needs to be needed."

Don't we all?

Take me, for instance.

When was the last time someone *needed* me? Besides Lucy-Maude or Jasper, I mean.

"Well," Slade answered easily, "Shea and I can sure fit the bill there. We definitely need her." He paused and grinned a little at the exuberant conversation Shea was carrying on in the backseat via her cell phone. Everything was so *important* at that age, life or death. "Opal's amazing—she's only been with us a few days, and already there's a place for everything, everything's *in* that place. I have all the clean shirts a man could ask for, washed, starched and ironed, and you can see yourself in the backsplash behind the kitchen sink."

Joslyn laughed. "That's Opal," she said. "I imagine you're eating pretty well, too."

"Too well," Slade admitted. "If this keeps up, I'll have a belly in no time. Give me a pair of mirrored sunglasses and one of those round hats, and I'll look just like Jackie Gleason in *Smokey and the Bandit.*"

The thought made Joslyn chuckle. She could imagine Slade years from now, with wisps of gray at his temples and deeper lines in his ruggedly masculine face, especially around his eyes, but it was almost impossible to picture Slade Barlow's hard body gone soft.

After that, they lapsed into an easy quiet, though Shea continued to field one phone call after another. She must have told a dozen different people that she was one, staying in Parable with her Dad—*yes, for real*—two, on the way to choose her very own horse, and three, she even had an actual *job.*

The livestock sale, it turned out, was being held at a big auction facility, just that side of Missoula. There were trucks, horse trailers and people everywhere, as many women as men, and plenty of kids and dogs, too.

Jasper immediately ran off to join in canine games, and Slade didn't seem a bit worried by that. Teenagers in jeans and boots and souvenir T-shirts from every conceivable kind of concert soon appeared, taking Shea into the boisterous fold as easily as if she'd been one of them since birth.

In the city, Joslyn thought fretfully, people kept their children in sight in crowds like this—even the older ones—and their dogs on leashes. She flung a perplexed glance in Slade's direction, and he gave one of those tilted-up smiles again, the kind that made her heart beat faster.

And then he read her mind.

"They'll be all right," he said with a nod to indicate his daughter and his dog. "There isn't a person here I haven't known since I got tall enough to see over a milk stool, Joslyn."

She nodded, reassured, and one of them took the other's hand, though Joslyn was never sure who actually made the first move. The jolt that went through her should have lit up her skeleton, like in a cartoon.

They reconnected with Shea inside one of several huge barns, where something like fifty horses were up for sale.

Shea, still surrounded by new friends, immediately gravitated toward a small chestnut mare with streaks of creamy beige in her mane and tail.

"This one!" she called over to Slade, her face shining. "Dad, *this is the one!*"

Slade gave the brim of his hat a casual tug—cowboyese, evidently, for "I hear you"—and turned his attention to a massive bay gelding with a deep chest and impossibly long legs.

Like everyone else except Shea, who stationed herself at the mare's pen and couldn't be spirited away, Slade looked at every horse, in every stall and pen. He checked out the ones outside in the corral, too.

But it was the big bay gelding he came back to.

He let himself into the stall, ran his hands over the horse's sturdy limbs, along his neck and flanks.

Joslyn, fraudulent former rodeo queen, was both intrigued by these animals and overwhelmed by their size and power. A week presiding over the Parable County Rodeo on a borrowed horse and a single ride through the countryside with Hutch Carmody did not change the essential fact: that she was a complete greenhorn.

Still, there was this golden palomino mare, in the last stall on the right. While other animals were restless, blowing and shying in the atmosphere of general excitement, this one seemed gentle to a degree that was almost Zen.

Joslyn lingered in front of the gate and tentatively reached out a hand to stroke the mare's long, beautiful nose. When she stepped back she collided, although not very hard, with Slade, who'd apparently been standing right behind her.

"Thinking of getting yourself a horse?" he asked, looking down at her with another of those small, crooked smiles that always made her breath catch like a hook in her throat.

She laughed, shook her head. "Where would I keep a horse?" she countered.

"Hutch would probably board her for you," Slade answered offhandedly. Then he went into that stall, as he had the gelding's, and examined the palomino more closely. "She's solid," he said. "Pretty calm, too."

Joslyn didn't say anything to that. No way was she buying a horse. She was there to watch, that's all.

An announcement was made over the loudspeakers just then—the sale was about to start, the auctioneer said amiably, and folks ought to find themselves a seat in the bleachers over by the arena, pronto. The spots under the big aluminum awning would go fast.

Shea reluctantly left the little chestnut mare to follow Slade and Joslyn out into the hot sun and the dust and the noise of old friends and longtime neighbors greeting each other. Gatherings like this, she supposed, were a kind of social event for a lot of these people.

After waiting in line in front of a long table set in the shade, Slade registered to bid, was given a number on a piece of paper stapled to a flat wooden stick, and joined Shea and Joslyn in the third row of the bleachers. By then, to Joslyn's secret relief, Jasper had found his way back to them, too, and he sat leaning against Shea's blue-jeaned leg, panting happily in the bone-warming heat and keeping a close eye on the proceedings.

The auction unfolded rapidly, and Joslyn enjoyed the deft chatter of the auctioneer, the festive, country-fair aspect of the whole event. All around them, people ate hot dogs and swilled soda from the concession stand, and studied every horse that was led into the arena as thoroughly as if they expected to ride the animal through mountain passes and across raging rivers.

Some of them probably did.

Joslyn felt the sun baking right through her T-shirt to turn her shoulders red, but she didn't care. It was perfect, sitting there with Slade on one side of her and Shea and Jasper on the other.

To the casual observer, they probably looked like any other local family, making a day of it.

After half an hour or so, Shea's chestnut mare came up for sale, and Slade was the highest bidder. Shea let out a joyous yell and jumped to her feet. "I'm naming her Chessie!" she cried, and then she and Jasper both took off for the barn again, wanting to hang out with Chessie when she was returned to her stall.

Slade smiled at that but offered no comment.

Another forty minutes passed, and then the big gelding was on offer.

Buying Chessie had been relatively easy—there had only been one other bidder, and the man had dropped out when the price went into four digits. There was more interest in the gelding, though, and the bids kept climbing. All but one potential buyer fell away as the numbers mounted, and Joslyn, narrowing her eyes, surveyed the crowd for the troublemaker.

She guessed she shouldn't have been surprised when she saw that it was none other than Hutch Carmody, seated a few rows down from them, where she hadn't noticed him before—but she was.

Slade had spotted him, too, and there was a hard line along the edge of his jaw as he bid and bid again.

Each time his turn came around, Hutch raised his number-on-a-stick or simply nodded to the auctioneer.

Joslyn was on the edge of her seat, sinking her teeth into her lower lip, when Hutch finally let the gelding go—for approximately three times his real value, Slade would admit later. The expression in his eyes went beyond stubborn and well toward implacable, and Hutch looked just as serious.

Obviously, this wasn't just about the horse.

In the end, though, the gelding was Slade's, and Joslyn fully expected him to sign the check and leave the sale then, since his business there was completed. He'd already arranged, she knew, to have any stock he bought transported to Whisper Creek Ranch, so there wouldn't be any loading to do.

Pay and go, that was the plan.

Except that he didn't budge from the bleachers.

Horse after horse came up for auction—Hutch bought several of them—and then one of the men helping with the sale led the palomino mare out.

Sundance. The name—perfect for this particular animal, with its gleaming golden coat—leaped into Joslyn's mind, and her heartbeat quickened.

Don't be silly, she told herself. *What in the world would you do with a horse?*

Sudden, inexplicable tears scalded her eyes, though, and a longing older than time swelled in her chest.

When the bidding began, Slade leaned forward slightly, his gaze intent, and watched people raise their numbers, which popped up all over the arena.

At the very last moment, when Sundance would have gone for a goodly sum of money, he nearly doubled the bid.

The auctioneer chuckled into his microphone. "Looks like the sheriff wants this horse," he commented. "Maybe he's getting up a posse."

Good-natured chuckles rippled through the crowd.

Slade simply waited. Hutch hadn't bid on the animal even once, but the tension thrumming in the air between the two men was almost tangible just the same.

"Anybody want to bid higher?" the auctioneer finally asked.

No one spoke.

"Sold!" shouted the man with the microphone, pointing to Slade.

Slade raised his number, so the bookkeeper could record it.

All during the exchange, he hadn't looked away from the mare or the arena. Now, his gaze landed on Joslyn's face.

"Every rodeo queen ought to have a horse," he said simply.

Joy filled Joslyn, quickly followed by a tsunami of reality. "Slade, I can't afford— I don't have a place—"

"She can live at Whisper Creek for the time being, along with my gelding and Shea's Chessie." There was a certain gentle finality in his tone, and Joslyn simply stared at him, completely at a loss for words.

After that, he took her hand and they left the bleachers—folks calling out greetings and congratulations to Slade all along the way—and they headed for the barns.

A large semitruck had appeared near the main building, with the Whisper Creek Ranch logo emblazoned on both sides, and men were already loading the horses Hutch had chosen.

Slade ignored the truck, nodded toward the barn. "Would you mind rounding up Shea and Jasper while I'm settling with the auction people and making sure the horses get to Whisper Creek?" he asked Joslyn.

Joslyn nodded and was about to turn

and head for the barn when Hutch walked up to them and gestured toward the fancy semi. "I'm headed that way myself," he said with just the merest touch of irony. The brim of his hat cast a shadow over his face, though, and Joslyn couldn't quite read his expression. "Back to Whisper Creek, that is. Might as well let me haul your cayuses right along with mine."

The tension between Slade and Hutch was so intense, Joslyn feared they might just lunge at each other, fists flying.

After a long moment, though, Slade sighed and said, "I'd appreciate that, Hutch."

Joslyn knew she ought to be headed for the barn, where she was sure to find Shea and Jasper admiring Chessie, but for some reason, she couldn't bring herself to leave Slade's side, not yet.

Hutch's gaze moved to her face, and one side of his mouth hitched up, briefly, in an attempt at a grin. "That fine little palomino mare is for you, I guess?" he asked.

Joslyn bristled, nettled by something in Hutch's tone or manner.

"Sundance belongs to Slade," she said.

Hutch shifted his weight from one booted foot to the other and adjusted his hat again. "Sundance," he repeated. "Nice name." His eyes moved in a lazy sweep from Joslyn's face to Slade's. "Never figured you for the poetic type," he drawled.

Slade's jawline tightened. "I'm full of surprises," he said, almost growling the words.

Hutch chuckled at that, shook his head. "No, brother, you're not," he said. "Fact is, you're about as unpredictable as tomorrow's sunrise."

A silent snap jarred the air, sharp as the crack of a whip.

Slade's shoulders were squared, and his chin jutted out just a fraction. "I guess it's a good thing," he replied slowly, "that I don't really give a rat's ass what you think of me."

Again, that hard pull of tension, tighter this time, stretched to the limit. Sure to break with the next tug.

Hutch merely smiled, though. Looked at Joslyn again. He might have been a stranger, she thought, instead of an old friend, one of the few who had stood by her after Elliott's long and dramatic fall from grace. "If you want any more riding lessons," he offered, "you know where to find me."

Inside the arena, the auction went on, the announcer's voice as rhythmic as a song.

Hutch nodded in farewell then, tugged at the brim of his hat and turned to walk away, heading back toward the ongoing sale.

Slade stopped him with a single word. "Hutch," he said.

Hutch paused, in no particular hurry to oblige, and looked back over one shoulder. "Yeah?"

"Thanks for running up the bid on that gelding," Slade said evenly.

"Glad to do it," Hutch answered with a grin. "You don't really think you can win the race riding him, do you?"

"I sure as hell mean to try," Slade answered.

Hutch chuckled, shook his head once and walked away.

Slade's jaw looked as hard as granite as he watched Hutch disappear into the shadows cast by the bleachers surrounding the arena.

Joslyn, having spotted Shea and Jasper approaching out of the corner of her eye, stood right where she was, watching Slade.

Finally, he looked at her.

"Meet you at the truck," he said gruffly, and she felt oddly dismissed, brushed aside. In the next moment, he headed for the office to pay for the horses.

Shea was beaming as she came to Joslyn's side, Jasper trotting happily in her wake. "I took a *thousand* pictures of Chessie with my phone," she announced, "and texted them to every single person I know. Even Mom and Bentley."

Joslyn, grateful that the strain had eased, now that Hutch and Slade weren't facing off like a pair of Old West gunslingers about to have a showdown in the middle of a dusty street, smiled. "I like the name you chose for her," she said. "She's beautiful, with that red-brown hide of hers."

"Thanks," Shea said. "It's not because of her coloring, though. Chessie is short for 'Cheshire.' Like in *Alice in Wonderland.*" A pause, spent looking around the immediate area. "Where's Dad? He promised we'd get lunch on the way home, and Grands is expecting me at the salon by two o'clock."

"He's in the office," Joslyn answered. "He suggested that we meet him at the truck."

Shea nodded and started toward the parking lot, Joslyn keeping pace as best she could. Although Shea wasn't very tall, she had long legs, and she walked fast, Jasper bounding alongside.

"Of course I'd lots rather go riding than sweep up hair and take care of the appointment book at the Curly-Burly," the girl went on, as though there hadn't been a break in the conversation, holding the door open so Jasper could jump into the backseat ahead of her. "But a job is a job, and Dad is big on responsibility."

"Well," Joslyn responded mundanely,

taking her place in front, "responsibility is a pretty important trait."

The woman-child, her face visible to Joslyn in the rearview mirror, had the good grace not to roll her eyes. "But it's not *everything,*" she said lightly. "Except, of course, to my dad."

Joslyn, recalling Hutch's gibe at Slade's predictability, felt a swift, sharp sting at the recollection. Except for Kendra, Hutch had been her closest friend all through school. He'd remained loyal even when the other kids in their crowd wouldn't speak to her, because of what Elliott had done.

For all that, today anyway, she could cheerfully have throttled Hutch Carmody with her bare hands. Not only had he goaded Slade unnecessarily, but he'd thrown out that remark about the riding lessons, emphasizing the word "more" to let his half brother know—know what?

"Joslyn?" Shea said, bringing her back to the here and now, where she came in for a hard landing.

Joslyn turned, looked back at the girl.

Waited for whatever it was she meant to say.

"Are you and my dad sleeping together?"

By the time he'd written a hefty check to pay for the three horses he'd bought that morning and returned to the truck, Slade had shaken off the effects of the near-row with Hutch. His breakfast— scrambled eggs, toast, fried potatoes and ham, prepared by Opal—was beginning to wear off, and he was thinking about lunch.

He climbed into the truck and stuck the key in the ignition before it hit him that Shea and Joslyn were both being unusually quiet.

"Everything okay?" he asked, looking at Shea first—she was playing some game on her cell phone, Jasper snoozing beside her on the backseat—and then at Joslyn.

Her color was a little high, and she stared straight ahead, through the windshield.

"Look," Slade said, after a heavy sigh

of resignation. "We're not going any-where until somebody tells me why this truck feels like the inside of a meat locker."

"I might have asked a personal ques-tion," Shea chimed, not even looking up from her phone.

Slade glanced at Joslyn again. "Like what?" he asked.

"Never mind," Joslyn said stiffly. "Can we just go now?"

"No," Slade said. "We can't."

"All I did was ask Joslyn if you and she were sleeping together," Shea in-terjected. "And just like that, she gets all huffy."

Slade closed his eyes for a long mo-ment and fought hard to keep the twitch in his lips from turning into a grin. "In-appropriate," he told his daughter, and he meant it, even though he still wanted to laugh.

Joslyn, he realized, wasn't angry—she was *embarrassed.*

What a strange—and enticing—com-bination of innocence and sophistica-tion this woman was.

"Sorry," Shea said, brightly insincere. The game she was playing on her phone came with an annoying little tune, made up of beeps and robotic "yahoos."

Joslyn didn't say anything, but she wasn't sitting quite as stiffly as before, and her cheeks weren't so pink.

Slade let out his breath. "I'll talk to her later," he told Joslyn quietly.

She relaxed a little, sighed. Looked at him, finally. "I probably overreacted," she said.

"Ya think?" Shea asked, amidst the merry beeps.

"Turn that thing off," Slade said.

The beeping stopped. "Dad?" Shea ventured, sounding almost timid.

"What?" Slade asked, grinding the key in the ignition.

"Thanks for buying me the horse," Shea replied. She reached forward, touched Joslyn's shoulder. "I'm sorry, Joslyn," she added, and this time, she sounded as if she meant it. "It's none of my business what you and Dad do together."

A slow smile broke over Joslyn's face,

and then she laughed. "Thanks," she said. "I think."

"Apology accepted?" Shea pressed.

"Apology accepted," Joslyn confirmed.

After that, the mood lightened up considerably. They ate lunch at a diner along the highway, Shea running on the whole time about how she'd rather ride Chessie than sweep up hair at the Curly-Burly for the rest of the day.

Slade, just back from taking Jasper a hamburger to eat in the truck, smiled at that. "If you don't work," he reasoned, taking his seat at the table again, "where are you going to get the money to feed a horse? There'll be veterinary bills to pay, too, and you'll need a saddle and bridle and some other gear on top of that."

Shea's eyes widened. "You never said I had to pay for anything," she said.

Slade chuckled and toasted her with his nearly empty coffee cup. "Some things," he told her, "go *without* saying."

Shea's gaze moved to Joslyn, who was sitting across from her, beside Slade, and the girl's thoughts were so clear that they might as well have been inscribed on her forehead.

What will Joslyn have to do to pay for the horse you bought her?

CHAPTER SEVENTEEN

Slade dropped Shea off at the Curly-Burly once they were back in Parable, along with Jasper, who seemed reluctant to leave the girl's side, and promised to pick them up when her shift was over.

Which left him with the meantime heavy on his hands.

He had the whole day off, and Sunday, too, a rare occurrence, and he didn't feel like hurrying back to the ranch where Opal was either baking up a storm or getting ready for bingo. Of course, he could head out to Whisper

Creek and help unload the new horses, since three of them were his, but the mood between him and Hutch was like tinder-dry grass, needing only a spark to set off a wildfire.

Simple prudence indicated that he and Hutch both needed some space, at least for today. Better to leave that alone till morning, anyhow, when he'd feel duty bound to drive out there and feed his own horses.

With luck, he wouldn't run into Hutch. His half brother was a busy man, after all, running one of the biggest ranches in the state.

He looked over at Joslyn, sitting rigid in the passenger seat. Her color was high again, and she was gazing straight ahead, at Callie's reader-board, as though fascinated by the offering of free haircuts for active-duty military personnel home on leave.

"I don't expect anything," Slade felt compelled to say, though he felt foolish for bringing up something that should have been obvious. "In return for the horse, I mean."

"I know," Joslyn said. Her voice was

soft as she turned her head to look at him.

For a long moment, they just sat there with the air pulsing between them, and then Slade sighed and started the truck, backed out of the parking space in Callie's lot and steered for the highway.

Neither of them said anything all the way back to Kendra's place. It wasn't far, but it seemed like a long drive to Slade, longer than the one down from Missoula.

He got out of the truck to walk Joslyn to the door, because that was what you did, taking a woman home, even in the middle of the afternoon.

When she took his hand, he felt that now-familiar charge, fit to knock him back on the heels of his best boots.

He swallowed hard. "Joslyn—"

She reached up, pressed one index finger against his mouth.

He was jolted again, even by the lightest of touches. It was like dancing in a mud puddle in the pouring rain, with both hands gripping an electric fence.

Still grasping his hand, she started toward the guesthouse.

Inside, where it was shadowy and cool, they stood practically toe-to-toe in the kitchen.

"This isn't about the horse," she said, and then, at his gruff chuckle, she blushed.

Damn, but she was even more beautiful when she colored up like that. Her eyes turned a deeper shade of brown, and flecks of golden light sparked in them, light that had to be coming from inside her, since the shades were drawn against the heat. He had to kiss her. So he did. And he felt her soft body melt against him, felt her nipples harden like stones against his chest, even through both their clothes.

He was careful at first, but as the situation developed, and their tongues became involved, he practically consumed her.

"This is—not—a good idea," he gasped out, when their mouths finally parted.

Joslyn spread her hands against his chest, fingers splayed. "It's absolutely the wrong thing to do," she agreed dreamily.

Then she stood on tiptoe, slid her

arms around his neck and kissed him in earnest.

The whole universe seemed to shift.

"I really ought to go—" he rasped the next time they came up for air.

"You really should," Joslyn replied, but she'd taken his hand again, and she was pulling him toward an inside doorway.

Sure enough, they wound up in the bedroom.

He figured he was either the stupidest man alive—or the luckiest.

Or both.

"You're sure about this?" he asked, watching as she removed her baseball cap, tossed it aside, raised her hands to undo the ponytail and send her hair spilling in rich brown glory around her shoulders.

"No," she answered with an honesty he could appreciate—even in those circumstances. "Are you?"

"I'm sure I want to make love to you," Slade said. "Beyond that—"

She hauled her T-shirt off over her head, stood there in her jeans and her sneakers and her lacy pink bra. "At least we can agree on that much," she said. "We both want to make love."

Slade wasn't usually tongue-tied with women, half-naked or otherwise—sex was a natural function, after all, like sleeping, eating and breathing—but this wasn't just any woman. His head reeled, and he was hard as tamarack, and if he loused this up, he'd have ruined something precious.

He was a man on a precipice, and he was about to lose his balance.

"Joslyn," he stumbled, "I don't—I didn't—"

She moved to the bedside table, unfastening her bra as she went, opened a drawer, took out a box and set it down.

"Condoms," he marveled. "Are you always this direct?"

She let the bra drop, revealing the most perfect pair of breasts he'd ever seen—not too big and not too small. "Actually," she answered, "I'm *never* this direct. And it's your turn to take off an article of clothing, by the way."

He laughed, though it was a raw sound, scraped from his throat. He untucked his shirt, worked the snaps, let the garment fall forgotten to the floor. He wanted to lay his hands—better yet, his tongue—on those lush breasts of hers.

And then proceed to do a lot more.

She moved toward him, there in that tiny bedroom, and they stood skin-to-skin, and Slade hesitated, then let his hands rest lightly against her shoulder blades.

Her flesh was soft and warm and smooth under his palms and his fingers, and her breasts pressed against his chest. A groan escaped him.

She cupped his face in her hands, looked up into his eyes and murmured, "This was inevitable, you know."

"Bound to happen," Slade confirmed.

He kissed her again, and there was a scuffle while they both grappled with the snaps and buttons on each other's jeans, and both of them ended up laughing.

When they were both naked, they did some more kissing and somehow wound up squeezed into a lilliputian shower together, under a lukewarm spray.

Whatever happened after this, Slade thought, he was never going to regret making love to Joslyn Kirk on that hot summer afternoon. He wouldn't *allow* himself to regret it.

They washed themselves, washed each other, and as the water drenched them both, Slade pressed Joslyn against the tile wall of the shower stall and kissed her yet again. Presently, knowing that the more slowly he went, the better this would be for both of them, he tasted her earlobe, her neck, the upper rounding of her breasts.

"If you're inclined to change your mind, Joslyn," he muttered, "now's the time to say so, because in another few minutes, you're going to be incoherent."

Joslyn *didn't* change her mind—she was in too deep for that—so she just gave herself up to what she'd wanted, *needed,* ever since she'd returned to Parable and subsequently run smack into Slade Barlow.

He kissed her breasts, tongued her nipples, slipped his fingers between her legs.

She moaned, and the cravings grew to an almost painful intensity, and she was exultant in her surrender.

When Slade moved to his knees, parted her and took her into his mouth, ever so gently, she cried out, plunging her fingers into his hair, holding him close against her.

He enjoyed her at leisure, bringing her to the brink, then letting her descend again, whimpering, while he kissed and caressed her thighs. Only when she pleaded did he come back to the core of her, only teasing her at first, but then devouring her.

He'd been right earlier—she *was* incoherent, her body flexing and buckling as he satisfied her, then satisfied her again, her cries joyous, her words nonsensical.

She was limp when he shut off the shower spray, hoisted her into his arms and carried her to the bed.

Both of them were still wet—they hadn't bothered with towels—but neither cared. By then, nothing mattered but being joined.

Slade laid Joslyn down in the middle

of the bedspread, fumbled for the box of condoms and was soon stretched out on top of her, careful not to let his full weight rest on her. His face was so open, so earnest as he looked deep into her eyes, asking the silent question.

Joslyn merely nodded, giving her permission.

Slade claimed her in one long, slow stroke, and she was already climaxing in soft, sweet spasms before he'd withdrawn to thrust again.

He kissed her eyelids lightly, whispered gentle words to her as she moved beneath him, ecstasy rippling through her as her body seized and then seized again. The releases were exquisite, but instead of sating Joslyn, each one led to another, steeper climb, another pinnacle, higher than the last.

She'd lost count of the peaks she'd reached when the big one came, the one that was off the Richter scale, the one that shattered her and left her in splinters, spinning in its wake like flotsam on a receding tide.

When Slade finally lost control, it was

with a low shout and a plunge that heightened Joslyn's pleasure until she exploded from the inside; she dissolved into a splash of light against an inner sky, trailing brightly colored sparks like the finale to some celestial fireworks display.

Slade fell beside her, breathing hard, stroking her breasts, her hips, her stomach as she slowly descended into the real world again, reassembling her soul piece by piece.

They were silent for a long time, exhausted and spent, and Slade, one leg thrown across hers, continued to caress her until she needed him all over again.

Deftly, so that she barely noticed the interruption, he replaced the first condom with a second, rolled onto his back, and brought her with him, and she found herself straddling his hips.

This time, there were no preliminaries. Slade entered her hard and fast and deep, wringing a gasp of welcome from her. Their lovemaking was wild, unrestrained, with neither one granting the other any quarter at all.

The friction grew greater and greater, and Joslyn, breathless, hoped it would never end, this giving and taking, this being more completely alive, more fully a woman, than she'd ever known she could be.

Slade grasped her hips and raised and lowered her along his shaft, faster and then more slowly, and then faster again.

Joslyn was neither promiscuous nor inexperienced, but she'd never been loved like this before, and somewhere in her frenzied daze of need, she knew she might never be again.

Whimpering Slade's name over and over, she crested the mountaintop and broke apart once more, raining fire upon her own inner landscape.

Slade bucked high as he erupted inside her. She felt the warmth of him, spilling life.

"Damn," she heard him mutter.

"What?" she gasped the word, and it took her a long time to work up the energy to do even that. She'd collapsed onto the bed, half blinded by pleasure, sweating and blissfully wrung out.

"I think the condom broke," Slade said.

She squeezed her eyes shut. "No," she said.

He left the bed, headed for the bathroom, returned a minute or so later.

"The thing blew out like a bald tire," he told her, stretching out beside her on the bed again.

Joslyn laughed at the allegory, but in the next instant, she was crying—not because she might be pregnant, but, against all logic and good sense, because she knew she *couldn't* be. There was the implant.

Slade gathered her close against his chest. "Are we going to let this ruin the mood?" he teased huskily.

She laughed again and sobbed, both at once. Was she losing her mind? She didn't love Slade Barlow, and he didn't love her. A baby would have been among the worst things that could have happened to either one of them.

So why was her heart about to crack down the middle?

"I'm not pregnant," she told him, and

briefly explained the precautions she'd already taken.

He smoothed her hair back from her cheek, where it was sticking to her tear-streaked, exertion-dampened face. "Well, that's good, I guess," he said doubtfully.

"You guess?" she asked, a puzzled frown creasing her forehead.

He kissed the crease away. "I can't say I'd be unhappy if you were," he said, with that stunning honesty of his. "It would be inconvenient for sure, but babies are *supposed* to be inconvenient, aren't they?"

She couldn't believe her ears. Most men would have been wildly relieved to learn that a condom malfunction wasn't going to result in untimely parenthood. Slade, to the contrary, almost seemed to regret that it was just short of impossible.

Resting on one hip and one elbow, his head cupped in his hand, he frowned at the emotions that must have been speeding across her face like clouds in a high wind.

"What's going on in there?" he asked,

thumping lightly at her forehead with the tip of his index finger.

"I was just thinking—well—how different you are from most of the men I know."

He waggled his eyebrows, grinned rakishly. "You know a lot of men?" he countered.

Joslyn blushed, then narrowed her eyes. "No," she said. "I don't. Not in the Biblical sense, anyway."

Slade threw back his head and gave a guffaw at that. His eyes, the color of cornflowers in the dim light of that small, shade-sequestered bedroom, danced with mischief. *"Biblical?"* he echoed.

"You're like the third man I've ever slept with in my whole life," Joslyn said, mortified. A pitiful count for a woman her age. There was no getting around it; she was a sexual underachiever.

He traced the outline of her mouth with the tip of the same index finger he'd used to tap at her forehead. "Do you keep a chart or something?" he joked.

She wanted to be angry, but she

couldn't help laughing. "How many women have you been with?"

"More than three," Slade replied, after a moment of comic concentration.

She laughed again. It amazed her that she could be this happy, when she'd just put herself into an entirely new kind of emotional jeopardy by giving in to her desire to make love with this man.

To her, this was a momentous occasion. To Slade, it was probably just summer-afternoon sex.

Laugh today, she thought, *cry tomorrow.*

That was when he kissed her, and the whole feverishly graceful routine started all over again.

Slade fairly crushed his hat onto his head as he strode toward his truck. He was late picking Shea up at the Curly-Burly, and she and Callie would probably *both* guess why he hadn't answered his cell phone all afternoon.

He'd left it in the rig, that was why, and he was furious with himself.

He was the *sheriff,* for God's sake.

What if there had been some kind of emergency, and nobody could find him?

His bones felt as pliable as warm wax as he opened the door of his truck, where he'd left it in Kendra's driveway, and given the choice, he'd have spent the whole night in Joslyn's bed.

But he had responsibilities, even if he hadn't remembered them any too soon.

He reached for the phone as soon as he'd started up the engine, thumbed in the numbers that would bring up his voice mail.

Three messages.

Maggie Landers wanted him and Hutch to come in for another meeting, concerning the further disbursement of John Carmody's estate.

"Further disbursement?" The man had left him over five million dollars and half of the family ranch. What else was there to disburse?

The second call was from some stranger, who wanted to discuss "exciting" investment opportunities. He deleted that one and moved on to the third message.

It was from Shea, and there was a

touch of little-girl panic in her voice. "Dad? Are you okay? You were supposed to pick me up an hour ago. Why aren't you answering your phone?"

He called her back instantly.

"Shea?"

"Hold on a sec, Dad," Shea replied breezily. "Tiffany's on the other line and I've got to tell her 'bye."

Slade grinned as he steered the truck around in a wide turn and headed down the driveway. She didn't sound all that traumatized after all.

She clicked off, and he sat at the end of the drive, waiting for her to come back on. When she did, she was in a state.

"I thought you were *dead* or something, Dad," she ranted. "You're *never* late."

"I'm sorry you were worried," Slade said reasonably. "I'll be there in a couple of minutes, and we'll go home and see what Opal left us for supper."

"Grands had to buy kibble over at Mulligan's so Jasper wouldn't starve!" Shea continued.

He swallowed a chuckle. "Come on,

Shea. Aren't you overreacting just a little, here? It takes more than one missed meal to starve a dog. Besides, I'm the sheriff, remember? For all you know, I've been out risking my neck, making the county safe for truth, justice and the American way."

Shea subsided a little. "Whatever *that* means." She drew in a breath. "Were you? Working, I mean?"

He couldn't lie, but, on the other hand, he wasn't about to tell his sixteen-year-old stepdaughter—or anybody else—that he'd been in bed with Joslyn ever since they got back to her place after the auction.

So he left the question hanging.

"I'll be there in a few minutes," he repeated.

They said prickly goodbyes, and Slade shut his phone.

By the time he pulled in at the Curly-Burly, it was nearly dark out, and Shea and Jasper were waiting in the shop's empty parking lot.

Slade frowned as he rolled down his truck window. "What are you doing out here?" he asked. He'd expected both the girl and the dog to wait inside with his mom, if only because that would have been the sensible thing to do.

"Grands invited us to stay to supper, but I said she needed a break from me and Jasper, and you were on your way, so we waited outside," Shea explained matter-of-factly, opening the rear door to hoist the dog into the truck. That done, she climbed into the passenger seat.

"Did the two of you get into it about something?" Slade asked. "Maybe you hit Mom up for a day off and she didn't like it?"

Shea gave him a look. "Grands and I," she said pointedly, "get along just fine."

He smiled. "But you're not so sure you and me do," he ventured.

"The jury's still out on that one, Sheriff," she told him.

This time, he laughed. "You're off tomorrow, right?" he asked, setting out for home. The shop was always closed on Sundays because, despite her poker-playing and her scandalous past, Callie Barlow was a churchgoing woman.

"Right," Shea confirmed, leaving the statement open-ended so it sounded like a question.

"Me, too," he said. "Maybe we'll go out to Whisper Creek first thing in the morning, feed the new horses, and take them out on the range, see what they're made of."

The freeze, such as it had been, was off. Slade was clearly forgiven for worrying the kid by being late—all it took was the mention of a horse.

"I can ride Chessie? For sure?"

"I want to try her out first," Slade clarified. "If she's used to the saddle, like the auction flyer says she is, you can take her for a spin."

"Except I don't *own* a saddle," Shea pointed out.

"We'll scrape something up," Slade promised.

That was when she ambushed him, came right out of left field with, "You were with her, huh? With Joslyn, I mean."

"Suppose I said that was none of your business?" he asked after a pause.

"I like her, you know," Shea persisted

coyly. "Even if we did get into that little tiff after the auction."

"Good," Slade said. "I like her, too."

"Grands told me Joslyn was involved in some kind of mess a long time ago," Shea fished.

"She was an innocent bystander," Slade told the girl. "And I'm surprised at your grandmother. She doesn't usually go in for gossip."

The eye-roll came then. "Get a clue, Dad," Shea advised generously. "Grands runs a *beauty shop.* The place is a regular clearinghouse for gossip."

The gate leading up to the ranch house was just ahead by then, and Slade signaled a turn out of pure habit, even though there were no other vehicles on the road. The porch light was lit, thanks to Opal, and the kitchen windows glowed in homey welcome.

As soon as Slade stopped the truck, Jasper started whining and scrabbling at the door with one paw, anxious to be released into all that inviting grass.

Slade let him out on his side, and the dog immediately lifted a hind leg to the rear tire. Shea, meanwhile, sprinted toward the house.

"What's the hurry?" Slade asked.

"Opal made peanut-butter-banana pie," Shea called back. "And, besides, I need to charge my phone. The battery icon is flashing, and it's bright red."

"God forbid," Slade said with a rueful grin. A person would have thought she was a lone astronaut, light-years from home, and the cell was her last connection to Earth.

Jasper, much relieved, trotted over to nuzzle Slade's pant leg with his nose.

Slade bent to ruffle the dog's ears, looked up at the first stars of the night. And he thought about Joslyn, the scent of her hair, the way she smiled, the sounds she made when he'd pleased her in bed. He shook his head, remembering the failed condom—and her quick assurance that there would be no baby. Strange as it seemed—he was old-fashioned enough to believe that people ought to be married to each other if they were going to have children together—the remark had left him with a hollow ache in the middle of his chest.

The back door creaked open as he and Jasper approached the house.

"Dad," Shea called. "Have you seen my phone charger?"

He chuckled. "No," he said, stepping inside the kitchen.

The room, like the rest of the house, gleamed with cleanliness, and something smelled really, really good.

A note from Opal waited in the center of the table. "A man called to ask if you were going to declare your candidacy for sheriff," she'd written. "I took down his name and number and left the paper by the phone. Chicken casserole in the oven. Martie will bring me home after bingo." She'd signed with a huge *O* with eyes in it and a smiling mouth.

Slade ignored the phone message, got out some pot holders and removed the foil-covered dish from the oven.

Shea was busy ransacking the place for her charger.

"Can the search wait until after supper?" Slade asked mildly, setting the food in the center of the table, which had already been set for two.

"As *if,*" Shea responded, starting toward the stairs. "Tiffany thinks Justin is *this close* to asking her out, and Melanie is pretty sure Aidan is going to break up with her any minute now. And—" her words died away as she pounded up to the second floor.

Slade gave Jasper more kibble, just in case he was still hungry, washed his hands and sat down to eat.

Shea returned momentarily in triumph, holding the charger like a trophy. "Opal must have put it on my dresser," she said. "I *know* I left it on the kitchen counter the last time I used it."

"Shea," Slade said patiently, "sit down and eat, will you, please?"

Shea plugged in her phone, washed up at the sink and joined him at the table. "I guess you probably don't want to discuss Joslyn," she said, dishing up a generous helping of supper.

"I guess you're probably right," Slade answered, speaking with exaggerated slowness.

"You think I'm too young to know what's going on, don't you?"

"I think you're too young for a lot of things," Slade said.

"You bought Joslyn a *horse.* Am I supposed to think you're not interested in her?"

"You're supposed to think about your own concerns," Slade reasoned quietly, a little amused and trying to hide it, "and leave mine to me."

She scanned Opal's note, still resting against the sugar bowl in the middle of the table. "Are you going to run for sheriff again?" she asked.

"Good," Slade replied. "A slightly less invasive question. The answer is—I'm not sure yet."

"What would you do for a job if you weren't sheriff?"

He smiled. Opal made one mean casserole, and he was nearly ready for a second helping by then. "I'd find a way to get by," he said.

Shea gave a long-suffering sigh, her fork poised above a chunk of chicken on her plate. "Were you this secretive with Mom? Because if you were, it's no wonder you two got divorced."

Slade chuckled again. "I'm not being secretive," he said. "I haven't decided, that's all. About running for sheriff again, I mean."

"You don't like the job?"

"I don't hate it," he said carefully.

"Wow," Shea replied. "*That's* a ringing endorsement."

"Okay. The truth is, I'd rather be a rancher."

"Then do that," Shea reasoned with a little shrug.

"It isn't that simple."

"Sure it is," Shea said. "Provided you can make a living ranching, anyway."

For the first time in his life, he didn't *need* to make a living. It was a startling concept for a man who'd worked since he was old enough to mow lawns and deliver newspapers. On what John Carmody had left him, he could live well himself, provide for his mom, contribute to causes he believed in and never so much as put a nick in the principle.

"I'll get by all right," he said, enjoying the magnitude of that understatement.

He thought about the big horse race—he had until Labor Day weekend to get himself and the gelding ready, and even though it was only June, he knew the time would pass quickly.

"I need a name for the gelding," he threw out.

Shea laid down her fork and looked over at him, her eyes bright. "How about 'Highlander'?" she suggested.

Slade would have gone with something less flashy, but Shea seemed so pleased that he couldn't shoot down her idea. "Okay," he said.

"Try to curb your enthusiasm, Dad," Shea responded, but she was still twinkling. "Highlander is a great name. So is Chessie. Joslyn's mare is—?"

"Sundance," Slade answered.

"That's good," Shea declared. "Does she even know how to ride? Joslyn, I mean?"

"Do you?" Slade countered, finding himself back on the subject he'd been hoping to avoid. Not that Joslyn had been out of his mind since he'd left her, even once.

"I rode with you when I was little, remember?"

Slade grinned. He'd never seen a happier kid than Shea had been, perched behind him on a horse. "I remember," he said.

Before she could turn the topic back to Joslyn—obviously, there was a lot Shea wanted to know about her—they heard a car coming up the driveway, saw headlights flash across the kitchen wall.

Cheerful goodbyes rang out like faraway bells, and soon the back door opened and Opal came inside.

Jasper rushed to greet her, and she laughed and patted his head as she took in Slade and Shea there at the table.

Remembering his manners, Slade pushed back his chair and stood.

"Oh, sit down," Opal ordered with a smile and a wave of one hand. "If we stand on ceremony around here, well, it'll just be too complicated."

Slade grinned and lowered himself back into his chair.

"How was bingo?" Shea asked eagerly as Opal set aside her big purse and hung up her cardigan sweater. "Did you win?"

Opal laughed, went to the sink and washed her hands. Then she fetched the apron she'd brought along from Kendra's and tied it around her waist. "No," she said, "but I had a fine time seeing all my old friends again."

"Opal," Slade said as the woman began running hot water into the sink. "Sit down and have a piece of pie with us."

"Just let me get these dishes started," she answered, approaching the table to collect their now-empty plates and utensils. "Anyways, I've got no room left for pie. Martie and I had a big supper over at the Butter Biscuit before bingo."

"Your workday is over," Slade said, gently but firmly. "Leave those dishes to me."

"Or me," Shea added.

Pleased and reluctant and shaking her head at all the fuss, Opal sat down at the table.

"I'm not sure I have room for pie myself," Slade admitted. "That was one fine casserole, Opal."

She beamed at the compliment.

Shea got up, cleared the table and brewed a cup of herbal tea for Opal.

"Why, thank you, child," Opal said with a gratified sigh. "Now, tell me all about that livestock auction you went to. Did you buy yourselves some horses?"

"Three of them," Shea said, bustling back to the sink and plunging both hands into the sudsy water. "Dad got a gelding—Highlander. I got a chestnut mare—Chessie. And even Joslyn got one—a pretty palomino she calls Sundance."

Slade saw Opal's eyes widen slightly as she took in the implications of that third horse.

"Well, I'll be," she marveled with a twinkle and commenced to sipping her tea.

CHAPTER EIGHTEEN

Joslyn sat up in bed, blinking away the last vestiges of a sound sleep, and reached for her jangling cell phone on the nightstand. The sun was barely peeking through the slats in the blinds, she noted, as Lucy-Maude, draped luxuriously across her ankles, displeased by the disturbance, bestirred herself with a petulant little meow.

Joslyn, meanwhile, struggled to pull herself together—making love with Slade the day before, for all its glorious and fevered frenzy, had left her loose-jointed with satisfaction and made her feel more like a small, expanding universe than a substantial person, bordered in skin.

Rummy languor was quickly replaced by concern, though, as full consciousness dawned—of course the caller was Kendra. Who else could it be at this hour? On Kendra's end, it must have been late afternoon by then, if not early evening.

Still, her friend usually took the time difference into consideration.

Had the end finally come—had Jeffrey died? Or had he revealed his big secret, the reason for her trip to England, whatever it was?

Joslyn's heart shinnied into her throat as she croaked out, "Hello?"

But the rueful chuckle on the other end of the line belonged to a man, not to Kendra. In fact, it was Slade's alone, as surely as if it had been trademarked to him.

"Morning," he said, and there was something intimate in the sound, as though they'd woken up in the same bed together instead of several miles apart. "Sorry to call so early, but Shea and I are about to head out to Whisper Creek to feed the horses, and we wondered if you might want to go along. Because of Sundance, I mean."

Relief swept through Joslyn, swiftly followed by the embarrassingly graphic recollection of how she'd responded to this man's lovemaking the day before, in the guesthouse shower and then the bed.

Joslyn hadn't had time to process everything yet, mentally, emotionally *or* physically, and she'd hoped for some kind of grace period before the next encounter with Slade. She was also, conversely, eager to see him again.

"Joslyn?" Slade prompted, when she didn't speak right away. His voice was throaty, and there was a smile hidden away in it, a private one meant for her alone. "Are you still there?"

She gulped and swung her legs over the side of the bed in the staff apartment.

Lucy-Maude, prowling the dresser top in lockstep with her own reflection in the mirror, issued a low, soft complaint.

As short as their acquaintance had been, Joslyn knew what that sound meant: the cat wanted breakfast—immediately if not sooner.

"Uh—yes," Joslyn stammered, pushing her hair back from her face with one hand. The thought of seeing Slade again so soon was daunting, but spending time with Sundance was another matter. "I'm here." She couldn't stifle a yawn. "Sorry—I was just—"

"Asleep," Slade supplied, with hoarse good humor that, for some incomprehensible reason, made her think of the long, hard lines of his body. He had a small tattoo on his right shoulder, she recalled dizzily, an eagle just spreading its wings to take flight. "I shouldn't have called. You go ahead and dive back under the covers—Shea and I will take care of Sundance, of course, right along with the others."

"No," Joslyn blurted, and then blushed, because she knew she'd sounded so eager. "I mean—I'd *like* to help. With the horses, I mean. Shall I meet you and Shea at Whisper Creek?"

"We'll pick you up at your place,"

Slade offered. His tone affected her like a slow caress—he hadn't said a single word about what had happened between them, and yet the conversation was starting to feel a lot like phone sex.

Joslyn sprang up off the edge of the mattress, only too aware that she had bed head, sleep-puffed eyes and probably a crease in her cheek from the pillowcase. "How long do I have?" she asked, trying hard to sound nonchalant.

Fat chance. She was totally "chalant"—if there was such a thing.

Slade chuckled as if she'd spoken that ridiculous thought right out loud, and she blushed again. "Take as long as you need," he drawled. "But we're only going to a barn, Joslyn, not a Saturday night dance." A pause. "Will twenty minutes be time enough for you?"

Twenty minutes? For a complete overhaul?

Just like a man to think such a feat was even possible.

"Sure," Joslyn was quick to say. She sounded perky in her own ears, which made her a little annoyed with herself.

She was behaving like a teenager with a bad crush, not a grown woman living her own life.

Such as that life was.

Another chuckle, inciting another ripple of fire between her pelvic bones. "See you soon," Slade said.

After brief goodbyes, Joslyn fed the cat, grabbed up clean clothes and underwear, darted into the overwhelmingly pink bathroom, pulled the shower curtain along the bar above the tub with a brisk rattle and turned on the water. She stripped, showered in record time, wrapped herself in a towel, and gave her hair a quick blow-dry. It came out frizzy.

She brushed her teeth, pulled on the jeans and long-sleeved T-shirt she'd gathered earlier, and semitamed her wild hair by putting it into another ponytail. By the time Slade and Shea arrived with Jasper along for the ride, Joslyn felt as breathless as if she'd just run a foot race.

Dressed for wrangling in old jeans, worn boots and a blue chambray shirt open just far enough at the throat, Slade crossed the sunporch and rapped lightly at the kitchen door.

His easy grin slanted as he looked Joslyn over, and, for a moment, she felt as though she was bared to him again, to his eyes and his hands and his mouth. . . .

Don't, she told herself sternly, silently. *Don't think about how good it was.*

Again, fat chance. Just being in the same general area as this man made her nerves pulse and then throb in rhythm to some silent song the cosmos was singing.

When they reached the truck, and Slade opened the passenger side door for her, Shea greeted her from the backseat with a smile and said, "Don't worry. I'm not going to ask any more personal questions. Dad said he'd ground me if I did, and that would mean I couldn't ride Chessie, go online *or* use my cell phone."

Joslyn grinned as she settled in and fastened her seat belt. "Sounds pretty drastic," she said.

Shea put on an expression of dramatic melancholy, but she couldn't sustain it, so it was gone in a flicker. "Dad takes this whole parenting thing *way* seriously," she confided.

"It would seem so," Joslyn agreed, still grinning.

Slade climbed behind the wheel, and moments later they were off, headed for Whisper Creek Ranch. It seemed so blissfully ordinary to Joslyn, riding in the truck with Slade and Shea and Jasper, as if this was something she did all the time.

They drove through town without saying much. It was early, after all, and Joslyn suspected she wasn't the only one who was still in the process of waking up.

Oh, for a cup of hot, strong coffee.

"What do you hear from Kendra?" Slade asked, when they left Parable behind for the open countryside. "Is she doing all right?"

Joslyn turned to look at him, and, for a moment, their gazes locked, and everything that had gone on the day before, in the cool sanctuary of Kendra's guest cottage, was silently acknowledged, but then he watched the road again.

"She calls to check in every other day, or so," Joslyn replied quietly. "We talk about what's going on at the office for a minute or two, but when I ask her how she is, she sort of pulls back inside herself."

In the back, Shea was laughing, oblivious to the conversation between Joslyn and Slade. She'd just discovered some cell phone app that barked, making a goofy, cartoonish racket, and that in turn made Jasper tune up, howling for good measure.

"This has to be tough for her," Slade said over the din.

Joslyn didn't remember how much she'd told him about Kendra's reason for visiting England and didn't want to say more than she should and further betray her friend's trust. In the end, though, she decided to answer, because she knew Slade's concern for Kendra was genuine, but she'd stick to the bare facts.

So she told Slade that Kendra's ex-husband, Jeffrey, was almost certainly dying, and he'd summoned Kendra to his deathbed, having sent word, by way of his mother, that he had something important to say, something that could only be addressed in person. No one except Jeffrey himself seemed to know precisely what that something was, though, and he'd been too ill to talk ever since Kendra's arrival in London.

"It surprised me when Kendra married that guy," Slade said. "Surprised a lot of people around here."

Joslyn nodded. "I expected her to wind up with Hutch Carmody," she told him.

Bare facts be damned.

"That's funny," Slade answered. "Because I thought *you* would. You and Hutch were pretty tight in high school."

"That was *high school*," she reminded him, perhaps a bit tersely. Did he think she had a thing for his half brother? That she was the sort to be sexually involved with more than one man at a time?

Had he been paying any attention *at all* yesterday, when she'd come undone in his arms, again and again?

Slade glanced her way, then shifted his attention right back to the road. Always so sure of himself, he seemed a touch bewildered all of a sudden—and stuck for an answer, too.

In the backseat, Shea's cell phone continued to emit sharp barks, and Jasper, purely delighted, yowled loudly in response.

Everybody laughed, and Slade said that would be enough of the noise, thanks, and one more difficult moment was behind them—for the time being, at least.

When they arrived at Whisper Creek, the pinkish gold light of the new day was spilling over the rims of the mountains to the east, pouring itself like shimmering liquid into the sprawling green valley below—most of which was part of the Carmody ranch.

Hutch was just coming out of the barn—he hadn't shaved and his shirt was misbuttoned, Joslyn immediately noticed—but when he saw her getting out of Slade's truck, along with Jasper and Shea, he grinned a friendly welcome.

When his gaze moved on to Slade, though, Hutch looked a shade less hospitable. She could almost see him dig his heels into the hard ground.

Shea, who must have met Hutch at some point when she was younger, nodded to him and headed straight for the barn. She was interested in Chessie and not much else.

Jasper, usually her shadow, wandered around the yard instead of following her, catching familiar scents. Perhaps trying to track down his former master. The thought, unlikely as it was, pinched at Joslyn's heart. Jasper was adapting well to life with Slade and Shea, but he surely remembered John Carmody and wondered where he'd gone.

"There's coffee," Hutch said, his voice quiet. He rubbed the golden stubble on his chin with one hand, then gestured toward the house. "Help yourselves."

It was an offer Joslyn wasn't about to refuse. She looked forward to that first cup of coffee every morning, and there hadn't been time to have any since Slade had rousted her out of bed with his phone call, and she'd had to rush just to make herself presentable, forget attractive.

Furthermore, she hadn't been about to ask him to stop for some along the way. He was a man on a mission—tending horses.

"Thanks," she said, taking a step in the direction of the house. "Slade?"

"I'll be fine without," he replied without looking at her. He was still watching Hutch. "Thanks just the same, though."

The brothers stood a few feet apart, facing each other. Horses nickered and whinnied, birds chirped in the tree branches, ranch hands went about doing morning chores. Everything *seemed* normal, but a strained and very private silence stretched between Slade and Hutch.

Joslyn reminded herself that they were grown men, and she was neither their keeper nor a freelance referee, and hurried into the house for coffee.

Hutch's kitchen was old-fashioned in style, with dark cupboards and floors, though the appliances, faced with shining steel, were probably custom-order.

There was a big fireplace on one

wall—a nice touch on a wicked-cold Montana winter morning especially, Joslyn thought—but the place felt oddly unoccupied, like the ranch-house version of a model home in some anonymous development, well kept and finely furnished—but not actually lived in.

You really need that coffee, Joslyn thought, shaking off the lonely sensation that had arisen inside her as soon as she stepped into Hutch Carmody's kitchen.

She spotted the coffeemaker right away, scouted out a plastic mug, wanting something unbreakable, and poured herself a dose of caffeine. There wasn't any artificial sweetener, at least not in plain view, so she indulged in a single teaspoon of regular sugar from the bowl on the counter, stirred briefly and headed back outside, sipping as she went.

Slade must have gone inside the barn, for there was no sign of him, but Hutch was still standing in approximately the same place as before, talking quietly to one of the ranch hands.

By the time Joslyn reached them, the

ranch hand was walking away, climbing into one of several work trucks.

Hutch grinned at her and rested his hands on his hips. Like Slade, he was leanly built, but powerfully, too, especially through the shoulders, and much to Joslyn's relief, he seemed at ease in his skin again.

This was the Hutch she knew. She nodded to him and started for the barn, which was a fair distance from the house, and he fell into step beside her.

"That palomino," he said, "is one good-looking horse."

"Yes," Joslyn said, pausing as she stepped into the barn to let her eyes adjust to the dimmer light. "She is."

"And, as I understand it, she belongs to you?"

What was he getting at?

Joslyn turned her head to look up at him. "Not really," she said. "I told you yesterday, Hutch. Slade bought Sundance—I'm just sort of borrowing her."

As she spoke, she was aware of Slade and Shea, saddling Chessie in the breezeway. Another of Hutch's ranch hands stood nearby—he must have fetched the tack.

"She's my horse," Shea was insisting anxiously. "*I* want to ride her, Dad."

Slade's expression was implacable, his jawline like granite. "Sorry," he said, clipping off the word. "Not gonna happen."

Hutch and Joslyn parted just inside the entrance, so he could lead the mare between them out into the sunshine and the sweet, soft breeze.

"Dad," Shea protested, double-stepping to keep up, "Chessie is *my* horse."

"Your dad's right," Hutch interjected, surprising everybody a little. "There's no telling how green that mare might be. You wouldn't want to get hurt, would you?"

Shea sighed, shook her head.

Slade's expression was storm-cloud dark as he gave an abrupt nod of agreement. It seemed to pain him to give Hutch even that much.

Outside, Slade stood beside the mare for a few moments, stroking her neck, talking to the animal in low words Joslyn couldn't make out, though his tone was reassuring.

The reins gathered loosely in one hand, Slade put a foot into the stirrup and swung easily up onto Chessie's back.

She snorted, and muscles quivered along the mare's gleaming barrel, as though she might be bunching her haunches to buck, but in the next moment, she settled down.

Watching Slade ride, Joslyn felt a whole new emotion, something akin to admiration and yet unique in and of itself. Together, the man and horse were like one glorious being, literally poetry in motion.

Even Shea, who had been peevish before, looked on with her eyes rounded and her mouth slightly open.

"It's in the blood," Hutch commented beside Joslyn again, and there was a rueful note in his voice as he, too, watched his father's illegitimate son manage that mare with a light-handed grace that was beautiful to see.

"Having second thoughts about that ridiculous horse race the two of you are planning?" Joslyn asked. Now *she* was the one who sounded peevish, instead of Shea.

Hutch chuckled, a raspy, humorless sound. Shook his head, his gaze still fixed on Slade and the chestnut mare. "Nope," he replied. "But it might be a whole lot more interesting than I expected."

Joslyn folded her arms. Barely moved her mouth as she replied, "It's a stupid idea, Hutch. And it's dangerous."

"Maybe so," Hutch conceded, "but I can tell you right now that the sheriff won't back down from it, and neither will I."

After that first morning, things fell into a pattern.

Joslyn, nervous at first, began to look forward to these early outings spent feeding and grooming Sundance, and especially to riding along the grassy banks of the Big Sky River, which bordered the Carmody property on one side, like a great curved arm, and fed the creek that gave the ranch its name.

Slade taught both Shea and Joslyn

to saddle their own horses and, though he still checked to make sure Chessie's and Sundance's cinches were pulled tight before they mounted up, he said they were a pair of natural-born riders and gave them the room they needed to learn.

Because Slade Barlow never said anything he didn't mean, Shea and Joslyn knew it must be true and rode with confidence.

Thinking back on the brief and long-ago days of her reign as queen of the Parable County Rodeo, Joslyn often wished she could go back and relive them, honestly this time. Back then, she'd been a spoiled, empty-headed child, more than passably pretty but with all the personal authenticity of a spray-on suntan.

Now, riding the Whisper Creek range every morning with Slade and Shea, she felt like a new person, capable of conquering new worlds. Her love life being the one glaring exception.

Since that fierce and blissful interlude in the guesthouse, she and Slade hadn't really been alone together, much less made love again. An awkward politeness had developed between them, strictly platonic, like her friendship with Hutch.

That troubled Joslyn and not just because she missed the sex—though she did, and sorely—but because she missed something harder to define, the closeness of it, maybe, the way she and Slade had connected, not just on the physical level, but somewhere deeper.

Somewhere sacred and eternal, where the body and the soul met.

The sensible thing to do, of course, would have been to talk openly with Slade, but on the rare occasions that the opportunity arose, Joslyn couldn't find the courage. She was afraid of upsetting the balance.

If it ain't broke, the saying went, don't fix it.

So June unfurled into July, and July rolled on into August, and nothing much changed, at least between Joslyn and Slade.

She and Slade and Shea went to Whisper Creek every morning.

And every morning, they tended their

horses and rode and talked about nothing in particular and finally went their separate ways, Joslyn to Kendra's real-estate office, Slade to fill his role as sheriff, and Shea to the Curly-Burly Hair Salon, where she seemed to thrive. When she wasn't there, she was with her flock of new friends over at the community swimming pool.

For all the time Joslyn spent in Slade's company, though, she wouldn't have known about anything that was going on in his life or Shea's if it hadn't been for Opal's regular reports.

He didn't want to run for reelection, for instance, and he was trying to persuade Boone Taylor, his favorite deputy, to throw his hat in the ring.

Practically every night, when he wasn't on duty, Slade went back out to Whisper Creek alone, saddled the big bay gelding and rode for hours by himself—getting ready for the race, most likely.

Lastly, he seemed okay with the fact that Layne and her new love were making marriage plans, Opal allowed. And she adored the girl. "That Shea," Opal would say, with a fond chuckle and a shake of her head. "She keeps life interesting, that's for sure."

For her part, Joslyn wondered, worried and crammed for her real-estate license exam, which was coming up at the end of the month. If she passed—and she intended to, with the proverbial flying colors—she could list and show properties instead of just fielding phone calls and emails and making excuses for Kendra's continued absence. And she was running out of superficial explanations.

The business had practically ground to a halt without Kendra there, but her friend didn't seem to register the implications of that. Her calls were frequent but invariably brief—Jeffrey was hanging on, she'd say, though he still hadn't spoken, she'd moved from her hotel to his flat in Knightsbridge, to save on expenses and, except for a visit to Charing Cross Road now and then to buy books to read while she kept her vigil at the hospital, she didn't go out much.

The whole situation sounded, well, *bleak,* to Joslyn, and, on top of that, it was vaguely mysterious. There was more going on here than Kendra was willing to admit, and even when Joslyn went ahead and confided that she'd not only gone to bed with Slade Barlow but enjoyed every minute of it, a fact she'd shared with no one else on the planet, Kendra still didn't open up. If she'd found out why Jeffrey and his family had asked her to come to England on such short notice, leaving her own life and business in suspended animation, she wasn't saying.

It wasn't until a few days before that blasted horse race, scheduled for the Saturday before Labor Day—Slade and Hutch had charted out the course together, apparently, and were in grim agreement that it would span a mile-long straight stretch on one of the ranch's back roads—that Joslyn found a chink in her friend's armor.

All she had to do to get a rise out of Kendra, she discovered, quite by accident, was casually mention that if Slade and Hutch didn't break one or both their necks settling this crazy bet they had by racing each other on horseback over what amounted to a rutted cattle trail, she, Joslyn, might break them herself.

Kendra's indrawn breath traveled the thousands of miles between them. *"What* bet?" she demanded. *"What horse race?"*

Joslyn explained what she knew about the agreement between John Carmody's pigheaded sons, which was little enough, as it happened, because even Opal hadn't been able to pry more than a few grudging details out of Slade.

"Oh, my God," Kendra gasped. "Are they crazy?"

"I think that much is obvious," Joslyn said mildly, though the pit of her stomach ached with dread, and she had an idea it was the same for Kendra.

"They can't have forgotten," Kendra ranted, in a breathless whisper. "Not Hutch, anyway."

"Forgotten what?" Joslyn asked, growing steadily more unnerved. By then, she was wishing she hadn't mentioned the horse race at all, even if it had gotten a bit of a rise out of the other woman, because Kendra clearly had enough on her mind without worrying about this, too.

"Two of Hutch's uncles got into a race just like this one to settle a score," Kendra said. "His father's brothers. It was years ago—but you must have heard the story, growing up in Parable. There was a terrible accident, and both of them were *killed,* Joslyn. Some people even said there was a curse on the Carmodys—"

"A curse?" Joslyn echoed, though she still felt as though she'd been punched in the stomach. "Surely you don't actually believe—"

"No," Kendra said, on a sigh. "Of course I don't believe in curses. But something bad is going to happen if Hutch and Slade go through with this—I can feel it."

A shiver trickled down Joslyn's spine. She'd never known her down-to-earth, superstition-free friend to make a statement like that.

She swallowed hard. "Kendra—"

But Kendra's tone was brisk, matter-of-fact, decisive. If it hadn't been for the circumstances, Joslyn would have been heartened by the change in her friend. "When is this *race* supposed to take place again?"

"Next Saturday," Joslyn said. Practically everybody in town planned to attend, she knew, and there were bets being placed at all the local taverns.

"I'm coming home," Kendra announced.

Joslyn blinked, both delighted and confused. "That's great, but—"

What about Jeffrey?

The question hung between them, unfinished.

"I'll be there as soon as I can," Kendra said, sounding more and more like her old self. "In the meantime, Joslyn, you need to do everything you can to talk some sense into Slade Barlow's hard head."

"He won't listen," Joslyn said sadly. "He's made up his mind, Kendra."

"God help us," Kendra said, "when John Carmody's sons make up their minds."

"Amen," Joslyn replied, her throat thick. She certainly hadn't liked the idea of the horse race herself, but Kendra's reaction heightened the urgency to a new pitch.

"Try talking to Callie, then," Kendra persisted. "Maybe *she* can get through to him."

"Maybe," Joslyn almost whispered. But Slade's mother must have already known about the race, and if she'd tried to reason with her son, she couldn't have succeeded, because the thing was still going to happen.

Joslyn seriously doubted that Callie or anyone else could stop it. Still, if only for Shea's sake, she had to make some kind of attempt.

The call ended with Kendra's assurance that she'd be back in Parable before Saturday, no matter what she had to do to make that happen. Her car was parked at the airport, so she wouldn't need Joslyn to pick her up.

It was midafternoon by then, and Joslyn closed the office early, locking up and shutting down her computer.

She gave Lucy-Maude an early supper, ratcheted up her courage a notch or two, and rounded up her car keys to drive to the Curly-Burly. She felt like a meddlesome fool—going to bed with Slade Barlow didn't give her the right to interfere this way and, besides, she was still convinced that stopping the race was a lost cause.

Reaching the parking lot at Callie's place, Joslyn sat behind the wheel, trying to figure out what to say to the woman.

Before she'd come up with anything that really made sense, Callie appeared in the doorway to the salon, smiling and beckoning to Joslyn to come inside.

"Here goes nothing," Joslyn murmured, getting out of her car, smiling hard.

Minutes later, after spilling her petition over a friendly cup of coffee at Callie's kitchen table, her expectations were confirmed.

"Nobody short of God Himself can talk Slade out of that horse race," Slade's mother said grimly. "It's something he's *got* to do."

CHAPTER NINETEEN

The Saturday of the race, the sky was ominously overcast, and both Boone and Shea were all over Slade as he led his gelding, Highlander, down the ramp from the Whisper Creek trailer.

Hutch was already there in that strangely desolate landscape far from the big house and the sturdy barn, with his tall paint, Remington, and a small crowd of spectators was beginning to gather in the leaning grass, the women hugging themselves and whispering to each other, the men somber as Judgment Day.

From the looks of the sky, Slade thought to himself, they might be right.

"Dad," Shea pleaded, clutching at Slade's arm and looking pale in the early-morning light. The rising wind blew her hair around her face. "Don't do this. Let Hutch *have* this stupid ranch—you don't really want it anyway!"

He'd long since explained the terms of his wager with Hutch to her, but his reasons for not letting this go, for not backing down, were harder to put into words. Besides, he was in an obstinate mood, having already had his ears pinned back twice that morning, once in his kitchen, by Opal, and once, via the cell phone, by his mother.

"This isn't about the ranch, Shea," was all he could think of to say. He knew the statement was inadequate, but there it was.

About that time, Boone stepped up. He wasn't on duty, and he'd made it clear what he thought about the race, but as a friend to both Hutch *and* Slade, he must have felt he had to be there just the same.

Dark-haired with deep brown eyes

and the stubble of a beard on his square chin and jaws, Deputy Boone Taylor gave Slade a restrained punch in the shoulder.

"Listen to the kid," he said. "She's making sense."

Slade slipped into sheriff mode, though of course he wasn't in uniform, either. Even when he was working, he seldom wore one, mainly because he felt it separated him from the very people he'd been elected to serve. "Get those folks to move back a ways," he said, inclining his head toward the small but growing audience. "I don't want anybody getting hurt."

Boone gave a raspy hoot at that, his voice void of all humor. "Well, now, sheriff," he drawled, "*that's* certainly ironic."

Just then, out of the corner of his eye, Slade spotted a little blue Beamer bumping overland toward them. The top was down, and he could see two women inside.

Kendra Shepherd was at the wheel, while Joslyn rode with her, not even buckled in but kneeling on the passenger seat, waving both arms and yelling something.

Overhead, the sky roiled and thunder clapped, and Slade couldn't make out what she was saying, but he had a pretty good idea.

Hutch, leaving the paint in the care of one of his many ranch hands, stepped up alongside Slade to watch as the women sped toward them.

"That can't be good for the shocks," he said.

A corner of Slade's mouth pulled upward. "Not to mention the seat belt violation," he responded. "I could cite her for that."

The Beamer screeched to a halt in the grass, died with a gasp and a series of clicks and disgorged Kendra on one side and Joslyn on the other.

Kendra marched straight up to Hutch, doubled up both fists and pounded unceremoniously on his chest.

He laughed and caught her by the wrists.

She struggled, but not, as far as Slade could see, with any real conviction.

"Hutch Carmody," Kendra sputtered, "you are a stupid, proud, bullheaded—"

He kissed her then.

The crowd cheered.

Joslyn stepped up alongside Slade and poked him hard in the ribs. "And you're just as bad," she said. "Don't you *dare* kiss me, either!"

He did, though. Hard and deep and with tongue.

There was more whooping and hollering from the onlookers.

Shea, by that time, had retreated to stand with Opal and Callie at the edge of the group. Jasper, usually his daughter's faithful sidekick, had been left at home. The girl's eyes brimmed with tears, and she was still pale, but she held her chin high and her shoulders were back.

"I love you," Slade told Joslyn.

She blinked up at him, and her mouth dropped open. Her hair was windblown from the drive out from town, and her eyes flashed with temper, with surprise, with the passion her body had already betrayed, however much she might deny it after the fact.

"What did you say?" she gasped, pushing her hair back from her face with one hand. The wind was picking up, and a few drops of rain spattered the hard dirt of the road that ran alongside the river.

"You heard me," Slade said quietly. "I love you, Joslyn Kirk."

A confused smile broke across her face, busting right through the frustration and the fury and the fine layer of dirt from the off-road approach in Kendra's car. "Oh," she said.

Her eyes shone, but then, like the sky, they clouded over. "I love you, too," she whispered, almost angrily. "Which is why I'm asking you to forget this race and settle things with Hutch in a sensible, adult way."

"Sorry, but that isn't going to happen," he told her with a wry glance at Hutch and Kendra, who were standing a few yards away, arguing nose-to-nose, with their fists clenched. He noticed, with further amusement, that Boone had eased closer to them, in case there was a need for riot control, evidently.

Hutch looked over at him. Like Slade, he wasn't wearing a hat.

When their gazes collided, there was another roar of thunder, as though they'd generated the uneasy weather themselves.

"Let's get this done," Hutch said.

Slade nodded in agreement.

Joslyn stepped back, shaking her head as though in disbelief. Was she crying, or were those raindrops sparkling on her face?

Hutch pulled away from Kendra, who might have tackled him and gone right on hammering him with her fists, if Boone hadn't taken hold of her shoulders from behind, and John Carmody's two sons led their horses to stand side by side.

"To the bend and back," Hutch reminded Slade when they were both in their racing saddles, bought specially for the occasion.

Slade nodded again, and, as if by reflex rather than intention, they shook hands.

A neighbor drew what passed for a starting line across the dirt road with a

long stick. Another raised a pistol,
pointed skyward and waited.

The rain came down harder, splotch-
ing the ground, raising the pungent
scent of wet dust.

Slade and Hutch bent low over their
horses' necks, waiting for the signal.

The pistol went off, and both Remington and Highlander bolted off the
line, first at a trot, then a gallop, then a
run.

The two geldings were side by side,
as though they might be pacing each
other, but neither Slade nor Hutch
slapped down the reins or nudged their
mount with the heel of a boot to speed
them up. There was time.

The course was simple, if rough. Half
a mile to the bend, half a mile back.

Slade felt pure joy surge up inside
him, loving the ride for its own sake,
loving the angry sky and the intermit-
tent rolls of thunder and the green Montana range grass, bent under the wind.
Loving the memory of Joslyn's testy
declaration, back by the starting line.

I love you, too, she'd said, looking as

if she'd wanted to slap him stupid in one and the same moment.

He laughed, remembering that, and the horses hit their stride, running full-out now, streaks of sheer, elemental power tearing along that rain-dappled road. Beside him, Hutch gave a wild shout, celebrating the race both of them had, on some level, been anticipating all their lives.

It was true, what he'd said to Shea, that this wasn't about the ranch. It wasn't about winning or losing, either, he realized. It was about being brothers, him and Hutch, whether they liked it or not, and acknowledging that fact through action, rather than just words.

It was about being young, too, in their prime. And it was definitely about being male.

They reached the bend, neither horse tiring yet, crisscrossed in a big loop of space and started back.

By then, both men were soaked with rainwater and laughing like a pair of fools, and the horses, instead of slowing down, ran even harder.

Hutch and Slade let the animals have

their heads at the same moment, it seemed—the race was between Remington and Highlander now, and both geldings were in deadly earnest. Both of them wanted to win.

Hutch gave another exuberant whoop and bent low again over Remington's long, lathered neck.

Slade did the same on Highlander, without the yell. He could hardly see now for the rain in his face.

The geldings shot across the line, Highlander barely a head in front of Remington, but it was enough.

Both men reined in carefully, giving the horses time to slow and then stop when they were ready.

Women and ranch hands and various members of the crowd rushed toward them.

"You win, Slade," Hutch said, so quietly that he was barely audible over the storm and the shouts of the approaching throng. Then, incredibly, he laughed, a raucous sound, with something broken in it. "But not by very damn much."

Slade's horse pranced and turned in circles as it cooled down, and he allowed that, easy in the saddle. "We're done with this?" he asked his half brother.

"We're done," Hutch told him, somewhat wearily.

"Good," Slade answered, just as Shea and Joslyn pulled ahead of the oncoming wave of people headed their way. "Then I accept your latest offer to buy me out—Whisper Creek is all yours."

Hutch's face changed, and his mouth fell open. "What—?"

"Maggie Landers will handle the deal," Slade finished. Swinging one leg over Highlander's neck, he jumped to the wet ground. His hair and clothes were plastered to his skin by then, and Joslyn splashed through a puddle just before she leaped off the ground and flung herself into his arms, sobbing that he was a fool.

He laughed and held her, kissed her temple and winked at Shea, who was standing nearby, looking up at him with a mixture of relief, admiration and indignation.

She smiled, though, oblivious to the

pouring rain, and then turned to walk away.

Slade kissed Joslyn soundly, and she kissed him right back with spirit. And when their mouths parted, she clung to his shirtfront with both hands and cried even harder, the sound strangely punctuated by gulping giggles.

"You're all right," she said, choking out the words. "You're safe."

"I'm better than all right," he told her. If he could have had his way, he'd have taken her straight to the nearest bedroom, peeled off those sodden clothes of hers, along with his own, and made love to her for hours.

But that would have to wait. He had to get Highlander back to the barn at Hutch's place, rub the animal down, feed and water him, along with Chessie and Sundance.

"Did you mean it—before?" Joslyn asked.

Hutch was swarmed by the spectators, though they seemed to be giving Slade and Joslyn plenty of space.

Slade touched the tip of Joslyn's nose.

Rain poured down in torrents, drenching them both.

"You know the deal," he said. "I never say anything I don't mean—especially not 'I love you.'"

"What happens now?"

"I tend to my horse, Opal and Shea spend the rest of the day with Callie at the Curly-Burly, the three of them discussing my stupidity and stubbornness the whole while, no doubt, and you and I meet at my place. We get naked, take a hot shower and do a whole lot of rolling around on my bed."

She smiled, tried in vain to wipe her face on the sleeve of her wet shirt and nodded. "See you there," she said, kissing him on the chin and then turning to walk away.

Kendra's car was stuck by then and had to be pushed onto the road, muddy as it was, an exercise in cussing that involved half a dozen men. Someone had put the top up, fortunately, and when the vehicle was on solid ground again, both Kendra and Joslyn got inside.

Slowly, the party dissolved.

Hutch and Slade rode their tired

horses back to the barn, so the animals could work the kinks out of their legs along the way, paying no heed at all to the steady rain. Conversation was virtually impossible by then, but it didn't matter.

They might never be friends, he and Hutch, but they'd settled something that day, and it brought a new and fragile kind of peace.

"You didn't throw that race, did you?" Slade asked, when they were both inside the Whisper Creek barn, unsaddling their horses.

"Hell, no," Hutch replied, leading Remington into a stall before he removed the bridle. "You won, fair and square. But just barely."

Slade chuckled, shook his head. "True enough," he said, as he preceded Highlander in the stall across from Remington's and reached for a grooming brush. "At the track, it would have been a photo finish."

Hutch murmured a few soothing words to his horse and took up a brush of his own. "A deal's a deal," he reminded Slade from the other side of the breezeway. "We agreed that if you won, you could move into the main house and run the ranch as an equal partner."

"I don't want half of Whisper Creek, Hutch," Slade replied forthrightly, still working with the horse, who was finally settling down, muscle by twitching muscle, munching hungrily at the fresh hay in his feeder. "I mean to buy the place I'm living on now, put up a barn and good fences, add on to the house."

Hutch left off brushing Remington down and left the stall, carefully closing the door behind him and then crossing to stand in looking in at Slade and Highlander. "Is that what you were planning to do all along?" he asked, resting his forearms on the stall gate.

Like Slade, he was soaked to the skin. Like Slade, he didn't seem to give a damn.

Slade considered the question, sighed before he answered, "Probably."

"Then why the race?"

"Because you challenged me to it, I suppose," Slade said with a grin. He'd finished with Highlander; it was time to let the gelding rest. God knew, the critter had earned it.

Hutch laughed, stepped back so Slade could leave the stall. "The way you laid that kiss on Joslyn out there on the road, I'm thinking she's got a place in your plans?"

Slade quirked his mouth into another grin. "Might be," he allowed, moving on to Chessie's stall. He had plans for Joslyn all right, but they were nothing he meant to discuss with Hutch. "What about you and Kendra?"

Hutch went into the next stall to feed Sundance. "She hates my guts," he replied cheerfully. "I think she would have spit on me if she didn't think it was a waste of saliva."

Slade chuckled. "And I took you for the world's greatest expert on women," he said. "Guess I was wrong."

Hutch's head appeared in the gap above the wall that separated Chessie from Sundance. "What the hell do you mean by that?" he asked, peevish.

Slade shrugged one shoulder, patted Sundance's gleaming, golden neck. Tried hard not to grin. "I figured you'd recognize passion when you saw it," he said. "But apparently, it went right over your head."

"I kissed her," Hutch reminded him, almost defensively.

"Yeah," Slade said, averting his face so his half brother couldn't see his expression. "I noticed."

"And you know how she responded?" Hutch challenged, stall to stall.

"No," Slade replied, folding his arms. "I was a little busy at the time myself."

"She *kicked* me, Slade. Square in the shin."

Slade grimaced. "Ow," he said.

"It probably cost me the race, in fact," Hutch went on speculatively.

"Dream on, cowboy," Slade responded, stepping back out into the breezeway as Hutch did the same. "Your horse was fast, mine was a shade faster, and your bruised shin had nothing to do with it."

Hutch planted his feet a little apart, folded his arms and glowered. But for all that posturing, he didn't seem to have an answer *or* a plan, and that made Slade want to laugh.

"We could always have another race," he offered.

"Now, what would be the damn point in doing that?" Hutch flared.

"Just trying to make you feel better—little brother."

For a moment, Slade thought Hutch might lunge at him, and they'd cap off the festivities with a good old-fashioned fistfight, right there in the middle of the barn, but in the end, Hutch just laughed and said, "You want to have a beer sometime?"

"Sounds good," Slade said. Were they bonding, him and Hutch? After all those years of enmity, would they wind up behaving like brothers? It was too soon to tell.

Slade slapped Hutch's shoulder as he passed him. Then he went outside, into the rain, to get into his truck and go home.

Peering past the windshield wipers, he drove away from Whisper Creek without so much as a backward glance. It was nothing more to him and nothing less than the place he'd never belonged.

With his back to all of it, felt as though a weight had fallen from his shoulders.

Although he couldn't have said exactly what had changed, Slade knew he'd been set free in some fundamental way, set *himself* free, and so had Hutch.

They were, each of them, their own man.

Finally.

Joslyn was waiting with Jasper, when Slade's muddy truck made its way up the slippery driveway that ran between his house and that decrepit old barn. She stood on the front steps, rain sheeting past her from the eaves of the porch roof, her clothes wet, her hair in dripping spirals.

She was too hot to be cold, but she shivered as she watched Slade get out of the truck, shut the door and move toward her.

The rain pounded down, but it didn't bow him—he walked upright, at an easy pace, his gaze burning blue into her face.

"About that implant," she began stupidly, as he mounted the steps to join her.

Slade merely arched an eyebrow and waited, looking down at her, already making love to her with his eyes.

"I had it removed a couple of weeks ago," Joslyn spouted, because this was something that had to be said up front. They both knew what was about to happen, and she wanted Slade to know there was a risk involved, even using a condom.

"That's fine with me," he told her gruffly, acknowledging Jasper with a pat on the head before taking Joslyn's hand, leading her across the threshold, where they both stood dripping rainwater on Opal's clean floor.

He kissed her then, and she lost herself in that kiss, gave herself up to it, to him.

When Slade lifted her into his arms and started up the stairs, Jasper didn't follow.

The shower was blessedly hot, but that was about all Joslyn remembered about the experience because Slade drove her right straight out of her mind, caressing her, kissing her and, as he had the other time, devouring her.

She was in a daze of sweet satisfaction when Slade shut off the water, dried her off with a towel and then bundled it around her, and steered her across the hall and into his bedroom.

His bed was big, with spooled spindles in the headboard and fluffy pillows, but Joslyn didn't notice much more than that. At her core, she was molten, but the wet cold had begun to seep into her bones, and she needed his warmth, his weight, his strength and, most of all, his love.

Slade drew back the covers and then somehow they were both beneath them, lying on their sides, facing each other.

He ran the backs of his knuckles lightly down her cheek.

Almost shyly, she slipped her leg over his, scooted closer.

He kissed her forehead, and she felt some kind of tremor go through him, opened her eyes to search his face.

"What?" she whispered.

"I'm selling my half of Whisper Creek to Hutch," he said, his voice gruff, his eyes almost painfully blue. "This place will be home from now on."

She blinked. "But you won—didn't you?"

"Yes," he replied. And then a grin crooked up the corner of his mouth. "But just barely, according to Hutch."

Relief swept through Joslyn, and she slipped her arms around his neck, moved closer still, into the heat radiating from that blatantly masculine body of his. "I'm glad," she said. "This is a wonderful old house."

His lashes were so long. It wasn't one damn bit fair for a man to have lashes like that, in Joslyn's love-fuzzed opinion.

"I'm glad you like it," he said. "The question is, do you like it enough to live here?"

Her heart leaped. She'd believed Slade when he'd said he loved her, and she certainly loved him back, but she'd been sure he'd want to wait, deliberate over every aspect of things, before making a move. After all, that had always been his way.

"Are you asking me to shack up?" she joked, but her voice trembled and she found herself holding her breath, maybe even her heartbeat, while she waited for his reply.

"I told you before," he said, his eyes shining. "I'm an old-fashioned man. I'm asking you to marry me, Joslyn. To help me build this ranch up to something we can both be proud of, to share this bed every night and to have my babies."

Tears filled her eyes. He was offering her everything she'd ever wanted, but things were happening too fast. She needed time.

Fifteen minutes, at the very least.

Slade frowned, stroking the length of her upper arm now, leaving a trail of fire everywhere he touched. "Unless—?" he began, as some thought darkened his face. *"Damn."*

"Unless what?" Joslyn asked, breathless, and not just because he'd moved his hand from her arm to her breast. He cupped her in his palm, prepared her nipple with the edge of his thumb, his touch idle and completely intoxicating.

"Shea will be living here," he said. "I promised her she could stay for the coming school year."

"Is that a problem?" Joslyn asked, feeling an overwhelming tenderness for Slade in that moment and for his step-daughter, too.

"Is it?" he countered.

She nibbled at his mouth, teasing him. "No," she murmured. "It isn't."

"You're sure?"

She grinned at him. "I never say anything I don't mean, Slade Barlow," she told him. "And now, since I've been per-petually aroused since the *last* time we went to bed together, would you mind making love to me?"

He laughed at that, rolled on top of her, his elbows and forearms pressing into the mattress on either side of her. "Why, ma'am," he said cowboy style, "I wouldn't mind that at all."

She spread her legs, hardly able to breathe, even though Slade wasn't put-ting any real pressure on her. "Good," she murmured and raised her mouth to capture his kiss.

There was no foreplay this time—the need to be joined was too great, too urgent. Slade put his hands under her hips, raised her slightly off the mattress and plunged inside her.

Immediately, her eyes rolled back in her head as the first release consumed her, wringing a long, low whimper from her throat even as she dug her fingers into Slade's shoulders.

"Just the beginning," he whispered, close to her ear.

The boast proved prophetic in no time at all. Joslyn was caught in the grip of one ferocious orgasm only to be hurled directly into the next. She gasped and cried out and gripped the rails in the headboard with moist palms, arching high off the mattress. She begged and threatened and, most of all, she *loved*—freely, wildly, with the whole of her being.

Finally, Slade's restraint gave way, and he flexed upon her, flexed again, his head thrown back, her name rasping past his lips over and over again.

Long minutes later, when Joslyn was

back in her right mind—mostly—she giggled into his shoulder.

"I hope the condom broke again," she said.

He gave her a light kiss. "What condom?" he retorted.

And they laughed together, with the rain beating down on that old roof and lashing against the windows, and their shared joy was a form of lovemaking in its own right.

The wedding took place two weeks later, in the church Callie attended, with the few stained-glass windows spilling colored light and the pews bulging with grinning guests.

Boone was Slade's best man, Kendra and Shea were co-maids-of-honor, and clad in matching organdy dresses they both claimed to hate.

Dana and Brian made the trip to Parable to attend, of course, and Dana sat with Opal and Callie, beaming. The three Graces, Joslyn thought.

It was all a blur, though, as she stood at the foot of the aisle, her arm looped through Hutch's. She felt beautiful in her carefully chosen, quickly purchased and slightly altered wedding dress, a froth of white lace and pearls. She wore a veil, too, held in place by a little crown of pale pink flowers, and carried a matching bouquet in gloved hands.

Slade stood up front with the minister and Boone, looking unbelievably handsome in his rented tux. Smiling at her across the pews full of dressed-up guests.

He would probably have been just as happy to elope, her tall, dark-haired, blue-eyed groom, but Joslyn had insisted on the whole works—white dress, bridesmaids, reception-to-follow and all the rest.

After all, this was forever, and that meant doing it up right.

The organ began to play.

"Ready?" Hutch asked quietly with a grin in his eyes.

"Ready," Joslyn replied, after drawing a deep breath.

As rehearsed, Shea went up the aisle first, proud and graceful.

Kendra, who had been studiously ignoring Hutch the whole time, soon followed, joining Shea to the left of the altar.

"Here comes the bride," Hutch whispered.

Joslyn smiled. "Let's do this," she said.

Slade had wanted to take Joslyn somewhere fancy for their honeymoon, but in the end, they stayed home instead. Although he'd already announced that he wouldn't be running for another term as sheriff—Boone was going up against Treat McQuillan in that particular race—there was a lot to do before the changeover took place.

Joslyn, having passed her exam and acquired a real-estate license, said Kendra was going through a rough patch emotionally and needed her to help keep the business afloat.

And then there was Shea. They couldn't simply go off and leave her, even in Callie's or Opal's competent care, now could they? Her mother and Bentley had married and embarked on a long cruise, so she couldn't go back to L.A., either.

As happy as Shea was about the marriage between Slade and Joslyn, this was a time of transition for her. The child needed stability, especially now, with all this change underway.

Slade, for his part, was glad to have his bride to himself, after the ceremony and the hectic celebration afterwards, in Kendra's elegant mansion. Mostly to himself, anyway, he amended, with a grin. Jasper was there to chaperone.

They'd come home to change out of their wedding gear, following the reception at Kendra's, both of them wearing jeans, boots and favorite sweatshirts.

Standing in that kitchen, with her hair down but still sparkling with a few stray rhinestone clips, looking like tiny stars swiped from a night sky, Joslyn looked every bit as beautiful as she had in all that lacy finery.

They kissed, laughed and kissed again. And then Slade whistled for Jasper, and they left the crumbling ranch house that would one day be stately again, and climbed into the truck.

"Happy?" Slade asked gruffly, as they headed down the driveway to the county road.

"Happy," Joslyn replied serenely. "And you?"

"Definitely."

She reached over, rested her hand lightly on his knee.

They didn't say much on the way to Whisper Creek Ranch, but they didn't need to. They communicated in so many private, subtle ways—linking their thoughts, smiling at each other in that special way that was theirs alone.

No one was around when they pulled up alongside Hutch's barn, which was not happy coincidence, but prearrangement.

They walked hand in hand into the barn, Jasper frolicking along behind them, and, once inside, parted to approach separate stalls.

Joslyn groomed Sundance, saddled the mare and led her out into the late-afternoon sunshine, crisp with the promise of autumn.

Slade did the same with Highlander.

They rode out onto the range with

Slade taking the lead at first, but Sundance quickly caught up.

"All we need now," Joslyn quipped, grinning at him, "is a sunset."

Slade chuckled at the image. "I was thinking more along the lines of making love somewhere out there, in the deep grass."

She grinned. "That would work, too," she said.

* * * * *